The
Dragon's
Doom

Tor Books by Ed Greenwood

The Kingless Land
The Vacant Throne
A Dragon's Ascension
The Dragon's Doom

The
DRAGON'S
DOOM

A Tale of the Band of Four

ED GREENWOOD

A TOM DOHERTY ASSOCIATES BOOK

New York

THE DRAGON'S DOOM

A Tor Book
Published by Tom Doherty Associates, LLC
175 Fifth Avenue
New York, NY 10010

www.tor.com

Tor® is a registered trademark of Tom Doherty Associates, LLC.

Library of Congress Cataloging-in-Publication Data

Greenwood, Ed.
     The dragon's doom : a tale of the Band of Four / Ed Greenwood.—1st ed.
        p. cm.
     "A Tom Doherty Associates book."
     ISBN 0-765-30223-3 (acid-free paper)
     I. Title.

  PR9199.3.G759D735 2003
  813'.54—dc21

                                                      2003040212

First Edition: May 2003

Printed in the United States of America

0 9 8 7 6 5 4 3 2 1

To Brian, who helped me to get it right

Esse Quam Videri

Yet folk who know Aglirta of old will know already what befell next.

For the people were unhappy,

The barons were no better than they had ever been

Sly tongues of evil were busy in the land

Fell magic had corrupted those who sought and wielded it

Without ever weakening their eager hands

This could be almost any year in Aglirta

So be thankful for the bards and heralds

Who look upon this Vale that is so fair

And yet so seemingly gods-cursed

For they at least help us keep our disasters straight.

From *A Year-Scroll of Aglirta*
by Jalrek Halanthan,
Scribe of Sirlptar

N

W · E

S

OLOSS BAY

PELAERTH

AROIND

THE WIN

D A

▲ GLOIT

▲ BALEIKRABAR

▲ ARLUND

BARONY OF LOUSHOOND

BARON OF CARDA

▲ DRANMAER OOL
IBRYN

SELT

ISLES OF IEIREMBOR

SORPH

▲ SIRLPTAR

SIRLPTAR

GLAROND POOL GLARONDAR

ILT

CASTLE BROS

IBRELM

BRIGHTSCAR

GILTH
(former)
BARONY OF
BRIGHTPENNANT

▲ SART

BARONY OF GLAROND

BA

NANTANTUTH

B

ZINDYILARATAR

▲ COELORTAR

ANUENEA,
The Spellgirt Sea.

ELGARTH

THE ULUMBILAER

▲ TELN

▲ ELMERNA

▲ URNGALLOND

ARAGALAR

ARANTARN BAY

ISLE of JARRADA

▲ HOULBO

▲ CARRAGLAS

OND BLAS

N G S

I R T A

(former)
BARONY
OF
TARLAGAR

TSELGARA

River Silverflow

LOAURIMM
FOREST

ARCH

(former)
BARONY
OF
BLACKGULT

BARONY
OF

CASTLE
SILVERTREE

(former)
BARONY
OF
PHELINNDAR

LAKE
LASSABRA

INDRA

(Ru

RITHRYM

GRIFFONGARD

SILVERTREE

TELBONTER

DARPANNEN

TER

BARONY
OF
MAERLIN

L A G L A T L A D

ver Sheiryn

FELSHEIRYN

Map of
a part of
ASMARAND
·Continent of Darsar·

The Dragon's Doom

Prologue

A hard, sudden rain was lashing the rooftops of Sirlptar as the evening came down, driven ashore by a home-harbor wind. The storm rattle on the slates and tiles of hundreds of roofs quite drowned out the customary chimney-sighs for which the Sighing Gargoyle was named. Flaeros Delcamper could barely hear his own harp notes, but—newly esteemed bard to the court of Flowfoam or not—this was his first paying engagement in the City of River and Sea, and he sang on with determination.

Yet even he knew, as he lifted his voice in the refrain of his newest ballad about the Lady of Jewels and the Fall of the Serpent, that he might just as well have saved his breath. Not a man-jack was listening.

Every patron of the Gargoyle was bent forward over the table that held his tankard, listening—or talking—intently. The mutter of voices held no note of happiness.

"And so 'tis another year gone, and how's Aglirta the better for it?"

"Aye, harvests thinner than ever, half the good men in the land dead and rotting when they should be plowing or scything—and now we have a *boy* for a king!"

"Huh. No joy there, yet he can hardly be worse than what we've had, these twenty summers now—wizards and barons, wizards and barons: villains, all!"

"Aye, that's so. Wizards have always been bad and dangerous—'tis in the breed, by the Three!"

"So we thrust a pitchfork through every mage we spot, and what then?

Who of our Great Lord Barons can be trusted not to lash out on a whim? They've all been little tyrants to put the most decadent kings of the old tales to shame!"

"And here we sit, thinner and fewer, every year, while their madness rages around us and Aglirta bleeds."

An empty tankard thunked down on a table, and its owner sighed gustily, clenched his hand into a helpless fist, and added bitterly, "And the great hope of the common folk, Bloodblade, turned out to be no better than the rest."

An old scribe nodded. "All our dreams fallen and trampled," he said sadly, "and no one cares."

A drover shot Flaeros a look so venomous that the bard's fingers faltered on his harpstrings, and growled, "Now we have some boy for a King, and his four tame overdukes scour the countryside for barons and wizards who took arms against him—and who cares for us?"

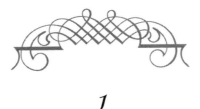

1

To Conquer a Kingdom

The rattle of keys awakened an echo in that dark and stone-walled place, and then a heavy door scraped open, flooding torchlight into a damp darkness that had lasted for decades. Old Thannaso, who kept the locks and hinges—and the manacles that waited on the gigantic wall wheel within, gleaming now in the leaping flames—well oiled, was as blind as deep night, and so had no need to light his way when he worked.

A lithe, slender man who wore skintight garb of soft, smoky-gray leather on his body and a half-smile upon his darkly handsome face held the torch high and behind his own shoulder, to peer into all corners of the cell. A little water was seeping in high on the south wall, glistening as it ran down the stone, but of intruders—beyond a small, scuttling legion of spiders—he saw none. Craer Delnbone was one of the best procurers in all Asmarand . . . which is to say that after too many years of escapades enough for a dozen thieves, he was still alive. If Craer's bright eyes saw no intruder, none was there.

The woman who followed at his elbow saw nothing either. She was much of Craer's size, and moved against him with the familiarity of intimate companions, but she was no thief. Tshamarra Talasorn was a sorceress from a proud family of Sirlptar, the last of her line—and her tongue could be every bit as sharp as her wits, as Craer had learned to both his fascination and cost. His "Tash" wore garments cut like his but of shimmerweave and silk, that flashed back torchlight every bit as much as her large and alert eyes. She, too, saw no peril in the cell—though most of her thin-lipped attention was bent upon the burden being carried behind her.

That burden was a large, stout man in rich garments, frozen in a pose as stiff and rigid as stone save for his furious eyes—eyes that darted this way and that, seeking to see all as one does who knows he will soon have very little to look upon at all. An armaragor of great size and thews carried the straight, immobile man, with the legs-steadying aid of a slightly smaller, older warrior who strode along with the easy authority of one born to command.

Hawkril Anharu was a gentle giant of a man, unless one crossed blades with him in battle. He carried their captive as lightly as if the man weighed nothing, and had to stoop and turn his broad shoulders at an angle to pass through the narrow door of the cell. He resembled an amiable bull in armor more than anything else.

The formerly raven-dark hair of the older armored man behind Hawkril was going gray and white now, but Ezendor Blackgult—once infamous across Asmarand as "the Baron Blackgult," a dashing warcaptain, decadent noble, and seducer of ladies high and low—was still handsome . . . and every bit as alert, as they moved through the dungeons, as Craer at the front of the band.

A radiance far paler than the torchlight flickered about their captive's head—the light of magic, lancing forth from a mottled stone carried in the palm of a tall, slender woman who walked at the rear of the group. Above a slight frown, her eyes were also fixed upon her captive.

Embra Silvertree had once been best known as "the Lady of Jewels" for her elaborately decorated gowns, but she much preferred the simple leather breeches, warriors' boots, and open silk shirt she was wearing now. Her long, dark hair swirled untamed down her back as if it was a half-cloak, and men best knew her now in Aglirta as the most powerful sorceress in the land.

Like the others who walked with her, she was an Overduke of Aglirta—and like them, she was carrying out a distasteful but necessary duty this day. Her gaze never left their dark-robed captive as Hawkril swung the frozen-limbed man upright—boots uppermost—as if he weighed no more than the petals of a flower.

Craer and the Baron Blackgult deftly plucked and fitted dangling manacles, the slender procurer trying the smaller key Thannaso had surrendered to him in each cuff. They locked and unlocked flawlessly, and with a nod to the baron, Craer fitted them to the arms of their captive, then accepted Blackgult's cupped hands to boost him to where the procurer could reach higher manacles, and so secure their captive upside down to the great wheel on the cell wall.

A tremor ran through those limbs as they were secured—gods, but the man must be part dragon, to struggle so in the thrall of Dwaer-magic!—and Embra let out a sigh of pain. Hawkril gave her a quick glance as he stepped back from the chained man, but she gave him a reassuring smile through the ribbons of sweat now running freely down her face.

"I'm ready," the shorter, darker woman murmured at Embra's elbow, and the sorceress gasped and nodded, gesturing to her to proceed. Tshamarra Talasorn smoothly cast a spell, stepping forward at the end of her weaving to hold her spread hands on either side of the chained man's head—just outside the flickering aura of Embra's Dwaer-spun magic.

That light promptly faded and died—only to be replaced by a brighter, more golden radiance flooding from Tshamarra's fingers.

"Spare your trouble," the chained man said, more wearily than bitterly. "I'm not going to try anything—not with a Dwaer-Stone that can blast me to spatters, or cook my mind like spittle sizzling into a fire, close enough to almost brush my nose. I'm guilty of occasional ambition, not utter foolishness."

"Indeed. Wizards rise and fall in the Vale as the years pass," Baron Blackgult said, "and the Serpent returns, and the Faceless and outlander mages alike clash and scheme—and yet the Master of Bats lives on. Powerful enough to hurl back those who'd seize your power by force, and wise enough not to step into anyone's trap."

"Save yours, Band of Four—and Blackgult. Or are you a member, good Baron, and this wench whose magic now constrains me the fifth, the outsider? I'd not heard that the boy king was proclaiming new overdukes . . . but then, I've not had the leisure to hear or see much of anything in the Vale this last while, with you hunting me. And if, as you say, I'm so wise as not to put a foot wrong, why this chasing and capturing? I was unaware that I'd slighted the Young Majesty. What quarrel has he with me?"

"None to speak of, Huldaerus," the Baron Blackgult replied grimly. "Yet your power is a danger to Aglirta of the sort we can no longer ignore. With shapeshifters busy and dozens of threats still menacing the River Throne like drawn blades, it's time—and past time—to scour the realm, collecting foes of the crown . . . or wizards who refuse to kneel to King Raulin and pledge loyalty. Your refusal was, you must admit, rather spectacular." He examined one of the chains critically, and told it, "At last, we're gathering enemies *before* they show up in the Throne Chamber with swords or flaring spells in their hands."

The Master of Bats made a face, his hands trembling from the force of a surreptitious attempt to tear free of his manacles. "So if I go upstairs right now and kiss the royal slipper and say the right words, I can go free? Surely 'twould have been easier to try that first, ere—"

"No, Arkle Huldaerus," the Lady Silvertree said softly but firmly. "Things might be different if you meant your pledge, and so swore loyalty in all heartfelt honesty, but this Dwaer can power spells I'd not dare to weave—or trust—by myself, and it has told me one thing very clearly, more than once since your capture: You feel no shred of loyalty or fair feeling to the King, or to Aglirta."

"So that's why you were forever asking me to swear fealty, or if I would—or could," the chained wizard murmured, his face now flushed deep red from his inverted position. "I thought you meant it as some sort of taunt."

"No," Embra told him calmly, "you thought nothing of the kind. You thought we were trying a new spell on you, to urge you to loyalty. You also thought that we were a lot of fools who'd be tyrants if we weren't so addle-witted, that this Dwaer was wasted in our hands, and that you'd been very clever thus far to hold back when Serpent and Dragon were contesting on Flowfoam, and in the troubles before that. You then went on to think that you were quite clever enough to weather this latest storm of foolishness on our part, and break free with the aid of the three bats that, even now, you're concealing upon yourself."

"My, my, that unlovely lump of rock shows you everything, doesn't it?" the Master of Bats replied, more wearily than mockingly.

"Three bats?" Craer snapped. "Where? I felt him all over, good and proper, and graul if I think he could have hidden even one of the little chit-terers from me. *Where* did he hide them?"

"Right now," Embra replied, "they're under his manacles, where the metal will best hide them from us. Before, when you were searching, they were in a dark place we all have, that's fashioned for expelling what our bodies are ready to be rid of."

"Why," Tshamarra murmured, "am I unsurprised?"

She watched Craer slip a long dagger under one manacle and slide it around the trapped wrist swiftly. A dark wing twitched momentarily into view, and then its owner exploded out of the other side of the manacle—and burst into blood that became threads of smoke in an instant, as Embra frowned, waved a hand, and her Dwaer flashed.

Anger darkened the face of the chained man, but he launched no futile struggle this time. Craer drove forth the other two bats, and they met similar ends. "He can fashion more of them from this, can't he?" he murmured, plucking at the wizard's dark and much-crumpled robes, and holding up his knife meaningfully, but Embra shook her head.

"No, Craer," she said. "I'm not going to be so cruel as to leave a man bared down here, to shiver in the dark and be dead in two hand-counts of days."

"No," the wizard told her flatly, "you're only going to be cruel enough to let me starve here, forgotten, until my bones fall out of these chains one by one onto yon floor—unless, of course, this dungeon has crawling gnaw-worms or other little welcoming beasts who'll come out to feed as soon as you take the torch away."

"I've almost as little liking for this as you do," Ezendor Blackgult told him heavily, "believe me. Or not, as is your right. You'll be fed regularly, rotated upright, and we will visit you from time to time, to ask questions—and per-haps, if your manner permits it, share news with you of events in the Vale."

"You realize," the wizard asked calmly, eyes moving from face to face, "how dangerous a foe you're making, don't you?"

"Huldaerus," the Lady Silvertree replied coolly, "we *know* how danger-ous a foe you already are. You may have forgotten your casual cruelties at Indraevyn and since—as they seem to matter so little to you—but I haven't."

Eyes that held coiling flames of fury fixed on hers, but their owner's voice was as icily calm as Embra's as he responded, "And so 'tis time for you to practice casual cruelties upon me now, is that it?"

"I can cast a spell upon you that will keep you in dreams, if you desire," the Lady of Jewels replied gently. "It will seem as if no time is passing, in the times when you're not being actively roused by someone."

"No," the Master of Bats said firmly, "I would rather hang here and brood. Perhaps I can come to see my folly and even to embrace King Raulin Castlecloaks in my heart, if you leave me here long enough. Perhaps."

"You're refusing a spell of dream-sleep," Tshamarra Talasorn asked carefully. "Are you sure you want to do that, Master Wizard?"

"Quite sure, Lady," the upside-down man chained to the wheel replied politely. "I am the King's captive, arrested and brought here to my impris-onment by his loyal overdukes, my freedom taken from me to make Aglirta the safer. I want time to think on that."

"Very well. We shall depart, and leave you to it," the Baron Blackgult said, and turned away.

Craer watched the chained man carefully, and saw what he'd expected: Huldaerus open his mouth to say something—anything—to keep their com-pany longer. Thereafter followed the next thing he'd expected to see: the wizard close his mouth again without saying a word, and smooth his face over into careful inscrutability once more.

Oh, yes, the Master of Bats was good at what he did.

Conferring with a few swift, wordless glances, the Band of Four and Tshamarra reached agreement and paced to the cell door together. Hawkril and Craer drifted to the rear, hands on hilts, to watch their prisoner narrowly.

He stared right back at them, his expressionless gaze almost a challenge. As Craer started to swing the cell door closed, the torch already behind him and the darkness coming down, the procurer saw the captive wizard's mouth tighten in angry anticipation of whatever taunt Craer might leave in his wake.

Craer shook his head, and said as gently as a nursemaid, "I wish you well, Arkle Huldaerus."

The heavy cell door boomed, and the Master of Bats was alone with the chill darkness. Not a kingdom many would choose to rule.

He waited, listening intently for the scrapes of their boots on stone to die away, as the darkness grew both heavy and deep around him.

And waited, growing used to the small, faint sounds of his new home. The whisper of seeping water flowing down stone, the slight echoes his own breathing awakened.

And waited.

When at last he judged that time enough had passed, and young and triumphant overdukes of the kingdom couldn't possibly have patience enough to still be lingering outside the cell door of a prisoner they knew to be helpless, Arkle Huldaerus murmured the word that released a spell he'd cast a dozen years back—and held ready from that day to this, through all the tumult since. *"Maerlruedaum,"* he told the darkness calmly, and patiently endured the creeping sensation that followed. Hairs pulled free of his scalp and slithered snakelike up his imprisoned limbs, to the place on his left shin where the legging under his boot had been so carefully soaked in his own blood: a place where that dark fabric was already stirring and roiling, rearing up . . .

Three bats lifted away from his manacled body, whirring reassuringly past his face at his bidding, and the Master of Bats smiled into the darkness. There was a jailer's slot in that door, to let someone outside peer in at prisoners, and in a moment or four his three little spies would be out and about in the cellars of Flowfoam, watching and prying. He'd have to take great care to keep them unseen as he saw where the little thief Delnbone returned those keys to, but th—

Sudden fire exploded into his mind, and in its shattering pain he felt first one bat, and then the next, torn apart. Desperately he tried to claw at the last one with his will, snatching it back from—from—

"Not so subtle after all, Master of Bats," Embra Silvertree whispered in his mind, as the last of his bats flared into oblivion. "I barely had time to get comfortable out here."

Furiously the manacled wizard thrust out at the sorceress with his will, seeking to hurl her out from behind his eyes, but the magic that had lanced into him, leaping back along the links of his own casting, seared agonizingly wherever it went, and he was failing, quailing . . .

"I'm not here to melt you witless," the lady baron said crisply, "or to bring you torment, Huldaerus—just to relieve you of all the magics you have ready to work mischief with. My thanks for providing so swift a road into your mind. This at least means I can leave you wits enough to remain yourself, and able to work magic in years to come."

"Mercy," the chained wizard hissed, his voice thin with warring fear and hatred, "I . . . I beg of you, wench!"

"Most charmingly begged, to be sure. Rest easy, Huldaerus. I'm not here to work you any personal harm, just to do away with any other little surprises you may have for us . . . *there.*"

The Master of Bats felt several tiny, icy jolts as other prepared magics were forced into wakefulness and then broken and drained away ere they could take effect—and then a curtain seemed to roll back in his mind, and he was left with a fair and sunlit view down the Vale from Flowfoam not long after dawn, as the last mists stole away like hastening wraiths above the mighty Silverflow on some day in the past. The tiny figures of women come down to the banks to do their washing could be seen at the first bend. He peered at them, trying to see their faces and hear the chatter amid their laughter, as a waterswift flew past overhead, and . . .

"I'll leave you this scene to brood upon," Embra's voice said to him, with a warmth and closeness whose affection shocked Arkle Huldaerus.

That and the shock of the blow of Craer's flung frying pan that had felled him hours before in the midst of his spells, with the Four all around him, had shaken the Master of Bats more than all the events of the year before this day. He shivered helplessly.

And then she was gone, and he was alone.

Truly alone, the last of his ready magic stripped from him and with no bats left whose eyes he could borrow. He plunged once more into that view of the Silverflow, with mists he could almost smell and merry converse he could almost hear—and then thrust it away again angrily. There would come a time when he would need its solace to keep away despair or even madness, but for now he had better things to think about.

The bitch had at least been true to her word. She'd refrained from blasting his mind and leaving him unable to work magic or know who he was. Ah, no. He knew all too well who he was.

He was a helpless, spell-drained wizard chained upside down in a dungeon cell under Flowfoam Palace. The beginnings of a dark storm of a headache were beginning to rage now, as the echoes of that frying pan blow were made monstrous by the blood pounding in his head. The Master of Bats clenched his teeth and spat a single furious obscenity into the surrounding darkness.

Rage and pain clawed at each other, doing battle inside him as he hung heavy in his chains, numb in some places and throbbing in others. Groaning from time to time, Arkle Huldaerus drifted in their stormy grip, letting himself be driven this way and that . . .

He slept, or thought he did. Yet it seemed that he'd not been alone with the darkness all that long when light arose around him again.

A cold, blue-white glow this time, with none of the warmth of firelight. It came from the wall of the cell across from him, hitherto hidden in the darkness, and it was *moving*. Moving?

Huldaerus stared at the glow. Was he asleep, and this a dream-fancy, or was that bitch Silvertree—or the other one, her slyskirt sidekick—at work with spells on his mind, trying to drive him into raving?

The glow had a shape now, as it stepped silently out of the solid wall—the shape of a skeleton, with two tiny stars of cold flame twinkling in its eye-sockets. Those eyes *looked* at him, and the chained wizard knew an old and fell intelligence lurked behind them, mirth that betokened good for no creature alive within them. A hand whose floating bones should all have clattered to the floor waved jauntily at him, the bony feet strolled across the cell, and the hand sketched another wave in his direction as the skeleton melted *into* the waiting stones, its glow dimming, and . . . was gone.

Arkle Huldaerus blinked at the darkness that reigned unbroken under his nose once more, shook his head, and sighed. This had not been a good day, nor did the morrow hold bright prospect.

He almost envied that skeleton its freedom to walk through walls.

The young man's bald head was slick with sweat despite the chill of the cavernous chamber. The snake fang–adorned bottom edge of his high-collared robe swirled above bare feet as risen magic played dancing white fires around them, shimmering across the mirror-smooth floor of the vast room. A pattern of intertwined serpents, jaws agape, encircled his wide sleeves, and scales were visible on the glistening flesh of his forearms and the backs of his hands.

The man took two measured steps forward, murmured an incantation, and flung up his hands as if to cradle a large globe of empty air. White sparks crawled tentatively from his fingertips to shape that sphere . . . and swirl about it . . . and then rise in tendrils around the Serpent-priest, building to silently raging brightness.

That growing light was reflected in the steady, watching eyes of two tiers of benches of expressionless priests along the chamber walls, well back from the spellweaving priest.

The cold radiance brightened as the incantation crafting it rose in volume—brightened and grew, becoming slowly writhing spirals of tentacles around the priest . . . and then coalescing into serpentine bodies shaped all of sparks. As those swaying serpent-forms grew snake-heads, they began to glide around and around the bald priest in an undulating, quickening dance.

The watching priests made not a sound, but some leaned forward eagerly. Not one looked away, even for an instant, as swiftly building spells erupted into bright bursts, one flaring atop another as the priest who stood alone at their heart cried phrase after phrase, his voice loud now with confidence, his fingers writhing like excited snakes in ever more rapid weavings.

White sparks sheathed the spellweaver's body, drawing in about him in thick coils, until it seemed a forest of large and ever larger serpents was lovingly encircling their creator. Their twining force slowly lifted the priest off the floor until he stood upright on empty air almost his own height off the ground, hands still furiously shaping spells.

Each new magic reached up, straining toward the lofty ceiling of the chamber. The unfolding spells seemed to draw upon something up there, unseen in the darkness, that sent down spiderweb-thin lines of force—force that blossomed into cold, bright fire when it touched the silently raging serpents woven by the lone priest.

In the heart of the light his incantations gasped and stammered on. Sweat drenched him, and his racing fingers were trembling now, his body shuddering as if fighting to stand against the snatching gusts of a gale.

A spell burst into a sudden shower of sparks, and there came a sudden, brief murmur—part consternation, and part satisfaction—from the watching clergy as the bald priest convulsed, shrieked something despairing, and clawed at the air as if to ward off a pouncing monster.

Sparks fell, and there came another explosion, bright and then dark, motes of fire raining down in all directions as the spellweaving priest sobbed bitterly. Burst after burst, in swift succession, tore the dancing serpents into a swirling cloud.

At its flickering heart the lone, sweat-soaked figure frantically waved fingers grown impossibly long, trying to shout words with a voice that had suddenly tightened into a loud hiss. A forked tongue darted from grimacing lips as the sparks raced aloft to shape many bright serpent heads—which then struck in unison, lashing down at the wildly gesturing man with terrible speed.

The bald priest screamed under those fangs of light, high and shrill. His suddenly long and rubbery arms flapped helplessly in the brightly boiling radiance—and then caught fire in a long gout of flame.

He screamed again, dancing grotesquely in the rushing conflagration, flesh melting and receding from bones with horrible swiftness. Smaller explosions bloomed and rolled all around that capering figure, and in the wake of each a freed spell fell away from the doomed priest and became a ghostly white serpent of flickering force, writhing and undulating in uncanny silence.

Within this ghostly circle of swaying heads and lashing coils, the dying priest danced on, his flesh melting. His screams became raw, faint and feeble . . . and he sank to the floor, still dancing—jerking back and forth, helplessly and horribly, like a stick puppet flailed about at a market fair for the amusement of small children.

Sprawled on the dark stone, the priest melted swiftly down to near bones—and as he became more skeletal, the freed, slithering spells dancing around him moved in, coiling into and out of the writhing bones. Where they passed, bones parted, dissolving into streamers of smoke, and shifting . . . twisting . . .

The skeleton was soon little more than a flaming skull atop a whirlwind of tumbling bones—remains spun into the undulating shape of a serpent by the ghostly Serpent-spells.

The fading serpent-shape coiled, reared menacingly—and the skull atop it exploded in a puff of bone-dust. The bones below faded, and out of that writhing collapse rose the last glowing wisps of magic, drifting up to whatever it was that hung high overhead in the darkness.

There they shone for one whirling moment around a mottled, hand-sized stone floating alone in midair. Glowed, and then sank into the stone, to glow no longer.

As darkness returned to the ceiling, the watching priests looked down from where the wisps had gone, tightened lips grimly, and sighed—some with wistfulness, and many more with relief.

"This failure was not unexpected," one man said into the silence, his cold tones loud, firm, and flat. "Shall we resume?"

Another priest lifted a hand. "We shall—and with Ghuldart gone, and his boasts and claims with him, one thing is certain: None of us has the might to master the Thrael. The Great Serpent is come not back among us. Yet."

A third, younger priest asked, "Could some of us not cast a few spells of the Thrael each, and so weld together a ruling council from among our ranks? Need it be one man?"

The first priest rose to his feet and replied, "There I hear the voice not just of you, Lothoan, but of all your ilk: the young, eager, and restless amongst us, who thirst for power and see change as no concern at all if it wins us more power swiftly. Hear me, now, all of you younglings. Hear and *learn.*"

Caronthom "Fangmaster" turned slowly to survey all the robed men on the benches. No women sat in the chamber; he and the knives of elder priests of like mind had seen to that. She-priests were vicious and treacherous, but alluring; there would be time enough to empower such when it came to open strife, and such qualities could serve the Brethren—and be the ready excuse for slaughtering the women as soon as it became needful.

"The Serpent who spawned us all was never a god. He was a mortal man, a great wizard—as were all his successors, Great Serpent after Great Serpent. None of us particularly loves serving a tyrant, but this is how it must be. Only one being can be master of the Thrael at a time. Once cast, the Thrael exists as a web of magic whose backlashes slay many linked to it if someone tries to wrest control of the Thrael from its creator, or craft a second Thrael that comes into contact with the first. When we pray to the Great Serpent, we send calls along the Thrael to him, calls he can hear. If he chooses to do so, he sends us back spells or healing energy or raw power, drawing on his own manifest power—which is that of all of us who are touched by the Thrael. Literally, our lives, and those of the sacrifices we slay in specific ways, empower the Thrael and the Great Serpent, and he returns power to us as he sees fit. Forgive this blunt speaking, but 'tis time and past time you heard it shorn of all the 'holy' nonsense we must always cloak it with, to conceal this central secret from lay believers."

Caronthom sighed, threw back his head, and continued, "So I say again: The Serpent was a man, not a god. Great elder magics create his recurring manifestation, and that of the Dragon who opposes him. Divine magics, if you prefer—magics we no longer understand or know how to control, augment, or destroy. From the Serpent we have his teachings, the secrets of the Thrael spells and of its working—and the sacred writings of what has gone before, which stand as lessons to us in what to do and not to do to win power."

He strode slowly along the benches, meeting the gazes of some priests thereon directly, and added, "Wherefore this council is met. As always, we must scheme and work and refine our plots, when seeking to win greater power in Aglirta—for no god aids us. We all saw Ghuldart try and fail to craft the Thrael, and witnessed his fate—and I feel no shame in admitting that, overambitious foolishness aside, Ghuldart was the most confident and powerful seeker amongst us who desired to master the Thrael. None of us is powerful enough to survive those castings."

The second priest rose. "Every word you utter is blunt truth, Caronthom. It should be clear to even the youngest and most restless amongst us that this council's most urgent business has now been determined."

He began his own slow walk along the benches. "You know me as Raunthur the Wise. Hear now my latest wisdom, and know it for no more than truth. We came here to discuss how to win power in the Vale, but could decide nothing until we saw if Ghuldart could ascend to the rank of Great Serpent over us. His failure means we must find and recruit a wizard powerful enough to become the new Great Serpent, so as to conquer Aglirta at last. Each of us—even as we work against the officers and authority of the boy king—must seek suitable men to become our leader. To borrow the words of the Old Viper who taught Caronthom and myself, 'The tyrant we must obey must be found.' "

One of the younger priests moved restlessly, and Caronthom pounced. "Yes, Thuldran? Speak!"

The young priest flushed and looked down. Both elder priests moved to stand side by side and glare at him. After a long, unwilling time of glancing up into their hard gazes and shrinking away and then looking up again to find their stares still fixed on him, Thuldran said reluctantly, "I-I like this not. We're to invite an outsider to power over us? Risking possible betrayal, and a rule none of us may favor?"

"Well said," Raunthur replied. "Of course none of us welcomes this situation. 'Tis right not to want or trust an outsider as our Great Serpent. To avoid disaster, all of us elder priests know very well that we must choose the *right* outsider. Finding and guiding him into office over us will be neither swift nor easy."

"In the meantime," Caronthom added, "be aware that we shall be ruthless in purging all misdirected ambitions from the Brotherhood. We elders are mages of some accomplishment; those who were not were the ones who perished. We may cower before the Thrael, but until it has been raised anew by a Great Serpent, *we* shall rule the Brotherhood. Speak freely, dispute freely—but obey when we speak orders, or we shall strike you down. In this leaderless time, treachery and internal strife are weaknesses we can neither afford nor tolerate. Heed my words, or die."

There was a stillness along the benches now that sang with tension. Raunthur smiled softly into it. "That's not to say we desire any of you to sit in hiding and wait for a new Great Serpent to come calling. Far from it. As we sit gathered here, we're still the strongest, smartest force in Aglirta, and we shall not be idle. If blustering idiot barons can hold power in the Vale, so can we."

"And so," the Fangmaster added smoothly, "we desire every one of you to aid in our chief plot to bring down the boy king. Some few among you, I've no doubt, have already gained hints of what this is. More than one of you is guilty of excessive prying in this regard that I'll henceforth reward with death. To quell consuming curiosity, know that before departing this place you'll be furnished with a spell. Others will follow, brought by fellow Brothers of the Serpent along with strict instructions as to when to use them and when they are not to be employed."

For the first time, the old priest who'd taught so many of them allowed a smile onto his face. "The first spell infects drinkables with something akin to the venom of some rare sorts of snakes, but stronger. Most who imbibe succumb to 'the Malady of Madness' told of in ancient times, the Beast Plague that makes victims lash out at others ere they die. Spread among Aglirtans with the words of 'divine punishment for misrule' you shall whisper, this will serve to weaken the rule of Flowfoam. When the time is right, all of you shall be properly placed, up and down the Vale, to supplant the local authority of the boy king."

Raunthur spoke up. "So much is the plan—so let your various spyings cease. You shall all hear the unfolding details anyway. Salaunthus?"

An old priest with a scarred face rose from the benches, nodded respectfully to Raunthur and Caronthom, cleared his throat, and said stiffly, "My tests have been a success. The spells I've worked with can now break the effects of the venom-spell, repeatedly and reliably. I—ah—there is no more to say." He sat down again.

The Fangmaster nodded. "Arthroon?"

A darkly handsome priest rose, smiled coldly, and announced, "Belgur Arthroon, from Fallingtree. The village is small, and accordingly I've been careful to enspell only a select few wine decanters and buckets of water. The results thus far are: success in every attempt. I'll soon be able to report fully on dosages and amounts of various sorts of drink to achieve specific results. As with all such castings, one must follow specific instructions or practice much to acquire a feel for the task."

The Fangmaster nodded, and Arthroon sat down again. "We've been absent from our holds and posts around the Vale long enough," Caronthom said firmly, "so let this council now entertain any other questions, concerns, or desires of the Brethren. Speak, Brothers, ere we break this assembly and confer upon each of you a scroll that holds the venom-spell."

No one rose, but an eager restlessness fell upon the benches. More than one priest leaned forward as if the promised scrolls could be snatched from empty air as a hawk takes a field rat. Caronthom watched, and smiled again. "Then let this council be at an end. Raunthur?"

The elder priest who was called the Wise strode to a door that glowed briefly as he placed his hand on it and then groaned slowly open by itself. "Scrolls, one to each," he said curtly. "No pushing."

Had any priest there dared to demonstrate so fatal a failing as a curious eye, he might have seen a younger priest clutching his precious scroll stride swiftly down a dark and little-used passage, duck through a lightless door and up a stair, and then pass through another door that glowed with guardian-spells every bit as powerful as those Raunthur had used to safe-guard the scrolls. Once through it, the young priest extended an arm that reached a full three feet farther than his other arm—or the arm of any human—should have been able to, and pushed at one end of a particular block in the stone wall. It pivoted, swinging open to reveal a cavity behind, and into this he thrust the scroll—and after it, his Serpent-robes.

Once the block was closed again, the naked priest turned away, his face and body sliding into something quite different than it had been. Again he reached out an arm that became much longer than any human arm had any right to be, and opened another pivoting block. A smock, trews, and boots were plucked into view and donned, deft fingers sketched guardian spells over both blocks and the inside of the door that had allowed admittance to this passage, and a farm laborer took six steps, made a particular gesture, and caused a whirlwind of coiling light to spiral into being in the empty air. Through it he stepped—and vanished, the spiral eating itself in his wake.

Only then did a dark, unseen watching eye floating high in one corner of the passage end blink twice, and perform its own vanishing act.

Its far end winked out in another chamber not far away, where another priest stood holding the scroll he'd just been given. "Well, well," he murmured. "A dangerous shapeshifter amongst us. Dear me. Something will have to be done about that."

His face melted and slid into quite a different visage. "Competition can be *so* harmful."

"Remind me," Hawkril rumbled, "why we must go riding blindly through the Vale again, offering ourselves as targets to all, to search out Dwaerindim. Can't you just use your Stone to seek them from afar?"

Embra sighed. "I can, yes, but unless the bearer of a Dwaer uses it for a very great magic, or is in the act of calling forth its power, or knows no better and is carrying it awake and aflame—for a light in a dark place, say—I cannot see it. If I touch not the powers of my Stone, and keep it hidden, someone using another Dwaer to seek it could stand beside me and not know I carried it. Some tricks offer themselves to anyone who can use *two* Dwaer in a search, but even then, must be very close to a sought Stone."

Tshamarra nodded. "More than that: One can only see raw Dwaer-power from afar—if its wielder uses it only to power spells of their own casting, one sees nothing."

"What if we sat you in a tower somewhere, guarding and feeding you, and you spent days using your Dwaer to search?" Craer asked.

Embra gave him a smile that held little mirth. "My Stone would be awake all that time. Someone—or *something*—would almost certainly see *me,* and come to snatch a Dwaer and slay."

"Thereby coming within our reach," the procurer responded triumphantly, "and allowing us to choose the battlefield!"

The Lady Talasorn sighed. "I doubt they'd herald their arrival, my lord. They'd watch and see just where we all were, and how best to slay us. The first you'd know of any battle would be a Dwaer-blast separating you from your bones."

Craer looked at her—and suddenly beamed from ear to ear, saying brightly, "My, but the Vale's lovely this time of year! I feel a sudden longing to take horse and ride."

Blackgult had said nothing, and continued to do so, but he did—almost—smile.

2

Stones Hunted, Trouble Found

The blacksmith shook his tongs to make sure of his grip, lifted the cooling, darkening bar, and thrust it into the bucket of oil. There was a roar of hissing smoke—into which he spat thoughtfully—and he set his hammer down, straightening with a grunt. "Be ye ready?"

Two men looked up from their last tightenings of the straps and buckles that held the great draft horse. "Aye, Ruld. He's in the harness."

The smith nodded. "Well, then, let's be about it. 'Riverflow stops for no man,' as they say."

"Aye," both farmers replied, completing the saying more or less in unison: " 'Not even if the Risen King commands.' "

Ruld snorted as he strode across his cluttered smithy. "Some 'Risen King'! Risen and gone, like that, an' some fool lad sitting the throne in his place. If they were going to choose any green youngling standing by, they'd've done better to pick a farmer—an' at least have someone who knows crops 'n' harvest and such."

"Aye! Better a Sirl peddler than this boy king," Ammert Branjack agreed, patting the vast flank of his horse in a manner that was meant to be reassuring. "They might as well have chosen a farfaring merchant from half the world away! What were they *thinking*?"

"Ah, that's just it," his friend Drunter said, spitting thoughtfully into a corner heaped with rusty scraps of old metal. "They *don't* think, up at Flowfoam. If they did, we'd not have half the realm dead, every third brute calling himself baron, and the hissing snake-heads *still* lurking behind every tree."

"Hoy, now!" the smith growled. "Untrustworthy as the rest an' beloved of talking menace they may be—but the Serpents pay good coin an' do no worse than any baron, an' I've never had a baron fetch me water before, just to be helpful an' not expecting anything in return!" He wiped his brow with a brawny forearm, blinked at the nails splayed out in his hand, and shook his head.

"B'y'Three, but I'm hot today," he growled. "Don't know why . . . shouldn't be wet as this, after so short at the forge . . ." He took a swig from the longpipe of water on the post two paces from his anvil, gasped, and shook his head again.

"You be looking pale, Ruld," Dunhuld Drunter said helpfully. " 'Tis all that wenching, I'll be bound!" He tried a grin, but put it away again swiftly when the blacksmith only grunted.

"Ah, but at least the weather's holding up," Branjack offered. "If this keeps on as it looks to, we'll have a good harvest, sure."

The smith spat and shook his head grimly. "An' who'll bring it in, with so many dead? Grain's nothing but a free meal for the gorcraws if it rots in the fields. Sirl merchants won't pay to reap an' husk—an' won't pay fair coin at all, if they can claim there's a glut. Some of them are claiming that already, an' not a plant in the Vale properly showing its own yet!"

"Ah, but Ruld, we've seen war and plundering outlanders and misrule before this—aye, and bad weather too—and there's still enough to fill every belly in Fallingtree, and Aglirta yet stands around us. Oh, barons rise and barons fall, and no doubt there's lives wasted and coins gone that could have been saved if the Kingless Land never saw strife, and a good strong king ruled well from Flowfoam . . . but what man alive has seen that, as the years and years pass? Yet we still have a kingdom that Sirl folk, for all their coins, covet dearly."

"Aye," the smith shot back, a strange green and purplish hue washing momentarily across his face, "yet I doubt me not if Aglirta had seen less foolishness of barons and blood spilled needlessly, the Vale would rule Sirlptar outright, long since, an' we'd all have coins to toss an' roll about in."

"And then ye'd only charge a dozen times what you do now, Ruld," Drunter responded, "as would we all, hey? And where would this golden Aglirta come from, where the gods make barons behave differently than barons have ever done, anywhere? And kept the weather grand, folk friends to all, and the reavers of all Darsar—aye, and the swindlers Sirl city breeds, too—far away?"

The smith shook his head like a horse seeking to drive off persistent flies, and growled again wordlessly as he snatched up hammer and shoe, and approached the horse strapped into the shoeing harness. "Tempt me not into clever answers, friend Drunter," he grunted, as he hung the shoe over the usual hook and caught up the massive hoof to be shod, "an' I'll spin thee no airy tales, hey?"

"Wise words, Ruld," Branjack said quickly, wary of the smith's tone of voice. "Wise words! We'd all do well to—"

The blacksmith straightened, shuddered all over—and then whirled around with frightening speed and laid open Branjack's startled face with one strike of the horseshoe.

With a bubbling scream, the farmer stumbled hastily back—and fell hard on his backside. He landed whimpering in fear and scrabbling to get up and out of the way, but the wild-eyed, sweating blacksmith bounded past him, hammer in hand, and smashed Drunter to the ground with a single blow.

Dunhuld landed hard, his skull crushed like an eggshell. Jaw dangling and eyes gushing blood and brains, he for once—and forever after—had nothing to say.

Branjack screamed again as he plunged out the smithy door. Men were trotting nearer, peering to see what was afoot, for Fallingtree was not so large a place that solid entertainment was to be had in generous plenty, and Ruld's smithy was where many of them were wont to gather in easy company, to talk in the din and glow where a man they all respected worked and held just opinions and shared them in a few short words, but suffered others to talk as long and as freely as they would.

Branjack clawed aside the first man who tried to talk to him—which kept him alive for as long as it took the blacksmith to slay that man, and the next, and another after that. Then everyone who'd approached the smithy was running away, and a sobbing, roaring Ruld was amongst them like a wolf savaging running deer. One man fell, spattering the ground with his brains, and then another, landing like a hurled grainsack with neck broken and head lolling. Swearing, a third tried to draw a belt-knife—and the smith rounded on him in a roaring fury and battered him to the ground in a rain of bone-shattering, brutal blows.

Branjack made it most of the way down the lane ere the horseshoe in the smith's hand laid open his smock across the shoulders and his skin with it, and then struck one of his elbows a numbing blow that spun him around.

Face to face with the staring-eyed smith, the farmer wasted no time in trying to turn, but ducked under Ruld's arm and sprinted back toward the smithy, seizing on some wild idea that the smith wouldn't want to break his own anvil, nor spill out the forge fire, so perhaps fleeting shelter could be found behind them . . .

That thought died on the smithy threshold with Branjack, the shoeing hammer driven so deep through his skull that it almost reached the top of his spine.

Howling, Ruld ran across the warm, familiar room, bloody hammer in one hand and gory shoe in the other—and began to madly belabor Drunter's draft horse.

It reared in the harness, belling and then screaming as loudly as any of the villagers had managed, and then some—and at its third bucking plunge worn straps parted, and it bolted, kicking out hard as it went.

The unshod hoof smashed Ruld's ribs like dry kindling, hurling him back into his tools with a crash.

The horse burst out through the half-door, still kicking hard, and the blacksmith rebounded to his feet in a dying daze, sobbing for breath, clawing weakly at the air . . . and seeming to see the blood all over him and the sprawled bodies of his friends for the first time.

"No," he gasped bloodily, stumbling forward with the hammer falling from his failing hand. Everything was going dim . . .

"No! Three Above, no . . ."

But the Three weren't in a hearing mood, it seemed. Bucklund Ruld managed two more steps before he collapsed on his face and died.

"The so-called Band of Four have defeated all our Brethren could hurl at them twice before, Brother Landrun—and prevailed. Don't be fooled by the buffoonery of Overduke Delnbone and the dim-as-yon-post front Overduke Anharu likes to present to the world. They're not the ineffectual fools they look to be."

"Yes, Lord—and knowing that, we shall—?"

"We shall make very sure of what the Blood Plague gives us, before anything else. You and I test, observe—and also watch over Scaled Master Arthroon and his Fangbrother, Khavan, as they conduct their own far more clumsy experimentations. You know the plague has no effect on a few, but plunges many into madness. Know this much more: it transforms others into marauding beasts."

" 'Marauding'? Mad, or hungry, or consumed by the urge to slay all they see?"

"Most of them, yes. Yet, if our most secret tomes can be believed, some may be suited to serving us in a greater way."

"And this 'greater way'—?"

"Patience, and we'll see."

"But . . ."

"Landrun, which of us two is a Lord of the Serpent?"

"My," Craer Delnbone commented, squirming in his saddle, "but there's one thing being a tirelessly roving overduke gives you a true appreciation of: just how blamed *big* the Vale is."

"I suppose," Tshamarra teased, "you'd prefer all the King's foes to obligingly show up at court and line up to receive us?"

"Well," Craer reflected brightly, "t'would save wear on my backside—and spare the horses, too. We could sword the enemies of the crown by appointment, be finished by evening, and celebrate in the wine cellar."

"Thereby considerately saving servants the trouble of fetching us bottles up and down stairs," Blackgult observed. "Your commendable consideration for others surprises me, Lord Delnbone—'tis a side of you I've not seen before."

"My good Lord Blackgult," Craer observed in shocked tones, "you amaze me. Why, you hired me yourself as a procurer in your forces, some years back. Can it be that you've forgotten the function of procurers? Poured out from the brimming flask of your memory the fact that procurers considerately relieve persons possessing too many valuables—or valuing same so carelessly that they safeguard them not—of excess items, and transfer those items to persons who think so much more highly of them that they're willing to pay to acquire same?"

"Craer," Embra observed pleasantly, "belt up. Procurer philosophy is far too arch to be entertainment even if one's tipsy—and all of us are very far from that now."

"*Precisely* why I evoked the image of the royal wine cellar at Flowfoam," Craer explained earnestly. "Scouring the realm for missing barons and anyone else who may have a Dwaer-Stone is thirsty work."

"I believe King Raulin used the phrase 'crucial and exacting' rather than 'thirsty,' " Blackgult told his saddlehorn calmly, "but your mention of refreshment brings up a point we may as well debate now as later. Once more we ride through the Aglirtan countryside seeking Baron Phelinndar, the Stone he presumably bears, and two other unaccounted-for Dwaerindim. Various tersepts and barons are demonstrably paying a minimum of loyalty to the River Throne—and despite our exalted titles, we are but five against all the forces they may muster. Accordingly, we should reach some decisions about where we should look next—hmm?—and how closely we should keep in touch with Raulin, to guard against courtiers either slaying or subverting him."

Craer sketched a bow. "My concerns exactly. As the overduke who's invariably in the lead when we get attacked—"

"This sounds all too much like a cue," Tshamarra murmured to Embra, peering into the trees that shaded their wandering cart track on both sides.

"—and upon whom shall fall the weight of the blame should we ride enthusiastically into a trap, it behooves me to share some of that blame by involving the rest of you in some decision as to where specifically we're headed. Now, *some* prudent Aglirtans—killjoys and shutter-minded sorts, to be sure, but fellow citizens of this fair realm nonetheless—cleave to the notion of deciding where they're bound even *before* they set forth, but—"

"Drowning's too quick for him," Embra observed. "Strangulation, Hawk?"

"If you insist, Lady Love of mine," the hulking armaragor rumbled, "though I should point out that he *does* have his uses. Occasionally."

"—on the other hand, it has been observed by sages writing well before my time that if you expected a hireling to do nothing stupid, you'd not engage the services of a procurer in the first place, and—"

"If he keeps this up," Blackgult observed, "his *horse* may strangle him."

Tshamarra shook her head. "Nay, drowning, definitely. Toss the rider, pin him down with one hoof, empty bladder downwards—and 'tis done, simply over, and avoids all that chasing about looking for a handy overhanging branch . . . Oh, my; such as the one approaching now!"

Craer made a rude sound and a ruder gesture in her direction. "Really, Lady Talasorn, such an old ploy is unworthy of you. Even street urchins in dusty backtrail villages like Fallingtree rise above such crude gambits. May I remind you that I'm no longer a mere vagabond and outlaw procurer, but an Overduke of Aglirta, bright-belted and apt to—"

"Be found loitering around ramshackle whorehouses by night," Embra supplied helpfully.

Craer gave her a wounded look, ignoring Tshamarra's urgent pointing gesture, and said grandly, "Lady Baron Silvertree, that remark is similarly unworthy of *you*. I can perhaps overlook the transgression of the Lady Talasorn, hailing as she does from an outland and some may say—though I for one do not—barbarian culture, but your lineage—"

"I withdraw my warning," Tshamarra told him with a snort, folding her arms in mock dudgeon. "Let yon branch have its way with you, sirrah!"

"—is much grander and could even be said to rise from the very roots of Aglirta, like that of my former employer Lord Blackgult here, and—"

Craer's horse trotted on, and the handy overhanging branch attacked.

Pounced, actually. The procurer let out a momentary and somewhat strangled yelp as it jabbed into his side and thrust him from his saddle, but Craer was as swift as many striking serpents, and twisted in the air enough to bat at the branch and so propel himself onto the back of Tshamarra's mount, right behind her.

His personally painful arrival upon the high rear cantle of her saddle more than startled the horse beneath the Lady Talasorn, and it reared, snorting in alarm. Embra laid a hand on her Dwaer to send a soothing spell if need be, but Tshamarra was equal to the task of wrestling her mount back to head-tossing complaint and then normalcy, despite Craer's distracting hands upon her, as he—or so he insisted—merely reached for reliable handholds.

"D'you think you could stop playing the fool, on this foray?" the Golden Griffon snapped at the irrepressible procurer.

Craer gave the glowering old noble a merry smile. "Lord Blackgult, in a word: no. If my . . . foolishness won me the title of 'Overduke,' then I shall cling to it. 'Tis not as if I could do anything else—and I refuse to become a grim, stone-nosed old noble . . . ah, like some folk I could mention. If Craer of the Wagging Tongue was good enough to rescue Aglirta from itself thus far, that same Craer shall see the Realm of the Vale safely through the *next* few days, as well. I'll not change into some bootlicking sobersides. Demand it of me, and farewell empty overduchal title and good greeting to the outlaw life once more!"

Surprisingly, the Golden Griffon merely nodded.

The moment the Lady Talasorn's horse quieted and Blackgult rode up close enough to get a hand on its bridle and prevent it from bolting, Hawkril spurred past and caught the reins of Craer's mount, bringing it to a gradual halt.

They gathered in a jostling huddle of snorting horses where their trail traversed a small and shady hollow. Tshamarra sighed, looked left and right with her hands on her hips as she sat in her saddle ignoring Craer's impudent gropings, and announced, "This *still* looks to me like a place all too suited for a brigand ambush."

Hawkril looked at his own lady. "Well?" he rumbled.

Embra did something with the Dwaer that made the air around them sing with a high, jangling note, and then shook her head. "We're alone."

"Then let us confer," Blackgult said firmly. "Craer, get back to your own saddle."

The procurer surprised them all by nodding and deftly doing so in silence, waving at Blackgult to speak.

"Mucklar was the market town we rode through this morn," the old baron said promptly. "Ahead is Osklodge, where there's been no tersept's lodge since a fire that raged when I was a boy. A mere trailmoot now. There, our trail branches into ways no grander than this one, heading southeast to the town of Stornbridge and west to the village of Jhalaunt. Unless things have changed since our last halt, our Stone warns of no other awakened Dwaers within its range. Still so, Embra?"

The Lady Silvertree nodded, and Blackgult continued. "As to the second concern, I've summoned Flaeros Delcamper—now reportedly on his way to Flowfoam—to stay by Raulin's side as both guardian and spy, and called on two certain courtiers to do the same. Men I trust, mind you, after extensive discussions with them eavesdropped upon by Embra and her Dwaer. They know of each other and of Flaeros, but the bard's unaware of their sworn duties. Thus escorted, I hope to give young Castlecloaks at least a fighting chance against treachery in our absence."

Craer snorted. "I know not which of your trusts is the flimsier: depending on the musical flower of the Delcampers to do anything—or counting on any Tersept of Aglirta to remain loyal when tempted by almost any lure."

"Judge not all men as nursing as dark a mind and morals as your own," Blackgult said rather sternly. "If we were all so self-serving, the Vale would have drowned in shed blood long ago, and this would all be beast-country, haunted by the restless spells of murdered mages and roamed by desperate outlaws."

"Now *there's* as good a description of Aglirta as I've heard in years," Craer remarked.

Tshamarra nodded. "Forgive my forthright speech, Lord Blackgult," she murmured, "but many in other lands would agree. 'Cursed Aglirta' is not an unfamiliar expression anywhere on the coasts of Asmarand."

"No doubt, and not without reason, either, but surely we know better—and work to make it doubly false."

"We stray," Hawkril rumbled. "Let us accept that the King is as well guarded as we can manage for now, and return to our personal progress: across country, or halt nigh Osklodge for some reason, or more likely on to either Stornbridge or Jhalaunt—but which?"

"Stornbridge," Craer said promptly. "More to do."

Embra lifted one eyebrow. "Steal, you mean?"

The procurer blinked at her. "Lady Silvertree, you wound me. You wound me deeply—"

"Not yet, Lord Delnbone, but the fate you anticipate may soon befall if your lips continue to spew such sly foolishness," Embra told him. "Quell the clever comments for once and speak plainly. You favor Stornbridge. For other reasons, so do I."

Craer grinned. "More places to buy gowns, sleep in decent beds, and shop?"

"Now who wounds who? I thought more thus: The larger place is more likely to house someone with a Dwaer, given that our fellow folk of the Vale seem unable to keep patient—and hide treasures—for long."

"Sarasper managed it," Hawkril rumbled. There was a little silence ere Craer sighed and turned to look upriver, as if his eyes could somehow pierce miles of trees, hills, and riverbends to the grassy mound on the far prow of Flowfoam, where their friend now lay buried.

"He grew old doing so," Embra said gently, "as did the Crow of Cardassa, remember?"

Blackgult half-growled and half-snorted in agreement. "I'm not feeling all that young myself, these days."

Craer grinned at him. "And so you ride with us to regain your lost youth. A chance once more to adventure, swagger, and rut again like a youngling!"

"Really? Is that why I'm here?" The man who had once been best known across all Asmarand as the Golden Griffon—the most handsome and dashing of all barons—asked mildly, as his saddle creaked under him. "In front of my daughter?"

Embra lifted her eyebrow again. "This hampered you before?"

Her father gave her a smile that held more than a touch of sadness. "I'm not one of those who shows a different face to different folk—though betimes I've been plunged into feuds and troubles for doing so. Many barons find such bright-faced acting the easiest way to rule, but 'tis a weakness that dooms them in the long run, for greater ease on this day or that."

"But what about a baron's duty to his people?" Tshamarra asked quietly. "If a baron invites the swords of a stronger neighbor if he says or does the wrong thing, what 'strength' is there in doing that thing—and dooming many folk who have no part in his quarrel, or chance to speak in its unfolding, one way or the other? I mean no disrespect, Lord Blackgult, but again: There are some in other lands who lie and smile through their rage daily, to get along with countrymen and avoid daggers drawn—and they look upon the Vale as a place harmed by its ever-warring barons."

"So Aglirta is," Blackgult agreed gravely. "I've never claimed to be a wise ruler, or even fit to rule. In the Kingless Land, power fell to those who could seize it. I used and misused it—throwing away far too many lives in a mistaken attempt to snatch the Isles was only my largest folly—and the blood of many men stains my hands. Yet I know and admit this, where many of my smiling, slydog fellow barons never did ere they were slain in strife that their own treacheries kindled and nurtured. I enjoy what I do, and have from the first. By standing proud, dealing bluntly, and paying the price for my misjudgments, I loved the passing days, and did the better for it—unlike those barons who cowered and schemed and feared poison and blades at their backs nightly, and passed their days like anxiously quavering rats."

"My, my," Craer said. "And here I thought being a baron was all snarling orders and bedding wenches and putting boots up on the best furniture. 'Tis not so different from being a procurer by choice, after all."

"No, 'tis not," Blackgult agreed. "But I fear we've crept back to procurer philosophy once more, and the Lady Silvertree is quite right as to its arch nature and lack of daily usefulness to those not yet standing trial for their misdeeds."

"Father," the Lady of Jewels said softly, "my name is Embra."

There was another little silence, there on the road, as Craer and Tshamarra looked from the sorceress to the tall, still handsome baron.

Blackgult made a little "say on" gesture with one hand. Embra nodded and told him slowly, "Were it not for Kelgrael's decree, I would have no claim whatsoever to the name Silvertree. I . . . was raised to hate you, schooled in your villainies, and sworn to slay you if I could . . . But I've never been anything but grateful to you since the day your revelation freed me from thinking the blood of the brute Faerod Silvertree ran in my veins."

Silence returned, broken only by a jingle of harness as a restless horse tossed its head, until Ezendor Blackgult said quietly, "Yet an awkwardness lies between us. Yes, I bedded your mother. Yes, I sired you in our joining. Yes, I did the same in many beds—"

"And barge cabins, and glades, and atop feast tables," Craer murmured, but was ignored.

"—up and down the Vale, with many a woman, and regret not one rutting. Women are my weakness, and my strength. Yet, lass—Embra—I have only ever acknowledged one child as my own. You were my pride long before you grew in grace and woman-curves and sorcery, because you stood alone against the Dark Three and the man you thought your father, and somehow survived. Survived with a mind of your own and a loving nature, not a cruel echo of those who held you captive, nor a broken slave. I . . . I long for your approval, and know I never dare hope for it, for giving you to such a cruel rearing, and doing nothing to deliver you from it." He hesitated, and then added in little more than a whisper, " 'Twas even in my mind to . . ."

"To wed me, once my fa—Silvertree was dead, and his wizards too, and so join our baronies," Embra said calmly, nodding. "I could see it as well as the folk of Silvertree could, as you wenched your way up and down the Silverflow. I used to dream of your bursting into my bedchamber with bloody sword in hand, and claiming me." A thin smile lifted one corner of her lips. "Half Aglirta—the female half—embraced similar dreams. Have you not seen the older ladies twittering and whispering as they glance sidelong at you, even now?"

Blackgult drew in a deep breath, as if a great weight had lifted from him, and protested mildly, "*Older* ladies? You wound me. You wound me deeply."

"Hmmph," his daughter told him. "Line up behind Craer—'twill save me on sword-thrusts. I can pincushion the both of you with one shrewd stroke."

There were chuckles and stirrings among all four riders in the hollow, and Hawkril growled, "So is it Stornbridge? Or Jhalaunt?"

"That sounds painful," Craer said to Blackgult, as they turned their horses. "I've never so much as felt a swordtip in my jhalaunt."

" 'Tis worse in the stornbridge, believe you me," Blackgult and Hawkril said in unison, and then broke off in startled and delighted laughter at both of their minds seizing on the same cleverness at once.

Tshamarra and Embra exchanged glances and shook their heads wordlessly. Craer held up his hand—quelling the mirth in an instant—and cocked his head to listen. "Wagons, more than one," he said briefly, pointing ahead along the trail. "Enough touching heart-baring for now; 'tis time to play grandly titled heroes again. Overdukes must impress."

Hawkril loosened his sword in its sheath, and grunted, "Ready to play."

"Likewise," Tshamarra said, sliding her reins up her arm and drawing back the sleeves of her jerkin to give her slender fingers full freedom. "Though 'tis sad we should expect a few carts to bring on swift war, I must say."

Hawkril shrugged. "Aglirta," was his simple reply.

As they rode forward, drawing apart out of wary habit to give each other fighting room should battle burst forth, Embra guided her mount close to Blackgult's and laid a hand on his thigh for a moment. "Father," she said, "we'll talk more later." Their eyes met, and she added swiftly, "Please?"

The Golden Griffon looked startled, just for an instant, ere he nodded vigorously and echoed firmly, "Yes. Please."

The distant thunder of rumbling carts and many plodding hooves grew louder as the five riders rode downriver, up out of the hollow and over another little rise and on. The creakings of protesting wood—the shiftings of old, heavy-laden wood in worn lashings—became audible.

Probably just a few open carts . . . local Aglirtans running goods they'd bought at market home, or their own unsold wares on to the next town to try turning coins there. The boy king's enthusiastic road patrols had at least brought this longtime habit back to the Vale, though men still went in larger groups than in olden days, and always well armed.

Another rise came and went beneath overduchal hooves, and into view came the expected: a trio of oxcarts, one open-topped and the others sporting low-slung weathercloak awnings, surrounded by a rough muleback escort of tradesmen and carters. A few nodded and flicked their drive whips in the usual bobbing salute to fellow travelers, but more than one looked tired and ill, reeling pale-faced in their saddles and wiping away sweat.

"Hard at the flask yestereve, looks like," Hawkril rumbled, as they drew steadily closer to the carters.

"Homebrew, probably," Craer murmured, "to make them that sick. Mind: they won't be in good temper. To the side, single-file, and grant them full room."

Blackgult gave him an amused look, but it was Tshamarra who purred sarcastically, "Really? I was *so* looking forward to riding head-on into yon ox yoke, and the wagon behind, and watching it cleave like butter before my royal authority . . ."

"This," Craer explained to Hawkril and Embra, with a wave of his hand at the Lady Talasorn, "is the savage tonguework I must endure every night behind closed doors, and—"

"No one could deserve it more richly, I'm sure," the Lady Silvertree told him sweetly, as the din of the wagons rose loudly around them. "Why, I—"

The foremost carter nodded curtly to Hawkril, who'd ended up at the head of the column of overduchal mounts—and Embra's hand closed over her Dwaer out of habit as the first wagon started to creak past.

The second carter on the near side of the group shuddered in his saddle, looking decidedly green, and his eyes were more than a little wild. Tshamarra's eyes narrowed as she gazed upon him, and she raised a hand as if to ward off something, or to be more ready to swiftly unleash a spell.

That carter seemed to look up and notice them for the first time as he drew level with Blackgult. His jaw wavered as if he was having trouble forming words he wanted to utter—and then he sprang from his saddle with a wild roar, clawing at the baron's leg and stirrup as he came down and snatching out a long, curved knife.

The Golden Griffon punched him hard in the face with a fist that had the hilt of a reversed dagger protruding from its midst, and the man's head jerked back like that of a child's doll.

He fell under their hooves without a sound—though he might as well have been blowing trumpet calls for all that he could have been heard in the sudden roar of a dozen throats. Men clambered up onto carts, drew swords and daggers with wild shrieks and shouts, and leaped at the passing riders.

" 'Tis because we're overdukes, that's what does it!" Craer explained to the unheeding world at large, as he drew a dagger and threw it in one smooth, flashing motion, while drawing another. "Like deer we wander up and down the Vale luring every passing man with a dagger to do us violence, helpfully baring our breasts and behinds to them with loud cries of 'Here I be! Strike at me! Strike now! I'm the best grauling eager targ—' "

Craer swallowed his words in a desperate ducking movement as a muddy boot swept toward his head. It belonged to a leaping carter who'd plucked Tshamarra from her saddle with the sheer force of his arrival—as her horse reared and kicked, and her desperate spell blew the man's head into spatters.

The blast spooked her horse into leaping forward into a cart with a mighty crash, and the world was suddenly a wild place of flying reins, lashing hooves, and raw-screaming men.

Craer sprang from his saddle to rescue Tshamarra, who was rolling and kicking in trail-dust amid plunging hooves and the bouncing, headless corpse of the man she'd slain. A carter sprang after him, howling.

The procurer struck aside a hoof with his shoulder, trying to get himself into a protective stance above the Lady Talasorn, but another crashing hoof nearly crushed her and sent him sprawling.

He came up right under a vicious stabbing downswing from the pursuing carter, and drove his own dagger hilt-deep into the man—only to have it snatched out of his grasp by the carter's shrieking spasm of pain. As he grabbed for the receding hilt, a lashing hoof nearly took his face off.

He threw himself against that horse, leaping as high as he could, and managed to get its head turned in another direction, so that its bucking took its deadly hooves away from him and his lady.

Another carter was coming at him, barking like a hoarse, angry dog. Craer ducked away from the first thrust of the man's rusty and much-notched old warsword, sprawled headlong to avoid being gutted by the second, and then managed to kick the man into a fall before his warsword could reach Tshamarra—who was grimly shoving a headless, gory body away so she could roll out from under it.

Craer plucked his knife out of the groaning, twisting body he'd left it in, cut that man's throat, and sprang away in time to meet the carter with the warsword head-on. They crashed together like two rutting bulls, blade to blade—and the procurer suddenly went to his knees, the man plunged helplessly over him, and Craer put a dagger into a passing crotch and clambered up to open another throat before the screaming became too shrill.

Tshamarra staggered to her feet—and promptly fell on her face again as a loose rein lashed her across the chest and throat with a crack that made Blackgult, sword-wrestling with two carters, three wagons, and many plunging horses away, wince and stare.

"Teeth of the Three!" Hawkril swore. "What's got *into* these mad-heads?"

Someone hacked at him, and he turned aside the blow with his own blade. The attacking carter snarled and hacked again, not even trying to protect himself, more like an enraged drunkard than any sort of warrior.

Steel clashed on steel anew, and the man staggered. Rather than slash the carter's throat open or run him through, Hawkril reversed his sword and rammed its pommel into the man's helmless head. The carter crashed to the ground like a falling tree.

Hawkril felled the next roaring, wild-eyed carter who came running his way with a kick to the throat, ere turning in his saddle to meet Blackgult's grim gaze. His onetime master pointed urgently over Hawk's shoulder, and the armaragor whirled around in time to see a trio of carters trampling down the awning of their own wagon to take up stances atop it as it crashed and clattered past, hauled by oxen in a hurry to be somewhere safer.

Three blades thrust down at Hawkril. He snarled and struck two of them aside with a savage swing, knowing even as he did so that the third was going to slice at his unprotected throat—

Embra shouted something, the Dwaer flashed in her hand—and the world exploded in blue-white fire that made every hair on Hawkril's tingling skin stand out like a needle. Atop the cart three men stiffened into helpless statues and started to topple, as Tshamarra screamed, Craer cursed . . . and Aglirta erupted in blinding, blistering flame.

3

A Plague of Magic

People called to each other up and down the muddy lane that ran through the heart of Fallingtree, and their voices were high, fearful, and dismayed. Men swore and snatched weapons from walls, or curtly ordered their younglings to "Get within!" Too excited to whisper, women cried the news over sty fences to neighbors, and everywhere folk were running.

"Now we'll see," someone said nervously, from the trees where they watched. A hand like an iron claw choked off his words, and laid a warning finger across his lips. The someone nodded violently, and made no more sound, not even when the bruising grip was gone from his throat.

Small groups of villagers were staring down the lane at the distant sprawled bodies where the flies buzzed. A few men of Fallingtree traded expressionless glances, hefted whatever served them as weapons, and then, slowly and reluctantly, strode toward the dead. They looked like a doomed warband going up against a dragon, knowing they were dead men but walking forward anyway.

"Three look down!" the foremost gasped hoarsely, counting his slaughtered friends. Drunter, and Gelgarth the miller's son, and Huldin . . . so much blood! Brains spilled like—like wet cheese . . .

He retched, turning away hastily, and more than one of his fellows swallowed, looked aside, and stalked grimly on, past familiar puddles that now ran dark red. The rest of the villagers watched in pale-faced silence. No one stepped forward to join the plodding men.

Fists clenched white around weapons, they walked on. There was more death on the smithy threshold, and that terrible quiet reigned over all. Ruld's hammer would clang no more.

The cobbler who dared to be the first to step inside came back out again with a face that was green where it wasn't bone-white. He moved his lips twice before the words came out. "None left living. Fetch the priests."

Slowly and reluctantly, but unable to stay back, the women and the bolder children started to drift down the lane, until most of Fallingtree was gathered in stunned bewilderment, staring down at the blood and carnage.

Two pairs of eyes watched that whelming through the bushes that flanked the smithy outhouse. "I'm well pleased," the owner of one pair murmured, fingering the tiny serpent-pendant he wore under his robe. "The Malady comes down both hard and swiftly. Now we'd best get gone—once the bereaved start their weeping and wailing, the menfolk'll look around for something heroic to do . . . and that'll mean someone to blame."

"And we're the strangers, and so the cause," the other watcher replied, daring to speak at last. His throat still hurt; he rubbed at it gingerly as he glanced down the tiny trail that led past the outhouse, down to the creek and the little pool where Ruld had been wont to wash off the oil, soot, singed hair, and sweat of his daily labors. In all other directions the trees had been thinned by much cutting, and the brush was too thick for anyone to move about without making much noise. "So down along the water and out of here, Belgur—then where?"

The senior Serpent-priest shook his head. "Out here, Fangbrother Khavan, I am 'Scaled Master Arthroon,' or just 'Master.' Hear my strict order: You are *not* to go fleeing anywhere. Nor shall I. We'd best escape notice for some time, lest these simple folk turn on us, the only strangers, as the cause of this, ah, 'dangerous puzzle'—but we must remain. Our work here isn't done. We must still see if some fight off the Malady, not falling into war-crazed rage, but instead are turned to beasts by it."

Khavan stared at his superior, and then nodded his head toward the gathered villagers. "So *that's* the 'lost magic' that spawns the Beast Plague?"

Belgur Arthroon stared at him in silence.

"Uh . . . Scaled Master Arthroon?"

The senior priest smiled coldly. "Indeed it is," he replied. "We must know who falls, who fights and is twisted into beast, and who withstands it altogether . . . before I go hunting barons, tersepts—and boy kings and over-dukes."

"The Band of Four?" Fangbrother Khavan gasped.

Arthroon's smile was as cold as ever. "Of course."

Sheets of roaring flame rolled out in a great wave, making horses rear and scream and stray branches crackle and fall—and then were gone, leaving nothing but smoke and a sharp burnt smell in their wake.

Thankfully, no trees fell and no field caught alight, though it might have been better for the five riders on the trail if some had. Burning grass hides relatively few brigands . . . or lurking wizards.

Embra peered tensely this way and that through the thinning smoke as the last of the wagons bounced and rattled away into the distance, with no living man left to guide its oxen.

Dead carters lay sprawled everywhere atop the grassy rise, in the dappled shade of the dozen or so old thornapple trees that lined the trail here on both sides. The Lady Silvertree muttered something over her Dwaer, still casting swift glances in all directions . . . but no lurking foe could she find. The stump-fenced fields certainly looked deserted.

"Whence came those flames?" she inquired of the Vale at large, as her Stone quieted the horses.

"Sorry," Tshamarra Talasorn gasped, from her knees amid the rolling dust of the road. "My spell . . . got away from me."

"Ah, but you won't so easily get away from *me*," Craer said gleefully from beside her, dragging her down atop him. She slapped him hard, and then turned within the space his flinch allowed and dealt him a shrewd blow in a tender place. Obligingly, he emitted a strangled chirp of pain.

"Let me *up*, dolt," she snarled. Craer's only response was a gasp. She frowned at him as she clambered to her feet. He tried to give her a smile, but Tshamarra turned her back on him, clapped dust from herself, and peered about.

Blackgult, Hawkril, and Embra exchanged puzzled glances with her and each other across the stretch of churned and littered trail that was fairly carpeted with dead carters.

And at least one who still lived. Hawkril used his sword to nudge the one he'd stunned, but the man remained senseless, eyes closed and mouth slack and drooling. A gentle slap with the flat of Hawk's blade brought no reaction.

By then Craer had found his feet, wincing and straightening slowly. "So what was all *that* about?" he demanded, voicing the bewildered exasperation they all felt. "They're not wearing scales or Serpent-tattoos or anything, are they?"

Hawkril drew on his gauntlets against poison or creeping things, and bent again to the unconscious carter at his feet. "Nay," he said briefly, after tugging aside none-too-clean clothing and peering here and there. He looked up at Embra from under bushy brows. "They were enspelled, though, aye?"

His lady frowned at him, and then traded similar expressions with Tshamarra. " 'Tis likely, given the suddenness of their attack, unless we deem them all trained Sirl actors—"

"And given the recklessness with which they fought," Craer's partner put in, swinging herself back into the saddle of her now calm horse.

Embra nodded. "But 'tis too late to be sure. Only when spells are very strong, or clash with other strong magics, or affect wards and other standing, spells, do they leave a taint of power behind that can tell us anything." She surveyed the sprawled bodies again and sighed. "If this befalls again *and* we've time and opportunity to cast the right spells before someone so war-crazed dies in the fray, we might be able to find out."

Craer had been conducting his own search of a handy body—that of a tall, well-dressed carter he'd seen hanging back from most of the fighting, doing more swaying and sweating than anything else. The man had the look of some wealth, so his purse might come in handy.

The procurer had drawn on one of the pairs of soft, tight leather gloves he always carried ready in belt-pouches. Those gloved hands had been gliding here and there up and down the corpse like busy spiders, but paused suddenly. "This one has scales," Craer reported grimly.

Embra exchanged unhappy glances with her father this time. By the set of Blackgult's jaw, he welcomed this news no more than she did.

"Magic, then," she said softly, "but what magic? Another evil Serpent sending, probably—but if not, whose dark reaching *this* time?"

Blackgult shrugged, and waved to Embra and her fellow sorceress to ride with him a little way on, to the crest of the rise.

Lacking shovels to do burials, Hawkril and Craer carried the corpses to the deepest part of the ditch, the procurer busily expropriating purses and serviceable-looking knives and daggers as they worked. Hawk propped the man he'd stunned into a sitting position against a tree, a little way along the trail from where they put the dead.

"We haven't seen any Snake-lovers recently," Craer said thoughtfully, taking the ankles of the corpse Hawkril was hefting.

"Oh?" the armaragor rumbled. "If they take off those robes and put on something that hides any scales, how would we know? They don't *have* to hiss and cackle, do they now?"

Craer grunted agreement as they let the body fall, and started back for another.

The merchant's wife set down her wine untasted. "What *can* be keeping him? Lessra, go you and fetch the master! Tell him the wine is poured, it grows late, and we've a long day ahead on the morrow."

Her maidservant hovered attentively, awaiting more instructions, until the goodwife lost her patience and snapped, *"Go!"*

Nathalessra went, passing out of the candlelit chamber like a hurrying shadow.

Her mistress sighed and gave the nearest candle a glare. Had Golbert got himself drunk again? How long did it take a man to dress in his finest? Why, he'd promised her this night of love on and off for two moons now! Always too busy, always another wagon to load or unload, until now there was just this last night before the ride to Sirlptar, and she'd put it to him bluntly—nay, begged him like a common trollop, almost in tears . . . truly in tears, after a frown had crossed his face. Why, 'twas as if—

Nathalessra screamed.

High, raw, and . . . cut off, abruptly. Wetly.

The goodwife frowned. "Lessra? *Lessra!* What've you found? What's he up to?"

There was no reply.

"Lessra?"

The candles flickered, but no answer came. With something approaching a growl the goodwife rose and made for the door. If Golbert had finally taken to pawing her own maidservant right under her nose, she'd—

Something came through the door before she reached it. Something low and long-snouted, with fur that glistened with blood. Its claws left bloody prints as it came, moving slowly and heavily.

Two yellow eyes gleamed hungrily at her over what was dangling from its many-fanged jaws: Nathalessra's staring, blood-dripping head.

It flopped loosely, still attached to one shoulder. The rest of the maid's body was nowhere to be seen; those fangs were long enough to pierce right through flesh.

The beast was still coming toward her menacingly, as large as the table behind her. As it came out into the full candlelight—long before she backed into the table and lost her footing and it loomed up over her—the goodwife screamed.

The beast was wearing the torn and shredded remnants of a tunic, vest, and breeches.

Golbert's tunic, vest, and breeches.

The Brother of the Serpent repressed a shudder—hopefully before it was noticed by the Lord of the Serpent who was standing beside him, smiling a soft smile.

That hope died swiftly as the senior priest asked, "Direjaws not a favorite of yours, Brother?"

"Ah, uh," Brother Landrun replied, swallowing, "no."

The Serpent-lord smiled and waved a dismissive hand. "No matter. I'm not as enamored of beasts as many Brethren, either. I prefer spellchanging those the plague plunges into beast-shape into more useful forms." He fell silent, obviously waiting for the Brother to ask what those useful forms might be.

Landrun did manage not to shudder this time. Every secret revealed to a priest of the Serpent was one more good reason why that particular priest might later have to die. He was not enthused to learn secrets.

Yet, eyeing his superior's smile, he knew he was being given no choice. "I've been considering, Lord," he said humbly, to excuse his slowness, "but I cannot think of what those more useful forms might be. This must be the 'greater way' you spoke of, earlier. May I be permitted—?"

The Lord of the Serpent smiled in a way very similar to the direjaws. In the scrying-whorl, Landrun could see it had now torn out the goodwife's throat and turned away, dripping even more blood. "Of course. Why leave some cobbler or herder plague-twisted into a direjaws or a wolf that prowls at your bidding, when he could act at your command, speaking just what you desire him to say—if you know just the right spells—while wearing the shape of this tersept . . . or that overduke?"

Blackgult and the two sorceresses had left Hawkril and Craer to the grisly work, and now sat in their saddles at a pleasant spot on the trail where they could look far down Silverflow Vale. Below, the broad, placid river glimmered back sunlight.

"So what do you think, Father?" Embra's voice sang with exasperation.

"The Serpents again—but rising in earnest—or a few priests working mischief and vying with each other for command of the faith? Whoever cast the spell is gone, or in hiding watching us . . . but was it a test of his spells, a strike at overdukes blundering by, or a coldly planned first foray against the crown?"

Blackgult shrugged. "You know sorcery—and those who work it, whether they trust in grimoires or scales and hissing-chants—far better than I do. I know how best to swing a blade or bellow at others to do so, the backtrails of the Vale, and reading and goading my fellow nobles . . . Must I now be your expert on Snake-worship, too?"

"Griffon," Embra snarled, "*help me!* I—I learned spells well enough, but precious little else, and Craer and Hawk now look to me to be their warcaptain! You roamed Aglirta for years before I was born, and as I grew up imprisoned in Castle Silvertree. Then you were regent, at the heart of the court . . . whereas I'm still learning blind-basic things about Aglirta as we travel, and know so little of what I should be doing that I often lie awake nights fearing I'll lead us all to our deaths—or doom Aglirta with a single wrong word."

Blackgult gave her a long look. "I'm glad to hear that. Good rulers and warlords spend much slumbertime worrying. Bad ones only fear for their own skins."

"Lord Blackgult," Tshamarra Talasorn put in softly, leaning forward in a creaking of saddle leather, "must your daughter beg more, or will my plea do? Speak, I pray you! Tell us your feelings about the realm as it stands now, and share something of what you know of its doings . . . Please?"

Blackgult sighed and threw up his hands. "And when I'm dead, who'll you turn to for advice then? The wind, to wait as battle comes down on you? Any smiling foe?"

"Without your counsel," Embra told him grimly, "there's little chance of us outliving you—I'm all too apt to get us all killed together."

The man who'd sired her looked away down the Silverflow for a moment, and then sighed again, leaned forward conspiratorially, and said, "For a long time, I've been in the habit of buying tankards for 'old friends' when stopping at inns, so I can listen to their talk. I learn as much from what they stop saying or lower voices on when they know who I am as I do from what's said to me. Though I doubt this tactic will work for either of you, given your looks and the fear of sorcery most folk have, you might want to try it in spell-disguise, from time to time."

Embra stirred, but Blackgult held up a staying hand and added, "I'm well aware that time is what none of us have to spare, these days—not when any afternoon can hold an attack like the one just visited upon us. So I'll share what's most telling of my learnings, this last while. Not that it should come as great enlightenment, mind. Neither of you lasses are dullards nor dreamwalkers through your days; I'm sure you know as well as I do how unhappy Aglirtans are, right now."

Tshamarra nodded. "The notion of a 'boy king' sits not well with them," she said. "They long for peace and plenty . . . and feeling safe in their own land."

It was Embra's turn to sigh. "They long for golden days none of us can remember, if they ever existed at all. Long years and many cruel and close-to-home examples have made them hate and fear barons and tersepts—and Serpent-priests, too, for that matter. Wild tales have served wizards the same, and built the Risen King into a shining crown of hope they now know is shattered and gone."

The Golden Griffon nodded in agreement, and waved at her to go on.

Embra took a deep breath and obliged him. "Bloodblade was their new hope, and he, too, went down into darkness—after showing enough of them that he was no better than the barons he overthrew to sour Aglirtans on even new hopes."

She waved toward the river in exasperation. "That'll change . . . folk *need* to believe in new hopes, and they will again, as soon as something acceptable comes along. Right now, though, times are hard, brigands are everywhere, and royal law and order scarce or unknown. *We* are all most Vale folk see of Flowfoam or the hands of the King."

"Three help them all," Tshamarra commented, twisting her lips into a mirthless smile as she gazed down at the beauty of the Vale laid out before her, between the rising ranges of the Windfangs to the north and the Talaglatlad to the south. She peered at the haze in the distance that hid the lower baronies, Sirlptar, and the sea, and sighed. "Such a beautiful land, and such unhappy folk. There's many a seacoast village where poor men battle storms to put to sea, to eat fish or starve, and would think themselves beloved of the gods were they delivered here."

She swung her darkly beautiful head around to regard Blackgult with sad eyes. "Yet it seems to me that Aglirta *always* knows strife, and its folk are always unhappy. Is this an affliction, a curse of wizards or gods? Or are the people who dwell along the Silverflow all crazed?"

Ezendor Blackgult shrugged and gave her a crooked smile. "You touch on a question sages and simple men alike—myself, for one—have thought upon in vain. Like all folk, we react with fury when outlanders point such things out to us, debate among ourselves with almost as much anger . . .

and in truth know nothing, whatever our conclusions. Some say the never-ending strife of Serpent and Dragon keeps the land restless, making peace and contentment impossible. Some agree, saying the Three decree this, while others claim 'tis all the work of men. Still others hold that Aglirtans have learned wisdom from the violence of the realm though others across all Darsar deny or cannot see this—but many say we are deficient, or gods-cursed, never to appreciate or be able to hold peace, that we *must* fight. Yet others say proudly that all folk of Darsar envy and desire Aglirta, and constantly send agents to try and take it or at least win influence in the Vale, either covertly or by open force . . . and that these grasping men are behind all of our strife. Whatever the truth in all these words, they serve in the end as excuses for why the fighting must go on, no matter what one Aglirtan or the next may do—so we may as well do as we desire, or whatever we can get away with."

He shrugged again, and added bitterly, "When I was young, of course, I knew all truths with fire-graven certainty—when I bothered to think at all beyond my loins, belly, and the point of my sword. Later, I saw I was no more than a hotheaded brawler . . . and then was caught in a Dwaer-blast that left me with but the shards of my memories and my thinking. Now I'm a simple soldier indeed."

He smiled at the Lady Talasorn. "I think many Aglirtans are like me. They've known so much disappointment and war that all they remember is their anger and their loss—and how to fight."

" 'Aglirta is the anvil upon which all hammers fall,' " Embra murmured, quoting the old Vale saying.

"I don't think the 'why' of the strife matters, particularly to those who puzzle when they should be swinging swords, and so wind up dead," Hawkril rumbled, leading his horse to join them with Craer right behind. "Our task is to defend the realm. As always. *How* we do that is our puzzle."

"Our task?" Tshamarra echoed. "As overdukes?"

"As overdukes," the armaragor agreed heavily. "Our work is simply put: Find whatever crisis tightens its jaws about Aglirta now, and deal with it before the next hungry trouble comes."

"My only real complaint," Craer put in, as he swung himself back into his saddle, "is that overdukes seem to spend their waking lives riding hard from crisis to another. Can't the things grow in bunches, or at least on the same bush?"

"Now, Cleverfingers," Embra said affectionately, "you'd miss these endless rides—ho ho—if ever you weren't racing wild-cloaked across the realm."

"Which brings us back to what I was yammering about before yon carters went mad," the procurer responded with something like triumph. "If discontent and lawlessness among Aglirtans are rife from one end of the Vale to the other, and we've already harvested all the bad barons and dangerous wizards we know of–hidden Phelinndar and his Dwaer excepted, I'll grant–where precisely should we now be racing to? Wouldn't it be easier to establish ourselves somewhere pleasant that's well supplied with wine, platters of good food, and willing wenches, and wait for the foes of Aglirta to come to us? We could rig up some traps or the like, to–"

"My Lord Delnbone," Tshamarra Talasorn said in a dangerously silky voice, "I hardly think I missed hearing you say 'willing wenches.' "

"Ah, I was thinking of Lord Blackgult's comfort, my lady!" Craer replied brightly and a shade too swiftly. "Truly! I–"

"Craer," the Lady Talasorn said coldly, "I can tell your lies from several hills away. I think you'll be sleeping in cooler and lonelier circumstances. This night and henceforth."

The procurer winced and looked imploringly at Tshamarra, but she turned her head away, to stare west, downriver.

"Cold place, this 'henceforth,' " Hawkril told the nearest tree trunk conversationally, into the deepening silence. "I never liked visiting it, myself."

"The less said, here and now, on any personal matter between the Lady Talasorn and the Lord Delnbone, the better," Blackgult said firmly. "At the risk of sounding like some doom-tongued old father, let us speak only of other things. I can see much crawling in Craer's future, and things growing only worse if more words are uttered now. For all our sakes, let there be fair feeling between us. Two of us were for Stornbridge, as I recall. Embra, pray give us the reasons a warcaptain might head there, rather than take the other trail."

His daughter nodded. "As Craer started to say ere his tongue rode away with him, the easily identified foes of the crown have fled, fallen into our hands, or lie well hidden. We need some honest answers as to their whereabouts, or doings, or odd happenings locally–and about how Raulin is truly regarded by the local commoners, *not* what self-serving tersepts and barons and priests may tell us of what the folk feel." She gave her fellow overdukes the beginnings of a smile and added, "Several of us know the Tersept of Stornbridge–well enough to take our measures of him, at least. He's a bit of a fool, weakling, and drunkard–agreed?"

"Agreed," Blackgult said, as Hawkril and Craer nodded, and waved at her to say on.

Embra acquired a real smile. "Some wine should loosen his tongue enough—with you, me, and Tshamarra all probing with spells, if need be—to get him to spout some truths. Even if he knows nothing but the lean of the nearest fencepost, we should learn how the folk of his terseptry feel about the King, and Aglirta in general. The ones whose words he hears, at least. Perhaps we'll learn more than we want to know . . . But we must begin turning over rocks in the Vale *somewhere*, now that all the easy chasing is done."

"There's one thing more," Tshamarra added, a little hesitantly. "At the risk of insulting you all by pointing out the rock-hurled obvious, we've been hunting wizards for a while now, and swording Serpent-priests along with half the realm before that. If we see none now, it doesn't mean we've scoured the Vale of them all—it just means they've learned to be wary and keep hidden. *We* ride all over the realm, and can tell when a face we last saw down in Drungarth is now happily settled in Overember—but villagers don't. They're used to wandering peddlers and to folk fleeing this or that baron elsewhere in the Vale coming to town, and won't suspect new arrivals of being anything more than they claim to be. Not all mages—or Serpent-clergy—are arrogant, swaggering dolts. Some can hide themselves very well . . . and I suspect more than a few of them have learned both caution and patience, these last few years."

"Well said," Blackgult agreed. "Wherefore we find the loose-tongued and ambitious, and see what they can tell us. Stornbridge may of course know nothing beyond what he likes at feasts and in his bed, and where his next sack of coins is coming from . . . but folk desiring power would soon see that, and try to use him. If they have, we should at least be able to get their names and faces; my magic is laughable scraps set beside the might of you two ladies, and even I could get that much from him."

"Well then," Hawkril rumbled, mounting up, "it seems we're agreed. Our chosen idiot's castle lies near enough to be easily reached before much more of the day is fled—crazed passing carters willing—so let's be about it."

So it was that they took the eastern trail at Osklodge, along the way meeting with only a lone farmer walking beside his mule cart. He gaped at them and then nodded, as one Aglirtan to another, making no bows for overdukes but also refraining from howling and charging at them with a sword.

"Blessing of the Three," Embra murmured sardonically at that, and her companions gave her various wry expressions of agreement. As they rode, they saw a few folk working in distant fields. Most straightened to stare, but only one waved.

From time to time gated farm lanes departed the trail, but as the overdukes rode on, the trees on either side grew from thin boundary stands one could see rolling fields through to dark forests that entirely hid the farms.

As the light grew dim and green, Craer turned in his saddle and silently signaled Hawkril. The armaragor nodded and waved to his fellow over-dukes to slow their mounts, be wary, and proceed as quietly as possible.

The procurer hastened ahead, opening up a large gap between his mount and Hawkril's. Tshamarra heard the faint rasp of Blackgult drawing his sword behind her. Frowning, she began to cast a slow, careful spell.

It was at about that moment that Embra realized there were no more birdcalls and whirrings of wings on either side of them. The forest had fallen strangely silent.

Their own gear creaked in its usual manner as they rode on, but the sounds were startlingly loud now as the overdukes listened intently, peered, and . . . waited.

Tshamarra suddenly stiffened in her saddle. At almost the same moment, the distant Craer threw up his hand in a silent wave of warning.

Silence held for a moment more—and then the trees flanking the trail erupted into snarling movement. Large, dark beasts burst out at the over-dukes through dancing branches, shredded leaves tumbling—six-legged monsters bigger than bears, gaping great wide jaws like the largest and ugli-est lurgfish hauled up in Sirl nets. Mean and hungry red eyes flashed as the beasts hurled themselves at the rearing, screaming overduchal horses.

Embra cursed as she fumbled for her Stone while trying to stay in her wildly bucking saddle—and Blackgult's blade slashed past her out of nowhere to hack at monstrous jaws reaching to close on her arm.

Orange blood fountained from the beast's sliced snout, accompanied by a loud, pain-filled roar—a roar echoed by other beasts along the trail, where Craer had raced his own frightened mount back to join them, busily hurling daggers into red eyes and down beast-throats as he came.

Hawkril stood up in his stirrups, reins bouncing free, and held his own fearful mount steady by gripping its head in one iron-strong hand. His other hand swung his warsword, hacking tirelessly, the sharp steel rising and falling in a blur soon marked by sprays of orange gore.

Tshamarra cried out and clutched at her head as three coldly hostile minds broke her seeking spell and then fled from her thoughts again, as swiftly as if three swords had slid icily through her—and as they departed, the surging, unified beast attack broke apart into a growling flurry of mon-sters fleeing in all directions.

Branches splintered and cracked as hairy bodies plunged through them, Hawkril riding hard in pursuit. More than one wide-jawed beast fell heavily, squalling, as the armaragor's blade hit home. Embra called up a burst of fire in the air under the nose of the only beast still menacing the two sorceresses, as Blackgult pursued another on its ungainly scramble back into the trees.

At the forefront of the chaos of frightened, plunging overduchal horses, Craer cursed softly as a six-legged monster wheeled away wearing one of his best daggers. Leaping from his saddle, he bounced once in the swirling trail-dust, sprang forward, and landed running.

His sprint was short but swift: he caught the beast as it was shouldering between two trees in pain-wracked haste. Catching hold of his knife-hilt as if it was a handle provided by the gods, Craer hauled hard—and found himself steered bruisingly by a tree branch up onto the thing's surging, stinking back.

Which was about the time he saw another beast-head turning toward him in the tree-filled gloom, jaws opening, and remembered that this was no bards' ballad—and that overbold heroes seldom live long.

Taking hold of his dagger with one hand and an overhead tree limb with the other, Craer jerked, twisted, and ended up dangling above emptiness, gore-dripping dagger in hand, as those wide jaws reached up for him.

He kicked out at hand-sized teeth, driving the snarling snout aside—and as he swung away and it whirled amid a great splintering of small branches to bite at him again, Hawkril arrived at a run.

The armaragor swung his great blade in both hands, down and in, like a woodcutter seeking to fell a tree with one ax blow—and the beast roared in pain and fell back, one leg almost severed. Wailing, it fled into the trees, disappearing with many crashings.

Meanwhile, Blackgult was swinging his own sword in a smaller but just as tireless metal storm, slicing and slashing at a beast as it turned its head repeatedly to try to bite Embra and Tshamarra.

" 'Tis almost as if someone's controlling it," he gasped, hacking a snout already raw, diced, and dripping flesh in four places. Moaning, the beast finally whirled and fled blindly through the nearest saplings, trunks shattering under its weight.

And then all the beasts were gone, and the anointed Overdukes of Aglirta were panting at each other across a blood-spattered ruin of hacked branches, trembling and snorting horses, and Craer's mocking comment, "My, but a stroll along a woodland trail in Aglirta these days is apt to be *awfully* entertaining!"

"W-what were they?" Embra gasped. "I've never seen the like before . . ."

"Dlargar," Hawkril growled. "Beasts sometimes called running bears and sometimes widejaws. Of the swamps nigh Elgarth—never seen in the Vale."

"So they were conjured?" Craer asked sharply. "By someone still out there?"

"Well," the Lady Talasorn replied, "yes, and they *were,* but . . ."

"No awakened magic or scrying near us," Embra reported. "They've fled."

"Serpents?"

"Yes," Tshamarra said grimly. "Three of them guided those beasts, and broke my tracing spell. Their minds were . . . not nice."

Hawkril frowned. "The same ones who turned the carters against us?"

The Lady Talasorn shrugged in reply.

"Will they try again right away, do you think?" Blackgult asked gently.

The sorceress shook her head. "They're nowhere near—gone by magic. One was very angry, a rage born of fright. He won't willingly face us again until he has better spells to hurl."

Craer rolled his eyes. "Then let's be on our way, before someone *else* decides overdukes are good hunting."

The five clapped spurs to their horses together. The still-frightened mounts were only too glad to flee, galloping wildly over a ridge and out of the thick trees. Their riders peered warily around when the horses slowed, snorting and pawing, flanks streaming with sweat.

Embra looked to Blackgult questioningly, indicating her horse, but the Golden Griffon shook his head curtly, and pointed ahead down the trail. Winded or not, the horses would have to wait for a chance to rest.

Not many words were exchanged as the overdukes descended out of gently rolling hill farms, the trail often running beside a chattering brook that gathered strength and size as springs joined it, until—over a broad green shield of intervening forest—they could see the roofs of Stornbridge ahead.

It was a fair-sized place, a market-moot surrounded by several twisting streets of cottages. They could see gardens amid the trees, and many folk at work in them. With the day well past its height, much of Stornbridge lay in the shadow of the tersept's castle, which rose like a cluster of stone lances out of a little lake that served it as a moat.

"We've been seen," Craer announced, pointing at someone only Black-gult saw before the tiny, hastening figure passed into concealing greenery.

"Let's hope we won't have to fight our way through the town," Tshamarra commented. "My spells aren't endless."

"Embra," Blackgult asked politely, "have you such a thing as a shielding-spell against arrows?"

"Of course," the Lady of Jewels replied, "but even with the Dwaer to source it, I can't hold something large enough to protect all of us on horseback, on all sides, as we ride. Not without many gaps, albeit shifting and unseen. If we stood tight together, more or less unmoving, yes, but . . ."

Her father held up his hand. "Forget it. 'Twas only a passing thought. Perhaps I'm being foolish . . ."

Craer looked back at him. "You mislike the look of yonder trees as much as I do?" he asked quietly, gesturing at the thick stand ahead, where the trail plunged into gloom, turning and descending swiftly out of sight.

"Yes," Blackgult replied simply, reaching for the small, almost useless shield slung across the high back of his saddle. Hawkril already had his own out. Embra looked at Tshamarra, who gazed back and shrugged.

"As usual, my sweet curves are all my armor," the last surviving Talasorn announced—as Craer spurred his mount to swiftness, the rest of them did likewise, and they thundered into the trees together.

Here and there woodcutters' glades opened out on either side, but for the most part the forest was old, dark, and thickly grown, branches interlaced above the road to form a dark tunnel. Wherever their steep descent revealed glimpses of what lay ahead, it seemed the five were always looking at the tall towers of Stornbridge Castle.

Slippery leaves forced them to slow, and Hawkril growled, "Made for brigand strikes," as he fell back to ride beside Embra. There was no room for anyone to shield her other side, even if they'd had armored riders in plenty to do such a thing. As it was, Blackgult fell back to let Tshamarra ride just ahead. Craer was left alone at the forefront, and he thanked his companions loudly and sarcastically for that as they plunged down through the last stretch of forest, spurring more swiftly again now as sunlight—and the waiting homes of Stornbridge—opened out ahead.

"We're turning into a lot of fearful shy-at-shadows," Embra told her man ruefully as the trees grew thinner, and the piercing rays of sunlight more prevalent. Tangleleaf and thrushtarn bushes grew thickly where the light fell, making hedges on either side of the trail, and they could hear the *thock* of axes on chopping blocks ahead, and the creaking of cartwheels. Hawkril made a small, noncommittal sound and raised his shield higher.

The next sound they heard was a loud hissing from the trees all around—and a startled grunt from Craer as an arrow struck his shoulder and snatched him out of his saddle, its bloody, glistening point coming out right through his back as he fell.

Tshamarra screamed and tried to ride right through Hawkril to reach the fallen procurer. As their horses jostled, the armaragor's shield rattled under the crashing strikes of three arrows—and an arrowhead burst half through it, to quiver not far in front of Tshamarra's nose.

At about that time a shaft thudded into her horse, and it reared. The Lady Talasorn clawed at its mane to try to keep her saddle as Embra snarled an incantation, Blackgult shouted something else, and Hawkril sprouted an arrow of his own.

As she saw hooves kick at leaves overhead and started the long, slow tumble down into darkness, Tshamarra screamed again. Arrows came hissing down like storm-driven rain . . .

4

A Stornbridge Welcome

The circular window of the study overlooked the finest and most extensive gardens in all wealthy and sun-warmed Arlund. A gray-bearded, dark-browed man in simple but expensive robes stood gazing in the direction of Aglirta, thinking of that nigh-Kingless Land.

Dolmur Bowdragon did a lot of that, these days.

There were great disturbances in the flow of the Arrada, as if mighty magics were being worked in secret . . . somewhere in Silverflow Vale. Of course. Such things *always* befell in Aglirta, land of reckless mages and those fell wizards who called themselves "priests of the Serpent." Which was why Dolmur kept spell-watch over that long, narrow green realm that had one great river at its heart—and not much else to remark upon.

So who in Aglirta was working sorceries that shook all Darsar . . . when the priests were dabbling in poisons and bribery, and the forces of the king were rounding up every wizard they could find?

Such puzzles were why he'd always watched Aglirta, and always would . . . even if it hadn't been a place that had made his heart dark and heavy with grief.

Accursed Aglirta—the realm that had swallowed most of the younger Bowdragons. Cut down in eager youth, their bright magic lost before they could quite achieve mastery . . . just a handful among the ranks of all the dead and forgotten wizards who'd fallen in the ongoing strife that had been the true ruler of the Kingless Land for as long as Dolmur could remember.

As long as his parents could have remembered, too, and probably their parents before that. Senseless, so senseless.

"They died," he murmured to the unheeding window, "because they were fools who went looking for trouble. Fools near and dear to me, but no less foolish for that."

The window was taller than a man, its frame set with gems inside and out—massive cabochon-cut stones there to hold enchantments that warded birds from the glass and kept the single huge pane from breaking under the sharpest weapon-blows Dolmur Bowdragon had been able to test it with. He smiled at the memory of the largest, strongest armaragor he could find running full-tilt down the long cellar passage in full armor, before leaping into the air to put his entire weight behind a great swing of his two-handed battleax. In the crash that had followed, the weapon had been chipped and its wielder numbed and winded, but the glass had held firm, unmarked. It was a good, strong spell, one of the last powered by the slowly ebbing life of the spellbound wizard entombed alive deep under this house. Someone called Eiyraskul, who'd been a foe of Dolmur's father.

Dolmur would have preferred to source his lasting spells from an enchanted ring, wand, or stone he could control rather than a slumbrous mage who might someday be freed of the binding enchantments and come looking to slay Bowdragons—but wizards weren't obligingly sacrificing their own lives to craft such treasures, these days.

Dolmur sighed aloud and told the window, "We must work with what we have. Yearning after desired dreams of what can never be is how the weak-minded waste their lives."

"Is it now?" came a quiet voice from behind him. A voice that should not have been there.

Dolmur Bowdragon whirled around. To a wizard, such surprises are armor-chinks of carelessness or misfortune that usually mean death. But no man can help but want to see his slayer or fate.

The ward-spells on the study and the house around it should have hurled away non-mages and warned Dolmur of the entry of any wizard powerful enough to break them . . . yet this robed man facing him, with the raven-dark hair and the soft, knowing smile, could be nothing else but a wizard.

An intruder standing in his own study, boots only a stride from a flag-stone that bore one of Dolmur's hurl-hard spells—that would snatch the man straight up to impalement on the spikes of the huge iron dragon-head candle cluster thrusting down from the ceiling above.

His visitor smiled more broadly, and carefully stepped around that flag-stone as he paced forward. "Forgive the abruptness of my intrusion—and for that matter the intrusion itself, Lord Bowdragon. I come with peaceful intent, to make an offer, not to try spells with you."

"Then be welcome, Lord Nameless," Dolmur said calmly, gesturing to the lounges by the fireplace as he turned and walked toward them. "Offers always interest me. Will you take wine? Or hot serbret, perhaps?"

"Neither, thank you," his guest replied, following. The stranger's route took him across a certain cluster of flagstones—as Dolmur had intended it to—but no alarm flourish of horn music swelled to life. This was no intruder, then, but a "sending." Solid-seeming but illusory, and so of course unable to drink. Able to spy on him for months, though . . . and wanting Dolmur to know it, by the avoidance of the hurl-hard flagstone.

"Then take your ease, and unfold your offer." The Bowdragon patriarch waved his hand toward the fireplace, offering his unexpected guest any of four lounges—or the more likely choice of standing against the mantel. Again his guest surprised him, taking a seat. There came a slight rustling of robes and a creak of furniture as he sat down, but Dolmur smiled inwardly. He knew of no natural way to make that lounge creak in that manner, given what it was made of—so his visitor must be using magic to "supply" sounds, to fool Dolmur into thinking this sending was solid. My, to have magic to waste so lavishly . . .

Dolmur took a seat of his own, briefly entertaining the notion of using the lingering spell that amplified his voice to summon servants to echo perfectly the rustling and creaking, to signal to his guest his recognition of their falsity, but—no. Mages whose greatest need was to impress did such things, and Dolmur Bowdragon was years beyond the need to impress.

Or so he hoped. Assuming a relaxed pose, he waited.

"I'm Ingryl Ambelter, a wizard once in the service of Baron Silvertree of Aglirta. I supported him in his ambitions to rule the Kingless Land, and confess myself less than enamored of the new King, the boy Raulin Castlecloaks—and of the overdukes and former regent who crowned him. They've done me much injury, though my sorcery has been powerful enough to keep me alive and allow me to flourish since. These foes of mine have also done much injury to you, slaying more than one Bowdragon without cause, warning, or so much as fair salutation. Now they're hunting wizards, slaying or imprisoning without cause—and when they've scoured Silverflow Vale clean of mages, they'll look in this direction and others, and reach for you. Not for nothing do your countrymen have the saying, 'Beware wizards of Aglirta.' The overdukes watch you even now, and remain a menace to you so long as they live."

"And so?" Dolmur asked calmly, wishing he'd fetched a decanter, but not wanting to interrupt this Ambelter now.

"I offer you a chance to avenge the deaths of your kin—and more. I'm here to entreat you to join with me to overthrow and slay Aglirta's new King and his overdukes."

Silence hung between them after that. It lasted a goodly time, both robed men staring expressionlessly into each other's eyes, before Dolmur slowly shook his head.

"As it happens," he told his unexpected visitor calmly, "I've no interest in slaying any royalty or nobles, and even less interest in overthrowing any ruler. Mastering sorcery is enough for me, and takes most of my time—and achieving as much power as possible in these arts would seem to be my only defense when these Aglirtans, as you warn, come looking for me. If they ever do."

"Oh, they will, believe me. I know they spy upon you with magic, even now. I say again: 'Beware wizards of Aglirta.' "

"Ingryl Ambelter, *you* are a wizard of Aglirta."

"Forgive my correction, Lord Bowdragon: I was once a wizard of Aglirta, neither born nor reared there, but merely hired by a baron of that realm—and cast aside when he deemed me no longer useful. I'm now an exiled foe of Aglirta."

"Correction noted; yet I remain a man who desires neither to slay nor to overthrow. Such actions create lawless strife, and the banishing of such must needs be by the imposition of new rulers . . . and in being such a ruler, or thinking myself responsible for placing anyone in such a position, whether they know of me or take counsel of me or not, are things in which I have no interest."

"Not even if it delivers into your hands one or more of the fabled Dwaerindim?" Ambelter held out his empty hand, palm up—and suddenly a mottled, round stone hovered or rather spun above it, acrawl with strange glows and fleeting lightnings.

Dolmur's visitor smiled over it at the patriarch of the Bowdragons. "This is but an illusion of the Stone I already control. I'm not foolish enough to think I can control more than two Dwaer. Wherefore I need someone I can trust, stand in common cause with, and respect, to wield the third and hopefully the fourth Dwaer, once we win them. I already know where one Dwaerindim lies: in the hands of one of the overdukes who seek us both. The Lady Embra Silvertree has it, and must be made to yield it . . . or neither of us is safe. I need your help, Dolmur Bowdragon—and the reward for your aid could well be what wizards of all Darsar dream of: an everlasting and mighty Dwaer-Stone."

Ambelter held out his hand, and the Stone spinning above it drifted toward the eldest living Bowdragon. Small motes of light sparkled into life, orbited it, and winked out again in an endless, excited cycle of eager power. Dolmur stared narrowly at it, and then drew his head back and said bleakly, "No. I'm not yet interested."

"Aha! Then the day will soon come when you are?"

"The day may come when I'm changed enough to be overly tempted by such power," Dolmur Bowdragon replied in a level voice, "but it is not a change I shall welcome. Or encourage."

"Then—"

"Then begone, Ingryl Ambelter. Take your sending, and your spying, too, and return my privacy to me!"

Ingryl Ambelter nodded, and the winking Stone vanished, leaving him empty-handed once more. "I respect your wishes, Lord Bowdragon, and have no desire to give offense or make of you an enemy. But by the names of your slain kin, I entreat you to remember my offer. Should you ever desire vengeance for—"

"Begone!" Dolmur Bowdragon snapped, rising to his feet. He took a swift, threatening step toward Ambelter, but the sending only sat, smiling faintly at him, until with a sudden furious incantation Dolmur banished it.

He was breathing heavily as he went back to the window, and stared out at the garden without seeing a single tree or flower. "So it's begun," he murmured. "Far sooner than I'd like . . . But then, things always do."

Mouth tightening, he whirled away from the window, silently calling on the binding to strengthen his wards. They sang and glowed in the air around him as he added reluctantly, "Wherefore I must make ready. Time to earn my share of the fell reputation that clings to wizards."

Shuddering, Embra clutched her Dwaer to her breast and snarled out a spell—and the gale that roared out from her swept away arrows like dry leaves whirled away by a winter-heralding storm.

Hawkril lowered his head against the hissing flood of arrows and sprinted forward, waving his warsword wildly as if he could bat speeding warshafts out of the air with it.

He could not. One arrow shrieked along the armor covering his shoulder and bit home deep enough to hang from him as he ran—and the next slammed home right through the lacings of his side-plates, driving the air from him and spinning him half around. His insides blazed up into numbing fire as he roared, struggling to keep going. Two more arrows found him, an archer dodged away through the trees in front of him, and then a howling storm caught the armaragor from behind and tried to hurl him off his feet.

Hawkril snarled at the fire now raging in his innards and leaped forward, seeking to reach another man in the trees—and the gale at his back plucked him right into the forester. They fell heavily to the ground together, rolling and growling like beasts . . . beasts trying to sink sharpened fangs of steel into each other . . .

The Lady of Jewels watched her sorcerous wind howl away from her. It slapped Tshamarra to the ground and rolled a groaning, cursing Craer away from Embra, too, but . . . 'twas that or they'd all be slain hosting half a dozen arrows each, or more.

Blackgult was whirled to the turf with a snarl, and even Hawkril struggled against her rushing wind, staggering through the trees bent over in pain and clutching at the arrows in him, so Embra reluctantly let it drop.

As soon as she did, a fresh volley of arrows came racing at her from all sides—aimed right at *her,* this time!

Gasping, Tshamarra Talasorn found herself able to move again, the moan of the gale dying as it slackened. She was wallowing in road mud, fighting for breath, and couldn't even see if anyone was running up to stab at her . . . hastily she rolled over onto her back, seeing a brief whirlwind of greenery and rushing arrows and sun-dappled sky. Embra's magic had left the air still roiling up twigs and old leaves, in a storm that began inches above her nose.

Sobbing for breath, Tshamarra tried to think of what spell she could use to deliver herself—and all the overdukes—from this now. She could hear a distant Hawkril roaring in pain, gasping to match her own that must be Embra, and Craer grunting with effort, grunts that moved rapidly away from her. She dared not even lift her head to look, as arrow after arrow hummed through the air just above her . . .

Embra threw herself into the dirt. Something struck her elbow a numbing blow as she went down—a burning that swiftly became a tearing, sickening pain. She bit at her lip to keep from retching, her ears full of the vicious, wasplike buzzing snarl of arrows whisking over her, only inches away. Her arrow-struck arm felt wet . . . wetness that was trickling between her fingers. She did not have to look to know it was blood.

Well, if Embra's little gale was going to roll him like an empty tankard, roll he would—into the trees where he might at least find *someone* to bury a dagger in. Anything to take his mind away from the numbing fire of the arrow in his shoulder . . .

Craer tumbled enthusiastically, drawing in breath for a whoop—and then spending it in a curse as the gale suddenly died, leaving him all too far away from the nearest tree, with movement behind it that just had to be a bowman shifting to see him better, so as to put an arrow—his next one—through a certain stranded procurer.

"Graul," Craer grunted, kicking off hard and tucking his head under so tightly it hurt. The world whirled, his boot heels slammed into the ground as he trailed his injured shoulder, and red pain blinded him for a moment.

He flung himself forward and out of that red mist, growling "Bebolt!" this time, and rolled on, bruising his knuckles but not daring to let go of the daggers clutched in both fists. If the—"Sargh!"—gods were willing, he'd live long enough to have a chance to use them, once he reached that tree . . .

"Enough!" the Lady Silvertree spat, and furiously hurled her will up and out at the trees above, willing the air to become not a gale, but a great hand that would slam and push.

A half-heard *heaviness* rippled in the air, rolling outward from above her. She heard Craer cursing softly, and then some startled, angry oaths from farther away.

A trunk as large around as one of the thrashing, dying overduchal horses cracked with a sharp, deafening sound. Embra watched it topple—and as if its fall had been some sort of cue, small branches splintered, tumbled, and then were hurled away in all directions. Most of the other trees she could see started to groan and then lean away from her, farther . . . and farther . . .

The ground heaved under Embra as a deep root was forced to the surface. She rode it upward in time to come upright and see fearfully crouching archers loosing a volley of shafts low along the ground at her.

Setting her teeth—Three Above, but her arm was hurting!—Embra slashed out with a sudden gust of wind that snatched the arrows far off to the right, well away from her companions.

The trees all around were leaning slowly outward like the spreading petals of an opening flower. One fell as the groaning of tortured wood grew as loud as a roaring bull, and its crash spurred some of the archers to startled shouts. Those angry, frightened cries were still rising when Embra heard something else: the sudden crashings of heavy-booted men fleeing frantically away through dead leaves.

Someone screamed in fear, someone else bellowed out a long, elaborate curse like a battle cry—and a third someone's rallying yell ended abruptly in the heavy crash of a tree slamming to earth. Boots kicked wildly from beneath its trunk—briefly, ere they went limp and still. Human groans mingled with louder protests of tortured wood as Embra's sorcery slammed fleeing archers helplessly into tree trunks. More than one bow splintered in such collisions, and watching archers saw their fellows battered, cast fearful glances at Embra, and then rose out of their crouches to flee headlong into the forest.

The Lady of Jewels swayed on her tree root, hoping her arm wasn't broken. It felt weak and useless, and she needed peace and quiet to fight past the pain and remember *how* to heal with her Dwaer. 'Twas easy when no battle was raging and a certain sorceress was unhurt, but right now . . . *Horns of the Lady, it hurt!*

Embra's gale had slammed into Blackgult's horse, driven it back a few stamping, frightened feet, and then—once it reared obligingly—flung it over on its side.

Out of that snorting, pawing confusion the Golden Griffon sprang, in a leap that brought him to the ground in the lee of his rolling mount. Crouching, he ran back down the trail the way they'd come, chased by two hissing arrows that were caught and sent tumbling by the gale . . . and then he was in the trees with his sword in his hand, keeping low as he whirled around and fought his way back toward Embra, from trunk to trunk.

Men with unfriendly faces and blades in their hands were waiting for him in the lee of the fourth tree. Ezendor Blackgult gave them a grin that held no humor, and launched himself into a charge.

When the gale died, his arrival among them was its own storm. Swordtips bit through his armor soon enough, but men were already down and dying around him by then, and he was on to the next tree.

He gave the men waiting there a cheerful smile, too.

·   ·   ·

Out of a blur of tears, Embra shook herself awake, wondering how long she'd been sliding into pain and letting her magic falter.

Well, no archers were running toward her, at least. Her companions were huddled together around her. As far as she could tell, Blackgult had suffered only swordcuts. Everyone else was nursing arrows . . . but one by one they all gave her the grim nods that told her they'd survive for now, if she needed to fight on.

Throwing back her head to gulp in air—it seemed she'd have to quell this thrusting-with-air magic soon, or fall asleep for lack of something to breathe—the Lady Silvertree called on her Dwaer to quiet and call back their horses.

Two responded, snorting and tossing their heads as they came back into view through the shattered trees. Only Blackgult's horse looked unhurt, though Embra's own mount might be more terrified than wounded. Craer's horse was down and dead, Tshamarra's was dying on the trail behind them, and the great beast that bore Hawkril limped so badly that no one could ride it, perhaps ever again.

Sunlight was flooding down into Embra's new-made clearing—and as she looked in all directions, seeking foes foolish enough to bend bows in her direction again, she caught sight of some astonished woodcutters far off in the trees, axes dangling forgotten in their hands as they gaped at her. None of them looked angry or likely to attack. Rather, they looked as if they wanted to stay a long, long way back from so deadly a sorceress—or perhaps dwell in a land that had never known wizards, and never would.

Embra turned to seeking foes again. Some of the archers had drawn their last breaths in Darsar; their sprawled bodies were already surrounded by buzzing flies. Other bowmen had taken hurt but yet lived, and were feebly trying to drag themselves away or at least into hiding.

"Who commands you?" the Lady of Jewels demanded as she glared at their frightened faces, her voice cold and level. They froze in unison, but no one seemed in any hurry to answer, so she asked again.

Silence.

"Well, then," she said curtly, "I'll have to assume that each one of you is the Tersept of Stornbridge—and guilty of treason against the River Throne. Wherefore I've no choice but to slay you all, one after another, starting *now*."

Taking a slow, purposeful step forward, she raised her hands above her head in two dramatic claws, a gesture of menacing magic that was spoiled by her need to hold the Dwaer in one hand—and use its power to clumsily lift her injured arm. The resulting pain was so sickening that she staggered helplessly sideways, and almost spewed up the contents of her stomach.

Shuddering, the Lady Silvertree held herself upright by magic, swaying and letting small sparks of light swirl around her. Those twinkling motes meant nothing and could unleash no magic, but Embra hoped they looked impressive.

More than one of the watching men mistook her twisted expression for fury rather than pain, and cowered visibly.

"L-lady," an older archer called hesitantly, from among them, "how can we win our lives? What must we do to have you spare us?"

Embra gave him the coldest and most steely look she could muster. "Bring me Tersept Stornbridge—or the man who ordered this attack upon us, if that man is not the tersept. Bring him *now*."

The man looked fearfully back over his shoulder, and so did some of his fellows. It mattered not if they ever summoned up the courage to obey her, for now the Lady Silvertree knew which trees to blast to flame and ashes if the pain threatened to overwhelm her.

Swaying, she turned toward that thick stand, on the far side of a wooded hollow a good distance down the road to the open fields of Stornbridge. "Come forth, Stornbridge!" she snapped, letting the Dwaer carry her quiet voice into the trees like a biting weapon.

Silence fell again, and she added almost lazily, hoping no one would realize just how close she was to collapsing, "Come forth. Or die."

There was a stirring, and a man rode forth from behind the trees—bareheaded and empty-handed, slowing his mount swiftly to a trot, and then to a walk. When Hawkril raised his blade warningly, he stopped his horse altogether.

"That's not Stornbridge," Craer muttered, out of the side of his mouth. Blackgult nodded, and smiled wryly when he saw that his daughter's eyes had already narrowed in suspicion. He crawled closer to her, so as to be within reach if she fell. She thanked him with the flick of an eye, her cold expression never changing.

"Stornbridge," Embra told the trees gently, "I want to see *you,* not your loyal armaragors and cortahars. I've felt one of your arrows, and my patience is dwindling. Very swiftly."

The man who rode into view this time was larger, and wore overly splendid armor—as did his horse, lavishly emblazoned with the arms of Stornbridge: scarlet hawk after scarlet hawk, perched on as many gilded bridge-arches in an unending tapestry of barding and freshly painted armorplate.

"Graul me if it doesn't look like a court costume," Craer muttered. Tshamarra laid a hand on his arm, and he winced as he tried to give her a smile.

"I–I humbly beg your pardons, Crown Lords and Ladies," the Tersept Stornbridge said grandly, sweeping his arms wide as he assumed an anguished expression. "Down bows, men of Stornbridge!"

He rode nearer, trying an uneasy smile. His elaborately curled shoulder-length locks of chestnut-hued hair warred with watery blue eyes and an awkwardly broken nose. "Forgive me, great Overdukes, but I've had to fight off so many brigands in this forest–here, before my very gates!–in recent days! I–I had no idea . . . if I'd heard even a whisper you were coming, or seen royal banners, or heard heralds' horns . . ."

"Is it then your custom to greet any five swift and well-mounted riders with arrows? Sirl traders, perhaps, or Flowfoam heralds?" Embra snapped.

"Well, I–I–"

"Or any tersept or baron of the realm, riding with his personal armaragors?"

"Lady Silvertree," Stornbridge blustered, "as a tersept myself, I'm charged by the same crown you serve and uphold with the duty of keeping safe my roads, lands, and people! Armed folk riding hard and fast around here are *brigands,* and if an honest man of Stornbridge doesn't put swiftly an arrow into any brigand he faces, he all too often dies!"

"I daresay," the Lady Embra replied. "And I also daresay that if you judge who's a brigand and who's not so swiftly, and with eyesight so poor, you shoot down more than your share of honest men of Stornbridge."

"Lady, I protest!" Stornbridge snapped.

"Lord, I *bleed,*" Embra snarled back at him, and lifted her Dwaer meaningfully. The tersept and the men slowly gathering behind him stiffened in unison, and both Blackgult and Hawkril struggled to their feet and stood where they could block any charge or bowshot aimed at the Stone or the slender arm that held it.

All of the overdukes stared coldly at Stornbridge, and he stared back at them, defiance warring with fear across his florid face. His words fooled none of them, and he knew it.

"Of course," the tersept said abruptly, raising his voice. "I quite forget both my manners and your peril. You have my word that you'll be both safe and treated with all courtesy, as we tend you in Stornbridge Castle. All

Stornbridge is ashamed at this terrible mistake!" He turned and roared, "Clear me yon wood-wagon! Let the overdukes be conducted to the castle with as much gentle care and dignity as we can give them!"

There was a general scrambling, all around the overdukes. Blackgult and Embra glared about as if expecting a stealthy bowshot or sudden sword-charge, but—aside from averting their eyes from the simmering displeasure of their overduchal guests—the Storn men seemed to be interested only in obeying Stornbridge's orders in almost frantic haste.

Amid the tumult, Hawkril reached out a long arm and hauled his friend Craer upright. Tshamarra sprang to help the procurer as he winced, swayed, and spat blood.

"Well, now," Craer asked her from between clenched teeth, as firewood was hastily swept off the wagon, and cloaks laid across its mess of bark and splinters for them, "did I not describe him rightly?"

" 'A blustering man in overly splendid armor,' " Tshamarra quoted in a disgusted murmur. "Yes, your words cover him quite well. Now keep *still*, Craer! You've lost blood enough!"

"Lady," Hawkril rumbled, leaning close to Embra.

"*Embra,* Hawk," she whispered, her lips trembling on the sudden edge of tears. "Call me Embra—and just hold on a little longer. Please." As hesitant hands ushered them up onto the wagon, the sorceress cast a warning ring of harmless golden sparks around herself, and in its midst leaned toward Blackgult and murmured, "Father, be ready if I falter. Tshamarra, hold to my hand. Together we must . . . must . . ."

Heal. Tshamarra silently sent that word into all of their minds with a swift, simple spell that kept them all linked, so any attack, word, or gesture one of them saw would instantly be shown to them all . . . and in that half-mazed state they rattled and swayed their way into Stornbridge.

Hawkril and Craer peered up at the looming castle, seeking to glimpse who gazed down at them from window and battlement—but never saw certain servants standing in the shadows behind the row of gawking maids who leaned and jostled along the sills. Four chamber knaves among those watchers in the shadows exchanged silent glances . . . and then slipped away. They hastened out of Stornbridge Castle by rear doors, crossing its moat by bridges unseen from the foregate where the wagon of wounded overdukes rumbled along in the heart of a hastily formed and untidy honor guard of battered archers and puzzled woodcutters.

The departing chamber knaves did not hasten as men do when they flee in fear, never to return. Rather, they hurried as men do who desire to deliver reports amid the cottages of Stornbridge, and then hasten back to their castle posts ere their covert expeditions are noticed by visiting–and somewhat battered–overdukes.

Fangbrother Khavan peered at the muddy pastures of Bowshun rather sourly. He'd seen more than enough dusty, muddy, dung-reeking villages of backcountry Algirta to last him the rest of his life. A thorny branch sliced ever so gently across his nose as he turned away from the incredible stench of a far-too-successful farmer's pig midden, and back to where Scaled Master Arthroon's iron grip on his shoulder was guiding him. A crowd of intently listening villagers, yes–quite possibly every last lad and lass of thinking age in Bowshun–but even if they were hanging on every word uttered by a Serpent-priest, this was very far away from where men dwelt who held real power in Silverflow Vale.

Yet here they all were: a Brother of the Serpent he'd never seen before; Khavan himself; and cold, implacable Scaled Master Arthroon. Wasting words on dungheads dragged away from their fields to stare uncomprehendingly at a snarling servant of the Serpent.

"Know you," the man was raging now, punching the air with his fists in emphasis, "that the Dragon was *evil*. Yes, the good Serpent defeated it–but at great loss. Your worship, your coins, and your strong, honest hands are needed!"

The Brother paused, looking around at his silent audience, waiting for at least a scattered cheer–and daring it to come. The silence held.

"Worship the Serpent!" he roared. "Give us your support, that we may cleanse Flowfoam of this boy king and the foul, decadent Baron Blackgult who lurks behind him, telling you what to do just as he always has!"

A mutter ran through the crowd, a murmur of agreement. The priest grinned, thinking he'd broken the mistrust and fear he'd seen in the villagers' faces earlier. "Oh, I know some of you dare not rally to our holy cause yet. You're honest folk, and I admire that. Dutiful folk, dependable. You're the backbone and ready hands and staunch heart of Aglirta . . . and you'll know, when the time comes, the right thing to do."

He leaned forward to whisper conspiratorially. From their concealment in the bushes behind the crowd, Scaled Master Arthroon and Fangbrother Khavan might have been two statues–but the Brother of the Serpent wasn't speaking to them.

"Some of you know already: the wisest of you, those who see first what's best for Bowshun, and for Aglirta. I'll welcome you this very night, when the moon falls upon Emdel's Glade, to worship the Sacred Serpent with me. In the glade I'll say more, and together we'll gaze upon a glorious future for Aglirta. I tell you that before you're another summer older, the Kingless Land shall be rich and mighty at last! *You* shall be rich and mighty at last!"

He drew himself up, robes swirling, and smiled down at them. "In the moonlight, in Emdel's Glade, you'll hear more. Wise ones, I'll await you there." With one uplifted hand the Brother of the Serpent traced the sinuous Sign of the Serpent in the air.

A few tentative hands echoed it—and he smiled at their owners from atop the haystack, whirled, and stepped down from its far side.

A breeze stirred, a bird flapped lazily over a nearby field, and still the folk of Bowshun stood still and silent, staring at the empty height where the priest had stood in silence . . . a silence that lasted a very long time before any of them stirred and moved away. It was even longer before they started to chatter, and for the first time, Fangbrother Khavan was impressed.

He still didn't see what a few toothless old farmers, dungpat-hurling youths, and sunburnt dungheads of the fields could do against armored cortahars of Aglirta. Now, however, he believed that they could be made to do something.

And that, after all, was what priests were for.

5

Feasts and Entreaties

This will be quite acceptable," the Lady Silvertree said coldly, waving the aged seneschal toward the door. He'd made the mistake of trying to be haughty to her—she was, after all, no more than a dirty and bedraggled woman claiming some grand upriver title, and accompanied by a handful of ragtag armsmen and vagabonds who could well have stolen all they'd brought—but his first glance had proven to be wrong. Very wrong.

Seneschal Urbrindur was old enough to have felt the sharp edge of two baronial tongues before the stormy bluster of his current master, and he knew real nobility when he heard and felt it. This icy wench was noble, Three take all. Was it *his* fault folk didn't look their proper parts anymore?

He strode stiffly out of the room he'd conducted the five wounded and furious "guests" to, and stared at the door after it closed in his face for only a brief, thoughtful moment before whirling away down the passage to deliver several sharp blows with his rod of office to heads and shoulders of the nearest handy chamber knaves.

Then he stalked off without a word to them, ignoring the hate-filled glances he knew they were giving his back. Such reactions were only fitting, after all—and Seneschal Urbrindur was very strong on what was right and fitting.

"They made a right and fitting end of as many of our horses as they could." Gloomily Craer surveyed the battered remnants of their saddlebags, flicking a last splinter of arrowshaft out of a torn tangle of leather. "I don't doubt roast horseflesh will feature prominently in tonight's feast."

"Later, Lightfingers," Embra Silvertree told him, her voice almost pleading. "I can't use the Dwaer if I fall senseless, now can I?"

Despite the arrows he still wore, Hawkril was at her side in an instant, awkwardly cradling her shoulders to hold her up. Embra sagged against him gratefully and asked, "Father?"

"Chairs, or to the floor together?" Blackgult asked, sword in hand as he peered about the room, seeking every possible spyhole and entrance.

"Floor, if we can get there *gently*."

Craer gave Embra a leer. "Lady, I never thought I'd hear you ask so plainly."

Tshamarra rolled her eyes and brought her hand down, ever so gently, on the broken shaft of the arrow that protruded from Craer's shoulder.

He doubled up with a shuddering sob, and she lowered him the rest of the way to the floor tiles, murmuring, "Lord Delnbone, you *mustn't* hurt yourself more than you have already. Please, submit yourself to my will for once, and behave sensibly—and so live longer. Possibly."

Hawkril snorted at those honeyed words—and then hastily went to his own knees as the last surviving Talasorn gave him a hard glare.

"Close together," Embra told them, "so we can all touch." *The Dwaer's power isn't endless,* she added silently, using the last fading tatters of Tshamarra's spell. *Not in so short a time. I've done much with it already.*

"You certainly have," Blackgult murmured into her ear as he lowered Embra to the floor. "Though if admittedly twisted memories serve me, 'tis more a matter of the wielder's mind reaching limits than 'tis a Stone becoming exhausted."

"Well, *that's* consoling," Craer hissed through clenched teeth.

"We're being watched," Tshamarra whispered, joining them on the floor. More than once she glanced straight up, as if to repeatedly make sure nothing deadly was plunging down from the ceiling.

"Of course. Magic?" Blackgult muttered.

"No. Eyes. Moving, in the wall tapestry behind you."

"As long as 'tis just spying, and not darts that strike. We must shield Embra, until—"

"Of course," Tshamarra whispered back, with a mocking smile. "Magic?"

"No," Blackgult replied, in a ghostly parody of his 'old baron' growl. "Those charming armored curves of yours—augmented by my old bones."

The Talasorn sorceress flicked an appraising glance up and down his body. "Hmmph. Well-fleshed ancient bones, I'd say."

The Golden Griffon struck a preening, feminine pose that would have done credit to the most alluring of court ladies, and then relaxed back into his customary wary lounging. "I'll take this side," he murmured into Tshamarra's amused—and astonished—face. "See if you can cover the rest without letting our stubborn lion of an armaragor rear up to try to do his duty no matter how sorely wounded he is, for once."

"Lord Ezendor," Hawkril protested, from somewhere beneath Tshamarra, but Blackgult waved a quelling hand.

"I'm your Lord no longer. Ezendor, yes—and as your friend I tell you: belt up and lie still. You've more arrows in you than the rest of us put together. Embra?"

"Forgive my selfishness, but this will go best if I'm free of pain. Now, Sarasper showed me . . . oh, yes . . ."

They felt her convulse, and then twitch and shudder from fingertips to toes. When it passed, Embra opened her eyes, smiled—and let the healing flow into them, like a warm and tingling tide.

As her four companions groaned and gasped, feeling pain ebbing from them, Blackgult moved like an attentive servant in response to looks she gave, gently drawing forth specific arrows at her bidding. Craer jerked when surrendering his shaft, mewing in helpless pain, but Tshamarra held him in a suddenly iron grip when he might otherwise have jerked away . . . and in both near silence and a surprisingly short time the healing was done, and they were whole again.

"We must be very careful not to lose that," Hawkril rumbled, patting the Stone as he flexed his arms and shoulders experimentally. "I'd not want to return to the days of pilfering trinkets from the Si—"

"Hush," Embra said severely, slapping his cheek gently with the tips of her fingers. "The walls listen, remember?"

"They also watch," Tshamarra said dryly, "which leaves me in strong need of Lord Delnbone temporarily shorn of his usual pranks, leering, and clever comments, to hold up a privacy cloak whilst I bathe—hmm, mintwater; they're not entirely uncivilized here—and don suitable finery for the feast to come."

"Ah, yes. Platters heaped with sleep-potions and poisons," Craer smirked. "I hope the seasoning, at least, is to my liking."

"I'll be using magic and expecting to find taints with it," Embra told him, turning to the saddlebags with the Stone glowing. "Now, let's see what the enthusiastic bowmen of Stornbridge left us."

"Not much of this one," Tshamarra said disgustedly, holding a torn fragment of gown up against her. "Ruined."

Craer winked. "Fallen, perhaps, but I'd hardly say ruined. The gown's had it, though."

The Lady Talasorn gave him a cold and level look. "Lord Procurer, I believe you're still on probation. Conduct yourself accordingly."

Craer glanced at Hawkril for sympathy, but the hulking armaragor gave him a grin, a wink, and the words, "Want to really unsettle our host? Wear that gown yourself!"

"Thousands of men in Aglirta," Embra told a ceiling thankfully still bereft of plummeting dangers, "and I have to travel with two afflicted with the delusion that they're uproariously funny jesters, fit for the courts of the South!"

Blackgult turned. "Two?"

Embra held up a warning hand. "Don't try to join their ranks. Just don't."

The Golden Griffon gave her a slow smile, and said merely, "This bids fair to be an extremely interesting meal."

"But, my Lord Overduke," the cortahar stammered uncertainly, "my lord the Tersept gave us very specific ord—"

"So," the hulking armaragor growled, glaring down from the burly height of a full two heads taller, "you choose to be as much of a traitor to Aglirta as he?" He hefted his warsword. "Well, then . . ."

"Ah, there's no need for bloodletting," the knight said hastily. "I'm sure—"

"Hurrh," the mountainous man in armor told him with grim humor. "So am I."

Behind a nearby wall, two men in robes adorned with crawling serpents traded glances. " 'Tis working!" Brother Landrun hissed. "He must never've met Anharu before—three breaths, and he accepts that this *is* the overduke!"

The Lord of the Serpent arched an eyebrow and displayed his direjaws smile. "But of course."

The young page pressed into service as a herald stumbled over their names and titles, but Blackgult said merely, "Enough, lad. They know who we are.

'Overdukes,' all, is as fine a way of saying it as any. Show us our seats and introduce these fine lords of Stornbridge to us, hmm?"

The young man stared at him, stammered something, and then hurriedly set about doing just that.

"Lord Blackgult," Tshamarra hissed, "I'm *not* a noble of Aglirta, nor—"

"You are now," he growled, "for this night at least. You can renounce your title of 'Overduke' in the morning, but try doing so now and I'll paddle your bare behind—*yes*, in front of all these Storn men. 'Tis the agreed-upon ritual; just ask Craer."

The Lady Talasorn gave them both withering looks. Craer grinned like a maniac, but Blackgult merely raised an unimpressed eyebrow. Surveying them both for a long, silent moment ere they turned to follow the herald, she sighed and followed them to the feast table.

Five men were already seated around its far end, regarding the overdukes expectantly. Six chamber knaves were ranged around the walls behind, but no Storn woman could be seen in the room—though none of the overdukes doubted that some of the eyes undoubtedly watching from the dozen or so high gallery windows were feminine. The tier of open balconies just above the chamber knaves, however, were as deserted as most of the places down the long feasting table. It seemed the Tersept of Stornbridge had little interest in displaying his humiliation to his people.

The young herald led each guest to a specific seat, named them, and then went to stand behind each seated man of Stornbridge in turn, reciting their titles carefully.

Each overduke mentally shortened the flow of grand words—how many high offices could a market town afford, anyway?—to simpler names. The old, bristle-whiskered man regarding them with open hostility was the local lornsar, or captain of cortahars, Lornsar Ryethrel. The more elegant and urbane man beside him was the castle official they'd already verbally dueled with: Seneschal Urbrindur. Next to Urbrindur, at the head of the table, was the tersept. On Lord Stornbridge's other side was his younger and more handsome echo, a man who proved to be both the Scribe and Coinmaster of Stornbridge, one Eirevaur. Beside the scribe sat a scarred mountain of a man with murderous eyes, who was introduced as the Tersept's Champion. *Enforcer, more like,* Embra thought silently. She suspected Champion Pheldane was well armed indeed under his satin shoulder robe. He looked at her as if she was a brothel-lass who'd set her price too high—a price he was looking forward to forcibly lowering. Soon.

Blackgult had drawn the seat beside the glowering champion. Across the table, Craer would be sitting beside the lornsar. Embra caught Tshamarra's glance, and rolled her eyes. Oh, this was going to be a jolly feasting, indeed . . .

At a curt nod from the seneschal, the stammering herald withdrew. The overdukes seated themselves, Hawkril casually swinging his chair up like a weightless toy to examine its legs and underside—and Embra not bothering to hide the faint singing sound of the Dwaer weaving a shield against archery around them all.

"Stornbridge is honored by your unexpected presence among us," the tersept said with a sunny smile. "I apologize again for the misunderstanding that greeted your arrival so painfully, but trust we can dine together cordially and forge true bonds of friendship, as loyal fellows of Aglirta."

"That is also our hope and trust," Blackgult told him gently, raising a goblet in salute but not putting it to his lips.

Craer sampled his wine very lightly, and then thrust his leg against Embra's, under the table. Unseen beneath the tabletop she touched the Dwaer to his hand and sent magic flooding into him.

The procurer swayed slightly as the burning sensation of the poison passed, and then smiled at Stornbridge. "You all enjoy mraevor in your wine? I find it makes most vintages too salty, but perhaps this pleases local Stornbridge palates."

"You *dare*—?" Lornsar Ryethrel growled, turning upon him.

Craer gave him a smile that could only be described as sweet. "Ah, no, Lornsar, I'm afraid someone else has been daring. Unless of course, you'd like to achieve that selfsame condition, by drinking of this goblet?"

He held it out, just beyond the lornsar's reach. The furious captain-of-guards slapped at it, as if to dash its contents across Craer's face, but then abruptly—at just about the time the procurer's other hand, under the table, put the very cold tip of a dagger against the upper edge of Ryethrel's codpiece—fell still and silent, sweating suddenly.

"Or perhaps you, Seneschal?" Craer asked mildly, proffering the goblet as if Ryethrel had said and done nothing. When Urbrindur gave him only stony silence, he lifted his brows and added mildly, "Anyone?"

"Perhaps the entire cask was tainted," Tshamarra said lightly, handing her own goblet to Craer. He sipped, nodded, and nudged Embra under the table again. Her healing was swifter this time, and was promptly followed by another spell unfamiliar to him.

The contents of Tshamarra's goblet promptly burst into blue flames under Craer's nose, so he put it carefully down. As he did so, his own goblet erupted, followed by those of the other overdukes. Those of the men of Stornbridge glowed briefly blue, but didn't ignite.

"My thirst seems to have quite fled," Embra announced calmly to the pale-faced tersept, a dark challenge in her eyes. Under the table, she let her spell fade, and the blue flames died away. If such menaces were going to be proffered all night, she'd need the Dwaer for more important things than feast table tricks . . .

"I–I know not how this could have happened, but–" Lord Stornbridge stammered, looking furious as well as frightened.

"Yes," Blackgult agreed, staring at him, "I can well believe that. The interpretation of orders all too often surprises those who give them–as I've learned often down the years, to my cost. Why don't we exchange platters and goblets henceforth, lords, and so quell all suspicions? I *would* like to form friendships here, this day."

Lord Stornbridge opened and closed his mouth without uttering a sound for a moment, and then in almost desperate haste gobbled, "Why, yes, let's do just that! I–I–"

"Can't think why that didn't occur to all of us before," Embra finished for him smoothly, coolly meeting the glares of the lornsar, the seneschal, and the champion in turn. The coinmaster merely looked thoughtful.

Tersept Stornbridge nodded in energetic agreement, and quaffed his own–safe–wine deeply. "If you don't mind my asking, and the answer's not too delicate a matter . . . what fair wind brings you to Stornbridge? We are, after all, far from the most important banner-stand in Aglirta!"

Surprisingly, it was Hawkril who made answer. "Lord," he rumbled carefully, "we have our duties to the River Throne, as you have yours. One is to travel the Vale consulting with common folk, visiting merchants, and local rulers alike, as to troubles that need seeing to and needs and wants Aglirtans feel. Even backcountry shepherds know Raulin Castlecloaks is a different sort of a king, but they're mistaken as to how. 'Tis not that he's a lad without royal lineage–'tis that he wants to *understand* what's afoot in the Vale, hearing from both high and low, and shape his decrees accordingly. Our eyes and ears are a part of that."

"Y-yes," Lord Stornbridge's smile was sickly as he saw reports of arrow volleys and poisoned wine.

Evidently the seneschal had more swiftly entertained similar thoughts. Seeing the tersept struggling for words, he asked, "Has the King yet shared any views on what he sees for Aglirta in the seasons ahead? We're all weary of warring barons, plundering mercenaries, and priestly strife, but what road can Castlecloaks—pray pardon, *King* Castlecloaks—see to take us out of all that?"

At that moment, servants came through the curtains behind the tersept bearing steaming platters of roast boar, garnished with medallions of sym-raquess—the tart and juicy orange fruit so plentiful in far Sarinda, but rarely seen north of Elgarth.

"We're moving first," Lady Silvertree replied crisply, breaking the custom of not talking politics in front of servants, "to drive out, capture, or come to strict and exacting terms with all wizards of power in the Vale. Any desiring to dwell in Aglirta must work closely with the crown—and not stand behind, or hire themselves out to, any warlord hungry for the throne."

"All wizards of power?" the lornsar echoed derisively.

"*All,* Lord Ryethrel," Embra said firmly, giving him a look like a swordthrust. "Myself included." A brief boiling of the air around them might have just been a warning of the magic she commanded—or a spell seeking magics and poisons lurking on the platters. Servants were bringing bowls of mushrooms swimming in spiced golden sauce, now, and breads baked in fanciful shapes, but Embra gave them no visible attention. More important to her companions, her foot sought none of theirs under the table.

"For the same reasons," Blackgult added, "we work against Serpent-priests who seek to instruct barons and tersepts. The King desires all who hold titles at his pleasure to stand alone, making their own decisions so long as they obey his royal decrees—not follow the whispers of those known to oppose the rightful rule of Flowfoam."

The lornsar nodded as if satisfied, but the seneschal scowled and asked, "And if one who happens to worship the Serpent presents us a fair idea or sound proposal?"

"Do as the King, his barons and tersepts, and yes, even overdukes always do," Craer spoke up. "Consider *why* he offers his scheme. What true gain does it offer you? And what real benefit, to him? If you accept or adopt it, what else has he moved you toward, and why?"

"There may not be any crime in a particular idea or counsel," Tshamarra said quietly, "whether it comes from Snake-lover, fell mage, or rapacious Sirl trader. There *is* a crime, now, in not informing royal messengers and heralds of such entreaties made to you. Normal private business dealings in the Vale aren't our affair—but dealings with all wizards, clergy, and outlanders, and all matters of acquiring magic, weapons, armor, and hireswords, *are.*"

The tersept and his seneschal blinked, but the Coinmaster shook a narrow scroll from his sleeve and made a swift note on it, murmuring, "That seems prudent enough."

The seneschal shot Eirevaur a look that had drawn daggers in it, but the handsome young man merely sprinkled a pinch of powder onto his ink to "set" it, nodded politely and expressionlessly to Urbrindur, and turned his attention again to the Lady Talasorn.

"I understand," Lord Stornbridge said gently to Tshamarra, his tone very careful not to reproach or deride, "that you are both a sorceress and an outlander. How is it that the King trusts you?"

The seneschal nodded in satisfaction at this thrust—and Champion Pheldane leaned forward, transformed in an instant from a coldly watchful statue to a hungry hound straining eagerly on its leash.

"He has his good reasons," the Lady Talasorn replied mildly. "As, I'm sure, you have to trust those who serve you. We all have our own tests for loyalty, do we not?"

Seneschal Urbrindur raised his goblet toward the ceiling and turned it, as if thoughtfully examining the shifting reflections of candlelight on its glossy flanks. He seemed almost to be dreaming as he asked it softly, "And how can one ever know when someone mighty in sorcery has fairly passed a test of loyalty? What sort of test can stand untainted by magic?"

"A test of deeds," Blackgult replied flatly, "when easy personal gain and safety lies on one side and battle peril, pain, hardship, and loyalty sit upon the other. All of us who bear the title of 'Overduke' have passed such tests, not knowing we were being tested." He helped himself to the platter before him and added calmly, "If you persist in proffering threats and insults in the presence of poisonings, my lords, we'll have no choice but to regard you as failing such tests . . . and we all know what happens to traitors."

"Yes, I believe we do," Lornsar Ryethrel said softly, from across the table. "They declare themselves regent, and then get made overdukes, and ride up and down the Vale speaking grand words and presuming to pass judgments on the few Aglirtans who survived their personal feuds and willful wars."

Craer regarded the lornsar thoughtfully. "He's from the Isles."

"I know," Blackgult replied, his gaze locked with Ryethrel. "He's the man who burned down Sea Rock Hall on Nantantuth with dozens of his countryfolk inside—most of them women—because a few of my warriors were searching the place, and he wanted the invaders he dared not face blade-to-blade dead."

The lornsar half-rose with a snarl—but came to a gurgling halt as a thin, whisper-sharp blade appeared across his throat from nowhere. No hand held it; it floated serenely with its keen edge against Ryethrel's windpipe as if by . . . magic.

Craer looked at it with surprise. The weapon was his, but he hadn't—

The sheath, nigh his elbow, was empty.

He looked up from it with a frown into the eyes of Tshamarra, who gave him an impish little smile.

"The simplest spells make the best table manners, I find. Don't you?"

Tersept Stornbridge had been fighting to find the right words to say during these last few moments; dismay, rage, and wincing fear racing across his face in clashing and rebounding succession. His champion, however, was a far more direct man.

"Magic!" Pheldane roared, and sprang to his feet, hands streaking to the hilts of several knives as he looked past Blackgult at Lady Talasorn.

The Golden Griffon vaulted the table, hands flashing out to catch Pheldane's wrists. The bull-necked Tersept's Champion was twice as large and half as old—but the graying baron held him easily, even when Pheldane roared in fury and wrenched toward freedom as hard and as suddenly as he could . . . and those blades stayed unthrown.

The lornsar lifted his hand in a sudden gesture, and the empty balconies filled with bowmen—but the Dwaer sang, and the archers promptly slumped into slumber, arrows and bows clattering down.

Pheldane snarled and brought a knee as broad as a tree trunk brutally up into Blackgult's crotch—only to scream in pain as the barbs on the Griffon's codpiece pierced his knee.

The champion fell back into his chair, sobbing. Blackgult kept firm hold of Pheldane's wrists and stayed on his feet. He let glowered slowly around the table and at each of the uncertainly hovering chamber knaves beyond it, and in a gentle voice that promised doom, if doom was provoked, announced, "I'm still seeking to make friends in Stornbridge, rather than fill graves. I hope you'll all work toward the same ends." He looked longest at Lornsar Ryethrel, before silently sitting down again.

The captain-of-guards was purple and trembling with rage, but Tshamarra's spell kept the sharp, slender needle of steel at Ryethrel's throat, and he said nothing.

Lord Stornbridge found words at last. "Lords and Ladies all," he began, favoring the table with another sickly smile, "I find Overduke Blackgult's suggestion to be a most sensible one, and—despite the unpleasantness that marred the arrival of Aglirta's overdukes in Stornbridge—believe that no tersept nor baron in all the Vale feels a sense of loyalty as sharp and bright as I do. I look upon the reign of King Castlecloaks as a new beginning, a new chance for our fair realm! To have a king who's not asleep for centuries is a great thing in itself!"

He tried a laugh that fell unappreciated into silence, and quickly faded— but almost as swiftly caught up his own enthusiasm and went on. "Yet I'm most heartened by the news you bring, esteemed Overdukes! To have a King who desires to know what we think—even unto blacksmiths and mushroom-pickers! Such wisdom, such a chance for a bright future! I—"

The tersept's enthusiasm faltered for a moment as he caught sight of Craer eyeing his platter dubiously and exchanging a look with Embra, and her swift unleashing of Dwaer-magic on the food, but again Stornbridge caught himself up into a beaming smile, and gabbled, "I find myself quite excited at the prospect of new ideas, a closely guiding hand at work in the realm making the roads safe and settling the many petty disputes that divide one town from the next, and family from family—not that you'll find any of that sort of thing here in Stornbridge, mind you! Ah, no, but I welcome you, brave Overdukes, and hope you'll take a good look around, and talk to many folk, to see the true quality of my stewardship!"

The tersept faltered again, and his undoing was more serious this time. Hawkril and Tshamarra were both visibly struggling to restrain mirth— though Stornbridge had no way of knowing that it was not because of his ridiculous words, but due to the reactions to them of Coinmaster Eirevaur (droll, eye-rolling impassivity) and Seneschal Urbrindur (openmouthed dis-belief, broken by silent winces of disgust).

Stornbridge visibly weighed the consequences of reacting with anger to the two miscreant guests, and finally asked, in a strained voice that held mingled coldness, stiffness, and diffidence, "Is there, ah, some problem with my sentiments I should know about? Or some affliction or condition befalling you, perhaps?"

"Horns of the Lady," Undercook Maelree whispered, from her hard-won perch at a high gallery window, "but this is better than a six-bard show!"

Mistress of the Pantry Klaedra chuckled, and then nudged Maelree. "Ssshh. Musn't miss a word!"

They grinned at each other and leaned toward the sill, made bolder by all the tumult below.

• • •

"Magic would be the problem," Embra told the tersept briskly. "Spying-spells have just reached into this room!"

"Wha—? But who? *Why?*" Stornbridge seemed genuinely astonished.

"To hear what we decide, obviously," Craer replied, in tones that unmistakably added the words "you idiot" to the end of his sentence.

Tshamarra and Blackgult both shot puzzled looks at Embra. "Able to pierce my shielding and elude your probings for the same reason," she told them tersely. "A reaching not directly to us, but rather to observe through the eyes and ears of someone in this room . . . the servant standing behind Coinmaster Eirevaur."

Craer promptly vaulted from his seat up onto the table, touching down once amid the platters, and sprang from it at the chamber knave. Servants ran forward to meet and stop him—all but the one he was seeking, who whirled around and fled through an archway. The procurer sprinted in hot pursuit.

"Be *careful,* Craer!" Tshamarra called, rising.

With a triumphant snarl, Lornsar Ryethrel struck aside the hovering blade at his throat and clawed at the hilt of his sword, eyes fairly flaming as he glared across the table at Blackgult.

The Golden Griffon never moved. The flying needle, however, did—and Lornsar Ryethrel found himself staring at its point, perhaps an inch away from his left eyeball.

"Unless you'd prefer to lose your right eye first?" Tshamarra Talasorn inquired sweetly.

The lornsar let go of his sword and sank back down into his chair in careful silence, the hovering blade moving smoothly with him.

"I see Champion Pheldane has almost recovered—so long as he sits still and puts no weight on his leg," Embra said, every inch the noble hostess. "Perhaps he could reflect on the ease with which I could enspell him to end-lessly enjoy the sensations he felt at the moment when he injured his knee . . . and so remain quiet."

"Graul you, you *bitch*!" Pheldane snarled. "You and all your bebolten spells!" He reached furiously for his goblet—but the movement was sudden enough to send fresh agonies shooting up his leg. He hunched over, seething and whimpering, sweat dripping from his contorted face.

"Alternatively," the Lady Silvertree announced, "I could deaden your pain, Champion, though the actual injury would remain. Shall I?"

"Sargh upon you, woman! Sargh right in your grinning face!" Pheldane spat. Without warning or any change of expression Blackgult swung his arm in a great roundhouse blow that smashed into the warrior's face, leaving him reeling. His body promptly twisted and jumped in spellspun pain.

The lornsar and chamber knaves tensed as one, but Seneschal Urbrindur snapped, "Steady! He more than deserved that. Peace be upon this table!"

The Lady of Jewels gave Urbrindur a warm and gracious smile. "My thanks, Seneschal. 'Tis such a pleasure to hear sense spoken among all this fury and bluster. I, too, would fain enjoy a civilized meal among men who reason and debate to wise ends, rather than snarling and showing teeth like dogs warring over a bone."

The Tersept of Stornbridge laughed again. It sounded no more genuine—and was no better received—than his previous efforts at mirth, but he soldiered on into converse once more, determined to salvage *something* from this disaster of a day. "Why, let us forthwith debate matters of Aglirta, then! As tersept, for example, I feel a constant shortage of coins constraining me from hiring and equipping men enough to patrol the Storn lands as diligently as I would wish. Were the reinstituted crown taxes lower, I could hire more men, and keep the King's law better. Fewer brigands would steal and fewer outlander merchants avoid paying the taxes *they* should. The royal coffers would be as full, whilst all benefited from greater peace and justice."

Embra nodded. "Every baron and tersept feels so, and most let us know it. Yet we've only to look back over these last ten seasons to know what happens when every ruler, large and small, is free to buy armsmen. War over every little dispute and disagreement—with crops ruined, much blood spilt, trade trammeled, *no* peace and safety on the roads, *no* justice for all, and in the end death for almost every baron and tersept, no matter how respected or wise they might be. Remember the Crow of Cardassa."

Lord Stornbridge signaled for his goblet to be refilled. "But Lady, we have a king now; surely such bloody days are behind us! Could—"

"We had a king *then,*" the Lady Silvertree reminded him. "My point stands. Whoever sits the River Throne looks up and down the Vale and sees many keeps—such as this one—full of cortahars and armaragors, each with its own ruler commanding their blades thus and so. If we give tax relief to those who hire more swords, what end can there be but more war? Lord Stornbridge, do you hire more cooks and not eat?"

The tersept looked as if he wanted to snarl something angry for a moment, and then his face fell back into anxious uncertainty. "I–I–Lady, you must realize I meant no dispute with the King's policy. I merely—"

"Of course." Embra lifted her untouched goblet to him. "I quite understand. I was merely demonstrating how Flowfoam must regard matters from other sides, when they can see the desires of all. 'Tis when we cannot hear, and thus not know, of local disputes or the wants and needs of Vale folk that we can't hope to make the right decrees."

"So you're saying you overdukes make decisions for the King, is that it?" Those harsh words belonged to Seneschal Urbrindur. "Or do you mean a little cabal of the wizards you've been gathering to Flowfoam so diligently these last few months? Or senior barons, like you and Blackgult here?"

"My, my," the Golden Griffon told the platter in front of him, "but I do *so* enjoy civilized discussions. Seneschal, I find your ignorance amusing. You seem to truly believe that senior barons—or a handful of wizards, for that matter—could actually agree on anything!"

Unexpectedly, the Coinmaster chuckled. After a moment of staring at him in startlement, Tersept Stornbridge joined in. Hawkril nodded approvingly, and noticed as he did so that smiles flickered across the faces of several chamber knaves.

The seneschal didn't bother to look annoyed. He merely waited for the ripple of mirth to die and said, "Yet we have peace—of sorts—in Aglirta right now because of such agreement, however reached. We also know King Raulin Castlecloaks is the son of a bard, a young lad of no lands nor coins, without influence or armsmen to his name to claim anything . . . least of all the River Throne. We also know that some folk reached agreement to crown him—or at least not to sword him down if he seized the crown for himself and proclaimed himself King—and that some folk, visibly including you overdukes, support him on that throne, or he'd not still be there. Why choose a boy? Might it be because he's easily biddable, so you can shape Aglirta as you see fit?"

Embra opened her mouth to speak, looking less than pleased, but Blackgult quelled her with a lifted finger and replied calmly, "That's indeed the most obvious explanation, soon occurring to anyone who considers such things. Had you been in the Throne Chamber at the right times, to see and hear for yourself, however, you'd know that I could easily have passed from regent to King—and was both urged and expected to do so, by some—and that Hawkril, here, was also asked to take the crown."

The seneschal spread his hands. "Yet we only have your word for that, my lord. We were *not* there—nor were the majority of rulers and officers, up and down the Vale. Most barons and tersepts, in fact, were appointed by Kelgrael or by you as regent or by King Castlecloaks, and so owe lands, coins, and power to Flowfoam, with very recent reminders of how suddenly and fatally such gifts can be taken away. Again, we bow the more easily to your bidding . . . those who would not are those now dead."

Blackgult smiled. "So you'd have us change the way of the world, Urbrindur? Tell the Three how to order things, differently than they've done these past dozen centuries, at least?"

"The Serpent-priests tried to do just that," Coinmaster Eirevaur said unexpectedly. "Though they failed as completely and as spectacularly as did Bloodblade or any baron."

The Golden Griffon nodded. "Mountainsides grow no softer if you scream at them—or hurl yourself against them a score of times or more. I've learned just one thing down the years about trying to make large changes in Darsar around us: All such attempts end up costing the lives of many."

Lornsar Ryethrel regarded him sourly across the table. "So what're you saying to us, Overduke Blackgult? That all Aglirta should accept one large change, the ascension of the boy king, and another: his new way of doing things . . . because any third large change would bring much bloodshed? That seems to me no more nor less than the sort of menace that barons have always spoken to us: *I* can do what I like, because I have the swords to back me, but if you dare try anything, you'll be the irresponsible butcher who brings ruin to all Aglirta. I'm not defying King Castlecloaks, nor belittling your mission or authority . . . I'm merely pointing out that to many of us, such pretty talk seems to veil the same old spiked gauntlet."

Blackgult smiled. "So it does, Ryethrel. So it does. In the end, for all our high-minded schemes, it always comes down to who can whelm the greatest force, does it not? I wish things were otherwise, but they're not." He glanced at the hunched-over Tersept's Champion. "Are they, Pheldane?"

"Graul you like a blinded boar, Blackgult," the champion gasped, not looking up. "Graul you and roast you in your own armor, you whoreson wolf!"

Blackgult smiled. "My fond love for you grows greater too, Pheldane."

"Lord Blackgult!" The Tersept of Stornbridge's voice was almost a whine, his pleading open. "Lady Silvertree! Harsh words and rough handling have you entertained since arriving here in fair Stornbridge, and I humbly beg your pardon for that when there can be no real pardon . . . But tell me: Do you deem us enemies of the crown for speaking with candor? Are we doomed, merely for our honesty?"

"No, Tersept, you are not," Embra told him quietly. "We value the truth, and knowing what folk really feel, over all the empty fawning and false smiles the Vale can give us. Do you think your views surprise us?"

Stornbridge regarded her silently, and then slowly shook his head. The Lady of Jewels gave him a faint smile—and then, as a flicker of movement from above caught her eye, she called on the Dwaer, the air sang and shimmered, and the few bowmen on the balconies who'd begun to stealthily reach for blades or quivers fell back to sleep again, arms dangling.

With one spell barely cast, Embra called on her Stone for another, bringing another probing spell down on platters all over the table. Faint sparkling radiances winked and crawled across the food. She put one ladylike finger into some nearby gravy, eyes narrowed, and then carefully licked it and turned her magic on herself.

"What is it?" Lord Stornbridge asked, as if he could not very well guess what she was doing. "What's wrong, Lady Overduke?"

"Many things, Lord," Embra told him, lifting grave eyes to his as she put another gravy-coated finger in her mouth. "Wherefore none of us can be too careful." Sucking her finger clean, she added approvingly, "Your kitchens are good. My thanks."

"Yesss," Undercook Maelree said fiercely, cramming a knuckle into her mouth to quell the shriek of delight she felt rising within her. "She's done it! 'Tis *in* her!"

"Quiet, now," the Mistress of the Pantry murmured beside her—but it was a gloating murmur. "We mustn't warn our overduchal heroes they've ingested the plague until they've all tasted it."

The Undercook nodded, and drew back a little from the high gallery window. In the shadows the two women exchanged soft, menacing smiles. "A good day for the Serpent," Maelree breathed, her fingers digging into Klaedra's shoulders with excited, bruising force.

The Mistress of the Pantry did not tear free of the painful grip and strike Maelree across the face for daring to touch her person—and that in itself was a measure of how delighted she was.

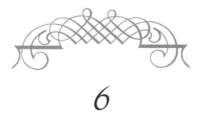

6

Madness and a Timely Flagon

"Though I do what lovely ladies say, this will get me killed some day,' " Craer Delnbone sang softly and mockingly as he plunged down an unfamiliar passage, the groans of the guard he'd just kicked in the crotch fading behind him.

Bebolt that overenthusiastic cortahar, anyway! He'd delayed Craer just long enough to let the chamber knave he was chasing whirl into this side passage, and through one of these nigh-dozen doors. At least the fool had slammed it, marking his trail *that* much. Graul and bebolt all!

"Now, if I was a foolishly avid and attentive guard, I'd wait about *here* . . . ," Craer murmured, springing high to catch hold of an old torch-bracket as he came to a corner. He grasped it for just the instant he needed to swing himself high and hard—

Yes! A blade slashed at where his face and throat should have been, the cortahar behind it snarling in cruel exultation. That snarl became a growl of surprise as Craer flashed past overhead, kicked off the far wall, and flung himself back in a twisting turn that brought his hand down hard on the guard's neck.

The cortahar grunted in pain—a grunt that rose into a whistle of alarm as Craer's waxed cord slapped across his throat. The procurer caught the garotte's far end, deftly pulled and jerked—and the gurgling, strangling guard's head was driven into the passage wall.

The man reeled, shaking his head and clawing at the air rather dazedly, so Craer bounced as he landed, bounding high to slam the cortahar's head into the wall once more.

This time the guard only managed to pull his face off the stone far enough to blink—before he went down in a limp, untidy heap.

"No, don't thank me," Craer told the senseless cortahar, retrieving his garotte. "Just enjoy your slumber. The Three know if you deserve it. Me, I just know what *I* deserve."

He ran on, sprinting hard but almost soundlessly in his soft leather boots. Their pointed toes were hard and sharp—sporting little crescentiform knife blades of which Craer, their maker, was quite proud—but the soles were as soft and supple as a high lady's boudoir slippers.

Behind any of these doors, Three take him, the chamber knave could be hiding. Well, a procurer's life wasn't for the peaceloving . . .

Craer snatched at the latch of the first door, but it wouldn't budge. He shook it, whirling away without pause to another door a pace farther on and across the passage. The first door yielded not a whit, and no sound of alarm came from beyond it—but the second door opened.

Dust, darkness, and linens: a closet. Craer snapped his garotte into the gloom like a whip, encountering nothing. The moment he could see it was empty of cowering chamber knaves, he rebounded across the passage again to the third door.

This one crashed open to reveal three startled needle-wielding maids bent over a sewing frame. They screamed in unison, so Craer gave them a rakish grin, slammed the door on them, and sprang to the fourth door.

It was bolted, and shuddered under his attack. From behind it came a feminine gasp of alarm and a low, furious man's voice: "Not *yet,* Thalas! You promised this room until candletrimming, graul you!"

Craer grinned and flung himself at the fifth door. It opened—and he hurled himself to the floor as something fanged and hissing spun right at him!

His plunge took him to the very toes of his attacker, so he snapped his garotte around handy ankles, jerked, and then shoved.

The man cursed, flailed his arms for balance, and caught at someone else to keep from falling. By then Craer was up the man's legs and stabbing hard with one of his handy knives.

The Serpent-priest shrieked and snatched out his own dagger—only to *really* scream and come to a shuddering, quivering halt, as Craer's knife transfixed his other hand. The dagger clattered to the floor.

Craer twisted his blade, sending the priest to his knees in a sobbing howl. With his free hand the procurer grabbed the throat of the other man: the chamber knave he'd been chasing.

"Is this the man who cast the spell on you?" Craer hissed, shaking his knife so the priest's bleeding hand was dragged cruelly through the air, trailing its weeping owner. "Aye?"

"Y-yes," the servant choked, trying to shrink back through a wall to get away from the procurer . . . and failing miserably.

"You know him?" Craer snapped, his hand tightening.

"N-no, Lord, truly! H-he only arrived . . . castle . . . two days ago. I don't even know his name!"

Craer shoved the chamber knave, sending the man stumbling in search of balance. The procurer used that time to pluck up the priest's fallen dagger—a wavy blade with an open-jawed fanged serpent-pommel—and menace the servant with it, to make sure the man had no weapon and no chance to draw it if he did.

The knave shrank back, paling. "N-no! Mercy! 'Tis poisoned!"

Craer shook his own knife to keep the pain-wracked priest helpless, and held the snake-dagger up to the light. A stain that should not have been there—a deep greenish-purple distinctly different from blood, fresh or old—covered its keen point.

Craer thrust it at the chamber knave. As the servant screamed and tried to claw his way up the wall away from it, Craer reversed it and brought the rearing serpent-head down hard on a cringing skull. The servant collapsed without a sound, blood trickling from his nose.

Craer nodded approvingly—and then turned and drove the poisoned blade hilt-deep into the belly of its owner, point-first this time.

The Serpent-priest didn't even have time to scream ere he pitched forward on his face and bade farewell to all pain, forever . . .

"Well, Craer, you're the best," the procurer exclaimed—and then mockingly replied to himself: "Why, *thank* you. I hope they haven't eaten everything that's free of poison before I get back."

Jerking his knife free, he strode back the way he'd come, pausing only to rap on a door and growl, "Thalas. Come out, or by the Three, I'm coming in!"

"Thalas, you *bastard*! You black-pizzled, lice-dripping, misbegotten son of a she-boar!" came the muffled but frantic reply, amid wordless feminine wails of alarm.

Craer grinned and set off down the passage before anyone could emerge. "Yes," he told himself fondly, "this is certainly going to get me killed some day. But not *this* day."

He paused a swift step later, thinking of the first guard, who must have recovered by now. "I hope."

.   .   .

In a palatial chamber of high dark bookshelves, blood-red walls, and many gilded wyvern-head carvings, a black-bearded man sat alone at feast.

The wine in his golden goblet was a shade darker than his crimson robes—and much darker than the flames of hot anger in his eyes.

The servants knew better than to tarry once they'd set his steaming platter before Multhas Bowdragon; the "Blackheart" (a name known across Arlund, though never uttered in its unwilling owner's hearing) possessed both a hot temper and a cruel, violent streak.

Multhas dined alone by choice, for it was his practice as he lingered over favorite dishes to gaze into scrying-crystals and see what was unfolding across Asmarand. Their shifting glows lit a sharp-nosed, thin, and handsome face that might have belonged to a king or a high priest, if not to a mighty wizard—but to no softer man.

Multhas the Blackheart often brooded over real and imagined slights that both men and gods sent his way. He was brooding now. Why was his elder brother Dolmur the more powerful? Dolmur the quiet, who wasted so much time on fripperies like flowers and kindnesses and the cares of others. How was it that such a one commanded so much more respect than his brothers without ever resorting to open threats?

Oh, men respected Multhas Bowdragon well enough. They just all seemed to want to do it without ever meeting his eyes or dealing as friends or even coming within his sight if they didn't absolutely have to. They treated him with careful, wary courtesy, no trace of love—yet not the abject, terror-driven haste a mighty wizard should command by his very presence, either.

He must study men of power more closely. What they said, their small mannerisms, their stride, garb, and manners of dealing. What good is being a great wizard if you must blast men to have them obey you? Other mages need only smile or frown, and men leaped to do things unbidden, to keep them pleased or make them satisfied.

"That's the secret of the Three I must learn," Multhas muttered, looking up at the grimoires he kept closest. Old, thick spellbooks penned by the most powerful archwizards of long ago: Coraumaunth, and Meljrune, and—

"The Three reveal their secrets in their own good time, Multhas. Is hunting them in old tomes your wisest course?"

Multhas Bowdragon whirled around, almost upsetting his platter. "Who *dares*—?"

An intruder clad like a traveling mage stood at the far end of the room, facing him. Black hair, a soft and wise smile—and one hand hidden from view in a slit-pocket of wizardly robes.

Unfamiliar, yes, but Multhas had seen him before . . . through a scrying-sphere. Yes! Years ago, when he still dared to look upon Aglirta, before—

"My name," the man said pleasantly, "is Ingryl Ambelter. I come in peace, to make an offer I trust you'll find both profitable . . . and enjoyable."

Fear struck a chill deep in the Blackheart Bowdragon. It was only by the strongest of trembling efforts that he kept from flinching, or showing terror on his face.

Yet his unbidden guest smirked, as if every racing thought Multhas wrestled with was shouted aloud. Oh, he knew of Ingryl Ambelter, darkest of Silvertree's Dark Three, and quailed—and Ambelter knew it.

Multhas Bowdragon shook, willing mounting rage to overmaster his fear. How had Ambelter reached this innermost spellgirt chamber, passing wards without contest? What awesome power—?

The man had proclaimed himself Spellmaster of Silvertree—of All Aglirta, now, if Sirl gossip heard through the crystals could be believed—and some said he'd killed Baron Silvertree, the Risen King, and even the Great Serpent!

Certainly he'd butchered dozens of Sirl mages, decades back, sending slaying-spells by night . . . stealing through their wards unchecked, just like . . .

The Blackheart drew a deep breath. It might, after all, be his last.

"Ambelter," he echoed, keeping his voice steady, slow, and without any hint of weakness—or welcome. "I've heard that name before. Faerod Silvertree's mages . . . you were reckoned the most powerful of those 'Dark Three.' "

His visitor smiled. "Indeed, and rightly so." Ambelter waved his visible—and empty—hand at the splendors around him. "Your wards are among the finest I've seen, and yet . . ." He smiled again, and let silence fall between them.

Multhas let his scrying-spheres fade to dark quiescence, not hurrying to say anything that would further reveal his fears. With a thought he activated wands hidden here and there in carvings around the room. If it came to battle between them . . .

"Evidently not fine enough," he replied in dry tones, assuming a relaxed pose that just happened to cover the ring on his left hand with the fingers of his right, so the faint glow of its awakening to hurl fires was concealed. "You mentioned an offer . . . ?"

"I propose alliance toward a specific end. This must needs involve some measure of trust between us. Hence this meeting, eyes to eyes, for both of us to see if trust is possible . . . or not."

Multhas Bowdragon regarded his visitor expressionlessly. "Unfold your offer."

"For years Aglirta has been where barons brawl, each kinging it over his few farms and forests and cow pastures. The Vale feeds great Sirlptar, but is in truth no kingdom at all—a place of battle madness rightly called the King-less Land. Yet the true rulers of Aglirta have always been wizards. Wizards who warred with each other, using barons as willfully as barons use their lowliest cortahars. I was Spellmaster of Silvertree, and even that greatest baron of all bowed to my will—and never knew he was doing so."

"And so?"

"And so I know the true measure of Aglirta's might. If ever it stood united under a strong king, a real king, Arlund would not be safe, nor Sirlptar, nor any proud land of Asmarand; Aglirta could conquer all. Those who squabble in the Vale could come for you and all Bowdragons on the morrow, if someone did but unite and lead them."

"The worlds of 'if' are countless, but even our most daring sea captains rarely reach them," Multhas responded. "I'm not afraid of cortahars, or full-mantled armaragors, or even howling hosts of hireswords. A few spells, and—" He made a dismissive gesture.

Ingryl Ambelter smiled. "Indeed. However, there's far more to Aglirta than swords—there's magic. The ruins of a dozen cities of sorcery lie beneath the green fields and wildwood tree roots of Silverflow Vale, and in family crypts, roadside hedges, and many abandoned palaces and high houses. Much magic has been carried off down the years, of course, but far more lies forgotten. Magic enough to make those who wield it archwizards greater than any Darsar has yet known. Fool-headed farmers turn over spellswords when they plow, and barons toss aside everything not encrusted with jewels."

Multhas Bowdragon swallowed, his throat suddenly dry. "And having stepped through my wards as if they were less than window curtains, you need my aid in this matter . . . how?"

Ambelter took a step forward—moving in utter silence, Bowdragon noted—and said eagerly, "That's just it, Multhas! Alone, I can make myself the tyrant king Sirl folk would have to fear—and the rest of Asmarand would come to fear, once Sirlptar fell. This I can do already, without you or anyone. Yet I want more. Much more."

He took another step forward, and Multhas Bowdragon called up the powers of his fire-ring. This could all be but a ruse, for Ambelter to get close . . .

The Spellmaster smiled. "Calm yourself, Bowdragon, and quell what you're planning to hurl at me. Believe me, I have means to prevent it." He waved his empty hand as if delivering a speech to an assembly, and urged, "Hear me! I want allies, and I need friends. Friends to join me in founding a new Aglirta: a kingdom of wizards!"

The master of Bowdragon Towers knew his eyes were narrowing, even as his heart started to pound with excitement. "You want me to be one of your loyal subjects?"

"No! I see a council of mages, a high table of equals, with apprentices serving beneath us and commoners under all. A land as strong and clean and peaceful as we can make it, so Aglirtans are happy and wealthy, earning us coins enough to live like kings and pursue ever stronger magics, making new books of sorcery to enrich all. What say you, Bowdragon?"

"A compelling vision," Multhas admitted, nodding. "Yet I still don't see why you need me—or how I can be sure you aren't just seeking my death, and my paltry magics to add to your own."

Ambelter smiled again. "I've never yet thought that any mage can be *talked* to death. If I wanted you dead, a spell to smash Bowdragon Towers would have come without warning, and you'd never even have known who sent it. Much magic binds together walls and furniture around you, Multhas—and such magic can be twisted or shattered at will, by those few who know how. But I don't need your death. I need you alive, as a colleague I can respect and talk to, and work with. As a friend."

He held out his empty hand in the soothing gesture many women make when they dare not touch the one they want to comfort. "I know this is both sudden and unsettling. You'll want time to think, to consider all sides. I won't press you for any pledge or agreement this day . . . But I do believe that once you consider all the implications of this dream of mine, you'll very much want to be a part of it. Just think: to be free of swaggering sword-swingers and owing your backside to sly-tongued merchants at last!"

"I already enjoy complete freedom in such matters, thank you," Multhas Bowdragon answered rather stiffly.

The Spellmaster shook his head. "Only through the work of your brother Dolmur, whom you thus feel the same indebtedness to—and who can compel you as surely as could a tyrant king on your doorstep, or a merchant you owed every stone of Bowdragon Towers to!"

"I believe," Multhas Bowdragon snarled, "that this interview is at an end."

The Spellmaster held up a hand. "Please, Multhas, take no hasty offense. I meant not to anger you, but merely to honestly refute—and how often do you hear another mage speak such plain truth to you, hmm? Is that alone not a rarity worth having more of?"

The master of Bowdragon Towers glowered, then nodded reluctantly. "You speak rightly there. Yet I still know not what you desire of me. Has Aglirta not taken leave of its senses enough to enthrone a boy as King? Use your spells to rule him, and you have your kingdom with no help from me!"

His visitor nodded. "I could—but would then be plunged into a struggle that would lay waste to Aglirta even as I won it. Have you not wondered how this unknown lad came to be King? He's backed by the senior barons, Blackgult and Silvertree, and the rest of the self-styled overdukes . . . and they're in league with the most powerful wizards left in Aglirta."

Multhas waved at his crystals. "Oh? I've spent some time scrying the Vale from afar, and have failed to notice any mages of note left there. In Sirlptar, yes, but Aglirta?"

Ambelter smiled again. "I trust you've heard of the Master of Bats?"

"Yes, but he's not Aglirtan, nor even in the Vale."

"Oh? Have you farscryed him lately?"

The Blackheart glared at his visitor, and then snapped, "So perhaps he's in league with this cabal of Flowfoam nobles—what then? Surely you can smite down *one* wizard, however notorious!"

"Ah, but there are many more. I can defeat them, yes, but once I work openly, they'll be at me like a pack of hungry wolves, watching day and night, and the long struggle will begin. The shrewdest attacks come from a surprise source—such as yourself. *You* could smite down my foes, seize their magics for yourself, and be gone again before the rest even knew a death had taken place, let alone who did the deed."

"So who are these 'many more'? Are they all skilled enough to hide themselves from me, all these months?" Multhas waved at the scrying-spheres, letting the ready fire of his ring show.

Ingryl Ambelter smirked at it, then let his face grow very serious as he met the angry gaze of his unwilling host. "Not all Lords of the Serpent perished when the Great Serpent fell. Surely a mage of accomplishment like yourself is aware that the Serpent is no god like the Three, but an archwizard commanding a great web of spells. His priests are mages—some like you and me, but most little better than the hedge-wizards of yore, who can be found in a threadbare and useless carpet over most of Asmarand, muttering mysteries from every back lane. That web of magic, however, welds them into a formidable army—a host that knows and watches me, but leaves its backside unguarded against you and others it knows not!"

"And how," Multhas Bowdragon asked very quietly, discovering to his surprise that he was sweating so freely that a droplet was about to fall from his nose, "do I know they aren't watching you right now, listening to every word that passes between us, and marking me as a foe to be struck down before my platter here has quite cooled?"

"Oh," the Spellmaster told him softly, "you need have no fear of that." Slowly and casually he drew forth the hand he'd kept hidden in his robes, and held it up as though faintly surprised at what rested in its palm: a small, mottled brown-and-white stone.

"I believe," he remarked, "you know what this is without my having to tell you—or demonstrate, by, say, snuffing out all the wands you've awakened around me, that little bauble on your finger, *and* every last Bowdragon enchantment at work in Arlund."

"A-a Dwaer-Stone?"

Ingryl Ambelter smiled broadly. "Indeed, and more. 'Tis very dangerous for any lone mage to carry more than one Dwaerindim . . . but I know where there are others. One could well soon be yours."

He took another step forward. "So you can surely see, friend Multhas, that I can blast you to ashes at will—and every other mage, baron, or plow farmer in all Darsar, too. I've had this Stone for years, and *have* hurled down barons and archwizards alike with it. I could have done that to you and all the Bowdragons years ago. But that's not what I want, and not why I came here."

He stepped back as a haze of tiny stars suddenly encircled the Stone in his hand. "I want allies. More than that: I want friends. Think about that, Multhas. I'll come calling again . . . and although I give you my word that refusing me will be a completely safe thing for you to do, I hope you'll join with me. Now fare you well. 'Twould be churlish of me to let the last of your feast grow cold."

And the man holding the Dwaer seemed to become a drifting, fading figure of smoke—a figure that was gone before Multhas could think of something to say. He stared at where it had been, and then cast a hasty spell to make sure Ambelter wasn't tarrying, invisible.

When that magic told him he was indeed alone in his most private chamber—and, what's more, had been alone therein since he last invoked it, right after sending out the servants who'd brought his feast—Multhas Bowdragon at last found the right word to shout: *"Dolmur!"*

His older brother infuriated and unsettled him. In Dolmur's presence, Multhas always felt like a young and irresponsible child—a child being silently judged, by one full of pity who always found him wanting—and reached that finding with a complete lack of surprise.

Yet, a Dwaer! A mage of Aglirta stepping through his wards at will! A war of mages and a *realm* of wizards!

Temptation, very great temptation. Anger, of course—so much anger that his hands trembled as he shut down wands and fire-ring and snatched up his most powerful rod of magics—but also fear.

Yes, bebolt it, he was afraid. Multhas Bowdragon whirled out of his spellgirt chamber like an angry black tempest, forgetting the last of his feast completely in his haste to consult with Dolmur.

A last few wisps of steam rose from the platter, but there was no one left in that chamber to see them.

They were, however, observed by someone not in the room. Someone who almost squealed with excitement as she wove spells in eager haste, barely able to breathe over the racing of her own heart. By linking three of her uncle's scrying-crystals in her ghostwatch-spell, its reach through his wards had been subtle enough to pass undetected these last two seasons—and why not? After all, Multhas the Roaring-Bearded Storm wanted to be able to look through his wards with them *himself*—and those same crystals could serve as anchors to a tracer-spell.

If this Ambelter revisited Uncle Multhas in the same room—and why not? Multhas spent hardly a moment anywhere else, these days—she could, with luck, magically follow him when he departed.

Uncle Multhas was a greedy, blustering fool. His sneering superiority blinded him to his own weaknesses as a wizard, and to the carelessness that would always keep him weak. Uncle Dolmur would never join anything that he could not control, and her own father was as gentle as a blubbering chambermaid, weaker in his sorcery even than Multhas.

No, if the Spellmaster of Aglirta wanted a *real* ally to win his king-dom—even, perhaps, a consort? he was not *that* old and ugly, after all—he should look past the elder Bowdragons, and see the most capable of the younger ones.

Herself. Maelra Bowdragon, aquiver with excitement now as her last deft spell fell into place and completed the subtle web that should trace Ingryl Ambelter, if he came again.

She drew in a shuddering breath, ran slender hands down over her hips to wipe them dry, and then hugged herself in sheer excitement. This might be the road opening before her at last. The road to power.

"And so," she whispered to her mirror, "there came the day at last when all Darsar knew—and feared—the name of Maelra."

The smile her mirror gave back to her then was truly frightening.

"Is there really much chance of Aglirta seeing the rise of another Blood-blade?" Lord Stornbridge asked, over the clatter of cutlery and the sounds of eager chewing. The boar *was* good, if he said so himself. It had a special something . . . yes, Maelree had outdone herself. Klaedra left all the roasts to Maelree for good reason. Very good reason.

The Tersept of Stornbridge sat back, smothering a contented belch, to hear what reply these overdukes might give. They were as strange as Vale talk claimed, to be sure.

Thank the Three for that. If he'd ever dared to treat old Faerod Silvertree—or even this Blackgult, in the old days—as he'd done these folk this day, he'd be dead now, or screaming his slow, agonized way toward a death he'd be longing for. Stornbridge shuddered and put such thoughts from his mind as the Lady Silvertree told him quietly, "So long as Serpent-priests walk Darsar, and cast ambitious eyes on the Vale, they could set another Bloodblade on the bloody road of swords that ends at Flowfoam. 'Tis the task of us all to stop that from befalling."

All of the Storn men listened to her in better humor than they had just a few breaths ago. Good food does that to men—and so does soothing magic of the sort Embra had cast upon Pheldane. No one would have called the Champion or the lornsar friendly toward their visitors, but they'd now found it in themselves to be civil.

Hawkril visibly brightened as a lithe, familiar figure strolled back into the room via the archway he'd recently raced out through. Craer Delnbone held a decanter in his hands, and wore a jaunty smile on his face. "Sorry I've been absent this long," he told the table. "The best vintages take some time to find, in cellars so extensive." He inclined his head politely to Stornbridge. "My compliments, my lord. Refinement of palate I of course expected of you, but I'd no idea your tastes ran so deep."

The tersept, who knew very well that his wine cellar consisted of a disused pantry stacked untidily with a dozen or so kegs of whatever wine was cheapest, nodded with a somewhat bewildered smile. The little thief had obviously plucked the decanter off the serving cart just inside that archway, but . . . what was he getting at?

"You should try some," Craer urged his friends, setting the decanter down on the table before them. "Bites like a serpent, it does."

Blackgult regarded the ceiling for the briefest of moments, as both Embra and Tshamarra rolled their eyes. "Subtle, Craer, very subtle," the Lady Silvertree murmured.

Craer shrugged merrily, gave the lornsar a cheery smile as he took his seat, and asked, "What did I miss? Barbed threats? Little gems of glowering menace? Or just a little tongue-fencing?"

Lornsar Ryethrel regarded his newly returned table companion sourly. "A little peace and quiet. My lord."

Hawkril snorted with laughter, and Tshamarra smirked at her platter and said, "He's got you there, Longfingers!"

Craer regarded her haughtily. "That'll be 'Lord Longfingers,' if you *don't* mind."

"Would it be impolite of me to inquire, as seneschal of this castle, if the Lord Stornbridge is, ah, short one chamber knave at this time?" Urbrindur asked.

Craer gave him a bright smile. "No, and no. He has a bit of a headache, and is sleeping it off—comfortably, I trust. There's another man lying beside him who is—or rather *was*—a priest of the Serpent. A man who arrived here but two days ago, I understand. He's dead now, and whoever pulls his own knife out of him had best beware poison on its blade. Oh, yes, two of your cortahars need some weapons practice, and someone named Thalas is being far too mercenary in his rental of certain rooms."

"I *beg* your pardon?" Seneschal Urbrindur asked, in the heavy tones affected by those so scandalized that they're really doing nothing of the kind.

However, on the other side of the uncertainly smiling tersept, Coinmaster Eirevaur smiled, nodded, made a note, and murmured, "Thalas again. *Thank* you, Lord Delnbone."

Craer gave him a wink, and then addressed the seneschal directly. "No, I'm afraid not."

Urbrindur gave him a baffled but nonetheless disapproving look. "You're afraid, my lord?"

The procurer took a healthy mouthful of boar and sluiced it down his gullet with a swig from the decanter. "I'm afraid I can't grant the pardon you've so energetically begged for, at this time. Still, the Three work in wondrous ways, Seneschal. Perhaps I shall, sometime soon—if you can overcome this regrettable tendency to *judge* everyone around you. Take folk as you find them—"

"Aye," Hawkril rumbled, "take them for all they've got, is the usual Longfingers manner."

Craer shot his old friend a look that mingled mock pain and shared mirth, and continued, "—and enjoy life all the more. Some wine, perhaps? A timely flagon comes never amiss." He waved the decanter, but Urbrindur shook his head curtly.

"To continue, my Lord Stornbridge," Embra said patiently, "we consider that what's most important for every noble of Aglirta is to take great care to *not* follow the dark road of ambition favored by some of their more foolish fellows in the past." She sipped daintily at her wine, and added, "There's no need for anyone to go whelming armies beyond what's needed to patrol his own territory, or to conspire with others up and down the Vale in petty little alliances that in the end will only be manipulated by the Serpent-worshippers or another Bloodblade desiring to snatch the throne."

Blackgult nodded. "If every noble of the Vale kept loyal to the throne, and bought peace with wise decisions, ready swords, fair justice, and vigilant patrols, Aglirta would soon know greatness again, and the peace would bring prosperity to all."

"Your diligence on the road this day may have been misplaced, but it speaks well for your regard for your own people, and for all Aglirta," Embra added. "Though this may surprise you, we are thus far well pleased with you, Tersept of Stornbridge."

The Lord of Stornbridge visibly sat straighter and taller, looking delighted. Craer saluted him with the decanter, and then bounded to his feet and skipped around the table. Chamber knaves started forward uncertainly to intercept him, but the procurer was already refilling the tersept's goblet with the bubbling words, "That's right! Celebrate! A most excellent wine, this. You must tell us more of life here in Stornbridge—the fishing, say, and how the crops are doing, and who stops by to trade in the market, and what trade goods your people never see enough of. Let's stop all this snarling at each other, put our boots up, and *talk!*"

"I—I hardly know where to begin," the tersept told him, a genuine smile on his face. He raised his goblet, and then said in a rush, "I know: with a good long drink!"

"Exactly!" Craer agreed, sloshing wine into the seneschal's goblet despite Urbrindur's irritated expression.

"Tongue-loosening time, eh?" the lornsar growled. "Well, why not?"

He held out his own goblet to the prancing procurer. " 'Tis not every night we entertain overdukes!"

"Well, thank the Scaled One for *that*," Undercook Maelree snarled, peering down from the window. "Ryethrel has it right—that's *exactly* what that little foulness is up to! Get the tersept drunk and listen while he spills all. We've got to do something!"

The Mistress of the Pantry smiled serenely. "Already taken care of, Ree. Josmer got my signal."

The cook peered at her, brightening. "You mean—?"

"I mean there's nothing our proud tersept likes more than baked sugar tart smothered in rubywine sauce, a generous helping of which will very swiftly be set in front of him and the rest. The tersept's only—that bitch is using her magic to check everything put in front of any overduke—will have Josmer's little addition. I give Lord Stornbridge about six yawns before he's facedown in his tart and snoring."

"Klaedra, you're a wonder!"

The Mistress of the Pantry smiled again, smugly this time. "I know. The Serpent-priest said the same thing." She drew open her bodice—and the cook gasped.

Klaedra always wore a black silk ribbon about her throat; from it a number of keys hung on fine cords, riding within her bodice. Maelree knew those keys—but she'd never before seen so many gleaming golden coins as the row of punched and laced-together Carraglan zostarrs that hung down from one cord between Klaedra's full, tanned breasts, disappearing from view beneath her belt. Maelree blinked. She'd heard no telltale clinking, nor seen the rope of riches moving beneath the tight, dark gown the mistress wore . . . which meant the linked coins must be long enough to pass under that broad black cummerbund, and descend still further. The priest had paid Klaedra a fortune.

She shivered suddenly, wondering how long he'd leave Klaedra alive to spend it.

7

Fangs in the Dark

*E*mbra raised anxious eyes across the table to her father, but said
nothing. She'd been vigilant with her magic—in fact, she was clutching her Dwaer under the table now, and setting her veins afire with
yet another scouring-spell. Yet something was not right, inside her. Something that clenched and then writhed, moving deep in her gut, climbing . . .
into her chest, leaving a trail of twinges, as if something with sharp claws
was moving within her . . .

Blackgult grimly gave her the slightest of nods. Embra drew in a deep
breath—yes, she *did* feel odd—and tossed her head to take her hair back out
of her eyes. Air. She needed air.

She felt . . . warm. Warm and numb. She reached for her goblet and
turned her head with apparent casualness to look at Tshamarra, whose
eyes—just for a moment—flashed back alarm.

A warning that meant her fellow sorceress was feeling the same discomfort. So they might not have much time left, if she didn't—

"Your arrival at our gates somewhat surprised us," Seneschal Urbrindur
was saying in the lightly jovial manner with which veteran courtiers make
politely meaningless conversation, "given that you were seen in Gilth not
two days ago, heading west on the road to Sirlptar. Or do you use magic to
leap about the Vale, traversing entire baronies at a single step?"

"*Someone's* using magic," the Lady Silvertree told him said shortly, "or
perhaps just overly vivid imagination. We haven't been through Gilth this
season."

"Oh, now!" the seneschal protested with a smile. "Your secrets are safe with us! I hardly think a herald of Flowfoam is apt to invent a meeting with all the Overdukes of Aglirta, however passing, or mistake your faces."

"Which herald was this?" Blackgult asked quietly.

"Thorntrumpet. He passes through Stornbridge often—so often, in fact, that we've often suspected him of keeping a very close watch on us for some reason. To report to the King, of course, but our loyalty—"

"Is above question," Embra said firmly. "At Flowfoam, Lord Stornbridge's regarded as one of the most diligent and loyal of tersepts."

The Tersept of Stornbridge blinked at her in delighted surprise, and grew a broad smile. "Well, my lady," he said grandly from the head of the table, "it gladdens my heart to hear you speak so highly of my conduct. I assure you that Stornbridge stands ready, and ever shall, to . . . tooooooo . . ."

Embra turned her head in time to see the Lord of Stornbridge Castle, already nodding over his sinking goblet, topple in earnest—and land nose-first, splashing gravy in all directions, in his roast boar.

"My lord?" she asked politely, as if minor nobles of Aglirta fell into their food and started snoring at table every evening in her presence. Embra took some small satisfaction in seeing the startlement of the four Storn officers, even the hitherto-imperturbed Coinmaster. Seneschal Urbrindur even looked scandalized again—and for real this time.

For a moment she thought Stornbridge was dead, or at least in the process of suffocating in his food, but he promptly gave the assembled diners proof that he wasn't, in the form of a soft and fluttery snore.

It was followed by another, succeeded by many more. They didn't stay gentle or muted, by any means.

"Sounds like a boar in rut," Craer commented amusedly, saluting the snoring tersept with a raised goblet. Hawkril and Lornsar Ryethrel chuckled politely, but the seneschal looked enraged again, and the Tersept's Champion seemed scarcely less hostile.

Seneschal Urbrindur lifted one hand in an obvious sign to the chamber knaves, who advanced in silent unison.

Blackgult and Hawkril clapped hands to sword-hilts, and Embra made her visible hand glow with sudden warning fire—cold flames that scorched nothing, but proclaimed ready power.

The seneschal shook his head sourly. "Such won't be necessary, revered Overdukes. We mean you no harm, but we do desire that you retire to your chambers now, as shall we. Our Lord Tersept has been taken ill, and 'twould be the height of rudeness to continue our feasting and chatter with him lying stricken in our midst."

He nodded gravely to the lornsar and then the Coinmaster, both of whom rose, nodded farewells, and strode out.

Eirevaur spoke to someone unseen as he entered an archway, and four cortahars hastened forth from it to lift Champion Pheldane, chair and all, and convey him from the chamber. By his startled movements and furious expression, this assistance took the Tersept's Champion entirely by surprise.

"Until the morrow, then?" Seneschal Urbrindur asked Stornbridge's guests, in tones that were not—quite—a firm dismissal, as the overdukes rose and glanced at the chamber knaves they each seemed to have suddenly acquired. Those servants carefully looked over overduchal shoulders, never meeting the eyes of Tshamarra or the Four.

"Until the morrow," Blackgult agreed, showing no outward sign of the faint nausea that was now clear upon the faces of his daughter and Lady Talasorn. Craer and Hawkril both wore unreadable expressions, but their unaccustomed silence bespoke their own troubled innards.

As the overdukes and their silent escorts set off together, the Golden Griffon asked the seneschal, "We're bedded in adjacent rooms, I trust?"

"Ah, I fear not," Urbrindur replied, his voice archness laid soothingly over quiet triumph. "The architecture of Stornbridge Castle unfortunately makes such a courtesy impossible."

"I'll bet," Craer commented in clearly audible tones, and noticed a fleeting smirk come and go on the face of the nearest chamber knave.

"No strangers to impossible courtesies, we," was Blackgult's formal reply. Uneasy silence fell, and in its throes they were led up a spiral flight of worn stone steps, in an echoing shaft that reached from an undercellar past six or seven floors to unseen battlements above.

Ascending two levels, the overdukes were conducted down a long, dimly lit passage. Its walls were studded with arched, magnificently carved doors, some of which were flanked by pairs of lit lamps hung from ceiling-rings, each with a cortahar standing guard beneath. "Behold me clearly, for I'm a target," Craer murmured to Hawkril, who smiled almost as tightly as the chamber knaves who bent close to hear.

Embra was ushered through the first such guarded door, and had just time to give Hawkril a silent look of alarm and appeal as she left them. Tshamarra was taken through the next, some sixty paces on and around a slight jog in the passage from Embra's chamber.

The servants took their three male guests up a back stair to another level; Blackgult's door awaited them across the passage at the top of it.

"Sleep well, my lords," he told Craer and Hawkril dryly, as he left them.

The procurer and the armaragor traded glances and shifted their gaits, Hawkril striding ahead so that his chamber knave had to hasten to stay with him, and Craer slowing so that the servant accompanying him unhappily fell behind his fellow.

"This door is yours, my lord," the Storn servant told Overduke Delnbone with clear relief in his voice, as they reached another lamplit and cortahar-guarded door. He swung the door wide.

An oil lamp glimmered softly on a stone-topped table flanked by a tall, narrow chair carved into the likeness of an arch of leafy vines. A canopied bed of similar style stood to the right, and a matching wardrobe to the left. Screens in distant corners discreetly concealed a tall mirror and a "thunderchair," respectively.

On a large table to Craer's left stood a ewer in a bath-bowl, and another ewer with a pair of goblets. Before them on the gleaming tabletop Craer's battered saddlebags and their contents had been arranged in a neat row. Nothing seemed to be missing.

The chamber had neither connecting doors nor windows. Unbroken walls of elegant dark wood paneling rose to a lofty ceiling on all sides.

Craer smiled at those panels. They were relief-carved in splendid scenes that offered a hundred hiding places for spyholes—and had no doubt been liberally endowed with such features. Some might fire dart-traps to dissuade prying eyes or fingers, or even permit access to small storage drawers. A room like this was great entertainment to a procurer.

"May I be of assistance, Lord?" the chamber knave asked the ceiling carefully. Craer followed the servant's gaze upward, seeking traps, entrances, and additional evidence of spyholes. None were evident.

So Overduke Delnbone gave his most charming smile and said, "But of course. Tell me where the various secret passages, traps, spyholes, firing ports, and the like are hidden, around this room."

"I . . . uh . . . I . . ." The servant gaped at Craer as if he'd made an indecent personal suggestion involving horses and gamefowl and possibly the Tersept of Stornbridge himself, reddened, and shook. Craer watched with a quizzical smile, awaiting an answer.

The chamber knave regained his composure, gave the procurer a look of anger, and in utter silence wheeled around and marched out of the room.

"Have a pleasant evening," Craer called merrily after him, and then sighed and began his examination of the room for those features he'd just mentioned, muttering, "Which is more than I'll do, if my gut gets worse. Embra's magic can't catch everything, it seems. Something in the food." He shook his head, and then his fist. "If I die spewing and filling yon thunder-bowl, I'll haunt my slayer and send him the same fate—only worse. *This I swear.*"

He cocked his head and listened, gazing at the ceiling, but if the Three had heard his declaration, they gave no sign of it. As usual.

So here Craer Delnbone stood, in a den of foes who'd happily murder him and his four fellow overdukes—whilst some false overdukes were evidently traipsing around the Vale, working mischief . . . mischief they'd be free to go right on doing if the real overdukes quietly disappeared here in Stornbridge Castle. The Faceless might impersonate a person here or there, for a short time, but not five nobles riding around openly. The false overdukes were magically disguised Serpents, of course . . . and the road ahead was what it had always been, in all of these dark little dances for the throne of Aglirta: stay alive, and slay the Serpent-priests responsible.

With a sigh, the procurer examined his belongings. They held no delights unfamiliar to him, but 'twas something to do until darkness came—and all the slaying and similar fun began.

"I seem to have been crouching behind bushes and trees forever," Fangbrother Khavan complained in a whisper.

Scaled Master Arthroon gave him precisely the cold and withering sort of look he'd expected. "When the Great Serpent comes, those who've been unwilling to do what's needful will be those considered expendable. You'd do well to remember that, Fangbrother."

Khavan nodded and flexed his cramping, protesting legs by extending one in a slow, soundless parody of a dancer's deep kick, and then drawing it back and doing the same with the other. The pain lessened but little.

They were crouching in the deep gloom of a thornvine-filled thicket behind Bowshun, on the edge of a little clearing where Aranglar the Weaver and his wife Thaelae split and stacked their firewood, kept their privy, and tossed things that had rotted. The happy couple were in the clearing now, but decidedly not engaged in any of the activities they customarily used it for.

Instead, they were trying to kill each other.

Grunts and shrieks of effort, triumph, and pain mingled with the crashings of their bodies rolling in underbrush, dead leaves, and formerly tidy piles of kindling.

Kicking, punching, and gouging, Thaelae and Aranglar tore at each other's hair, tried to smother each other, attempted stranglings, butted each other like enraged bulls, and even tried to batter each other's limbs and heads against handy trees—while ignoring a handy ax buried in Aranglar's chopping block. Gasping and shuddering, they snarled and spat, wild-eyed, and literally raked and tore with their fingers at each other.

Fangbrother Khavan winced, more than a little sickened—and well aware that Arthroon was watching *him*. The weaver and his wife were streaming blood from dozens of places, now, and Thaelae had just gouged out one of Aranglar's eyes with hideous ease.

Khavan set his teeth, gorge rising, and risked a look at his superior. The Scaled Master was smiling, obviously amused at Khavan's discomfort.

"Come, Brother Softguts," he purred. "We've seen enough of this particular plague affliction. There's someone else I want a look at. Keep low and quiet unless you'd like to lose *your* eyes too."

Skulking around the fray, the two priests scuttled hurriedly back to Aranglar's cottage.

"Why the rush?" Khavan gasped. Arthroon's reply was to throw himself flat behind moss-covered rocks, catch hold of the Fangbrother's leg with cruel force, and drag his fellow priest down to join him.

"Three people live in yon hovel, not just the loving pair we've been watching," he murmured, ignoring Khavan's gasps of pain. "That gives us a good chance of seeing a different plague effect than mindlessly seeking to slay, taking hold of the third person. Right about . . . now."

The ramshackle back door facing them banged open, and an old man lurched out, his wrinkled and unshaven face twisted in pain. He retched, clutched at his ribs, bent over, and spewed what looked like a very large meal onto the ground, groaning like a woman astonished by the pains of her first hard labor. Then he stumbled off down the narrow track that led to the stream and the deeper forest beyond.

"Who—?" Khavan asked, more in an attempt to appear alert and interested than out of any true interest.

"Thaelae's aging father," Arthroon replied, rising like a hunter stalking a beast of which he must be wary—and yet get very close to, to make his kill. "Follow *quietly*. 'Twould be very unwise to let him see or hear us, if my suspicions are correct."

Like wary ghosts they drifted along the trail from tree to tree, keeping to dappled shadows well behind the old man—who was staggering along feebly, bent over like a man on the verge of collapse, but groaning with ever greater vigor.

Anon those groans become rougher and deeper, until they were almost growls. Khavan gave Arthroon a "what now?" look, but the Scaled Master merely smiled and continued his patiently stealthy pursuit.

The Fangbrother took care that his resulting sigh was silent. He was shaking his head and hastening to catch up with Arthroon—and yet do so silently—when the Scaled Master held up a hand to indicate that Khavan should halt.

The old man was still wandering along the forest track, growling like a beast, but now he was tearing at his clothing. As Khavan peered, he could see hair—reddish-brown, profuse hair, not sparse gray and white—cloaking the man's hands and neck. More of it could be seen wherever clothing had been torn away—and "torn" was exactly the right word: the old man's fingers seemed to be lengthening into claws! That stooped, frail body was growing taller, broadening to split its well-worn tunic . . .

Khavan took a careful step back, but Arthroon whirled and gave him such a glare that the Fangbrother froze, trembling, and remained in that quivering hesitancy even when the old man—or rather, the *thing* that the old man had become—stopped in its amblings, sniffed, raised its head to sniff again, and then turned with a roar to confront the two priests.

That weathered old face was gone, replaced by something with great long-fanged jaws and a snout. The body below it resembled some sort of long-tailed bear, its only traces of humanity being a few rags of tunic and the flopping remnants of boots it still wore.

It strode forward slowly and menacingly, stalking the Serpent-clergy. " 'Tis gathering itself to charge," the Scaled Master observed, as calmly as if he'd been identifying a flower in which he had no particular interest. Khavan eyed it, gulped, and more than agreed.

Hurriedly he cast a spell, almost stumbling over the incantation in his haste to get it out. Khavan's hands tingled, his fingers went numb—and the air around them shimmered.

As if his casting had been a signal, the bear-creature charged at them, howling and snorting horribly. It swung those gnarled, long-clawed arms forward and back as it came.

Khavan retreated another step, swallowing hard. Was his spell not working? Why hadn't . . . ?

And then the shimmering before him collapsed into sudden dark, solid clarity. A shield of hissing, snapping snakes was abruptly hanging in the air, coiling and writhing around each other, biting at the air, and slithering along on nothing but emptiness.

The serpents formed a floating wall in front of both priests, most of their jaws reaching for the onrushing bear-beast. Forked tongues flickered and baleful eyes glowered; a fearsome sight even to their creator.

Khavan gasped in relief as he backed hastily away, trying to calm himself enough to recall the incantation for his "lance of acid" spell—in case this bear-beast burst through his conjured serpents, and he found himself facing those long-taloned claws directly.

Arthroon merely nodded in satisfaction as the monster thundered up to him and reared to awesome height, pawing the air. The snakes hissed in unison, and it recoiled from them and then froze, wavering and hardly daring to wave a paw at the floating, writhing mass.

The snakes arched and lunged, seeking to reach this creature that loomed so close to them . . . and yet was just beyond the reach of their fangs. It roared at them, eyes wild—then turned on its haunches with a long, slobbering snarl, and plunged off the trail into the trees.

The Scaled Master wore a faint smile as the crashings of the beast hastening away from them faded into the forest. Khavan returned to his shield of snakes almost as swiftly, fearing his superior more than a beast who was no longer charging in his direction.

He'd just reached the spot where he'd cast the spell when the receding crashings of dead leaves, trampled underbrush, and splintering dead tree limbs suddenly erupted into the challenging roars of two contesting beasts.

These were swiftly followed by more crashings, a horrible snapping and gnawing, roars and squeals of pain, sharp splintering sounds, and several heavy thuds, as if large, hurrying bodies had fallen, rolled, and scrambled about. Then the crashings of movement resumed, swiftly dying away into the distance.

The Scaled Master turned to Khavan. "Good. We've truly recreated the Blood Plague of old. Some victims fall to the Malady of Madness, but others turn into beasts and forthwith attack all creatures they see."

He wagged his finger at the Fangbrother like a tutor enlightening a particularly stupid pupil. "Soon," he said flatly, "Aglirta will be ours."

"Ours?"

"Ours," Arthroon repeated firmly, "to keep forever, once anyone who drinks anything in this land is either under our protection or swiftly dead."

"And the overdukes?" Khavan dared to ask.

"We shall see. They bide in Stornbridge, feasted by the tersept there. Some who bow before the Scaled One serve at that table. Yes, we'll soon see."

Lord of the Serpent Hanenhather shook his head. "Clumsy, Arthroon, very clumsy. Let a plague-beast just wander and slay whilst you chatter? How then is it a weapon in your hand? Or for our faith?"

The bear-beast lay sprawled and dead, torn bloodily open by the plague-monster Brother Landrun had been spell-tracking.

The monster that was lumbering toward the Serpent-lord right now. Another unfortunate villager twisted into a new shape by the plague . . . a peak-stalker, this one: all massive gray head and claws, stonelike skin, and size and weight to overmatch any two oxen.

The Serpent-lord shook his head again. Arthroon didn't even know of their presence—and obviously cared nothing for the fate of the bear-beast, which could have served the Brethren well in the days ahead. And such men preened under titles like Scaled Master these days. Ah, well . . .

"Be still, Landrun," he snapped. "Blunder forward now, and *you* may be forced into another shape rather than yon stalker."

Brother Landrun froze and turned fearful eyes to his superior. Lord Hanenhather was smiling slightly as he wove his spell, but his eyes were as cold as ever—and Landrun shivered more than once as the peak-stalker twisted, dwindled . . . and was suddenly a man.

Lurching and stumbling, it turned away from them, into the trees. The Lord of the Serpent smiled after it. "Go, Tersept of Ironstone, and give the orders I bade you," he said softly, "and war will soon rage in Aglirta again—ah, such a realm of bloodthirsty, restless hotheads!"

Brother Landrun swallowed. "And the real Tersept of Ironstone, Lord?"

"Oh, he died rather suddenly, I'm afraid. You remember what our pet direjaws devoured by the roadside, last night?"

"A slithersnake as long as a wagon," the Brother of the Serpent said slowly, frowning—and then looking horrified. "You mean—?"

"Yes." The Serpent-lord's smile wouldn't have looked out of place on the face of the direjaws. " 'Twas a noble slithersnake, to be sure."

Landrun fought down nausea. "But if no one can trust his lord or wife to really be themselves, then . . ."

"We can spread blood-chaos from one end of the Vale to the other," Hanenhather replied, "and watch overdukes and boy kings—and clumsy Scaled Masters, for that matter—fall."

He chuckled. "Good feasting for some. Come, Landrun, we've work to do. You need more practice controlling these beasts. I think it's time a few simple farmers had their chances at playing overdukes."

There'd been just enough warm water in the wash ewer for a pleasurable soak in the dark. Craer had brought on that darkness the moment the bowl on the floor was full, by snuffing out the oil lamp. He'd long since lifted his dripping feet out of the bowl, dried them on the robe left ready, and pulled on his boots again. He'd never so much as disarranged the rest of his clothing. Doing so would have been less than prudent, if even half the events he expected to befall this evening started to happen.

On his first stroll around the room he'd found the usual chamberpot under the bed, in addition to the thunder-chair. He hooked it forward in case his complaining innards desired sudden emptying. Then Craer stretched like a cat and began to prowl his unlit bedchamber, looking at the carved wall panels for any hint of lamplight, an approaching candle, or the like. After a time he traced a particular carving with his fingertips, in a vertical line from about the height of his head to his knees. As he did so, a soft smile appeared on his face, and he nodded almost imperceptibly.

There came a soft rap upon his door. Craer took three swift steps to one side of it, drew two of his knives, and used the point of one to pluck up a spare boot from the table of belongings and toss it gently to the floor just inside the door.

There came no thrusting blade under the door or through the suspiciously wide gap down one of its sides, and no spell blasted through the doorway. After a moment Craer called softly, "Who is it?"

"Me, you dolt," came a familiar whisper.

Overduke Delnbone smiled in the darkness, sidled a few paces closer, and asked, "And whom might me be, this time?"

"You bastard," the soft whisper came back. "You know perfectly well 'tis me, Tshamarra."

"Oh? I know several Tshamarras," Craer whispered merrily back. "Where does this particular one wear a scar shaped rather like the mark of my bite?"

"On the underside of my left teat, where you bit me, Craer. Now open this damned door or I'll blast it down!"

"Are you alone, and acting freely?"

"Yes, bebolt you!"

Craer sheathed his knives, and then plucked up a third: the blade he'd driven between two flagstones just inside the door as a doorstop. Drawing forth the two wedges he'd slipped into the doorframe, he lifted the small, ornamental brass bar Lord Stornbridge provided to his guests and swung the door wide, moving like a knife-wielding shadow to stay behind it as it opened.

Tshamarra Talasorn stood alone in the passage, fully dressed in dark leathers like those many thieves favored—Craer leered appreciatively—and bearing a small, shielded lantern. The two passage lamps flanking Craer's door seemed to have gone out, and the guards standing under them to have suffered some common misfortune that had left them sprawled on the floor. It must have been a silent mishap—but then, with the right magics, almost everything can become an "accident" of roughly the desired main effect.

"Pray excuse my caution, Lady Talasorn," Craer murmured, as Tshamarra stepped carefully into the darkened chamber. "One can never be too careful—a thinking you seem to share with me, given your garb and demeanor. To put it plainly, you must be expecting trouble as much as I do."

"Even more than that," she replied grimly, closing the door behind her and leaning against it for a moment in either weariness or nausea. "We must find Embra without delay. I feel less than well; the food, of course."

Craer bent to his boot, plucked something from within it, and held it out, deftly untwisting a stopper. "Would you like some? 'Tis half empty already, I'm afraid."

"And this hitherto-unrevealed drink would be—?"

"My 'timely flagon.' " Craer touched the metal to her palm. His fingers, cradling it, found her skin shockingly cold. "I bought it years ago in Sirl town," he added with an inviting smile, concealing his alarm at her chill, "from a crone who swore 'twould purge all taints and poisons."

Tshamarra lifted an eyebrow. "And you believed her? Are you in the habit, Lord Craer, of believing the claims of old crones who keep shops in Sirlptar?"

"Lady Talasorn," Craer replied with dignity, "she was of the Wise, and I'd just rendered her a service. Buying myself armor for the morrow, as it were. I drank the uppermost half not long ago, and—see?—still stand before you. Have all that remains. *Please.*"

Tshamarra nodded—and a sudden shuddering shook her entire body and left her in an anxious crouch, halfway to her knees. "It can hardly make me feel worse," she muttered, putting her lantern on the floor and taking the flask. She sniffed it suspiciously, and then drank.

The shuddering that seized her this time was much worse. Tshamarra gasped, reeled, and put out a hand to clutch the wall, shaking her head and wincing.

"Ah," Craer said sympathetically, "forgive me. I forgot; 'tis strong stuff."

"Tell me no tales I know not already." She fixed him with tear-starred eyes that were both baleful and amused. "Let's find Embra before this night brings any *more* fiery little surprises."

Craer nodded, stepped to the carved wall panels where he'd traced a line with his fingers earlier, and did something to a carved stag-head. The wall split soundlessly and sagged open, to reveal utter darkness behind.

As Tshamarra lifted her lantern, the procurer gestured grandly at the hitherto-hidden passage its faint light revealed. Then he made a gesture that indicated that Tshamarra should move herself to one side, and then another that bade her hood her lantern.

As the Talasorn sorceress swiftly did both of those things, she saw Craer draw a dagger from one sleeve and glide to the opening, stepping to one side—and then the flash and gleam of the procurer hurling his blade sidelong, into and down the passage.

There followed a soft thud and a hiss of pain.

Then, softly and from very close by, a whisper of movement came to Tshamarra's ears. She reared back from it but did nothing else . . . and almost immediately saw a flare of light as Craer lifted the hood of her little lantern just enough to get the wick from another lantern under it. He drew it forth flaming, and softly let the hood back down again. Tshamarra watched the wick bob across the room in silken silence. As Craer settled the wick back into place and his lamp caught alight, they exchanged silent glances over its dancing radiance. The procurer winked solemnly, swept up his lit lamp, and strode back to the passage.

The moment he showed himself in the entrance, there came the snap and clack of bowguns—the hand-sized crossbows so favored in Teln and the cities of the South—from down the passage.

Craer sprang back, wielding the lantern like a buckler to strike aside the darts that came hissing at him, and grinning fiercely. Another trap anticipated. The luck of the Three—which any good procurer knows is no luck at all, but the result of preparation, suspicion, anticipation, and a certain nimbleness—was with him.

And making its usual mocking laughter. Flaming oil dripped between the procurer's fingers, now; a dart had shattered the cauldron of the lamp.

Overduke Delnbone snatched one hand free of his blazing burden—which must have been blistering the other—shook it to be sure it was free of flame and oil, snatched something from his belt, and hissed at Tshamarra, "My chamberpot, under the bed! Fetch *quick!*"

She spun and fetched, and he shook what he'd snatched into it. "Flash powder," she breathed, comprehending.

Craer grinned at her as he snatched up the chamberpot, ran back to the secret door, and hurled it around the corner, aiming high and throwing hard.

They heard it shatter against the passage ceiling—and Craer set his teeth and flung the flaming wreckage of the oil lamp around the corner to join it.

Tshamarra hurled herself flat to the floor.

Darsar exploded right on schedule.

The blast flung the last of the Talasorns against the wall, bruising her shoulder, but the room soon stopped rocking.

Tshamarra found her little lantern on its side, the floor already hot beneath it. She righted it and unhooded it just enough to make sure it was still lit and unbroken.

Craer gestured furiously to her to quench even that tiny flash of light, and she did so, watching the dark shape of Craer crouching in the glowing smoke.

The passage spewed that silently drifting smoke in profusion, and the procurer kept very low as he stepped into it, moving with the eerie silence that so awed Tshamarra. Oh, she knew a spell that could quell noise, but she could still hear her own swift breathing, the dying echoes of the blast still rolling and rebounding in distant, unseen passages, and even the faint roiling of the air around her . . . but not Craer.

She waited one long, drawn-out moment, realized she was holding her breath, and carefully let it out in a gently measured sigh, still waiting for—

The passage exploded in a sudden bright inferno, and raging flames burst back into the room. Magical, they had to be!

Tshamarra ran frantically to meet them.

"Craer!" she screamed—and the roiling flames spat a blackened, struggling figure at her, spinning in a ball of flame!

8

Many an Unquiet Knight

The moon had not yet risen over Bowshun, so the night was very dark. Wherefore boots blundered, branches snapped, and men swore softly as they gathered by Marag Spring, halfway up the trail to Emdel's Glade. They were few, but all carried unsheathed, ready weapons.

"Eregar?"

"Aye, Thunn. Who's with 'ee?"

"Braumdur," hissed a deeper voice. "With my best blade. 'Twill be a pleasure to let air into the innards of that snake-priest!"

"Aye," Eregar the hunter agreed, feeling his way to his favorite stump in the darkness. Then he stiffened and leaned into the night, muttering, "Who comes?"

"Narvul," came the fierce reply, "with my ax!"

"Good. That's all of us. Time to sword this snake of a priest 'fore he has time to wag his jaws o'ermuch, and turn our wives and lads into strangers, and set them to spying on us. I had a bellyful of that *last* time—and this 'Brother of the Serpent' is far less sly-tongued and handsome than the snakes hissing at us then. I'll be damned by the Three if I'll let Bowshun be torn apart again by the likes of him."

"So you shall, indeed," said a new voice, dark laughter in its cold tones. The four Bowshun men barely had time to gasp before ale-brown fire blossomed all around them.

It lit up Marag Spring, and showed the men of Bowshun each other frozen in gasping terror—literally frozen, only their eyes obeying their utmost straining efforts to move. Though the brown radiance was already fading, it held them like an iron-hard, unyielding claw—and its source was a cold-eyed man in robes now stepping carefully around trees until he could set foot on the trail. Other men walked with him, some in Serpent-robes and some in the motley armor of down-at-heel hireswords.

"Fangbrother," Scaled Master Arthroon said in satisfaction, "make ready." A robed priest snapped orders, and hireswords lumbered forward to each of the four mute captives, drew a knife, and looked to Arthroon. He nodded and said flatly, "Now."

Four throats were cut with savage ease, gurgling bodies slumped and toppled, and full darkness returned to the trail.

"Kick them into the stream," Arthroon said sharply. "Off the trail, every trace of them. The moon's rising, and I want us gone from sight before the good folk of Bowshun answer the Serpent's call."

Fangbrother Khavan conjured up a glowing, floating serpent's head that moved at his bidding. The Scaled Master gave it a sour look but said no word of rebuke, as the hireswords bent swiftly to work.

By the time they were done, moans of awe and cries of "Look!" were coming from down the trail. The serpent-head had been seen.

"Off the trail," Arthroon ordered quietly. "Stop as soon as you cross the spring." Obediently the Serpent-party melted into the trees.

Cold blue moonlight was growing steadily stronger, and by its light the silently watching Serpents saw folk of Bowshun hastening past the sprawled, unseen bodies of four of their own men, to reach Emdel's Glade and hear the Serpent's call.

Maelra came out of her scheming with a start. There! A throbbing, a twinge of awakened power!

Intruding magic was trying to enter the largest scrying-crystal she'd enspelled. It couldn't be Uncle Multhas, for her own covert use of his smallest crystal was at this very moment displaying a wavering image of him hurrying up the staircase where Uncle Dolmur hung all those splendid paintings, through veil after veil of Dolmur's strong wards.

She dared not continue that scrutiny for fear of being detected by whoever was sending this new magic. For a moment she raged—she *must* hear what Dolmur said—and then let her magic lapse, waiting for the contact she knew would come. Maelra emptied her mind, seeking calm by holding to a mental picture of glowing flames.

For all her effort at control, she fell into a brief imagining of herself as a baleful rat crouched at a corner where two passage walls met while a guard came tramping past . . . and then the contact came.

The spy was probing all of the crystals, to give himself—yes, the mind-touch felt male—many vantage points rather than one, and better chances of hiding from angry Bowdragons.

It *was* Ingryl Ambelter, come to spy on the Bowdragon brothers. Triumphantly Maelra pounced on his probe, riding rather than challenging it. Images flooded into her, and she waited, letting the scenes flow over her, doing nothing as Ambelter made his own reaching to Multhas, found the hurrying black-robed wizard, and witnessed the entry of the Roaring-Bearded Storm into Dolmur's inner chambers. There came a little lift of excitement in Ambelter then, and Maelra used it to slip into his linkage, transferring her own spying from Uncle Multhas to the Spellmaster.

Then she firmly withdrew her awareness, returning to herself sweating and eager. The spell lay ready, written out for this moment, and she was pleased to see that her hand trembled but little as she reached for it.

It took a moment to dare to whisper the first words of the incantation—and then the spell was unfolding, and there was no time to look back, and this was all so *easy* . . .

Alone in a plain and disused cellar of Maransur House in Arlund, Maelra Bowdragon finished her spell with a flourish, and began to magically trace the Spellmaster of Aglirta back to his lair.

"Lady look down, Hawk," Embra murmured, putting her hands over both of her breasts to keep them from getting torn by passing hilts or buckles, "not your *armor!*"

" 'Twould be wiser," Hawkril growled, settling heavily back down beside her in the great bed. Though she couldn't see him properly in the darkness, made all the deeper by the bed draperies, she could hear and feel that he was in his feast clothes, now adorned with the crisscrossing belts and baldrics of all of his blades scabbarded to him, and his great boots were still on his feet. "They'll have handbows when they come for us, if my guess is right."

The Lady Silvertree sighed, patted her hip as she thought about how easily a dart or arrow would pierce the leather breeches covering them or the still-unbuttoned jack she wore above it, and murmured, "And plenty of time to fire them, while I'm still buckling and hoisting up plates and tightening them around you . . ."

"Lass, lass, you make it sound as if I wear more barding than three horses! I haven't spells or a Dwaer-Stone to keep me safe when traipsing around Stornbridge Castle barefoot, like you do!"

"I put my boots on as I was taking the nightgown off," Embra told him teasingly. "I thought you'd be looking."

The armaragor snorted. "I was." He half-drew his sword experimentally and added, "But for secret doors popping open, and panels sliding to show me ready bows, and such, not at your feet—or a pair of boots slung fetchingly around your neck, either. You look marvelous in leather, mistake me not, but your own bare hide's far more to my liking."

Embra smiled. Ah, but 'twas nice to be wanted. By the strongest and yet most gentle man in all the Vale, too. "I wonder how long it'll take the seneschal to find my guards entranced, and charge in to hack apart the fell sorceress."

Hawkril chuckled. "Well, we're certain to hear it when he does. You left the usual blast-trap spell as your welcome?"

"I did," Embra said a little grimly. "How *dare* they give us rooms apart? And treat us like prisoners? After donning my leathers, I put my gown back on over them, opened the door to stroll out—and they set steel to me, forbidding me to set foot outside my chamber doors until escorted out come morning! *Forbidding* me! What do they think 'Overduke' means, anyway?"

" 'Enemy,' probably," Hawkril grunted. "And after all, they'd be right about that, wouldn't they?"

It was Embra's turn to snort. "After someone tries to arrowfall us on the road like a brigand, and then threaten and belittle us in converse, and then feed us poison on our platters, that someone should hardly expect us to think of them as anything less." She sighed, and stroked his arm. "I'm sorry, Hawk. I'm squawking like a chambermaid. Even after using the Dwaer twice, I don't feel right. Something's still *crawling* through me. I . . . I wish Sarasper was here, to heal us all properly."

"*I* wish that winter never came again, and that everyone in all Darsar was so happy and wealthy that they'd never have to raise sword or ax or hoe, and that every day would have splendid weather, with all tables in every realm constantly groaning under the weight of food put there fresh and ready by the Three without anyone having to sweat in a kitchen," Hawkril replied, "but do the gods listen to me?"

"No," Embra told him dryly, "they're always too busy listening to Craer. His tongue provides endless entertainment enough." She yawned, and then turned to bury her nose in the warmth of Hawkril's doublet and added sleepily, "Wake me when the trouble starts."

Hawkril reached a long arm across them both to pat his lady's behind affectionately, and rumbled, "To do that, I'd've had to start slapping and jostling you when you were about nine—and that's only counting the trouble you personally started, on purpose."

"Don't remind me," the Lady of Jewels muttered, yawning again. "We none of us get to choose our lineage, only whether or not we'll be like our parents. That wasn't much of a—"

There was a creaking or cracking sound from one side of the room, echoed by a like sound from the other direction.

"Under," Hawkril snarled in Embra's ear in a clear order, giving her a shove into the darkness. He plunged in the other direction, and Embra heard the scrape of his shield being plucked up from under the bed. She almost lost hold of the Dwaer in her haste to get under the bed without transfixing herself on the dagger on her own belt—and by then, the clash of steel had begun, shockingly loud and very close on Hawkril's side of the bed, and the thunder of many boots racing toward her was growing loud indeed . . .

"Craer!" Tshamarra hissed, rolling him over. "*Craer!* Speak to me!"

The smoldering man under her hands made a husky, rattling cough, and then spat something onto the floor and gasped hoarsely, "I'm alive. I think."

The Lady Talasorn snatched back one of her hands from him as his leathers beneath her fingers suddenly flared up into open flame. She sprang up, whirled to snatch the ewer of drinking water, and emptied it over him.

The result was a loud hiss, much smoke, and a sharper stink than had been arising from him up until then. Craer groaned, and the sound almost made Tshamarra miss the scrape of a stealthy footstep in the passage.

She rose, quivering in silent anger, and stepped carefully forward in the near darkness, as catlike as she knew how. Though she could hear herself moving, the noise she made was far less than the stealthy sounds of someone advancing cautiously along the passage toward her.

The Lady Talasorn mouthed an incantation, uttering all but the last word. She had few enough battle-spells left, and several overduchal lives might depend upon not wasting a single one.

Behind her, Craer groaned again and rolled over, shedding flakes and ashes of his scorched leathers. He reached his hands and knees and swayed there, head down and softly spitting curses, arms trembling in the after-shock of violent magic. The stealthy advance in the passage continued.

Tshamarra watched with icy eyes, waiting . . . waiting . . .

Something moved amid the darkening smoke still eddying in the mouth of the passage, and the sorceress breathed the last word of her spell as tenderly as any lover: *"Harandreth."*

And from her outstretched fingers streaked tiny teardrops of wriggling flesh, surrounded by their own twinkling trails of force. They flew like vengeful wasps, growing little fanged jaws and dark smudges of eyes as they went. Plunging into the drifting smoke, they darted and—struck.

A hitherto-hooded lantern crashed into brilliant life as it tumbled, its bearer staggering back with a hoarse cry and clutching at his face. Something dark and wriggling was gnawing at one of his eyes, and he shrieked and tried to tear it from his face. The skin of his cheek bulged as he tugged—and then his cries sank into desperate, strangled gurgles as another of Tshamarra's spellspawn darted into the man's throat, striking as hard as any arrow, and started its own gnawing.

The shattered lantern spilled flaming oil across the floor, and in its light Tshamarra saw the boots of other stumbling men—cortahars, a hostler, and a chamber knave, still in his livery—behind it. They seemed to have lost any enthusiasm for proceeding out of the passage as they hacked, tore, and slapped at her conjured attackers.

Tshamarra had never found the more powerful spell that gave the wizard casting it some of the life force drained by the spellspawn . . . so the poison raging through her might still bring her death before dawn. With that savage thought bitter in her mouth, the sorceress helped her dazed and burned Craer to his feet.

He was dying, too, all because they'd taken one road at Osklodge and not another. Still, the Dwaer they were seeking and the foe wielding it might be lurking somewhere in this cold, hostile castle. Aye, and perhaps Sirl ladies were wearing their sashes a fingerwidth shorter this month, too . . .

Staggering under Craer's lurching weight, the Lady Talasorn called back one of her spellspawn to dart ahead of them and light a way to the door. It faded and flickered, her spell almost spent—which was why she had to get out of here, and find Embra and the Dwaer. It could power the simpler spells for both of them, and old Blackgult too, if his wits weren't too wavering . . .

The spellspawn collapsed into sparks and then nothing as they burst out of Craer's room together, the procurer wincing and cursing but running more steadily now, getting back his balance.

"On, Lightfingers," Tshamarra hissed in his ear, dragging him around to the right. "We've got to find Hawkril and the rest!"

"Hawk's this way, yes," Craer gasped. "Blackgult . . . back behind . . . 'tother way . . ."

They rounded a bend in the passage, and lamplight flickered ahead. Standing in it, waiting with grim smiles and swords drawn, were a dozen cortahars, with a handful of chamber knaves behind them.

"Those who do murder in Stornbridge can expect but one fate," one Storn guard called—as they started to stalk forward, in careful, menacing unison.

Ezendor Blackgult had lived long enough to earn himself vivid dreams. Dying faces, stabbing blades, cold battlefield mornings, and slender hands clutching ready daggers behind welcoming thighs. All of these were familiar visitors, frequently shattered with bright Dwaer-fire, remembered explosions, and the hate-filled faces of shouting mages. Nor was the Golden Griffon any stranger to coming awake shouting himself, in a cold sweat or with a sleeping fur clutched in his hand as if it were the throat of a hated foe.

But this time the pain seemed real, as he was jolted from dark slumber by agony as great as he'd ever felt before, a red tide of burning pain that brought him awake and straining to rise—in a sticky wetness of his own blood enlivened by two snarling faces above him, in the glaring light of a lantern.

Those faces belonged to men he'd never seen before, but their intent was clear enough. He was staring at the ceiling of his sleeping chamber in Stornbridge Castle, between the tall and lancelike cornerposts of his bed—one that lacked a canopy, thank the Three, or it'd be aflame right now, and cooking him!

The intent of the two chamber knaves above Blackgult was clear because their hands were on the hafts of the two spears that had pierced right through him—one from either side; orderly fellows—to pin him to the bed.

The eldest baron of Aglirta, and sometime Regent of the Realm, could only writhe as they laughed and bore down. Already he was both numb and afire, red mists of pain threatening to overwhelm him entirely.

"Bring that lamp *here!*" someone snapped from the foot of the bed, as Ezendor Blackgult slapped his hands against the two spearshafts, and fought to close trembling fingers around them. They glistened with his own gore; his hands slipped, and then slipped again. He fumbled his way higher up the shafts as the lamp bobbed around from his right to somewhere beyond his knees.

"Ah, the great Griffon struggles," the same voice gloated. "Fitting. Let him die struggling, knowing the Serpent has collected his life at last!"

A head came into view above Blackgult's knees—a bald, cruel head, of a man who stood with the cowl of his serpent-adorned robes thrown back. A small, vertical coiling serpent was branded on one of his cheeks; it gave his smile a crooked appearance. The man was smiling now, as he slowly drew a wavy-bladed dagger and held it up to the light for Blackgult to see.

Blood was flooding into Blackgult's mouth. One way or another, this would end soon. He'd accumulated a few little tricks and magical gewgaws down the years, but nothing he could reach now, unless . . .

He tried to shove himself up off the bed, and learned two things: that great pain can force an overduke to instantly retch and spew blood and bile into the faces of anyone close above him, and that his left side wasn't pinned to the bed. That was the side where his boots stood, if someone hadn't moved them, and a sheath inside one of those boots held a very slim chance of taking his slayers down with him.

The chamber knave drenched in Blackgult's spew moaned in disgust and tried to back away, his weight leaving his spear—but the Serpent-priest struck him hard across the shoulders, and snapped, "Let go, and *die!*"

In the hand that wasn't walloping servants, the priest still held his dagger. He smiled down at Blackgult, turned the blade with leisurely slowness until its point menaced the pinioned overduke's breast, and then slowly— very slowly—stabbed down.

That glittering point was moving far too slowly to pierce skin; the man must mean to slice away Blackgult's silken nightshirt, and lay bare the overduchal chest for another thrust.

But no. As the blade descended, it seemed to writhe, ripple, and *grow*, twisting into . . . a silver-hued snake-head, whose fanged jaws opened to bite!

Ezendor Blackgult was not a man to surrender to any fate. He caught hold of the two spearshafts as high up as he could, and with a sudden jerk— and agonized roar—of effort, he pulled the two embedded spears toward each other.

The chamber knaves holding them staggered, gave startled exclamations, and then crashed together, shoulder to shoulder, with the priest's arm caught between them.

The Servant of the Serpent screamed, his fingers springing open, and the snake-headed dagger spun away to clang off a wall nearby.

Now. It had to be *now*. Sobbing, Ezendor Blackgult kicked the servant on the left off one spear, plucked it forth from himself, and smashed it across the face of the other chamber knave. Blood spurted as a nose broke, and the servant roared and staggered back, leaving Blackgult free to heave himself upward, and . . . tear . . . bloodily free of the blood-soaked bed.

The pain drove him to his knees, the world whirling around him in a yellow mist . . .

Shuddering, with one spear still through him and his hands like limp dead things, Blackgult felt for his boots—and managed to knock them over.

"Lady, smile upon me," he snarled, reaching again. "Old One, aid me . . ."

He tried to get his fingers inside a boot, and failed.

"Dark One, smite my foe," he prayed, trying—and failing—again.

Across the room, the Serpent-priest wept and danced in pain, clutching at a flopping hand that bespoke a shattered forearm.

"Aid, fools! Aid, or taste the curse of the Serpent!" he spat, but the other servants crowded into the bedchamber doorway—and a hitherto-hidden door, where a section of the paneled wall stood open across the room—hung back, gaping, swords and daggers forgotten in their hands.

The third time, Blackgult got his fingers into a boot and felt . . . the hilt of the little dagger he kept sheathed there. Horns of the Lady! The wrong boot; his flask of healing was in the other one!

Across the room, the Serpent-priest swayed, murmuring a healing spell upon himself, and Blackgult saw what lay right at the man's booted feet: that snake-dagger.

Healing—for both of them—would just have to wait. The Golden Griffon plucked forth his bootfang, hefted the spear until he got its far end up off the floor, and launched himself into a lumbering run across the chamber.

Watching servants murmured as the butt of the spear caught the Servant of the Serpent low in the ribs, ruining his spell and slamming him into the wall.

The pain of the impact made Blackgult scream, or chokingly try to scream, and he went to one knee, the yellow mists flooding in again. Through them he dimly saw the priest snatch up the snake-head dagger in his unhurt hand, and glare at Blackgult, his eyes flat with hatred. "Now," he spat, "you're going to *die*!" And he launched himself into a run across the room.

The overduke staggered to his feet, turned away from the onrushing

Serpent—and then at just the right time swung around to face him, bringing the spear butt into the priest's path again.

The Servant of the Serpent dodged aside to keep from running onto the spear. Blackgult kept on turning until the priest was running along the bloody spearshaft, raising his arm to reach out and stab.

Blackgult feigned faintness, bending his knees in a sagging that forced the priest to reach farther and farther—and left his wrist open to the sudden slash of Blackgult's bootfang dagger.

It must have burned like fire. The fingers flew open, the snake-head dagger spun away again, and the Serpent-priest opened his mouth to scream in pain.

Blackgult turned that shriek into a feeble bubbling with his backswing, slashing open a holy throat with the tip of his bootfang.

Then he turned away, not waiting to see the priest fall, and staggered back across the room to where his other boot lay. White-faced servants shrank back from him and the bobbing, bloody spear he wore, and when the Golden Griffon's numb fingers came up from the boot carefully cradling a vial—a vial that glowed when he pulled the stopper with his teeth—there was a general cry of fear, and the room emptied in a thunder of booted feet.

Ezendor Blackgult carefully drank down the icy-cold liquid to the last drop. It soothed like velvet, cutting through the fire, and gave him the strength he needed, sweating and reeling, to tug the spear out of himself. Sitting down heavily on the bed as it fell, his own blood fountaining after it, he stared dazedly at the walls. Everything was growing dark as the yellow mists receded . . .

Dully he watched the snake-headed dagger turn back into an ordinary blade again.

"Embra, if I die, go on to glory! Blackgult is yours, or Hawk's if you prefer, and may the Three protect you both," he gasped, tasting more blood and wondering if this healing would be enough . . . and if he'd taken it in time.

Embra rolled and twisted desperately under the bed, trying to get her legs under her and move away from the edge—where dark swordpoints were already stabbing hungrily down through the straw mattress, like fangs reaching for her face. The front of her jack was still unbuttoned, leaving only light silk over her breasts and nothing over her throat—the dangling gorget kept banging against her neck as she rolled—and she had to move fast. A moment more and they'd be sure her side of the bed was empty, and be bounding up and across it to stab Hawk from behind.

"Back!" she snarled, more to focus her will than out of any need to incant, and called on the Dwaer furiously, thrusting all living things away from her as hard as she could. There were startled shouts and wavering, fearful cries, and the thuds and scrapes of boots ended abruptly—only to be replaced by meaty thuds of bodies striking walls and doors and each other. This din was enlivened by a few shrill shrieks as men were impaled on the weapons of others, or laid open by blades they were tumbling past.

Embra set her teeth and reminded herself that *she* hadn't wanted this violence, any of it, and would just as soon dwell in an Aglirta where she'd never have to lay hand on a Dwaer, and men had better things to do than swagger around by night putting their blades through sleeping guests.

Bearing down with her will, she held the unseen men where they were, all around the chamber, and called on the Dwaer to do a second thing at the same time. She was getting better at this. Slowly. What she wanted was to hurl the bed above her over on its side, freeing her to stand up, and that was such a similar force as she was already holding unleashed that she thought she could manage it. To call on the Dwaer in this way she must have cast spells that worked very similar effects in the past, so as to recall just how it felt. Recapture that feeling closely enough, and the Dwaer-result would copy the long-gone spell. Luckily, hurling things about was something every novice sorceress did, in her earliest days of working brutish "shove at the world" spells.

The bed whirled up and crashed against a wall on the side away from Hawkril, its posts splintering with loud crashes. Judging by the thunder of its impact, men had been standing on it when its violent journey began—but as none of them could have been Hawkril, she cared not a whit.

Embra stood up, cradling the Dwaer, and from all sides came little moans of fear. Some radiance had leaked from the Stone in her use of it, and now outlined her in a softly flickering halo. From end to end of the Vale men heard tales of the Lady of Jewels, and here she was, among them. Frowning.

Embra breathed deeply, feeling the magic flowing through her that kept all of these armed and furious men motionless against the walls. Now to do something harder: cause the air to glow, to make her bedchamber as bright as day and show her where Hawk was, as well as all their foes.

Making an object emit radiance—what old grimoires called a "cold torch"—was easy, a magic mastered early by would-be wizards: it needed only the right visualization and incantation, and a flame to "drink." The Dwaer could replace fuel and conjuration, if she could hold a "mind seeing" of the brightness, *thus* . . .

Slowly, in a silent, rippling wave, the air grew bright. The Lady Silvertree saw her beloved right away, and Hawkril managed a wink to tell her he was unhurt. The shuddering of his neck and shoulders told her how much it had cost him to twist his head around so she could see his face. Around him—and trapped between him and the wall—were seven or so men of Storn. Dozens more were plastered against the walls on all sides: chamber knaves in livery, men in plainer garb bearing Stornbridge shoulder-badges—verderers and stablehands, perhaps—and fully armored cortahars with the scarlet hawks perched on gilded bridge-arches of Stornbridge bright upon their breasts. All of them had blades in their hands, and were staring silently at her in fear and hatred.

"Overduke Hawkril Anharu should be flattered, I suppose," she murmured. "So many of you, all come to claim his life—just one poisoned, sleeping noble. Whereas I'm the surprise sent by the Three to twist your scheme awry, as so often befalls in life. All of you came here seeking to take the life of the man I love, and I can't trust any of you not to try to take it again. Wherefore I'll now end yours."

She strode to where Hawkril was, turned her back on him to face the rest of the room, closed her eyes, and silently told the Dwaer what to do.

The force holding the men against the walls was reversed—violently—and then reversed yet again. Bodies slammed together in the center of the room with loud smacking sounds, clangs of metal, deep thuds, and one ragged cry. Then they were hurled back against the walls with another crash.

Again. Bodies slammed together, some still-conscious men having the sense to throw away their blades. Swords clattered to the floor here and there, but there were more grunts and sobs of pain as the Storn men slammed together once more.

Many of the bodies leaving the walls this time hung limp, senseless, or broken of limb. More of them made wet or cracking sounds when they tasted the stone walls once more.

Hard-faced, Embra hurled them again, and again. Her gorge was rising, but this was war, and she didn't want a man still able to stand or bend a bow or throw a dagger when she released Hawk and the seven Storn men trapped with him. Again. And again.

Many of the forms were shapeless now, and trailed blood as they went. More and more of them slumped, not responding to her magic . . . which meant that they must no longer be living.

Embra Silvertree drew in a tremulous, unhappy breath, strode to the center of the room with the Dwaer ready in her hand, and ended her magic. She stood somewhat off to one side of Hawkril, and as he staggered away from the wall, she sent a gout of fire in front of him—washing over the groaning Storn men following him.

There were a few screams and struggles from within those flames, but most of the men toppled without a sound, blazing.

When Embra and Hawkril were the only moving things left in the room, the armaragor turned to his lady and murmured, "My thanks for my life, Em. Remind me, please, never to get you really angry."

Embra stared at him, white-faced and trembling—and then flung herself into his arms, sobbing bitterly. Hawk held and rocked her gently as she wept, turning her slowly around and around—so as to look in turn through each of the six open doorways he could see, for any signs of more attackers. He'd known about only two of those doors when getting into bed.

The Dwaer, pressed between them, was hard and cool. Hawkril stole a hand up under it to make sure it didn't fall when they did draw apart—and discovered that one of Embra's hands was clenched around the Stone as tightly as any beast's claw could grip.

The touch of his fingers on it made her draw back in alarm and glare at him—and then dissolve into fresh tears, and embrace him all the more fiercely. Hawkril let her cry while his eyes roved about the chamber. His armor there and there, his boots over yonder beside the shattered, face-down wreckage of a wardrobe with two crushed servants sprawled half out from under it, and a blade Em could probably heft over there, by the splintered wreckage of the bed.

When his lady mastered her tears, Hawkril said gently, "Lady Silvertree, 'tis best we be going. We must find the other overdukes and make a stand together. Stand ready with the Stone whilst I salvage what we need, and think you on which doorway we should leave this place by."

Embra gulped, sniffed furiously, gulped again, and nodded. Her face was as white as moonlit snow, but she managed a lopsided wreck of a smile when he looked at her.

Hawkril gripped her shoulder reassuringly for a moment, and then hurried to his task, holding out his breastplate to her in the space of three breaths. "Hand me the Dwaer, and start buckling."

He stood patiently through the wild, helpless flood of laughter and fresh tears that followed—and for that, Embra knew, she would always love him.

She buckled and tightened and adjusted as fast as she could, heedless of cut or pinched fingers. For his patience and his kindness, most of all, she so loved this great bear of a man. . . .

9

Impressing Overdukes to Death

"Wake *up,* my lord!"

The voice above the candle was insistent and young. The Tersept of Stornbridge knuckled his eyes and growled, "What *is* it? Get that flame out of my eyes, man!"

"Get up! The castle's under attack!"

"The—*what?*"

"The overdukes are slaughtering your people, Lord—up and down the passages. They're setting fire to things, too! You're needed—before they bring all Stornbridge Castle down on our heads!"

Lord Stornbridge spat out a heartfelt curse and rolled to a sitting position, running a hand through the matted mess of his hair and recoiling from what he saw in his bedside mirror. A sword-hilt was suddenly thrust between him and his reflection—a familiar sword-hilt. His own.

"Your sword, sir," the servant said unnecessarily.

The tersept looked at it and then peered at the man, eyes narrowing. "Where're Alais and Jhaundra? I don't know you!"

The face of the man holding out the sword to him rippled and changed, and in quite a different—and much colder—voice its owner said, "Oh, but you do."

Stornbridge winced. "Fangbrother Maurivan!"

"The same," the Serpent-priest said coldly. "Now get up, strip down, and stand away from your bed, or this'll hurt even more than it should!"

"What will?"

"Move!"

Stornbridge moved. He'd heard that tone of voice only twice before from Maurivan, and each time, men had died for disobedience, or lack of anticipation, or for being a trifle too slow.

When he was standing shivering in the darkness—for the priest stood between him and the lone, flickering candle—the Fangbrother snapped, "Arms out! Legs apart!"

"What're you—?"

"Silence!"

A moment later, this furious order was joined by the words, "And stand still unless you want to be maimed!"

Frightened now, the tersept managed to keep still, save for some uncontrollable trembling. He managed to continue to do so even when he saw the pieces of his own armor drifting toward him from various dim corners of the room, floating along as if they could fly, and see. Maurivan's magic, of course.

The Serpent-priest stood silently watching as plates clacked and skirled into place, buckles did themselves up, and boots thudded to the floor in an unspoken command, right in front of the tersept's bare feet. He stepped into them, sweating in his armor—and wincing as his movements made metal dig into him here and there. He'd never worn his armor without any of its underpadding before, and it hung loose and awkward on his body. Rattling, pinching—and sharp.

He tried not to let his irritation—and a small, mounting worm of fear—show, as Fangbrother Maurivan held out the sword again, scabbard and all, and his baldric, with its usual four daggers, came flying silently up.

"I'm ready," Lord Stornbridge snapped, putting up his hand to catch his flying helm before it could do something painful to him, trying to get itself down over his head.

"Where—?"

"The Lornsar's Forechamber."

"Ryethrel? You've awakened him, too? Then why couldn't *he*—?"

"He's dead, that's why. He led a foolish attack on the one they call Hawk, and died with all the others, spattered around the walls of the bedchamber you put that man-mountain in. That bitch he beds keeps her Dwaer ready, and wastes no time in using it."

The tersept opened his mouth to say something, found his mind empty, and settled for clapping down his visor instead, and starting the painful tramp out of his room and down the stairs toward the lornsar's rooms.

He didn't bother to look and see if Maurivan was accompanying him. Stornbridge had no doubt that wherever he went and whatever he did, the priest would be watching. He'd long suspected that the Fangbrother's eyes were always upon him.

That was no more reassuring a thought now than it had ever been.

"Just a little farther," Tshamarra gasped, hauling at Craer with all her strength. He groaned and sagged back down a step. A hard-thrown sword clunked against the paneled wall not far to his left, and the procurer snarled a pain-wracked curse and clawed his way up to join her, as more shouts came from below.

They'd fled down one stair and then back up another, with cortahars in pursuit. Tshamarra had no spells left worth thinking about—she could conjure light, and work a minor illusion to make one face look like another, and that was about it—and Craer was failing fast.

The lower passage, where the two sorceresses had been given rooms, was crawling with dozens of cortahars, armsmen, and chamber knaves who held their weapons awkwardly and looked like they'd rather be in bed several towers distant.

That left two overdukes on the run with rather slender choices. They'd fled back up here, after sending most of the castle men pounding off down the passage in pursuit of a false Craer and Tshamarra spun with the best Talasorn illusion spell she had.

The cortahars waiting outside Hawk's room were still there, and Craer had stopped a swordpoint in his shoulder while killing two of them, to win Tshamarra time to yank open doors enough to find stairs up.

That had sent the two youngest overdukes staggering along in the moonlight and gloom of an unfamiliar upper level, trying to stay ahead of these few but persistent Storn blades—and wondering how painful their fate would be when dawn came and the rest of the castle woke up.

More doors had been opened, a few snoring servants awakened, and this latest stair found. It led farther up still, hopefully to some turret they could barricade themselves in.

Tshamarra no longer much cared. She felt as if fire was raging inside her. Sweat was pouring off her so swiftly now that her boots were filling with it, and its flow had brought numbness, a drowsy lack of caring overmuch about anything, and, under all, a growing anger. A wrath unlike her own sharp and sudden tempers, but dark and hot and deep, rising like an incoming tide. She could taste it at the back of her throat now, and wondered what would become of her when it rose to overwhelm her.

Behind them came a sudden strangled cry, as if someone had suddenly felt a sword slide right up through him, and didn't know what to do. Tshamarra looked back, conjuring light to see by.

That was exactly what had made that sound. A dying cortahar was sliding limply down the steps as Overduke Blackgult, every inch the dark and sardonic Golden Griffon despite being covered in dried blood from boots to throat, withdrew a glistening sword from the man's backside.

Behind Blackgult, Embra stood looking up at her, Dwaer in hand. "You're readily traceable when you use magic," the Lady Silvertree called, "but you move too fast to be easily caught up to."

"Craer's hurt," Tshamarra called back. "Badly."

"We're coming up, lass," Hawkril rumbled, from somewhere below. "Worry not. The Griffon here was gutted like a half-butchered stag when we found him—and he's whole now."

Tshamarra looked down at Blackgult's face, as wet with sweat as her own, and said quietly, "Or not, as that poison may have it."

Blackgult climbed the steps to her. "Embra took care of the poison, but yes, I can see you're suffering the same taint or sickness I am. Some advice: Don't ask her to try and cure you with the Dwaer unless you like feeling like you're being roasted on a spit—on fire inside and out."

"Leaving you as before, when it passes?"

Blackgult nodded. "As you see. Now, let's look at this lad of yours." He bent and sniffed. "Smells cooked."

Tshamarra snorted. "Some comforting elder *you* are."

"Lass, I leave that to Hawkril and my daughter, who're among the best comforters in the realm. I'm more your grim, bitter old man whose dark rutting past is catching up with him."

"Oh? Can I watch?"

Blackgult gave her a wolfish grin. "Oh, you'll live a while yet—if you don't say the right smart words to the wrong person, that is."

Embra knelt over the procurer sprawled on the steps, and then looked at Tshamarra. "Leave off fooling with my father, now, and hold Craer. He may buck and twist—Father, take his feet—and I want you with me, to feel and see what I do. If your own sickness starts to twist things, and I order you away, break off touching any of us just as fast as you know how." Without turning her head, she asked, "Hawk?"

"Standing guard," came the calm reply. "No Storn swords in sight yet."

Embra sighed. "They'll find us soon enough." She bent her will, her long dark hair stirred around her as if plucked by a wind no one felt, and the Dwaer rose an inch or so from her palm and started to spin.

Tshamarra hastily let her light spell lapse as the Stone tugged at it, glowing with its own brightening fire—and Craer suddenly leaped under her hands.

"*Hold* him!" Embra snapped, as the procurer made a sound that was half-gasp and half-sob, and writhed under her. Without hesitation, she flung herself atop him like a farm lass wrestling a pig, clutching the Dwaer in both hands and using her elbows, knees, and thighs to try to keep him down.

Tshamarra ducked her head to avoid Embra's boots and clung to Craer's shoulders, biting her lip as she saw Blackgult being battered back and forth by violently kicking feet.

And then, as suddenly as it had begun, the spasm ended, and Craer was smiling up at them. "More, more! Clothes off, Lady of Jewels, and let me enjoy this properly!"

"He's better," Hawkril observed, as Tshamarra dealt the procurer an affectionate slap and he grinned unrepentantly up at her.

"Up, Craer," Embra ordered crisply, clambering off him. "Your lady needs you—'tis her turn."

Tshamarra barely had time to blink before Craer sprang up and over her, to clutch her wrists as Blackgult pounced on her ankles—and Embra called on the Dwaer again.

"You . . . you know," Tshamarra gasped, as she bucked and twisted and tried to speak without biting her own tongue, "we'd be lost without this thing. I hope it has no limits we'll ever find . . . We've been . . . calling on it heavily enough . . ."

Then white fire seemed to storm through her, and she lost all means of speech or sight for a moment, as fire claimed her.

When she could see again, shuddering and drenched with her own sweat, Embra was saying gravely, "I hope so, too, because our only hope to see the morrow is for us to stand together now, so we three can all source our spells in the power of the Stone. Craer and Hawkril must be our merry warriors again, guarding our fronts and backs—and *no* clever comments, please, Craer."

Overduke Delnbone looked mournful. "None? Not even a little one?"

"*No,*" Blackgult and Hawkril said in sudden unison.

"Give the ladies a rest, Longfingers," the armaragor added. "They've got to be thinking of spells and the like, not your jests, or we'll never get through all this creeping around in the dark." He looked at Embra, and added, "This stair must end in a turret—a trap for us if there're Serpent-priests or wizards about, I'm thinking."

The Lady Silvertree nodded. "Agreed. You and Father work out where we go and what we do; you know castles better than the rest of us."

"If we're trying to just stay alive," Blackgult put in, "getting to the battlements so you can spelljump us out of here would be the best scheme—though dangerous in itself, given cortahars with bows standing nightguard."

"I heard an 'if' there," Tshamarra murmured, flexing her hands and wondering what could be wrong with her to make her feel so hot again, this soon after being Dwaer-healed.

Blackgult smiled. "Yes. We can try much more than that. If we find Lord Stornbridge, we won't be far from also finding any Serpent-priests lurking in this town or keep, if there are any at all."

"We'll probably have to wade through all of the rest of these Storn-heads to get to the tersept," Craer said darkly.

"So, what're we waiting for?" Hawkril growled. "Even if we're still hacking down seneschals and tersept's champions when the sun comes up, we'll have accomplished *something*."

"So we go back down this stair," Blackgult said, "slay anyone we meet who waves a sword at us—and put to sleep anyone running to raise the alarm about our whereabouts. If we keep moving, stay out of places where we can be cornered, and lead them a merry dancing tour around their own castle, I'd say we can do fair damage to the ranks of Storn swordsmen before we're done. If you think you see a Serpent-priest, cry it out without delay."

"Ah," Embra said with a sigh that was only half-mocking. " 'Tis *so* nice to have clear orders and a plan."

"Careful," her father warned sardonically. "That love of clear direction is what's let evil men rule large parts of Aglirta these last fifty summers or so."

Embra stuck out her tongue at Blackgult. Surprisingly, he returned the pleasantry, as he followed Hawkril down the stairs.

"They may be clumsy fools in Stornbridge," Lord of the Serpent Hanen-hather observed, "but thankfully, the poisons of our faith are neither foolish nor clumsy. I suspect Aglirta is short a few overdukes by now."

Brother Landrun chuckled tentatively. Hanenhather's temper had been chancy these last few days, and his hands were raised to weave a spell right now.

"Begone, longfangs," the Serpent-lord said crisply, as a glow of quickening magic outlined his fingers, "and arise, Lady of Jewels. An Embra Silvertree, Landrun, far more biddable to my will than the real one will ever deign to be."

Landrun watched the furry, wolf-headed beast dwindle into a slender, shapely human woman. Nude and placid, she blinked at them in blank bafflement, and the Serpent-lord rubbed his chin and said, "Those eyes seem wrong, yes—no fire behind them. Yet."

He raised his hands again. "Drag yon wench into the next room before you go and fetch the rock-cat, Landrun. We don't want it gnawing on our lovely sorceress, do we?"

"Fetch the rock-cat, Lord?"

"Yes, Brother. Let it chase you in here, and then get out of the way—unless you want me to transform you into that little thief of the overdukes. Not more than two bites for the rock-cat, though, by my reckoning."

Landrun cast a quick glance at the Lord of the Serpent. Hanenhather was smiling faintly, as usual.

"Where now, Father?" Embra gasped, as they drew breath at the head of a stair now littered with bleeding Storn bodies.

"Aye," Tshamarra agreed, panting. "We're listening with interest."

"Listening, aye, but heeding?" Blackgult replied. "Now that *would* be rare and bright. Hearken, then: We go to the end of this passage and through the tower beyond, thence to the north gatetower, and descend it—by the servant's stair, not the grander one guards use. Then we double back along the ground floor and go hunting Serpent-priests. Above all, keep together."

Tshamarra frowned. "What north gatetower? I don't—"

"First rule upon entering an unfamiliar castle," Hawkril rapped out. "Look how it lies, and keep track of where you go, within."

Tshamarra sighed. "Things were much simpler before I came to Aglirta. Hold out hand, accept what servant puts into it, and move on."

"And *that's* just how kings get slain, here in the Vale," Craer told her.

She rolled her eyes in response, and pointed at Blackgult. "So we do as you suggest. Let's move!"

"Ah, at *last*!" Blackgult and Hawkril said, more or less in unison—and then traded looks of surprise, followed by chuckles.

Tshamarra looked disgusted. *"Men."*

"No," Embra corrected her. "Boys."

Their first guardpost was a drowsy, half-asleep armsman who came awake in sudden alarm as Craer jerked his spear sharply out of his hands, sending him sprawling—and Hawkril thoughtfully plucked up a couch every bit as large as the guard and dropped it on the man.

He groaned once, twisted, and then sighed into senselessness beneath it. The overdukes were already racing on, through the door on the far side of the guardroom and along another passage.

This way, at the narrowing end of Stornbridge Castle, had no half-towers on its courtyard side, and its wall of windows let an ocean of bright silver moonlight into the room. That cold radiance highlighted some frowning portraits of presumably dead former owners of Stornbridge, none of which so much as moved—let alone attacked—as the overdukes ran past.

Then came another door, unguarded this time, and entry into the gate-tower, where voices coming up its two stairwells—which lacked doors of their own, opening directly into the chamber they now crouched in—told the suddenly cautious overdukes that folk were awake and about.

"Look, Chalance," an exasperated voice was saying. "If they try to flee, they *have* to come to South Tower, Storn Tower, or here. I can't see high-and-mighty overdukes willingly plunging off battlements or bursting through windows to plunge into the moat—nor can I see them getting all the way around the castle to the other gatetower without word coming to us, and every cortahar we have being flung against them, first. So they'll be along, fear you not. Our task is to wait with our bows, keeping quiet and out of sight, firing when we see the chance and *only* when we see a chance, until the blood price of coming down *this* stair is so high that they take the other one—into the arms of the priests. We're to try to leave one of the ladies alive but unable to cast spells—break her wrists and fingers, or cut out her tongue, or suchlike. The Champion was most insistent about that."

"My, what a surprise," Embra muttered sarcastically. "He was the one I wanted another long look at, too."

"If *I'd* been mounting this guard," Tshamarra whispered into Embra's ear, "I'd have put a spying eye up here, so they can see our arrival and which stair we take."

"Serpent-priests have a pet spell that hunts the spying eyes of others, so they think everyone else does the same," Embra breathed back, falling silent and using the Dwaer to mind-talk. "There'll be an eye somewhere, all right—my bet 'tis above the other side of yon arch, to warn the priests if we use *their* stair. I don't think they care what happens to the archers—and the archers know it."

"And so?" Craer asked, touching Tshamarra's hand to join the silent discussion.

"River of flame down the archers' stair, all of us scream like we're in agony, and then quick and quiet back out through that door and close it *quietly*—and wait for them to come to us."

Blackgult shook his head. "Good plan if there weren't dozens of Storm crawling around the castle behind us. I'd say we send a false Dwaer flying down the priest's stair, our own spying eye after it, *but* give a gout of flame up above the arch first to take out their spying eye. Then Hawk with shield up and Embra behind him down the archer's stair, flame at every turn in it to take out bows before they can fire. Get to the bottom, big rolling fireball, and then back up to join us and we go down the priest's stair after all, knowing how many priests are waiting to hurl doom at us. Keep looking at the ceiling, Hawk and Craer—Serpents love to use a spell that drops biting snakes on heads."

"Ugh. I *hate* snakes in my hair," Tshamarra announced, in a mind-voice so firm that several of her companions winced.

"Agreed?" Blackgult asked. Their mind-touch flared with accord, and they hastened.

The priests' eye was just where Embra had thought it would be. It vanished in an instant, to the accompaniment of shouts from below—shouts that rose into an excited crescendo when the Dwaer-Stone sailed into view. Spells and hurled weapons surrounded it in a cloud, snarled orders making it clear that at least one Serpent believed an invisible Embra was flying and holding a Stone she couldn't hide with magic—and by then flames were roaring on the other stair, and archers were running up its steps and firing before they had anyone to shoot at and then bounding down and away again, just to avoid the fate of sudden fire rolling over them.

"Behold, tower stairs," Blackgult gasped, after what seemed an eternity of running and slaying later. "Up or down, lads and lasses?"

"Down," Craer growled, hefting blood-drenched daggers.

"Up," Embra panted, "because it gives us more choices of ways on, and because the Serpents will be up high. Priests prefer to be above, looking down, in command. You're a thief, and so think of skulking—"

"Lady Silvertree! 'Procurer,' *please!*" Craer protested, in mimicry of a scandalized matron. "Agreed: up 'tis."

"Where we'll meet them teeth to teeth," Blackgult said in satisfaction, "and get our first strike at our *real* foes."

"Conjure a shield first," Tshamarra panted. "One for each of us, to float and flank Hawk's real one. There may be bows ready."

Embra nodded, and they hurried up the stairs with unseen shields shimmering before them.

The uppermost passage was deserted, but the Lady of Jewels urged them on. "If we can get to yonder room first and make ready by its doors, they'll be coming through in haste, thanks to all the fires we've set, and we can—"

The door at the far end of the passage burst open, and armaragors in full battle armor clanked hastily through, swords out. Seven—no, eight—knights, with shields at the ready, forming a neat, practiced—and menacing—wall. Craer whistled and grinned. "A proper fight at last!"

"Embra! Shields high, on edge, and fly them forward," Tshamarra hissed. "We might just be able to break a Serpent-worshipping neck!"

The Lady of Jewels replied with a smile and nod, as Blackgult and Craer hurried to flank Hawkril, and the two groups of armored men hastened to meet each other.

Coming through the door behind the Storn armaragors, as the over-dukes had expected, were the Tersept's Champion, in gleamingly magnificent armor, and a haughty-looking man in robes adorned with wriggling serpent designs. Champion Pheldane drew his sword with a flourish and stood guard before the priest, who raised his hands dramatically and began to intone a loud, slow incantation.

"Lady look down, he's trying to impress us to death," Tshamarra murmured. Embra chuckled at that as their unseen shields flashed over Pheldane's shoulders . . . and struck the priest's throat, edge-on, from two directions at once.

They did not behead the man—quite—but broke his neck in an instant, leaving a gurgling head to loll on suddenly blood-spattered shoulders, ere the corpse toppled headlong.

It struck Pheldane's arm, and he whirled, aghast—at about the same time as Tshamarra snatched the magic of the invisible shields into a new spell, using the Dwaer to send lightning crackling through the Storn armaragors, a step or two before their swords reached the trio of overdukes.

Hawkril and Blackgult sprang back, swearing, but the Lady Talasorn's spell had been precise: their foes were still alive—barely—but quite helpless. To a man, the Storn armaragors crashed to the passage floor and lay there, twitching uncontrollably.

"Safe to proceed?" Craer called. Tshamarra shouted reassurance, and the three overdukes rushed over the stricken knights to confront Pheldane, who licked his lips, backed away, and then turned to flee.

Craer raced past him, eluding a wicked side thrust as he went, and spun in midair to fetch up barring the door with his blade raised. "Is this a Tersept's Champion I see before me?" he taunted. "Or a craven coward?"

Pheldane snarled and hacked at him furiously. He must hew down this little thief before the two armored overdukes reached him, and *get out that door!*

Craer deflected one mighty blow. The force of the next bent the procurer's parrying blade and drove him to the floor, where he overbalanced onto his back. The glittering point of the Champion's blade drew back to slay.

The procurer beneath it kicked out at the Champion's legs before Pheldane could skewer him. The Champion staggered, roaring in rage, and almost fell on his face atop Craer—but caught the door handle as he toppled forward. Gathering his great strength, he plucked the door open, crashing it hard into Craer's shoulder.

It was Craer's turn to roar, as bones splintered and the door drove him helplessly across the floor. The Champion wasted no time on trying to slay his foe, but trampled the procurer in a frantic rush to get out and away and—

Hawkril Anharu's diving lunge caught Pheldane's elbow, and whirled the man around against the wall with a crash. The Champion staggered, caught his balance, and sprang for the door again—only to find the edge of Blackgult's blade barring his way, at throat height. Recoiling, Pheldane found himself spun around by Hawkril's hand, as the armaragor clambered up from the floor.

Together, the two armored overdukes herded the Champion into a corner, away from the moaning, writhing procurer. It was Hawkril who withstood Pheldane's frantic sword blows with his own sword, while sparks flew and metal belled deafeningly—and it was Hawkril who in the end ducked low and then came lunging back up in the same motion to bury his blade hilt-deep in the gap between the Champion's gleamingly fluted codpiece and the tasset beside it.

Pheldane screamed, fountaining blood and trying to beat Hawkril aside with the hilt and quillons of his sword. The overduke stood firm.

For a moment they stood nose to nose, the one quivering in agony and disbelief, and the other blazing with anger.

"M-mercy," the Champion gasped. "Get me a healer, and chests of gold'll be yours! I—"

"You," Hawkril told him in a voice of doom, "are all that is wrong with Aglirta. Men like you, who kneel to the Serpents and take their coin. I have no use for chests of gold. Die, and so rid this fair realm of one small stain!"

And he twisted his blade, ramming it upward with all his strength as he did so.

Pheldane sobbed in pain and stared wide-eyed at the ceiling, making the Sign of the Three with trembling fingers. But no healing stirred within him, nor shining cortahars appeared to deliver him from his foes. It seemed the gods were as hard of hearing as always.

10

A Night of Destroying Castles

*H*awkril Anharu twisted his blade again. The man transfixed on it sobbed, choked, and then stared over the armaragor's shoulder at Tshamarra and Embra, seizing the chance to gaze on beauty one last time.

They stared coldly back at Onskur Pheldane as his gaze became fixed, his jaw fell slack, and his sword slipped from failing fingers.

Hawkril tugged out his blade and let the body fall. It crashed heavily down the wall to sprawl beside the groaning procurer.

"Bones broken," the armaragor snapped, looking from Craer up at the two sorceresses.

"No doubt. Did he damage the door?" Tshamarra asked wryly, as she and Embra hastened forward. Hawkril and Blackgult stood watchful guard as the Dwaer shone and spun again, and Craer came wincing back to his feet, muttering, "I've got to get me my own magic Stone, really I do!"

"Later," the Golden Griffon told him with a grim smile—as shouts arose from the passage behind them. The overdukes whirled around.

Dozens of Stornbridge cortahars, bright blades gleaming in their hands, were advancing toward them, a Serpent-robed man snapping orders at their rear. Craer eyed the foremost knights and observed, "Just now, Lady Silvertree, would be a very good time to do something destructive."

"Indeed," Embra replied with dignity. "I'll turn this shielding into something deadly, if our friendly priest yonder doesn't—"

It seemed the Lady of Jewels was fated never to comfortably end a sentence during this early morning excursion through Stornbridge Castle. Fire roared up into a thundering sphere at the far end of the passage, a shouted command made all the cortahars scatter and crouch by the walls . . . and the passage shook as the ball of flames started to roll forward.

Embra smiled. "He's bound to send at least one more firesphere, right behind the first. We must await just the right moment . . ."

"Mages always say that," Craer complained, "and then never say what the right moment is, or why. 'Tis all part of acting too mysterious for their own good, or ours, I say . . ."

Embra gave him a withering look and did something that made her Dwaer-shield twinkle with tiny dancing motes of light—as the firesphere roared up to them.

It thundered against the shield, intense heat licking overduchal faces—and then rebounded away, back down the passage, rolling considerably faster than before.

"So did he cast a second sphere?" Tshamarra murmured.

Embra gave her a wolfish smile. "Touch the Dwaer here, and help me steady the shield. We're going to need—"

The blast that smote their ears then made the stone floor leap upward, spilling them all onto hands and knees. Pieces of armored cortahar were flung through the air like rags, tongues of flame stabbed in all directions, flagstones burst into deadly hurtling shards—and everything struck the unseen Dwaer-shield with a force that drove Embra and Tshamarra back up to their feet, up and bowed over backwards as if unseen and brutally raging men were shoving at their breasts and shoulders . . . and then fell away from that barrier, leaving the overdukes and their end of the passage unharmed.

Obviously, there had been a second sphere. Dust, flames, and smoke roiled in an impenetrable cloud in front of them. Then, amid shrieks of grinding, rending stone, the floor above gave way with a great, gathering roar—and crashed down into the passage.

"Back!" Embra screamed, turning to run. "I can't stop rolling sto—"

Craer stared openmouthed at the sight of riven chambers from the floor above slowly tilting and spilling their contents—furniture, tapestries, silver bowls, and portraits—toward him, but Hawkril closed a numbing grip on a leather-clad shoulder, plucked the procurer bodily off his feet, and ran him back along the passage scant instants before a chunk of wall as large as a coach bounced out of the cloud of destruction and tumbled ponderously toward them, shedding blocks as large as their bodies as it came.

"I believe," Blackgult shouted, as they ran down the passage together, "I was going to have some words with you about destroying castles, daughter mine. Now I believe I'll need some time to craft *new* words in that regard!"

"Claws of the Dark One!" Hawkril shouted. "The roof!"

Tshamarra looked up, stumbling and almost sprawling headlong in doing so, and saw cracks—dozens of cracks—racing overhead, blocks of stone already falling from between them. *"Embra!"*

"Just . . . get . . . yon door . . . open," the Lady of Jewels gasped, as they neared the end of the passage. "I moved the shield . . . to be a roof above us . . . but . . ."

Hawkril threw the procurer forward. Craer landed running like the wind, clawed open the door, and then stood beside it like a servant, gesturing each of his fellow overdukes through with a flourish. Embra tarried until last, holding up the shield—and then gave him a friendly swat to make him move when he started making silent "No, after thee" gestures. As she plunged through, the last of the ceiling came down with a crash.

Panting, the overdukes turned and stared at the cloud of dust and tumbling stones beyond the doorway.

"In answer to your question," Embra said briskly, dusting her hands on her hips and smiling at Tshamarra, "yes, I do believe he *did* cast a second sphere!"

The Lady Talasorn laughed a little wildly, and then broke off suddenly. "I—I'm not used to this much fury from you four. You're changing." Four overdukes looked her way, and she added in a low voice, "And I'm changing, too."

"Later, lass," Blackgult told her gently. "Now is the time to do and be. If we're very good, this next little while, we may win ourselves time to judge and hone philosophies."

Craer looked up. "Warn me when you get to then, and I'll go fetch wine, hey?" Then he turned his head. "Forgive me, Embra, but why can't we use the Dwaer to trace the priests running around this keep?"

Embra sighed. "In the countryside and most towns and villages, of course we could, but in any Vale castle there're so many enchantments, old and new, laid atop each other, that tracing all but a particular spell you've seen cast and hooked talons onto right then, is well-nigh impossible. Add to that the echoes of all the magic unleashed here this night, and . . ."

The procurer nodded. "So we're back to sidling along with our blades out, trying not to be seen. Right; sidle where?"

"We must keep moving, even if we just blunder around and around the castle," Blackgult put in. "If we take a stand in one spot, or allow ourselves

to get cornered, the Storn folk can close in around us as they please. Standing still dooms us."

"Now that last sentence," Craer said thoughtfully, "would make a court
saying many a king might be proud of."

Tshamarra rolled her eyes. "*Craer!* We're in a hostile castle, surrounded
by foes trying to slay us, and—"

"Enough," Hawkril rumbled, in a voice that made them all fall silent and
look at him—whereupon he gave them a little smile, and started down the
tower stairs. "We go down a level, along to the next stairs, and back up to
the battlements, aye?"

"I care not, so long as we get out of Stornbridge," Tshamarra snapped,
"so I can find more of this fun in the next village, and the next!" She glared
at Blackgult. "Why exactly did you make me an overduke, again?"

"I needed someone to hold Craer's reins," the Golden Griffon replied
unsmilingly, "and you seemed willing. Now hush and trot like a good lass."

The Lady Talasorn gave Blackgult a look that promised she'd remember this—and not fondly—but did as he'd suggested.

When they opened the door on the first landing below, they saw only
darkness. Embra frowned and did something with the Dwaer. "Magical
murk, this, and newly cast . . . with many foes beyond, waiting for us."

Craer grinned. "So what're we waiting for, exactly?"

Embra found herself grinning back at him. She strode forward, her fellow overdukes with her.

Light promptly blossomed at the far end of the passage as lanterns were
unhooded; in their glimmer the overdukes could see armor gleaming on
dozens of plate-armored cortahars, gathered around a familiar figure.

"Well, well, what have we here?" Seneschal Urbrindur's voice was loud
and cold. "Traitors to the crown and murderers of honest Storn men, who
break guest-rights with the bloodiest of crimes, and make war on us in our
own castle. The penalty for such behavior is no less than death, and in the
King's name I sentence you five false nobles to—"

Craer yawned, turned away politely to mask it with one hand, and then
whirled around and hurled a dagger with all the force he could muster.

It was a long throw, and the cortahars had time to see the flash of spinning steel and get their shields up. The dagger clanged off one of them and
shot harmlessly aside to clatter down a wall.

"Delnbone! Bring him to me alive, but maimed. For that attempt on my
person, little man, your death shall be slow and painful!"

Craer yawned again. "You," he said severely, strolling forward, "have
been reading too many bad Sirl chapbooks. Next you'll be telling us that we

must die, foul villains that we are, that Aglirta may live! Or couldn't you afford to purchase that particular tale?"

"Kill him," the seneschal ordered the cortahars curtly. "I've no desire to listen to his insolent mouthings."

The Storn knights advanced in careful unison, adjusting shields and blades to form a solid, moving wall. It was clear by their mutters and narrowed eyes that they didn't like the look of their foes.

Not that the overdukes were all that impressive—it was that they were walking unconcernedly forward with no semblance of battle readiness at all. The two women whispered together like town gossips behind old Baron Blackgult, and all three male overdukes seemed relaxed and smiling, slouching along for all the world as if they were crossing a manor lawn for their third or fourth feast of the day.

The two forces were perhaps six paces apart, with Craer busily buffing an invisible blemish on his shortsword on one sleeve, when an invisible force of frightening intensity plucked at the cortahars, tugging them irresistibly into each other. They wavered, leaning and struggling—and then crashed together in a huge, ungainly, and silent knot.

An utter lack of sound now reigned over the passage. Men shouted and dropped their blades unheard, and Blackgult raised a hand as he smilingly sidestepped the frantic, entangled knot of cortahars—and cast a silent spell Seneschal Urbrindur did not recognize.

He discovered what it was as Craer and Blackgult closed in on him and he turned with a pale attempt at a sneer and tried to open the door into Storn Tower, right behind him. It was sealed as solidly as if it had never been there. The wall was as unbroken stone.

The seneschal gabbled soundlessly, and then frantically clawed out various daggers from about his person.

As iron-strong hands encircled his wrists and forced him to drop the two knives he'd managed to fumble forth, Malvus Urbrindur discovered the spell of silence wasn't absolute: if you were touching someone directly, the two of you could hear each other. He could hear Blackgult right now.

"You were correct in one matter," the Golden Griffon told him almost jovially. "The penalty for treason is death, as is murder done or ordered against nobility, by commoners not acting upon royal justice. Overduke Delnbone will now enact sentence upon you."

Craer reached up, put the tip of a wickedly sharp dagger against Urbrindur's throat, and then said, "Ah, let him go. It feels ill to gut a man like a hog, when he's held—and besides, 'tis more fun to chase him."

Blackgult nodded, released the seneschal, and stepped back. Urbrindur stared at the procurer for a moment, trembling—and then whirled away, viciously snatching out and hurling something as he did so.

Craer struck the hurled dagger aside with his own drawn fang, watched it bite deep into a window frame, and noted the greenish sheen on its thrumming blade. "Poisoned," he said contemptuously. "You snake."

The seneschal had run out of places to run to, and turned in a daze of desperation as Craer threw his own dagger. It sprouted under Urbrindur's chin.

The seneschal stared at him, gave an ugly, wet gasp, and then choked and gurgled his dying way to the floor, as the five overdukes assembled around him.

"Well, we're pruning the Vale of corrupt local officers, at least," Tshamarra observed, "though I suspect you'll be more satisfied when Stornbridge is dying, or the Serpents guiding him."

Embra nodded. "Behind it all, in the Vale, if you set aside the lurking Faceless, 'tis always the Serpent-priests." She indicated the door. "Shall I? Given that spells or drawn bows may be waiting for us the other side of it?"

"Ah, open it!" Craer growled. "I weary of creeping caution."

"You," Tshamarra said severely, "wearied of sanity long ago, and now seem to be wearying of something else: continued life!"

Blackgult's spell melted away before the glow of the Dwaer, and Embra spun another spell into curling, drifting existence before she opened the door.

Their first look at Storn Tower was of a sumptuously furnished room—cloth-of-gold and red silk adorning glossy-polished furniture. Bookshelves crammed with interesting-looking tomes ascended into dimness, and the floor was covered with a lush rug bearing scenes of brave knights swording a variety of fantastical beasts.

Seated behind an ornately carved table facing them were Coinmaster Eirevaur and two scribes, wearing black robes with the arms of Stornbridge on their breasts. Impassive Storn cortahars in livery rather than armor stood guard behind their chairs, with spears held in formal rest position.

Eirevaur gave the overdukes a half-smile and nod, folding his hands together on the table. An array of parchments lay before him, but there was no sign of a weapon.

As Embra stepped into the room, her spell curled around her like a cloak, moving with her. She held the Dwaer as a high lady might clutch a tiny purse as she strode to the table, glancing briefly at the ceiling overhead, the empty stair curving up into it, the similarly empty stair leading down, and the closed passage door across the room. "Fair morn to you, Coinmaster," she said politely. "Are you, too, under orders to slay us as traitors to the realm?"

The scribe shook his head. "I've refused to play such games," he announced a trifle sadly, "and am therefore under arrest myself, in the custody of these two gentlesirs."

He inclined his head to either side of him—whereupon the robed scribes came up out of their seats in lunges, spellspun disguises falling away in momentary shimmerings to reveal gloating faces, and flung serpents out of their sleeves at the Lady Silvertree.

"*Die,* witch!" spat the two Serpent-priests, as fangs bit deep into Embra's breasts, and thrashing tails whipped to and fro exultantly.

The Lady of Jewels sighed, calmly pulled back a vacant chair, and took her own seat at the table. The spell around her flared momentarily into gold-tinged white radiance—and the two snakes burst into flaming gobbets that flared and then were gone into wisps of smoke before they struck the floor.

Embra stared coldly at one priest, and then the other—and they flared up into flames too as her magic struck, screaming for but a breath each ere they became oily, drifting smoke.

Ignoring her bleeding wounds, the Lady Silvertree asked wearily, "Am I supposed to believe you knew nothing of their intent to slay me?"

The Coinmaster's face had gone very pale, but his answer was steady enough. "They did in fact discuss their intentions, which were to kill the Lords Craer and Hawkril, and take the rest of you captive. They spoke of sparing your lives in return for surrender of your noble offices and the Dwaer, but these were apparently the schemes of others, conveyed to them as orders. I believe this throwing of snakes was a personal invention—and it *did* come as a surprise to me." He sighed. "Slay me if you must. I'm guilty of my own crimes against Flowfoam, though they involve absent coins rather than bloodshed."

"I believe you," Embra replied, the Dwaer flaring into life again between them. "Treat us with continued honesty if you would, Eirevaur, and tell me: What other orders regarding us have you been given? Where's the Lord Stornbridge? Are there other Serpent-priests in this keep—and if so, where?"

"You're going to kill me, aren't you?" the Coinmaster asked in apparent terror, as he pointed silently up at the ceiling and then spread his fingers twice, counting out: *Five.* Then he touched the carved and painted arms of Stornbridge adorning the back of a chair recently vacated by a priest, and pointed up again. So—as far as Eirevaur knew, if he was dealing in truth—

five priests and the Lord of Stornbridge were above, either in this turret or on the adjacent battlements.

"Not yet—if you sit in complete silence, unmoving, until we say otherwise." Embra reached back as she uttered these crisp words, and when her fingers brushed Hawkril's hip, she mind-spoke: *Say nothing. Touch the others, so we can all mind-talk.*

He swiftly did so. When the overdukes had gathered close together around Embra's chair, she mind-said: *We must be very careful. Twice now, something—another Dwaer, I think, used in a way I know nothing of—has tried to drain power from this one. I don't think the Serpents here have it, but whoever does is watching us directly. What I want to do now is make this man an offer of escape, and after we've dealt with him, one way or the other, we three who can work spells will use the Dwaer only to negate and oppose Serpent-magics, whilst Hawk and Craer go up and reap priests and a tersept with sharp steel. Agreed?*

Can you send us aloft another way besides up yon stair? Craer thought back at her. *I'm betting they've bows ready.*

Of course. We'll need to peek at the battlements, to properly see a spot to deliver you to.

Then let's take your road. Craer's reply was echoed with wordless affirmations from Blackgult and Tshamarra.

Lass! Hawkril's mind-voice burst forth like an anguished shout. *Those serpents! How fare you?*

His lady's mind-voice sounded wry: *Let's just say I've been reminded how painful venom can be, and how much like being on fire Dwaer-healing feels like. I'll live, love.*

Then Embra called on the Dwaer with a force they all felt, and it spat forth tendrils of thick mist. Out of them she beckoned the Coinmaster.

The scribe rose, swallowing several times, and moved reluctantly around the table. When he was standing amid the overdukes—painfully aware that Craer was holding a dagger to his codpiece from one side of him, and Hawkril held another blade not far from his ear on the other—the mist suddenly swirled all around them in a sphere, and changed into something deeper and stranger.

Embra gave the trembling Storn officer a steady look. "So, Inskur Eirevaur: Do you prefer to live, this day? Or die?"

"L-live, of course."

"In Aglirta, making full report to King Castlecloaks on Flowfoam—or in exile, to an anonymous alleyway in Sirlptar?"

The Coinmaster stared at her, swallowed, and said, "In exile. Nowhere in the Vale is safe for me, once they know my treachery."

" 'They'? The Serpents?"

Eirevaur nodded mutely. The overdukes exchanged glances.

"Are they that widespread, then?" Craer asked. "Serpents in every village and town?"

"Y-yes."

"How do you know that?" Tshamarra snapped. "They've told you, you've gained that impression, or—what?"

"L-lady, many of them have dined at Stornbridge, passing on reports and orders. Threescore and more, coming singly or in pairs. Add to that the names of never-seen-here fellows they've uttered, they can't muster less than fourscore. They still come, often—and they're building up to something. I know not what, but 'tis something soon and very important. Something they believe is going to give them power over nearly every commoner of Aglirta."

"What sort of something?" Blackgult asked calmly.

The Coinmaster spread helpless hands. "Lord, if I knew, I'd tell you, believe me. Something that will spread, and that—according to a report a few days back that occasioned much celebration amongst them, the first time I've seen them here drunk and merry—has been tried somewhere in the Vale, and has worked."

"Coinmaster Eirevaur," Embra said, "have the thanks of Aglirta. Craer, give him something tangible of that."

The procurer frowned at her. "Em . . . ?"

"Coins," the Lady of Jewels said bluntly. "Those purses you stuffed into your boots not so long ago? A man needs coins to get anything in Sirlptar."

Craer gave her a hurt look, then took off one of his boots and upended it. A slithering pile of purses spilled out onto the floor. He spread them with his fingers to make sure no daggers, lockpicks, or the like had fallen out with them, and then pulled his boot on again.

"And now the other one," Embra said flatly.

"*Graul*," Overduke Delnbone told his second boot, as he slid it off and another pile of purses started to appear. "I suppose you want me to give him a dagger, too?"

"No," the Lady of Jewels said calmly. "I can see from here that Coinmaster Eirevaur has a perfectly good one at his belt, and he walks like a man who has at least one sheathed down a boot. He also acts like the sort of man who'd carry at least one hidden dagger up a sleeve, probably more. He might even manage to stay alive in Sirlptar long enough to thank us."

The treasurer stared at her, and around at them all, disbelievingly, and then down at the pile of purses.

Craer gave him a disgusted look and Embra another, and plucked a wrinkled carrysack of thin cloth from his belt. He tossed it into the air and let it settle over one heap of purses.

"Try not to spend it all at once," he growled, and turned away.

11

A Bowdragon Comes Calling

man whose robes bore the arms of Stornbridge stood blinking in the shadows of a stinking moonlit alley in Sirlptar, a small but heavy sack of coin-purses in his hands.

Though strewn with rat-haunted rubble from the collapse of two buildings, the alleyway had been entirely empty of men—blinking or otherwise—a moment before.

At first, Coinmaster Eirevaur just looked in all directions, fearing immediate attack. Reassured by the still emptiness of his surroundings, he shook himself like a dog awakening from dreams, and looked up at the sky in wonder, smelling the sour sea air and reassuring himself that yes, this must be Sirlptar.

Then he seemed to recall that he was holding a sack of money—and that this could be a danger in itself. With slow, exaggerated care, seeking to avoid any telltale clink or metallic shifting of coins, he thrust the sack under his robes and folded his arm over it. Moving slowly and bent over, as if he was a beggar or an old destitute, Eirevaur shuffled out into the moonlight and off down the alley, seeking a place of safety—but too happy to entirely hide his wide grin.

He was away from the coldly spying Serpents at last, and his cruel, increasingly treacherous Storn fellows, too. Not far enough to be comfortable, of course. His first move must be to take passage on a ship, and get well away from Aglirta before it erupted in war once more.

A scribe who could keep honest count could readily find work in any port of Asmarand—and any port comfortably distant from Silverflow Vale beckoned warmly about now.

Coinmaster of Stornbridge no longer—gods, yes, he must get rid of these arms on his breast; best turn his robe inside out in this next doorway—Inskur Eirevaur went on down the alley, daring to hope for the first time in months.

Out of a doorway that had seemed quite empty when he passed it slid something that looked like a cat, only larger. It rose, shifting smoothly into manlike stance, but remained black and furred as it loped silently along after Eirevaur, padding closer . . . and closer . . .

When the scribe reached his chosen doorway and glanced quickly up and down the alley again, the loping thing had thrown itself onto its face in the refuse, and he did not see it. It risked scarring no features on the littered cobbles by its swift dive, for its otherwise human head had a smoothly featureless face.

Once Eirevaur set down his sack and hoisted his robe up over his head, however, the faceless beast rose up from the cobbles like a great black claw, growing huge fanged jaws and curving talons as long as scimitars—talons that reached out in almost loving anticipation . . .

The moon was sinking, but would shine brightly on the high battlements of Stornbridge Castle for some time yet. Occasional gentle breezes ghosted past the nervous Storn cortahars who kept watch there, but the starry sky had been clear since sunset, and bid fair to remain so.

Or had, at least, until a moment ago, when a drift of cloud as thick as river-mist had unaccountably formed above the moat, curling around itself with deceptive lassitude . . . and then suddenly flowed up the castle wall and flooded through the merlons, to drift among the warriors.

There were words of wary alarm, and a call through a turret window for a Serpent-priest—but before any robed figure could stride forth to deal with the mysterious mist or impart some sharp words to overly fearful cortahars, two figures appeared in the lee of the mist, seemingly born of nothingness, on a part of the battlements where the usual bored wallwatch sentries were absent thanks to the unusual gathering of fully armored defenders around the turret of Storn Tower.

"A snake'll be out to clear it soon," Craer murmured. "By then we must be right in their midst, or 'twill be farewell, surplus overdukes!"

The armaragor glanced over his shoulder. "The one from the gatetower's seen us. He's . . . aye, he's on his way here—with his alarm-horn."

"That's unfriendly of him. He's alone?"

"Yes," Hawkril said. "Should I—?"

"No, we need him taken silently. His helm and tunic would be useful, too. Get down here."

The armaragor stooped, puzzled, as Craer laid himself on the flagstones and asked, "Did you bring that cloak the Coinmaster left behind? The one I pointed at?"

Hawkril snorted. "Of course. My mind may not follow yours down every devious twist and trail, but I trust you—the Three alone know why." He plucked a wadded bundle of cloth.from behind his shield-strap, and shook it out to full length. "Here 'tis."

"Right. Draw your sword and lay it ready here." The procurer patted the flagstones just to his left. "Then keep hold of that cloak and lie down on top of me—and *don't* crush me, you great ox, or as I die groaning, I'll curse you to die doing something much worse. How close is our enthusiastically approaching guard?"

Hawkril glanced again. "Starting along the last run of battlements now."

"Good. Spread the cloak over us. I don't want him to see anything of me but my boots. Leave the talking to me, and don't act startled."

"You're the madman," the armaragor agreed amiably, lowering himself carefully onto his elbows and shaking the cloak out over them both.

"Ready?" Craer murmured from beneath him. "Shift your left arm a bit, so I can peer out under it. Yes."

A moment later, he gasped in a high, feminine-sounding voice, "Oh, yes! Oh, love me! More! More! Don't stop, my stallion! Oh, don't stop!"

Hawkril moved atop his friend as if they were lovers, hearing the nearby scrape of a cortahar's boot coming to an uncertain stop.

"Oh, yesss! More! Oh, give me *more* of you, you great—oh, ohhh, *ohhh!*" Craer cried, setting Hawkril to trembling with suppressed laughter.

"Graul!" the cortahar exclaimed, his voice a mix of disgust and wonder, and the overdukes heard the tip of a grounded sword grate on stone. "Who's that, Orsor, and where did you find her?"

Craer laid a finger across Hawkril's lips, reminding him to be silent. "Oh, my Horse!" he cried in apparent alarm, sounding so much like Embra playacting that Hawkril nearly collapsed into guffaws. "Someone's *watching* us! Oh, hurry! Uh! Hurry!"

He paused for a moment, and then added with a girlish giggle, "Unless he's one of your *friends* . . ."

"Forefather above," the cortahar growled, leaning closer. "Orsor, who *is* this wench?" He peered, leaning on his sword as if it was a walking stick, and then stiffened. "*You're* not Or—"

The rest of whatever he'd intended to say was drowned in gurgling—the only sound the Storn knight could make over the hilt of the dagger that had come whirling up from under the armaragor's arm to bite deeply into his throat.

"Catch him, Hawk!" the procurer hissed, and Hawkril spun around atop Craer with fearsome speed to thrust a hand into the knight's gut ere he collapsed.

"Stand him up and lean him back," Overduke Delnbone added, springing to his feet. "We need to keep his blood off the helm and tunic."

"Neither will fit me," Hawkril observed, plucking the helm from the dead cortahar's flopping head before it could fall off.

The procurer snared the alarm-horn from around a limp, dead arm, and gave his friend a sour look. "You just dislike Storn gear. Put them on." He glanced back along the battlements, and snapped, "Lower him, quickly! A snake-priest is back there, sternly commanding Embra's cloud to begone."

Hawkril did so, dragging the tunic up with one hand as he held the corpse's belt firmly with the other. Craer swarmed over the garment, and in another breath had relieved the guard of two daggers and a slender purse. "Drop him into the moat," he hissed. "*Drop,* don't throw."

Hawkril gave his friend a weary look. "I'm not completely stone-headed, you know."

Craer blew him a mock kiss. "I *know,* my Horse."

Hawkril rolled his eyes and lowered the body between two merlons, dangling it at the full length of his arm before letting go.

The splash was louder than they'd hoped it would be, and they both saw the priest's head jerk around to stare directly at them.

Or rather, at Hawkril. Craer was crouching down behind his friend, hissing, "Act like a Storn cortahar standing nightguard."

"Like an idiot, you mean?" the armaragor growled. "Or do you mean stare out from the walls with a bored look on my face?"

"Bebolt him, he's casting a spell! We'll just have to hope Embra quells it. Stride toward him like a guard. I'll be right behind you, but remember: I'm not here. No turning to look to me—and no talking, either! Breezes take our words too far."

"Aye, Mother. Any more advice for the witless warrior?" Hawkril growled, settling the cortahar's helm over his head and smoothing down the front of the scarlet hawk-adorned tunic as he started walking, slow and purposeful, along the battlements. "Like perhaps what you want me to do when I get nose to nose with this particular hostile holy hand of the Serpent?"

"I'll think of something," Craer muttered, from a foot or so behind the armaragor's shoulders.

"That's *exactly* what I'm afraid of, Longfingers," came the dry, flat reply.

A few steps later, Hawkril finished refolding his cloak, tucked it back into his shield, and added, "We're past halfway there, and yon priest's starting toward *us,* now. Think faster, little thief."

"Anyone with him?"

"Of course. Four cortahars. You don't think Serpent-clergy dare to do anything dangerous alone, do you?"

"Any bows? Handbows?"

"None I can see. Swords and grim looks—oh, and his spells, of course."

"We have to trust in your lady-love to break those. Mist all gone?"

"Aye, but Embra's sending more now. There're about a dozen more Storn swords by the turret—that's who's calling to the priest. He's turning back to see, and 'tis coming up over the battlements like an eel, right in front of him. Aye, he's going to be mightily suspicious of this mist."

"My, my, another chance to practice his mighty suspicion. How nice for him."

Hawkril sighed. "Craer, as much as I love your familiar leaden wit, how about reassuring me just a trifle? In the matter of just what, by all the Three, I'm supposed to do now? These battlements are quite wide enough for them to come at me six or seven at a time, you know."

"Keep walking. I need us to be much closer."

"Craer! I've dined quite heavily enough from your 'Trust me and my mysterious little stratagems, thick-headed warrior' platter. I can act far more effectively if I know what you're planning, and want me to do—beforehand!"

"Ah, a fair point. A fair point, indeed. There's just one little problem, Tall Post."

Hawkril waited, striding on. And waited.

Finally, he sighed and came to a stop, turning to peer out from the battlements.

"What're you doing?" Craer hissed, from beneath him.

"Waiting for you to tell me what your little problem is, *without* my having to ask, 'And what would that be?' "

"Ah," the procurer responded jovially, "I'm glad you asked that. The little problem is this: I haven't the faintest notion what we're going to do, beforehand. I just go—and do."

Hawkril bent over and gave Craer a very cold look. The procurer smiled crookedly up at him, bright-eyed, and spread his hands. "Well," he added, "you must admit that thus far every one of our battles has worked out all right in the end, yes?"

The armaragor straightened up and squared his shoulders. *"Right."* Then, ignoring the frantically hissing procurer behind him, he strode to where the priest was furiously dispelling mist (with only passing success) and called: "Orsor? Orsor?"

The priest turned and fixed him with a glacial glance. "Get back to your post, fool! You heard the orders, did you not? Whatever business you have with Orsor, it can wait. *Go!*"

"Sorry, Lord, but I'm afraid not," Hawkril replied. "Someone calling himself the Great Serpent wants Orsor back at my post right now. 'No matter what' were his words, and meaning no disresp—"

"The *Great Serpent?* You're sure he called himself that?"

"Oh, yes. Twice he said it, like he was afraid I'd not get the title right. He's a right scary one, too, Lord—uh, meaning no disresp—"

"Yes, yes! *Where is he?*"

"Orsor, Lord? I know—"

"Not grauling Orsor, you ox-brained lummox! *The Great Serpent!*"

"Ah. Here!" Craer said brightly, popping up over Hawkril's shoulder by the simple expedient of bounding up and perching on the armaragor's shoulder-plate with both hands.

The Serpent-priest gaped at him—and the procurer swung on Hawkril's shoulder, launching himself into a drop kick that put the toes of both his boots into the cleric's throat.

That throat exploded in blood as the dagger points protruding from Craer's boot tips plunged into them. The priest staggered backwards, head bobbling loosely on the shoulders it was almost separated from.

"Now I'm going to have to ask someone *else* where Orsor is," Hawkril complained in mock exasperation, as the two cortahars able to see what had happened through the billowing mist stared at them in amazement. Craer put a dagger through one of those open mouths, and then sprang off in pursuit of the other knight, who whirled and fled into the clouds of mist. Hawkril bounded after him, drawing his warsword.

Craer's favorite tactic in mist or smoke, he knew, was to dive at any ankles he saw, toppling foes. Already, just ahead, Hawkril could hear the startled grunts and thuds of men falling. So as long as he slashed with his blade above Craer's head height, anyone he struck should be a foe. "Longfingers?" he called, just to be sure.

"Fallen again," Craer sang back, and Hawkril grinned and waded forward, slashing at mist, great blade-sweeps that cut only air once—twice—and thrice. The fourth time, he struck flesh and armor hard enough to numb his arms. Someone toppled with a wet, squalling sound, and a sword clattered away across unseen flagstones.

Hawkril moved toward that noise, guessing Craer couldn't be crouching anywhere that a sword could slide through unimpeded—and that a cortahar might approach the sound.

Hawk's boot soon struck the sword, and he promptly hacked the mist around him like a madman, in case someone charged. When nothing happened, he carefully plucked up the sword, and hefted it to throw.

Someone cursed and then screamed, ahead to his right. Craer hamstringing or neck-stabbing, no doubt. An unseen door grated open and someone else inquired coldly, "What's going on out there?"

A Serpent-priest, for all the gold in Asmarand! Hawkril threw the sword he'd just acquired as hard as he could at where the voice had sounded from, whipping it end over end into the eddying mist.

He was rewarded with a strangled cry—and an angry shout. "Get that door closed! The overdukes must be out there! Bowmen, up here! Brothers of the Serpent, to—*Eeeee!*"

The scream that ended that cry was cut off abruptly by the slam of a heavy door, which in turn was followed swiftly by an urgent call of "Tall Post! Over here!"

"Coming," Hawkril rumbled, hefting his warsword and advancing into the mist.

"Tall Post!" the call came again. Something was moving to his right . . . a striding swordsman, taller than Craer . . . hidden again by mist . . .

An armored shoulder, the scarlet hawk of Stornbridge—and Hawkril thrust his sword in under that arm with all his strength.

His victim screamed and thrashed, trying to turn and hack but pinioned on Hawk's blade . . . Hawkril shoved and twisted his steel as he thrust forward, trying to keep the man off-balance.

The cortahar screamed again, far more feebly, and dropped his sword, stumbling—and then something flashed in the mist, the knight's head jerked back, and Craer grinned at Hawkril over another slit throat. "Greetings, Overduke Anharu. Charmed, I'm sure."

"Tolerated, I'd term it," Hawkril growled, "but let's use your word. 'Tis more flippant, and that's fitting, hey?"

"Indeed. Come on!"

The armaragor hastened to follow Craer, off around one side of a turret looming up in the mists. Its massive walls sported frequent tall, narrow slit windows, all firmly shuttered with covers made of vertical rows of overlapping shields. The door Hawkril could see was also sheathed in old shields, hammered flat and nailed together.

"As quiet as you know how," Craer murmured, "get up yon ladder onto the banner platform. We both need to get there without a sound to let them inside know where we've gone. They'll be letting fly with everything in a moment, and we don't want to be here!"

In careful silence Hawkril did as he was told. They reached the small banner-platform atop the turret without incident, and lay down flat around the cluster of banner-poles a bare breath before the door below flew open with force enough to bang against the turret wall.

The air was briefly full of the angry hum and thrum of dozens of bows. The bowmen inside the turret must be moving with smooth precision, firing in pairs and then diving aside to let the next pair stand by the door, pair after pair.

Their reward was at least two groans from the mist, as they shot down their unseen fellow cortahars. Most of the shafts cracked off stones or whistled down over the moat to thump to earth as deadly offerings from the clear night sky.

Behind the twang of strings, thudding of boots, and hissing of arrows, the two overdukes could hear an angry, rising chant: Serpent-priests casting a spell, probably to banish the mist.

A bright and evil green radiance spun forth like spiraling tentacles from the door below when the chant ended. Those tentacles started to bleed smoke almost immediately, but mist fell away at their touch, and in a trice the moonlit battlements were clear once more.

Clear—and strewn with pools and smears of blood, most of them adorned with sprawled, motionless cortahars.

Out from behind a merlon ducked a lone figure—Embra, in a tattered and bloodstained but glowing gown, holding the Dwaer to her breast.

"Parley!" she called. "Lord Stornbridge, let's talk! There's—"

Bows twanged and two shafts sped through the Lady of Jewels, vanishing as if they'd never been fired. Another pair of arrows followed—as Hawkril, raging up to his feet atop the turret despite Craer's frantic clawings, saw she must be an illusion, and sank down again, breathing heavily.

"Spare your arrows," Embra cried. "I come for peace, not more bloodshed! Already you've slain most of my fellows, and—"

The ball of raging flame that burst out to consume her roared along the battlements as far as the next tower, where the changing course of the walls left nothing beneath the fire but air—so it plunged down to the moat below, a fall that ended in a hissing that briefly drowned out all other sound except Craer's snarl of "Keep still!" in Hawkril's ear.

The armaragor did just that. Together, the two waited for those in the turret to emerge or send forth more magic.

Instead, the turret shuddered under the sudden impact of a spell from the other direction, that flung fire past the overdukes. Startled shouts from below told Craer and Hawkril that the magic, whatever it was, was both unexpected by the Storn defenders and that it had destroyed or flung open the metal doors and shutters, handing sounds made inside the turret to the passing night breezes.

The response was predictable: another furious volley of arrows along battlements that—as far as Craer and Hawkril could see—were occupied only by a few openmouthed Storn cortahars on wallguard duty. The few who survived that hail of warshafts vanished in the heart of another ball of flames.

"We're wearing them down until they fall asleep, or we die of old age, is that it?" Hawk whispered.

Craer grinned. "You might just be right about that. Time to spice up the cauldron." He drew a steel vial from inside one boot, another from his belt, and a strange little glass globe from behind his belt-buckle—a globe that bulged at the center of a short glass tube. Uncorking one vial, he slid it carefully onto one end of the pipe. Then he repeated the process with the other.

Hawkril smiled. "My arm's long enough to reach down and throw yon assemblage to the floor inside the turret. The glass has to break, hey?"

Craer's answering grin was fierce as he handed over his contraption. "I can't admit that. Professional procurer's secret, this."

Hawkril's snort was eloquent, as he leaned over—and threw. "Close your eyes!" Craer snapped.

Someone snarling orders inside the turret broke off and screamed, "Down! Get—"

And the night exploded into bright white light. Hawkril waited for the turret top to heave upward or shatter under them . . . but instead, all of the turret's occupants began screaming.

" 'Tis only blindflash," Craer hissed. "Time to get down there and thin Storn ranks. The best way's to guide them out the doors with lots of 'This way, my lord' stuff. If they're cortahars, just keep going and tip them over into the moat. Snake-priests we slay right away, and Lord Stornbridge we save in case Embra wants to use magic on him. Oh—and watch out for priests turning themselves into snakes and slithering away. One of them just told another to try that magic."

Hawkril smiled and started down the ladder.

"Ambelter," the Baron Phelinndar said bluntly, from the chair by the window, "you're at it again."

The Spellmaster halted abruptly in his swift striding across the dimly lit main cavern of their shared lair, his mind full of something complicated and as yet incomplete called "the Sword of Spells." Putting such thoughts away with an inward sigh, he swung around. "At what, my good Baron?" he asked politely.

"Scheming and meeting with folk and casting spells and manipulating events all over Aglirta and not involving me in the slightest, or telling me a single thing. We have agreement on this, remember? I am *not* a piece of furniture."

Ingryl Ambelter forebore to make the obvious reply linking baronial usefulness and immobile items of furniture. Instead, he came forward into the light of the window he'd tunneled out of the earth, glanced out at the pleasant vista of the Vale it afforded, and took the other chair. "You're most correct, Phelinndar. My apologies; this is but long habit and no deliberate attempt to belittle you or leave you ignorant or uninvolved. I assure you that I've done a lot of thinking and scrying, but made very few . . . ah, aggressive actions beyond the Bowdragon visits. You observed every moment of those, I trust?"

Phelinndar nodded. "I did. Your spells worked admirably. Yet here I sit, eating eggs and fryfish—I kept some warm for you under yon dome—whilst you scurry and mutter. Wizards aren't the only folk in the Vale with brains or imagination—or Dwaer-Stones, either."

"Point taken," the Spellmaster agreed gravely. "Well, then, here's what I've been thinking about—thinking, mind, more than doing. Thus far, I've met with failure in all attempts to sway the Bowdragons into action. Much of my present scurrying, as you put it, involves trying to discover how to move them into aiding us—or if the powers of these remaining elders are feeble enough that we can abandon attempts to bother. Can we wrest their spellbooks and enchanted items from them, and have done—or is that the swift way into another feud, and more peril?"

He waved a hand that bore many rings at the dark and yet somehow glowing crystal spheres that floated in a curious, unmoving cluster above a small circular table across the room. "You've made good use of the scrying-spheres since I linked them to you, I trust?"

The baron nodded. "Unrest is rife, up and down Aglirta—neighbor turning on neighbor in mad violence, folk becoming beasts and savaging everyone . . . it *can't* be natural. Either the gods have cursed the Vale, or there's dark magic at work. And dark magic either means crazed wizards— an army of them, to cause this much bloodletting—or the Serpents. Unless you believe all those bards' tales about the Faceless rising to slaughter us all."

Ambelter shook his head. "Oh, the Faceless exist, to be sure, but this is not their way. No, this is the work of the Servants of the Serpent."

Phelinndar shook his head. "*Why?* Why destroy? Many a baron exe-cutes and tortures and spreads terror, but to loose something that harms many folk—crafters who could make you rich, farmers who feed you, loyal retainers as well as those who'd smile to see you dead—where's the sense in that? Why do the Snake-lovers always lash out to do harm in all directions, like reckless boys on their first sword-raid?"

The Spellmaster shrugged. "Mad folk, obeying mad orders? Who knows?"

The baron leaned forward in his chair suddenly, and burst out, "Ah, but we *must* find out! How can we proceed if the Vale is full of reckless idiots who could be unleashed upon us at any moment? Or commanded to work some idiocy like burn all the crops or poison the Silverflow itself?"

Ambelter nodded. "There's truth in what you say. I must confess I've been trying to ignore the priests and work around them—judging that any sort of assault would be attracting a foe to myself who could prove endless and all-consuming of my time—but yes, we should try to learn just who's leading the Serpents, and judge for ourselves their aims and probable forth-coming orders."

"Precisely!" Phelinndar agreed, letting the Dwaer roll down his sleeve into his hand and hefting it. "After all, what are half a dozen outlander mages compared to an army of ruthless fanatics already spread the length of the Vale? If we can steer *them* . . ."

The Spellmaster winced. "Experience tells me they'd never be more than a treacherous weapon in our hands, at best. Yet knowing what they plan, that I do agree to. Now, given their reckless and active nature, num-bers, and the magical knowledge senior priests among them undoubtedly possess, do we dare risk scrying to find out? They may well be waiting for us to use the Dwaer for such pryings, so they can trace it."

"They may also be kings of far lands, every one of them, with their armies arriving in Sirlptar right now to bring them their favorite fresh morning eggs, or eels, or tree-worms," Phelinndar snarled, "but I doubt it, and we can't sit here growing old worrying about what they might—"

A shimmering occurred then, in the air beside the Spellmaster's chair. Astonished, he snapped an incantation and raised his hands like claws to smite—never faltering when the rippling radiances resolved themselves into an unfamiliar, darkly beautiful young woman who stood facing them, her hands clasped together like a dutiful and abashed daughter being presented at court. Long, raven-dark hair fell in a smooth sweep down over a clinging black gown. Slender hips, great dark eyes—flashing now from one man to the other, above a mouth that opened uncertainly . . .

The baron gaped at this apparition, who stood unharmed and seemingly unangered in the midst of a lashing fury of spells hurled by Ambelter. Phelinndar even felt the Spellmaster plucking at the Dwaer—which rose and flickered in the baron's grasp—to power greater scourings.

The air around the wench caught fire, flames that raged and then fell to ice, leaving behind the sharp stink of burning. Tiny lightnings stabbed like tavern-brawl daggers . . . and then fell away, leaving the lass unmoved.

A sending, she must be.

Ambelter mastered his fear and astonishment, and addressed the stranger sharply. "I know not who you are, sending, but I am the Spellmaster of Aglirta, and I can destroy you—not merely this your seeming, but through it your true self. I intend to do this only after I've traced you and brought you here to us, to learn how it is that you found us, and all you know . . . and how you can be made to serve our pleasure. Prepare, rash one, to taste the first moments of your doom!"

The Dwaer tore free of Phelinndar's grasp and rose up before him, spinning and brightening. The baron let his hand fall, not daring to try to reclaim it.

"Lord Ambelter," their visitor said firmly, not moving, "these acts of rough—and all too traceable, by those who even now search for you and the Dwaerindim—magic won't be necessary." For a moment Phelinndar thought she was an immobile image, a portrait sent to hang before them, but then he noticed she was trembling—with excitement, by the sound of her voice, not fear.

"I'm called Maelra Bowdragon, and I believe you know my lineage. I witnessed your meetings with my uncles—and know who and what you are."

The Spellmaster's eyes narrowed. "And?"

"And I want you to know that not all Bowdragons are afraid of the Vale. I . . . I want to work with you."

Dark magic boiled up around them again. Hawkril winced, staggered, and dropped the bowman he was carrying. "Craer?"

"Keep at it," the procurer snapped. "Trust Embra to quell such, or we'll never be done here. I've not seen so many bowmen in one place since the Isles!" A splash announced the culmination of his latest guiding journey.

As the dark cloud faded, thinning rapidly, Craer came back dusting his hands together. "That's two dozen cortahars I've sent swimming. Possibly the first baths they've had this season. You're cutting all bowstrings?"

Hawkril nodded, and waved into the turret behind him. "A dozen or so are lying there yet—every time I bend to reach for a bow, one of these damned snakes tries to put its fangs in my face. Why couldn't Em stop them turning themselves into slitherers? I can't hack any of them without letting the rest fang me . . . which I suspect would be a *very* foolish tactic." With a grunt he heaved the limp cortahar onto a growing pile of senseless Storn warriors. To drop them into the moat now would be to slay helpless men—but the moment he saw one moving, he intended to pluck and toss.

"Very foolish," Craer agreed, "and I don't know why. Our ladies could probably do more if they could touch the priests directly, but . . . I long ago left the details of matters magical to others. I may be crazed enough to earn my coins as a procurer—but I'm not wolf-howling mad, like every mage I know."

Hawkril chuckled. "I'm sure Em and Tash will be happy to hear they're howling mad—just as I'm sure they're listening to us now."

"Truth," Craer replied with dignity, "is its own reward."

Hawkril swung around abruptly and dragged the third cortahar—who'd been stealthily but vainly trying to draw a dagger that was no longer in its sheath—out of the pile. Ignoring a stream of curses, he heaved.

There was a despairing, fading cry, and then a splash. Hawkril looked along the moonlit battlements of Stornbridge Castle, but the surviving wall-guards had long since disappeared down various towers. "I hope no one's rallying the Storn—"

"Hush!" Overduke Delnbone said severely. "Don't give these snakes any ideas!" He whirled around suddenly with a footstool in his hand, and flung it.

It crashed down into a corner as snakes whipped and wriggled frantically away. One of them writhed in pain, half-crushed, as dark blood slid like a gleaming ribbon across the floor.

"Oh, dear, another Servant of the Serpent gone," Craer said mournfully. "Such a loss."

Overduke Anharu saw further movement out of the corner of his eye, turned with a sigh, and hauled another awakened cortahar out of his pile.

Protesting and cursing, the man clawed at Hawkril—only to find himself sailing up, arms and legs flailing in the moonlight, and then down, down to the waiting moat below.

"So where's Lord Stornbridge?" the armaragor asked, as the sounds of the splash reached them. "You think this whelming was all a trick to draw us here, whilst he goes to ground, or rides across the Vale to raise alarm?"

"No, he's here somewhere," Craer replied. "Behind one of these panels with the highest Serpent-priests. These are underlings, left to delay and entertain us whilst they cook up something especially dastardly. Something Em's probably keeping a firm lid on."

A snake struck at Craer's face, missing narrowly. "That does it," the procurer announced, heading for the door. "Hawk, I'm burning this turret out. Sooner or later, one of these slitherers is going to get us!"

Hissing sounds arose from all around the turret. Hawkril swore and hurried after the procurer.

"Hawk!" Craer snapped, from the door. *"Run!"*

Hawkril sprang into a thundering sprint as snakes boiled up into human shapes behind him, reaching and hissing, retaining their serpent-heads for one last chance at a bite as they . . . caught hold of nothing, fingertips sliding helplessly over curved armor.

Snarling human faces were spitting out incantations as the armaragor joined Craer out in the moonlight. The procurer flung a dagger, and then another, at a dodging priest who gave him a sneer—until Craer's third knife sprouted in his eye.

Then the armaragor dived one way and the procurer hurled himself in another, scattering across the width of the battlements as fire flared up in the turret room—and roared forth to stab at them.

Hot flames were suddenly all around Hawkril. He thrust his face tight into his knees and rolled, his hair sizzling. The fire flung him over and aside and snarled on along the flagstones, leaving him staring at fresh flames in front of his nose: the wadded-up cloak was burning. Hawkril shook the shield off his arm as he scrambled up, fearing the next spell might be a bolt of lightning instead of fire, and glanced across at Craer.

The procurer was flinging daggers through the turret door and windows in a constant stream of whirling steel, buying them both time. Hawkril saw a discarded cortahar's sword lying on the flagstones. Plucking it up, he thrust it through the blazing cloak, skewering the bundle, and then ran up to the turret door and flung it inside, aiming high and far.

The flaming bundle struck a tapestry on the far wall and rolled down it, in a spitting of sparks and flaming scraps of cloth that gave Hawkril a momentary glimpse of three Serpent-priests weaving spells in hissing haste.

Another cortahar in the pile was moving, struggling to drag himself out from under the weight of his fellows. Hawkril yanked him free, stood him up like a child's doll, and ran him at the door as a shield. A few running steps away from the doorway, the cortahar started to scream.

A priest hit him with a spell anyway—a beam of flickering dark fire that almost cut the man in half, reducing a hand-wide slice of the man's gut to bare bones, but leaving the body untouched above and below. Hawkril flung the cortahar headlong through the door, bowling over a shouting priest, and then ducked low and ran in himself.

Two priests backed away hastily, trying to get to where they could unleash spells on the armaragor without endangering themselves—but Hawkril dived over the dying cortahar and in under the table in the center of the room, rising up under it to fling it with his shoulders, up and over.

Its legs sent a priest flying, to twist and groan against a wall. Craer came leaping through the door as the table came down atop the tapestry, tearing it and feeding the rising flames. Craer stabbed the groaning priest and then flung the same dagger—his last—across the room, into the face of the remaining priest. It laid open the man's forehead and spun away. Gasping in pain, the priest ducked out the far door of the turret and fled along the battlements.

"Right," Craer snarled, snatching up two broken bows, "burn the place!" He plunged after that last priest.

Hawkril cut down another tapestry and added it to the fire. Then he kicked aside chairs and stabbed into dark corners, making sure no snakes still lurked unseen.

Outside, the last Serpent screamed despairingly as Craer's second flung bow tangled between his legs, sent him crashing helplessly onto his face, and Craer pounced on his back.

A wall panel burst into Hawkril's face, hurling him back across the room—and two men raced for the door that Craer had taken: a priest, face contorted in fear and rage; and the Tersept of Stornbridge, in full armor, with a gleaming sword in his hand. Reeling, Hawkril ran after them.

"Stop him!" the priest ordered sharply. The overduke saw Stornbridge look back nervously, run on a few paces, and then turn, sword flashing.

Hawkril didn't wait for the tersept to take a stance. He swerved, clawing at the night air for balance as Stornbridge slashed at him, let the tip of the tersept's sword whistle past him—then leaned in, still running hard, and slammed his arm across the tersept's throat.

Lord Stornbridge crashed over backwards and bounced, sobbing for breath and feebly clutching at his windpipe. His warsword clattered away, but Hawk ran on. He had to get to the priest before that Serpent-lover had time to stop and cast a proper spell, or he and Craer would be dead in a few breaths.

The priest looked back, and Hawkril slashed at the air between them with his warsword, not slowing a whit. The Serpent grimaced, and swerved toward the line of merlons that guarded the moat side of the battlements. Hawkril thundered after him, still unsteady, his sword slashing back and forth.

"Fangbrother Maurivan!" the tersept sobbed from behind Hawkril, his voice raw and feeble.

The priest ran on, giving no sign he'd heard that cry—but in front of him Craer rose up, grinning like a fox, and said merrily, "Good evening, Serpent! Shall we dance?"

Fangbrother Maurivan swerved again, whirling to dive between two merlons. Craer and Hawkril both sprang to the wall, peering, but there was no splash. The robed figure plunged down, down—and vanished in a soundless flash of light, a moment or so before he should have struck the cortaharstrewn water.

"Magic!" Craer said scornfully. "Are we done?"

"Stornbridge," Hawkril growled, and they hurried back together.

The tersept was on his feet, still clutching his throat, his recovered warsword in his other hand. "Don't—don't you dare!" he croaked, backing away from them.

"Lord Stornbridge," Craer replied reproachfully, "we could hardly butcher and maim your faithful cortahars and these snakes you've made welcome in this castle, and not exact the proper punishment on you, now, could we? Hey?"

Stornbridge moaned in despair, and then charged, hacking wildly at the procurer. Craer dodged left—that magnificent blade smashed down on the flagstones, striking sparks—and then right—the blade clanged down again—and then drop-kicked the tersept, aiming his knife-toed feet high.

Those points skittered harmlessly across the tersept's steel breastplate, but sent Stornbridge back on his heels—and Hawkril's lunge, arriving a moment later, caught him flat-footed.

Through the space between two plates of the tersept's splendid armor the armaragor's warsword bit, only going in an inch or so through the underleathers, but Stornbridge reeled back again—and Craer, still on the ground by the tersept's feet, hooked his legs around Stornbridge's ankle and flung himself over on his side.

Lord Stornbridge toppled like a felled tree, crashing hard onto the flagstones and losing his warsword once more. Hawkril kicked him hard, rolling him clear of Craer, and then kicked him again, forcing the tersept into a frantic crawl that brought Stornbridge to his knees and then to triumphantly seizing on two fallen cortahar's swords.

With a bark of triumph he spun around, blades glittering in both hands. Hawkril charged, smashing one aside with his own warsword and then ducking after it, so Stornbridge's vicious thrust with the second blade stabbed only air.

Hawkril kept on circling, striding around behind the tersept until Stornbridge was forced to wheel around, leaving his back open to Craer.

The procurer promptly sprang onto the tersept's back and perched there, slapping Stornbridge's eyes with his fingers until the frantic noble flung himself over backwards to try to crush Craer on the flagstones.

The procurer leaped nimbly away, landed, and then sprang back, landing with both feet together and as hard as he could on Stornbridge's right wrist.

The tersept screamed as bones crunched audibly and his fingers spasmed open, letting fall one of his borrowed swords. Hawkril stalked forward, his warsword gleaming, but Craer called merrily, "Hey, now! You got to carve up Pheldane, and the lornsar, too, whilst declaiming grand doom—this one's mine!"

His next bound brought him down with crushing force on Stornbridge's other wrist—or rather, on a few fingers, as the tersept twisted desperately away.

Stornbridge screamed again, rolling over, and then found his feet and tried to flee, running desperately along his own battlements in the moonlight.

Craer sighed and pursued, springing once more onto Stornbridge's back. Off-balance, the tersept staggered, still running but trying at the same time to claw the procurer off his back.

Craer reached around and quite deliberately broke Stornbridge's nose.

Snarling, the tersept came to a halt, elbowed Craer free of him, snatched out his own dagger, and slashed wildly.

The procurer grinned, just beyond the reach of Stornbridge's fang—and then sat down suddenly and kicked upwards, slicing the tersept's arm with one of his toe-blades.

Stornbridge howled, staggered—and then stabbed down in a blind, frantic fury, again and again, seeking to bury his steel in the infuriating little man beneath him. Kick after kick thudded against the tersept's armor as Craer twisted, rolled, arched, and spun, always avoiding that dagger. Eventually the tersept lost his balance and staggered back until he fetched up against a merlon.

Panting, he glared at the procurer, gathered himself—and then rushed at Craer once more. The procurer ducked sideways, toward the crenellations, and the snarling tersept whirled to follow, reaching out with his dagger—

His wrist was gripped in one strong hand, and another clamped down on his arm above it, tugging in the direction of his thrust, but also turning . . . and, with a sob of sudden fear and disbelief, Lord Stornbridge was forced to stab his own armpit.

Moaning in pain, he staggered back along a merlon, and felt the dagger ripped from his fingers.

"Enough sport," the procurer told him quietly. "You've lived quite long enough for a man who hurt my Tshamarra, Stornbridge. Oh, yes—and betrayed Aglirta, too. Die, now, and feed some fishes. You might as well be of *some* use."

A line of liquid fire seemed to erupt across the tersept's brow. Blinking through his own blood, Stornbridge felt tugs at his armpits as straps were deftly cut. Striking out feebly with his fists, he drove his assailant away, hearing a grunt of pain but also the clang of his own breastplate dangling and clashing against his other armor.

Again the deft slicing, and this time cool air touched Stornbridge's sweating chest. His leathers! The little fox must have—

And then something that was both fire and ice together drove into his chest, and he could no longer breathe, could no longer move, could only sag into the warm, waiting chill . . .

Craer hooked one boot behind the tersept's knee and hauled on the dagger-hilt like a handle, shoving—and the battlements of Stornbridge Castle were suddenly short one tersept.

From somewhere, Lord Stornbridge found the breath and strength for a dying scream, as the cold waters of the moat rushed up to receive him.

The splash was satisfying. Craer straightened up to trade glances with

Hawkril—and their gazes were caught by a sudden tongue of bright flame flaring into the night sky from a nearby hilltop. As they watched, it began to curve, changing from a pillar of raging fire to a fiery serpent, swaying as its head cast about for foes, forked tongue licking forth repeatedly.

"All hail the Great Serpent," a weak voice husked from nearby. The overdukes turned to see the priest Craer had felled earlier lying on his side, with the fire-serpent reflected in his dying eyes. The man swallowed, struggled to speak as blood welled from his mouth, and then managed a single word: *"Auncrauthador!"*

As the two overdukes traded grim shrugs of foreboding, they felt the prickling of magic, and then the cold weight of hostile regard.

Some Serpent-lover was watching them from afar. Probably from yon hilltop, because now they could also hear—as if borne on a faint wind, but against the breeze sighing over the battlements from behind them, blowing toward the hill—chanting . . . a hissing chant: Serpent-worship.

Sudden shrieks arose in the castle yard below. Hawkril and Craer looked down, and saw cortahars and Storn folk stabbing each other with blades, clawing each other barehanded, and running wildly here and there.

Two strides took Craer to the dying priest. He slapped the man's face, and those dull eyes flickered. "What's causing this? This butchery and fighting? Hey?"

Bloody lips trembled to shape a last smile, and the priest whispered gloatingly, "Blood Plague. The Blood Plague is come at last."

12

A Surfeit of Plague

Fire leaped up in the night. Flaeros Delcamper stared at it—and then at another tongue of flame, shooting up to scorch the stars some distance away, probably at the next village. He frowned. "T'isn't festival time. What's going on?"

There were only three other paying passengers on the trade barge. One was asleep, but the other two were gawking at the flames just as he was. "What's going on?" he demanded again, but one of them—the trim-bearded Sirl merchant in green—just shook his head in silent bewilderment.

The barge crew had been rowing steadily against the steady flow of the river, keeping the barge to the most placid bankside shallows, but they'd seen the nightfires, too—and their response, without waiting for orders, was to stroke more swiftly.

For a moment the barge moved raggedly, and then settled into a new, faster rhythm. The breeze was quickening, too, and for the first time those afloat heard faint screams and shouts.

Flaeros strode toward the barge captain, sitting on his high perch and staring into the night ahead. Several of the hired Sirl guards moved to block his way, but the captain said a single quiet word and they drew back to allow the bard through.

Master Rold did not halt his ceaseless scanning of the way ahead as Flaeros approached. He'd caught up a double-ended metal spear from somewhere, and was holding it ready across his lap.

Even before the bard could open his mouth to repeat his queston, the master of the *Silver Fin* gave him a flat stare and said, "I don't know either, sir bard—but I'd much appreciate it if you'd stand quiet and just watch and listen, until I tell you different. Panic aboard makes our tasks no easier. So look sharp for archers or others on the banks who could menace us, and otherwise . . ."

"Keep my jaw shut?"

The barge captain nodded once, and resumed his steady scanning of the waters ahead and the banks around them.

Flaeros sighed, then said, "Very well. I agree if you'll tell me one thing—full truth, mind. I promise not to share your answer with . . ." He waved his hand to indicate the other passengers, now pacing nervously as new fires sprang up in the night—strange tall, narrow pillars of flame. The sleeping man had awakened, it seemed, and was going about asking very much the same thing Flaeros had been.

The barge captain watched those askings, sighed, and said flatly, "Ask your one thing, Lord Delcamper."

"Why are we on the water? Silverflow barges don't normally travel by night, and I remember us tying up and bedding down. When I came awake, there were one or two of these fires and we were under way again. Why?"

The breezes brought them more screaming; the folk doing it sounded terrified. "Is Aglirta at war?"

The barge captain shrugged. "As to war, the shouting and the fires, I know no more than you do. *Something's* going on, aye, but all I can tell you is that we cut our moorings in fair haste, and left Sabbar dock as fast as we could."

Flaeros cast a look back at the grimly rowing sailors, and saw sweat glistening on them in the reflected firelight. It was a clear night, but more warm than chill, even right on the water. "Why?" he asked again, when it became clear the barge captain was in no hurry to say more.

"Sir bard," the man asked reluctantly, "have you ever seen lions with two heads, that turned into great snakes halfway down their bodies, and slithered along with no rear paws? Or things like walking spiders as big as mules, but with dozens of snake-heads sprouting from the tops of their bodies?"

"N-no," Flaeros replied. "The lion-things are known to heralds, though, and are called *krimazror,* or *krimazrin* in the singular. The desert backlands of Sarinda were once full of them, the tales say."

"Ah. Well. That's very nice. Remind me never to take it into my head to go faring into the deserts of Sarinda."

"Master Rold," Flaeros asked firmly, "are you telling me you've seen such beasts this night? Here, in Aglirta? Real beasts, and not some wizard-spun illusions to drive you off a dock he was keeping open for someone else, say?"

"I saw no wizards," the barge captain replied stolidly, "or at least, no men in robes who waved their arms as they sneered and declaimed, but I did see beasts of both these sorts. Real beasts, Lord Delcamper. They burst onto the docks and bit the heads off some of the crew—and sleeping passengers, too—of the *Taratheena,* out of Dranmaer. It was tied up next to us, and when a lion-thing looked our way, I yelled at the lads to cut loose and push off into the Silverflow."

They were rounding a great bend in the river, and there were more flames ahead. Flaeros shook his head. "I don't doubt your word, master—but I can scarce believe it."

"Huh. You're not alone in that," the barge captain replied. "Now, Lord Delcamper, I'd best devote my full attention to avoiding sandbars and swimming monsters, and suchlike, so if you'll . . ."

"Of course," Flaeros said, turning away from the raised bow under the watchful eyes of the guards.

As he did so, a weird hissing call arose, faraway down the Vale, and seemed to sweep closer, picked up and echoed by unseen folk—or beasts—nearer at hand. As if in response, the pillars of flame bent, wriggled, and took on the shapes of serpents, snake-heads questing this way and that. Flaeros could just make out the heads and arms of a ring of worshippers gathered around the base of the nearest bright serpent of fire.

It bent toward the bank, a forked tongue of fire licking forth, and Flaeros felt its heat on his face. Instinctively he shrank away, murmuring, "I might have known! Always, 'tis the Snake-lovers!"

A low moan of recognition and fear arose on the barge. Flaeros looked back downriver, and then forward, and shook his head. Much of the Vale seemed to have erupted in whatever mischief this was.

Abruptly, a hay-barn perched high on the bank they were passing burst into flame—a blaze set by whoever was crying out in triumph, not a serpent-shaped fire, at least not yet—and in its sudden bright light, Flaeros and everyone else on the *Silver Fin* saw people running. Vale folk were fleeing other Vale folk, some of them staggering strangely.

Staggering, and sinking down into things that grunted and snorted and ran now on all fours, reaching out with tentacles or crablike claws or spindly, barb-limbed talons.

People were screaming, people were falling and being eaten.

"Three take us all!" someone gasped, as a tall, elegant lady in a torn gown ran down the bank, hotly pursued by two youths. Almost at the water's edge they caught and clawed at her, raking her face and arms into bloody ruin. She bit them, snarling and pummeling, as the last shreds of her clothing fell away, and then flung herself atop one of them and held him down and drowning as she battled the other.

Flaeros and his fellow travelers on the barge stared in horror as hair was torn out and kicks and punches thrown recklessly. Everyone seemed enraged, one screaming man even turning with a roar to bite and claw the monster chasing him. Everywhere, folk were battling in barehanded, reckless savagery, like maddened animals.

"What's *happened*?" someone on the barge gasped.

"Magic," a barge guard said grimly, and spat disgustedly into the river. "The same blight that always afflicts Aglirta. Fell magic, from wizard or Serpent-priest. To rule it, they rush to destroy or maim it. Until Aglirtans rise up and rid themselves of such vermin, this is going to happen again and again. My father told me it raged in his time—and here we are forty-odd summers later, and how far has the Kingless Land come?"

"Well," Flaeros replied quietly, "they have a King now."

The guard looked at him. "Hah! And do they heed him? Do the Serpents bow, and the barons obey, and the people know peace?" He waved at the fires and screaming people on the shore, and added wearily, "Oh, for a true King! This land could be so great!"

"I think it *is* great," Flaeros said firmly, "to have survived at all. The Dwaer-Stones lost and lost again, Faerod Silvertree and his Dark Three, Bloodblade, the Rising of the Serpent, the death of King Snowsar . . . Aye, Aglirta has survived much."

The guard slowly surveyed the fires and the maddened folk busily slaying each other, and then grunted, "Survived? Well, aye, after a fashion, Lord Bard. After a fashion."

They exchanged grim nods as the barge slid on through the night of blood and madness. Here and there, bodies were bobbing in the waters now.

"Is that you, Tash?"

"It had better be," the Lady Talasorn told Craer, as she swung around a corner to embrace him, and unhooded a lantern. "We . . . we're a little weary."

"Huh," the procurer muttered, "*you're* weary. Who's been swinging swords and jumping around like jesters while you three lounged around humming to yon Dwaer, I'd like to know?"

"Charming as always, Overduke Delnbone," Blackgult observed from across the chamber.

"One has one's reputation to maintain," the procurer replied, sketching an elegant bow.

"Evidently," the Golden Griffon replied in weary rebuke. "We felt the castings dwindle and end, so I presume the priests are all dead or fled, but I hope you sent Stornbridge to a fitting end?"

"One priest fled, aye," Hawkril replied, shouldering into the room, "and Craer did his usual dancing justice upon the unlamented tersept. But we've some grim news to report: The Serpents have unleashed something they call the Blood Plague, all over the Vale."

Embra nodded, looking pale and drawn. "It does seem widespread, yes. Fell and mighty, laying madness on folk who've never bent a knee to the Great Serpent as well as those who've come to his altars, so far as I could see. The altar fires . . ." She winced at the memory. "We had to leave off using the Dwaer, or be overwhelmed. So much magic, and so . . . *twisted*."

Craer nodded. "So, does anyone have anything trustworthy we can eat or drink?"

His fellow overdukes stared blankly at him, and then Blackgult—followed by Tshamarra, and then Hawkril—started to laugh.

"Well?" the procurer asked, folding his arms. "Are we now the masters of Stornbridge Castle? Should we find some chamber with food and drink that we can readily garrison, and get some sleep?"

"Now *that* is a very good suggestion, Craer," Embra muttered, and there were sounds of agreement among the mirth of the others. "Before someone expects me to stagger around this interminable castle, however, suppose we discuss where we might find such a place. If it helps, with what little I could tell through the Dwaer, all the guards, servants, and Serpent-priests seem gone from nearby."

Craer frowned. "Fear, or our hacking and spellhurling, or just freedom from dead masters—or did this plague touch them, too?"

"Some of them, yes," Embra replied. "Through the Dwaer, I saw one servant claw another, without warning, and the two of them fell to fighting like beasts."

"And I," Blackgult added, "saw an armsman in the castle start to stagger and hunch over—and by the time he reached his fellows, he was something lizardlike and slithering. They put spears and swords through him, of course, and then tossed the corpse into the moat."

"Might I suggest," Tshamarra said quietly, "that before we take on all the troubles of Aglirta, we see to ourselves? I'm . . . there's still something wrong with me, inside, and it could well be this plague, or something akin to it . . . and I know I'm not the only overduke in such a state. We should use the Dwaer to purge ourselves of its taint, if we can."

"Eat, drink, and sleep—sleep above all," Hawkril growled. "Some place you ladies can spell-seal."

"We need safe sleep more than anything else right now," Embra agreed. "But where? Those kitchens are quite a stroll back that way. And how do we know the food's untainted? And the water?"

"Sausages and pickles," Craer suggested. "Mad spellweaving Serpent-priests rarely take the time to stop and taint those."

"No more splitting up," Tshamarra said firmly. "Where we go, we go together."

Hawkril looked at his lady. "If you've strength left to blast down a door or two with the Stone, I propose we descend to the courtyard, walk along to the right tower to be close to the kitchens, and blast its door in. Take what we want, and then . . . Well, if we're far enough away from any fires or folk who could start new ones, another turret-top room might serve us as a refuge."

The Lady of Jewels smiled wearily. "Fine. Let's do that. Agreed, all?"

"Agreed," Blackgult said firmly, more or less drowning out the affirmative noises made by the others—so they went and did that.

Four guards met them in the passage outside the kitchens, grimly raising swords and striding forward. Hawkril and Blackgult strode to meet them, but were still a good three strides away from the foremost guard when the man suddenly screamed in terror, went to his knees, and started to sprout fur.

The overdukes backed away again—and so did the guards behind the stricken one. Both sides watched in wary silence as armor fell away from the hairy, increasingly wolflike body that quivered on all fours between them.

After a time it roared, shook itself, and prowled forward, snarling. Hawkril and Blackgult took up stances shoulder to shoulder, and waited, but the beast sprang right onto their waiting blades. A few moments of wrestling aside snapping jaws, and watching blood pump, and the beast went limp.

The overdukes traded glances, and then carefully stepped over the corpse. The guards beyond eyed them uncertainly—and then turned in unison and ran.

Craer grinned. "Ah, we've finally found the wiser ones. I was wondering where Stornbridge kept them hidden!"

"What I don't want to know," Tshamarra murmured from just behind his shoulder, "is what sort of monster the cooks have turned into."

The kitchen, however, proved to be deserted—abandoned in haste, by the looks of things: spilled condiments, burnt food on cooling spits above the dying coals of untended fires, and half-sliced onions upon a none-too-clean cutting block.

Embra sighed. "Go find your sausages and pickles."

"Hey, 'tis not that bad," Hawkril rumbled, looking around. "There's one end of a roast here not burnt—and sarrago stew, if my nose doesn't fail me."

"And it rarely does," Craer agreed, rummaging. "Tash, grab yon pot, hey? There's a wheel of cheese here, and roundloaves in plenty. We'll not go hungry, to be sure!"

"Couldn't we just garrison this room?" the Lady Talasorn asked. "Is there something especially scenic about a round room up six or seven flights of stairs?"

Blackgult sighed. "We need a strong-walled room that we can't be burnt or flooded out of, that gets air, preferably with only one or two entrances that can't easily be blocked from outside. Oh, and with a floor some of us can sleep on. There might be suitable pantries hereabouts, but I doubt it."

Hawkril shouldered a door open and peered in. "Hmm. I feel less and less enthusiastic about eating another feast in Stornbridge, no matter who's tersept and how far across Darsar we've scoured the Serpents out. Phaugh, as they say!"

"Agreed," Craer said, wrinkling his nose. "How about this next one?"

"Three preserve," Blackgult said grudgingly, after a moment, "but it seems ideal." He peered around again, and nodded. "Bear in mind, though, that anyone left in the castle will come here foraging, ere long. We have to be able to wedge this door against considerable force—and it has to be able to withstand a ram, and lots of arrows."

"Well, there's only one way to find *that* out, as they say," Craer commented brightly. "However, there's a harder test yet."

"Hey?"

"Embra has to say aye to it. Naught else matters, hmm?"

"I'm not," the Lady Silvertree said frowningly, "quite so much of a surly dragon as you make me out to be, Craer." She looked around the old stone room, reading what was painted on some of the jars. "Olaunt. Sar-fruit. Gaddorn. Yes, this will do."

There was a general murmur of approval—that lasted for as long as it took Craer to fetch two shallow tureens down from a kitchen shelf and present them to Tshamarra and Embra with the grand words, "Ladies—your chamberpots for the night. No, no, I'll accept no payment for this thoughtful service!"

"Tash," Embra said wearily, "kick him. Somewhere where it hurts."

"More!" Craer said grandly, dropping two bulging sacks beside Blackgult and trotting back through an archway again before his fellow overdukes could say a word.

Tshamarra sighed. "Been a day or two since he last had a chance to practice looting, would you say?"

Embra chuckled. "He's not done badly. I hope we can find a wagon in the stables to carry all he's gathered."

"Lass," Blackgult said reprovingly, "wheels of cheese and kegs of wine are wise booty to anyone. Be not so hard on the lad. We may even need yon chest of coins—if we need to buy a spare castle or two, for instance."

They stepped over more sprawled and gnawed corpses, and Embra shuddered. Stornbridge Castle had become one great charnelhouse, with bodies lying everywhere, fires smoldering unchecked, furniture and belongings broken and strewn, and transformed folk prowling the rooms and passages in their bewildering newfound lives as wild beasts.

By the cries of the suffering, unmilked cows, the town and the farms around were in much the same state. Anyone who'd survived the plague-fury had fled far away or was keeping well hidden.

"Let's hope some horses have been left uneaten," Hawkril muttered, advancing into the gloom of the stables cautiously, his drawn sword ready. Bright scratches on his armor bespoke the power behind the claws of the last beast he'd battled. It had pounced on him from above—and it had been a long time since the armaragor had been taken that much by surprise.

Some stalls had been torn open, and dead and half-devoured horses lay within most of them. Grimly Hawkril stalked on, seeking danger first, and beasts they could ride second. Two monstrous things of many claws and turtlelike body shells lay twisted together in death in one end stall, their jaws still locked in each other's throats, and an evil carrion smell wafted down from the loft above, but no foe remained alive to pounce or menace—

only trembling, snorting horses who were more inclined to kick than to welcome being led out of their stalls into all the slaughter.

"Seven beasts worth looking at," Hawkril growled, returning from his survey. "No wagons, Lord Delnbone."

"No wagons? Then we take every horse and saddlebag. What we don't fill, we sling over top, tied down, and take empty—we'll find uses for them, never fear."

"Aye, I'll bet," Embra murmured. " 'Tis those in our path who own anything attractive or valuable who'll have to fear."

"By the Three!" Blackgult agreed with a smile, in quavering mockery of a doom-saying old man.

"Help me get reins and saddles on these horses, you jesters," Tshamarra said from her perch on the rail of a stall above them, where she stood eyeing a horse almost as uncertainly as it was eyeing her. "*If* 'tis not too much trouble for you high-and-mighty folk, that is."

"Lady Talasorn," Embra said in mock-offended tones, "*everything's* too much trouble for we high-and-mighty folk. That's what's made Aglirta the glorious center of peace and prosperity that 'tis today!"

Tshamarra gave her a sour look. "Get in here and show me which end of the horse I put this on, hey?"

"Hey, indeed," Embra agreed. "Father?"

"Of course," Blackgult agreed, striding into the stall, striking aside its frightened occupant's deadly foreleg kick with one blow of a practiced hand, and ramming himself against the breast of the horse, crowding it back until he could get the bridle on. "Easy, see?"

Tshamarra and Embra looked at each other and rolled their eyes in heartfelt unison.

Fires were rising here and there in Stornbridge town, and half-eaten bodies and the stains of pools of blood were everywhere. The horses snorted and danced, even under Dwaer-calming, and their disgusted riders glanced around warily in search of danger. No dogs barked . . . probably because they'd been eaten, perhaps by the dark shapes that slunk from bush to bush and tree to tree, following the five riders and their pack horses, but never coming near.

"So this is a Blood Plague," Tshamarra said slowly, looking around at the devastation. "If it was what tainted us, it can be visited on folk in food or wine . . . but what is it, really?"

"Aye," Hawkril growled. "Foul Serpent-work, to be sure, but *how*? What spell, and how to undo or stop it?"

Embra sighed. "And so we're back to the problem that always besets us: not knowing." She held up the Dwaer. "If I knew what I was doing with this, and how to make sure the other three Dwaerindim were lost forever, I could rule Darsar quite handily, were I subtle and cunning enough."

She smiled thinly at the looks she received. "Worry not, friends—not only have I no desire to rule Darsar, I'll never know this Stone properly. They fight you, you know, quietly—things you've done before with them become harder to remember how to evoke, not easier."

Blackgult nodded. "That's true. I've never voiced it before, but . . . yes. The Dwaer *do* fight their wielders."

Craer glanced at the mottled Stone in Embra's hand with new respect. "Well, now," he began, "that makes dreams of snatching one of these baubles for my own—"

He was interrupted by a ragged shout from among the cottages to their left. A wild-eyed man charging at them, pitchfork in hand, with several boys running along in his wake. They clutched stones, and echoed the man's roar of challenge as he ran right at the horses, fork leveled.

"Hold!" Hawkril bellowed, drawing his sword, but the Storn folk didn't seem to hear him. Straight at the overdukes they ran.

Embra sighed, the Dwaer flared in her hand—and when the first stones came, they struck something unseen in the air and bounced away. The fork halted suddenly in midair, causing its wielder to emit a startled "Ooof!" as he folded up around it. The overdukes spurred their horses and rode away, up the road where they'd been greeted by arrows the day before.

Today, there were no woodcutters, or bowmen, though they all kept a sharp watch as they rode up through the trees, heading back to Osklodge.

"Whither now?" Craer asked quietly, as the trees gave way to fields around them. No carts, no beasts in the high meadows; this part of Aglirta seemed to have emptied.

"Glarondar," Embra said firmly. "We go right back the way we came."

"Well, that's a relief," the procurer said with a smile, cutting into a small wheel of cheese that seemed to have fallen out of his saddlebag into his hand a moment before. " 'Tis nice to have a clear destination for once. The barony of Glarond, where they've at least heard of decent wine, food, and hospitality."

Blackgult and Hawkril both cast looks at Embra, but said nothing. If she was choosing not to share her reason for heading to Glarond with them yet, that was all right. They had to search for missing Dwaer somewhere—and seemed to have found something more pressingly important that just might be *everywhere* in the Vale, so one direction was as good as any other.

Moreover, every last one of the Overdukes of Aglirta was weary of constant wrangling over deeds and destinations.

"We have the 'where,' now, but what shall we be doing there?" Tshamarra asked quietly, after they'd galloped along the road for some time, leaving Osklodge behind and losing all sight of Stornbridge.

Craer shrugged. "What we always do—draw our swords and chase them around the kingdom."

Tshamarra smiled and sighed. "Yes, but doing what?"

"Causing trouble, blundering along not knowing what to do next, and offering ourselves as targets for all foes of the crown."

"Craer!"

"Well," the procurer told her with an ingenuous grin, "it's worked so far."

"Well, Brother Landrun?"

"Ah . . . isn't Overduke Anharu *taller* than that, Lord?"

The Lord of the Serpent peered at his most recent transformation. The armaragor did seem to loom a little less than the real Anharu did, in his remembrances, but . . .

"You may be right, Landrun," he said slowly. "Make it stand beside our Embra. I should have done Blackgult first, because he's about half a head taller than his daughter, and Anharu overtops him by about the same . . . or a little less, perhaps. Hmm."

Brother Landrun hastened to obey—so quickly that there was a stumbling thud as he hastened down the side passage.

He strode into view soon enough, looking none the worse for wear, and towed the shuffling Anharu over to where the false Embra stood. Neither of the transformations looked at the other, but stood shifting aimlessly from one foot to another. Landrun gazed at them for a moment, and then returned to the passage.

Lord of the Serpent Hanenhather peered narrowly at the two false overdukes. How much of the real Anharu's hulking size was his armor, bulking up those massive shoulders? Or did folk really look closely enough at him for it to matter? Casting the spell took but a moment, but getting the results right, now . . .

Brother Landrun came up beside him, and Hanenhather sighed. "What do you think, Landrun?"

The tentacle that slapped across the Serpent-lord's mouth did not—quite—break his neck. A second tentacle was already ensnaring his wrists, crushing them ruthlessly even as it gathered them in, and a third wrapped around his waist and snatched him up into the air, to stare helplessly down at—at something that no longer looked much like Landrun at all.

For one thing, it had no face. Just smooth flesh where eyes, nose, and mouth should be . . . yet its voice was clear enough as it said coldly, "We Koglaur are feared and hated enough in the Vale without your shapeshifting mischief, Serpent-priest. Plague-monsters are one thing, but making doubles of tersepts and overdukes—or kings—is *our* province. Die, overclever Lord of the Serpent."

The last thing Melvar Hanenhather saw, as tentacles slammed his head floorwards at breath-snatching speed, was a trickle of blood coming around the corner from the side passage. Landrun's, of course.

There was a guard at the Flowfoam docks that hadn't been there before—with ready strung bows, too, the customary spears relegated to the banner-display stands at the back of the docks. The dockloaders and pages were frightened and eager for news; barely had the *Silver Fin* tied up at the jetty than excited whispers arose in a hissing chorus, as every passenger and bargehand was queried.

Flaeros Delcamper bounded up the steps before any servant could ply him with questions of fires and slaughter and marauding monsters. His haste earned him a barrier of crossed spears at the first terrace, with an officer of the guard aiming a bowgun at him from behind them. "Hold hard! Your name and business?"

Flaeros frowned. "I am the bard Flaeros Delcamper, of Ragalar; here in Flowfoam at the personal invitation of my friend, the King."

"Your 'friend'?" a spear-wielding guard asked skeptically, but his older fellow guard had already lifted his spear and stepped back.

"He tells truth," the veteran told both the officer and his fellow spearman. "This is the man who faced down the nobles, and made them swear fealty to our new King. He practically ran this palace for a month or so, until things settled down."

The enlightened guards eyed Flaeros with new respect, and the officer clapped his hand to his shoulder in salute as the bard nodded and resumed his ascent to the palace. As he glanced up at Flowfoam, its ravages now entirely repaired or concealed, he was aware of cold and unfriendly scrutiny from several sides—but who was so regarding him, he could not see. He gave his unseen observers a smile and a shrug, and went on into the waiting bustle of the court.

The request to present himself to the king earned Flaeros a hard-eyed escort of suspicious guards, before and behind, and a thorough search of his person for weapons. Lighter by the weight of his dagger, his best quill-case, and the tiny trimming knife he used for cutting quills, Flaeros was taken through three guarded doors, so weighed down by the glares of guards that he found himself moving slowly.

Even when he reached Raulin—seated behind a small desk, head down and writing furiously, with piles of parchments on both sides of him—the blades of two bared swords separated them. "May fairer days come, Your Majesty," he said gently.

Raulin Castlecloaks looked up with a frown, trying to place the voice— and when he saw Flaeros, he smiled broadly, tossed down his pen, and strode around the desk to embrace his visitor, laughing in delight.

Even then, the guards kept their blades pointed at the bard's back. When he turned, hugging the king, they moved in haste to keep behind him—until Raulin shooed them away with sharp words and waving hands.

They took up positions about four strides distant, swords still drawn, as the king gleefully swept a pile of writs and proclamations onto the floor to free up a stool, and presented it to Flaeros with a flourish. Grinning, the bard took his seat.

"Wine, some of that Craulbec, and apples!" the king called, to a servant nervously hovering just beyond the ring of guards.

Flaeros raised an eyebrow. "Craulbec? Since when did you take a liking for cheese strong enough to outreek dead goat?"

"Since you left some behind in the larder when you went home. Three Above, but I'm glad to see you, Flaer! I . . . I've been going wizard-witted here, what with all"—Castlecloaks lowered his voice abruptly—"the troubles in these halls. Writs and treaties are bad enough as daily fare, without all this . . ."

"Yes," Flaeros murmured, leaning in close to the king despite the stiffening, advancing reaction of the guards. "Tell me: *What* troubles? What's been going on? Why all the menacing swords?"

"Snakes," Raulin murmured. "Slithering into my chambers at night.

Three guards have died from their venom, and more have been bitten. They must come by magic—and you know who *that* means—because it matters not where I sleep, and how carefully the walls are chinked and sealed. I've even ended up in bare chambers on rope-sling mattresses with nothing but blankets, and still they come. And folk here in Flowfoam are going mad! Without warning, time and again, a servant or courtier or guard who's been perfectly pleasant to me for months will draw a blade and start stabbing and hacking—at me, or whoever's nearest!"

As if the king's words had been a cue, an approaching platter of wine, cheese, and apples suddenly went flying, two terrified servants were flung aside, and a guard burst forward, waving his sword and howling.

Astonished, Flaeros stared as the man charged right at them, wild-eyed. Two guards stabbed him from either side, were dragged along, and then frantically wrestled with the roaring man, who staggered up to the desk, battering the heads of the men clinging to him with his sword, and thrust out at the king.

Flaeros swept up his stool and smashed the steel aside—and as Raulin reluctantly drew his own sword and the snarling man tried to claw his way along the desk toward it, Flaeros swung the stool again, as hard as he could, into the man's head.

There was a dull crack, and the guard crashed down face-first onto the heaps of proclamations, riding them bloodily to the floor and trailing the pair of grimly clinging fellow guards.

The bard and the king stared at each other and then down at the lifeless man at their feet. Then they lifted gazes to stare at each other again, helplessly.

"I wish the Four were back here with us," King Raulin whispered. "They'll know what to do."

13

Too Many Monsters

Tshamarra sighed as carrion-birds flapped heavily away from something sprawled in the muddy trail ahead, and slowed her nervous mount. "I knew Glarond was a populous barony, but—gods—this many corpses? Is there anyone *left*?"

"Yes," Craer told her brightly, turning in his saddle. "The survivors!"

"And the worst of it all is," Embra murmured from beside the Lady Talasorn, "he thinks himself funny."

"He is," Blackgult said from behind them both, "so long as we're speaking purely of looks. 'Tis his words and deeds that swiftly stray from amusing to annoying. Yet the Three must love him dearly—what other procurer takes such care to be memorable and ever noticed? Most skulk through life in hopes of going unnoticed and living longer. Yet this mad Delnbone . . ."

Tshamarra nodded. "Truth, bluntly put. So can my Beloved-of-the-gods see us all safely through this Blood Plague, do you think?" She waved a small and slender hand at carrion-birds pecking busily at several motionless lumps in a field, and added quietly, "Or repopulate Glarond?"

Craer turned in his saddle, growing a broad grin, and without sparing a glance from his ceaseless peering at their surroundings, Hawkril growled, "Lady, encourage him not! D'you know what you said? 'Repopulate' hath but one means, remember?"

Tshamarra rolled her eyes. "Spare us your comments and gestures," she told her beaming man firmly, as he opened his mouth to say something clever. "Just—spare us."

"Shields up," Hawkril snapped. "Folk watching us, in the trees."

The two sorceresses hauled at the unaccustomed weight of the shields the armaragor had insisted on strapping to their saddlebags ere leaving Stornbridge, and looked at the trees ahead. The road plunged into their midst, and the two women exchanged wary glances, remembering arrows hissing . . . and thudding home . . .

Tshamarra caught sight of fearful eyes and cowering bodies. "By the Forefather, Hawk, they're just . . . frightened folk, staring at us!"

"Aye," Hawkril agreed, waving his drawn sword so that everyone could see it and standing tall in his saddle to peer farther into the treegloom ahead. "The problem with this plague is—"

Someone in the trees suddenly snarled and pounced on the man beside him. An unfortunate head was jerked back by a cruel tug on hair, a throat was cut, and in its wake that same someone howled and lashed out in all directions, steel flashing under the boughs amid wild screams and the crashings of fleeing folk.

"—this sudden falling into madness," the armaragor added grimly. "Prudence is swept away, threats and good sense mean nothing, and so 'tis wise to keep your *shields up!*"

His last few words were snapped back over his shoulder as he spurred forward to meet a wild-eyed man running out of the trees fumbling with a loaded crossbow. Shaking hands checked the quarrel, a ceaselessly murmuring mouth spoke reassurances to itself as the weapon was aimed—and Hawkril's warsword slashed the bow aside in a whirl of sliced strings, tumbling quarrel, and severed fingers.

The man screamed and ran, shaking his gory ruin of a hand and staring at nothing.

Embra winced, even as Blackgult snapped, "Craer! Guard the ladies!" and spurred past them to join Hawkril. Many folk were coming along the winding road ahead—fast. Eyes wild and unseeing, running hard, too winded for their screams to be much more than endless, raw groaning . . .

"What're they running from?" Embra muttered, clutching the Dwaer in one hand and trying to manage reins and shield in the other.

Hawkril looked back, guiding his nervously sidestepping horse, and the Lady Silvertree saw that he and her father were carefully positioning themselves to shield Tash and herself. She looked to the other sorceress, and found Tshamarra's eyes already on her. Tshamarra's face held the same helpless sadness she knew must be written across her own.

"Easy, now," Craer said from behind them. "Just don't go blasting things if it bids fair to involve trees toppling on us, hey?"

Embra risked a withering glance back at the procurer, and saw that the slender little man had a dagger ready in one hand to throw, and a fistful of glittering replacement fangs in the other.

And then the panting, stumbling tide of Aglirtans was upon them, Hawkril grunting under the battering of so many men impaling themselves on his lowered swords at full run. Blackgult was using a broken length of banner-pole he'd found at the stables like a quarterstaff, leaning low in his saddle to thrust and fend off. All the overduchal horses were rearing, Craer cursing as he fought to hold the lead reins of the riderless spare mounts. Tshamarra turned to help him, Embra gathered herself to try to quell equine minds with the Dwaer in despair at her own ignorance of how to properly do such a thing, and—

The running people were gone, crashing on through the brush and down the road behind the overdukes. Several of the stragglers howled and fell as the five riders watched, only to rise sprouting claws and snouts, limbs shifting and twisting sickeningly under their skins.

Hawkril grimly kicked a dead but still gurgling man off his warsword and told the Vale around him, "This is the worst foulness the Serpents have worked yet—making war on all Aglirtans, war-trained or not."

"Perhaps they've wearied of failing to conquer the realm," Tshamarra said a little wearily, "and have decided to just destroy it. The wolves'll dine well this year."

"Aye," Craer agreed from behind her, somber for once, "but I wonder if, having done so, they'll remain wolves?"

"Three forfend!" Embra gasped. "If birds and beasts can carry this plague, the land will never be cleansed of it!"

"We could just keep riding," the Lady Talasorn suggested in a small voice, "to other lands, and . . ."

"Aye," Hawkril snapped, "and do what? Wait for the plague to reach us there? Leaving Aglirta torn and laid waste? We've got to stop this, even if it means begging and promising every last mage in Darsar whatever they want to aid us in breaking this magic!"

"Father," Embra asked quietly, "are they all dead? Or is there someone down but alive and likely to remain so until, say, dusk, that you could bring me?"

"Quite likely," the Golden Griffon replied, swinging out of his saddle and tossing her the reins to hold.

"Lady Embra," Craer snapped, "I thought we Band of Four were leaving the 'Obey me, fools, for I am a great and mysterious mage' act behind us! We trust you, yes, but I do expect you to tell us *why*? Why d'you need some poor wounded idiot?"

"Well, I could say we have an immediate and pressing need to learn what lies ahead of us, that drove all these folk to flight, but the truth is, Craer, I can't learn anything more about this plague-magic unless I can probe an afflicted mind with *this*." Embra hefted the Dwaer, and added bitterly, "Whereupon I'll probably learn more about my own ignorance than anything else."

"You'll be sharing their wound-pain, if you probe someone who's hurt," Tshamarra murmured, struggling to keep her horse quiet. "That much I do know, from my own mind-touch magics."

Embra nodded grimly. " 'Tis all right. I won't get lost in agony—I'll have the remarks of an overclever procurer to anchor and goad me."

Craer looked down, and then away into the trees, and sighed. "I'm sorry, Em. I—My tongue, it just rides away with me . . ."

He fell silent, and so missed the looks of amazement both sorceresses gave him. They'd never thought to hear any sort of apology from Overduke Delnbone, who delighted in saying the most merrily rude or scornful things to the wrong folk at the very worst of moments, and—

Blackgult was turning over moaning, twitching bodies as Hawkril watched over him, a sword held ready to throw. Suddenly there came a fresh crashing through the trees, and the Golden Griffon hastily backed away to where he could stand free of corpses or almost-corpses, and took up a defensive stance.

Another man burst into view, running raggedly. He was barefoot and straggle-bearded, and the homespun of a backcountry Aglirtan farmer, torn and covered with mud and blood, hung from his limbs. He groaned with each breath, his eyes wild—

"Craer!" Hawkril snapped. The procurer plunged from his saddle, raced through the underbrush, and took the running farmer's legs from under him in a deft tackle that spilled both of them through a thornbush, into a welter of wet dead leaves and moss-cloaked, rotten deadfalls.

The man tried to rise and run on, arms flailing, but was too weak and dazed to resist Craer's swift ensnarement of his wrists. The procurer hooked a leg around the man's thigh, rolled him over into a helpless trussed state, and kept him there, panting, as Embra rode carefully over and dismounted.

"Thank you, Craer," she said warmly, clapping a hand to the procurer's arm as she knelt beside them both.

" 'Ware! He's changing!" Tshamarra snapped, pointing. The fallen man's limbs were acquiring scales, here and there—and as the overdukes stared, they thickened and shortened.

"But of course," Blackgult murmured sarcastically. "The Three cease not to smile upon us, hmm?"

"You stand guard," Hawkril told him, "and I'll hold the horses. Tash, watch for anyone approaching, hey?"

"My," Craer said, shifting his grip to keep tight hold of the panting body in his grasp as its shape altered, "*this* is a new feeling. Very strange."

"Don't get any ideas," the Lady Talasorn told him in a voice at once both soft and iron-hard. "Just don't."

The procurer gave her a swift, fierce grin. "I hadn't. Truly. But thanks for that one. Hmm."

"Belt up, Lightfingers," Embra snapped, busily casting swift, wary glances at the trees above and all around. Satisfied, she held out the Dwaer and put a firm hand on the brow of the moaning farmer.

The Stone in her hand glowed, silence fell, everything was falling and . . .

She was plunging into warm red darkness, at once pulsing with life and quivering with fear. It was a darkness that should be brighter, that knew this and was alarmed, and yet could not think, could not hold to thoughts, could not . . .

Could not . . .

Shuddering, the Lady of Jewels threw herself over onto her face in the forest loam, breaking the contact.

"Em!" Hawkril cried, bending toward her with force enough to drag seven horses in her direction. "Are you–?"

"F-fine," his lady told him, managing a wry grin as she rose with dirt all over her forehead and an array of leaves in her hair and sticking to her chin. "Just . . . whew. It feels . . . different from what afflicted us. 'Tis a magic that twists the mind–and its unraveling is beyond me, without time and quiet and the right books and such, to cast the spells I'll need. It seemed almost as if the plague itself can sense, and think, there in his mind . . ."

"A Serpent-priest, watching us through him?" Tash asked sharply.

"No, not that sort of awareness. Just the plague itself, stirring and flowing. Craer, let him go. He means us no harm–and no, he's not running from anything he remembers, he's just seeking 'away' as strongly as he can cling to the thoughts he has left."

"Can he . . . give the plague to someone else, by biting or touching them, or . . . ?"

Embra sighed. "I think so, Tash, but I don't *know*. That's why I wanted us in Glarondar. If the Three smile on us more widely than they've ever been known to do before, we just might find some answers in certain books in the baronial library there."

"Might?" the Lady Talasorn echoed with a smile.

"And how is it," Craer said gently, freeing the man and letting him stumble away, "that you know the contents of a library in Glarond? Not meaning any offense; I'm just ruled by curiosity, that's all."

The Lady Silvertree gave them both a thin smile. "The 'might' is because those books may not still be there. All my knowing of Glarondan libraries is that these particular books were once held by a previous Baron of Glarond. Ambelter wanted my fa—that is, Baron Faerod Silvertree—to send agents to steal them, long ago."

"There've been several Barons of Glarond since then," Hawkril rumbled gently.

"So we mustn't get too hopeful," Craer agreed. "All right: what was or is in those books that you're after now?"

"Castings of, and notes on, some spells associated with the Blood Plague that afflicted Aglirta long ago," Embra replied. "Now please find us a hollow, here in the woods, or some other place the horses can't easily get free from."

The procurer rolled his eyes. "But of course, lady fair," he fluted, flawlessly aping the elaborate gestures of a mincing courtier as he strolled forward. "Might I ask why?"

"You might," the Lady Silvertree agreed, and then chuckled. "I . . . saw enough inside that farmer to know I must use the Dwaer on us all, as soon as possible. The plague still lurks in us, awaiting future weakness to rage again—and ready, even now, to spread to others we have dealings with."

"Ah. Upon reconsideration," Craer announced solemnly, "I've concluded that I won't ask you why, after all."

"Get thee to a hollow!" Tshamarra snarled, pointing into the woods.

The procurer rolled his eyes again and fled. His return was almost immediate. "There's one just beyond yon stump. Go around to the right a bit, to lead the horses down; there're moss-slick boulders everywhere else. If Hawk and Lord Blackgult shift one of the dead trees down like a bar behind us, the horses'll be penned in. Right where their hooves can do us the greatest harm, might I remind you, if we get them scared. That *is* why you want a horse-pen, hey?"

"It is," the Lady of Jewels agreed rather grimly, and they descended into the hollow.

·   ·   ·

"Link to me, Tash," Embra said gently, "and see just how I do this."

"So I can do it to you?" Tshamarra asked softly.

Blackgult looked up sharply at something in her voice, and put his hand on the hilt of his dagger.

Embra nodded. "Last, after I purge you. On the ground, all of you men."

Cheek to cheek and hip to hip, the two sorceresses touched the Dwaer to each of their companions in turn. Each man shuddered, stared wide-eyed at nothing, and then convulsed and started to flail and writhe, clawing at the ground in pain. Craer whimpered, but the two larger men growled, loud and long, like angry wolves. The horses snorted and stamped nervously at that, tossing their heads.

"Burning it back," Tshamarra murmured, going reluctantly to her knees and then sinking down into a sitting position.

"Yes," Embra agreed. "No, right down. This'll hurt some."

"No lie?" the last living Talasorn replied sarcastically, giving the nearest horse a doubtful look as she took herself to the ground. Then she bit her lip at the Dwaer-touch, shook, and sobbed, thrashing and arching back and forth. Embra shielded her head from a root, and waited for Tash to recover.

The horses tried to bolt several times, and had taken to milling about the hollow in great haste, neighing frantically and recoiling whenever Embra used the Dwaer to shove them away from a human shuddering on the ground, ere Tshamarra Talasorn drew in a deep, tremulous breath, blinked eyes that were awash with tears, and reached out to clasp Embra's hand.

"I'm . . . I'm almost ready." She drew in another deep breath, shook her head with a rueful smile, and added, "Yes. I'm ready."

Somewhat unsteadily she found her feet, and with a flourish indicated the ground where she'd been thrashing. Embra smiled, handed her the Dwaer, and laid herself down.

Tshamarra stared at the Dwaer in her hand with a sort of wonder, smiling faintly—and never saw Blackgult's burning eyes on her, as he clawed his way upright on nearby rocks, and drew his dagger.

Like a patient mountain, Hawkril also found his feet, and eyed the horses, wondering if he'd have to charge and wrestle them back to protect Embra or the still-groaning Craer.

Tshamarra drew in a deep breath, threw her head back like a lass preparing to dive deep into a pool, made the Dwaer flame, and plunged her hand down onto Embra's breast.

And the Lady of Jewels screamed.

Loud and long and raw, the throat-stripping shriek of agony set the horses into a thundering gallop away from the two women, at Hawkril's barrier tree.

The scream was promptly answered by a roar of challenge from above, a great thunderous cry that echoed and rolled around the hollow—and made the horses skid to a stop and cower in a trembling heap.

Embra writhed in heedless pain, but the roar brought Craer back to cursing awareness, lying on his back and staring up at the suddenly darker sky. Something huge and dark was blotting out the sunlight, vast wings spread. Branches splintered and cracked under clutching claws far too large for them to support, trees bent aside and then broke, and with dust-stirring beats of its great bat-wings the nightmare came down to earth, stretching forth its heads to snap down at all the moving meals in the hollow.

Yes, heads: three of them. A dragon or nightwyrm twisted into a three-headed abomination such as had never been seen in Aglirta before. Tshamarra rose out of the fires in Embra's mind blinking in disbelief, the Dwaer forgotten in her hand, as searing, smoking spittle fell like rain, and three scaled necks plunged down at her, great jaws agape!

The Baron of Glarond hadn't been master of Glarondar for very long. Riding its streets was still a thrill, even if folk no longer cheered at the sight of him. It was his, every balcony, spire, and merlon of it. Oh, various of his subjects owned this house and that shop—but if he took a liking to a particular building, a few moments of strenuous stabbing by his guards led to the goods of dead traitors devolving into waiting baronial hands.

Not that he wanted most of the dirty, leaning houses in Glarondar. He was used to grander buildings from his days as a courtier in Flowfoam. The glitter of gold, the sheen of expensive cloth, the cold fire of gems—all of these he was used to seeing, but not actually having.

Not until now.

His castle vaults held a coffer of gems and at least three sacks of gold coins as large as he was, as well as several chests of lesser coins. He'd pawed through them more than once, despite the carefully expressionless scrutiny of the ever present guards—*his* guards, now—and looked forward to acquiring more. Much more. But he hadn't expected this much, so soon.

Like a golden mirror the tray gleamed up at him. He looked down at it, seeing his own bright-eyed reflection peering up at—at sixteen gleaming new Carraglan zostarrs, their gold as rich as that of the thick, chased-edge tray;

nine rubies larger than his thumb; and a gold wristlet that must hold as much metal as fifty zostarrs.

"Beautiful, yes?" the Serpent-priest asked gently. "And all yours, plus rule over half the Vale, if you obey me and not the doomed King in Flow-foam."

The Baron of Glarond looked up, suddenly dry-mouthed. He'd sent his guards away to make this a truly private audience at the priest's request, and now there was no one to shield him against the spells of this man Arthroon—if he *was* a man, and not some magic-driven shell used by the Great Serpent he claimed to serve.

He licked his lips, and then from somewhere found the strength to ask, "And if I refuse?"

Arthroon's cold eyes did not smile, even if the mouth below them slid easily into a mirthful curve. "Then death will come to Glarondar. The mad death of the Blood Plague, wracking you and all your courtiers with agonies and gnawing at your minds!"

The baron looked again at the gleaming tray, and then back up at the smiling Serpent-priest, and said carefully, "I've heard of this Malady, yes. Yet Glarondar has been spared the plague thus far, despite busy Vale merchant traffic, and my advisors assure me that spells laid on this town centuries ago by the mage Laerlor keep such perils at bay, and will continue to do so." He tried a smile at the priest, though he could not—quite—keep his eyes from straying to the tray of riches again.

Belgur Arthroon's own smile widened. "Good Baron," he said gently, "Laerlor's spells were broken seventy years ago, by the archmage Golkuth of Sirlptar—better known today as the Skull That Does Not Sleep. Know this truth: everyone in Glarondar is infected, including you! All that prevents the plague rending you, right now, is *this*!"

The priest's right hand shot forth from his left sleeve, cradling a rounded, mottled stone—a stone that was glowing a flickering, pulsing white, and hovering a finger-thickness above Arthroon's palm.

The Baron of Glarond was not a learned man, but courtiers heard much—and even a fool could have felt the raw power pulsing from the stone. This was one of the fabled Dwaerindim, the War Stones . . . the Stones of Power!

Sensibly, he fainted.

Belgur Arthroon's lip curled. So *this* was what ruled baronies in Aglirta, these days. It was more than time for it all to be swept away, in the rightful rise of the Great Serpent.

He bent his will to the Stone, and used its fire to lash Glarond.

The slumped man trembled, hands opening and closing, and then swayed upright in his seat again, wild-eyed. He started to scream, but Arthroon choked it off into a strangled, bubbling whistle, and forced the man to slap himself.

The baron's head reeled, the eyes trapped and wild. Arthroon smiled grimly into them and made Glarond slap himself again.

And again. Then he forced the man to rise from his chair. Limbs twitching and jerking like a clockwork Carraglan automaton, Glarond fell over twice, but the priest forced him to his feet again, stumbling and swaying.

"Thank me for my generous gift," Arthroon commanded, pointing at the tray and letting slip his control over the baron's head.

Glarond burst into tears, but managed to stammer thanks through the flood of sobbing terror.

"Silence," Arthroon snapped, not bothering to hide his disgust—and used the Stone's magic to force the despairing noble's obedience.

"Now, come!" he added, rising from his own chair with an angry swirl of serpent-adorned robes. "We've much to do!"

"Craer!" Hawkril roared, as gaping jaws came down at him like the descending roof of a cottage. "Throw your fangs at its eyes!"

"I'm not an idiot, Tall Post," the procurer replied, reeling to his feet and snatching at hilts here and there about himself. "So have some like advice: Hit it with your sword! Use the sharp edge!"

"Shield-spell, Tshamarra!" Blackgult snapped, running toward her. "Use the Dwaer!"

The Lady Talasorn hadn't stopped to think or to weave magics. Aghast, she'd simply lashed out with the fire still roiling around her mind— and the Dwaer spat forth flame.

One of the dragon's jaws filled with bright fire, roiling flames that spat and curled around its great fangs. Shuddering, that neck spasmed and snatched its head away, leaving just two—one closing around Hawkril with a vicious snap, and the other turning to engulf horses.

Belatedly, Tshamarra tried to spin a shield, using the Dwaer to power what she remembered of such spells.

The result was a failure of whirling sparks, but it struck the descending snout like a great unseen fist, driving fangs aside from the terrified horses.

And then Blackgult was there, large and solid, slapping his hand to the Dwaer beside her own. His mind was like a great sharp sword, dark and knowing, torn and yet storm-strong.

Rouse Embra, he commanded. *Use this, thus.* He showed her bright threads within the Dwaer's unfolding power, and then his attention whirled away from her, back to the dragon above them.

It had drawn in its wings, arching its burned head in pain, but was breaking trees down and aside with its great claws, settling down over the hollow like a ceiling.

"What eyes, Hawk?" Craer complained, springing from rock to rock like a mad jester, trying to reach the lip of the hollow. "There's this big scaled *body* in the way! Hawk? Hawk? *Hawk!*"

Only one side of the hollow was free of covering dragon now, and down through that remaining sliver of sky one head quested for prey, snapping wildly. Blackgult struck at it with unseen, slashing edges of Dwaer-force, short-lived whelmings that shouldn't rob Tshamarra of too much of the power she needed to finish Embra's healing and drag her back to wakefulness.

The burning dragon-head was thrashing somewhere up out of sight, but the third head hung over the hollow, closed and quivering—and Blackgult saw the point of Hawkril's warsword protruding from it, dark with glistening gore.

The armaragor had wedged his blade across the jaws to keep from being crushed, and the dragon had bitten down on it anyway. Blackgult could see an armored arm stabbing and hacking behind the not-quite-closed teeth—Hawkril was still alive and had his dagger out.

"Cut its tongue!" he roared. "Hawk, cut its tongue!"

There, the pain would be greatest, and the beast should try to spit the armaragor out, if only to bite him the better . . .

Craer snarled in satisfaction as his third hurled dagger slashed across an eyeball before spinning away. The dragon screamed.

Heads ringing from the din, Blackgult and Tshamarra wrestled with the Dwaer, the Golden Griffon spinning a shield of shimmering force to fend off dragon jaws, and the Lady Talasorn to get Embra back . . . "to join this mad mayhem," she gasped aloud, ruefully, watching the head that held Hawkril shaking violently, and the burned head swoop down again, trailing smoke, while Craer capered about, hurling daggers in an enthusiastic and largely futile flurry.

Where by all the Three had this beast *come* from, anyway? It was obviously no spell-spun illusion, but . . . Serpent-magic? The wilds north of the Silverflow headwaters went on for unmapped miles, rugged ridges of forests split by rushing rivers and lakes beyond number, enough to hold a dozen realms and dragons to spare, but nothing like this had ever been—

"Where's Hawkril?" a quiet voice asked, from beside her waist. Tshamarra looked down, and drew in a deep breath of relief. Embra was awake and seemingly whole once more.

"Inside yon head, fighting," the Lady Talasorn told her, pointing.

Embra shivered, and then said briskly, "Father, unhand the Dwaer. I need it all." Wordlessly Blackgult complied, and they watched the shimmering of his shield dart under the head. The dragon was still shaking it violently, rather as a dog frees itself of water.

That shimmering flared into brief brightness, broke into two, and one half soared up to slice at the dragon's neck like an ax blade.

Gore sprayed, scales flew, the dragon roared—and its jaws sprang open. Hawkril tumbled out, still hacking as he went, and fell onto the waiting first part of the shield. Embra lowered him swiftly away from the wildly thrashing head—and used her improvised ax of force to strike aside the burned head, which had nosed perilously close to the descending armaragor.

"A vicious beast," she murmured, as they watched Craer scamper along the lip of the hollow, easily evading snapping bites of the third head, "but clumsy. Almost as if it doesn't know how to fight—or even use its jaws with any precision. And there's no way it could have fed all that bulk to grow this large and not be an expert with those fangs, if its mind is its own."

"Or if it's been a dragon for very long," Blackgult commented.

Embra shot him a glance. "That's so, Father!" Then she looked at Tshamarra. "My thanks for bringing me back. For now, at least, I'm free of the plague."

The Lady Talasorn managed a pale smile. "I thought the Dwaer made magic so easy. I know better now. Lady, I salute you."

Embra smiled wryly. "Hah! You think *I* know what I'm doing with this? I just wish we weren't always fighting, so I could explore the implications of half the unleashings I do. What if using the Dwaer harms Darsar in some way we don't even know about?"

"*Later,* Daughter," Blackgult said firmly. "There's this three-headed dragon, remember?"

Hawkril stumbled onto the rocks rising to the lip of the hollow, climbing to join Craer. Embra whisked the shield that had carried him back up into the fray, jabbing it into another neck.

The dragon recoiled, snatching its third head well away from Craer. Eyes narrowing, Embra struck it again with both shimmering shieldwedges. The dragon reared up, letting light back into the hollow and causing a fresh frantic turmoil among the trapped horses.

"Not a dragon long," Tshamarra murmured. "Could it be *the* Dragon, sent by the gods and destined to oppose the Serpent? And if it's come again, is the Serpent itself risen again, too? Can we spend our lives slaying that snake and never truly kill it?"

The Lady Silvertree shook her head. "This is neither that dragon nor a real dragon at all, I'm thinking. As for the Great Serpent, we can probably never slay it. There'll always be both Serpent and Dragon, but their power comes from the awe or fear or worship folk give them. Shatter the priesthood, and reduce fear of the Serpent to old tales, and the real Serpent won't be more than a big beast."

"Like this?" Tshamarra asked, waving at the rearing three-headed monster, now snapping furiously if gingerly at Embra's tormenting force-arrows. "I'd say this sort of big beast could destroy any Vale town, or even Sirlptar, if it got going!"

"Not this big," Embra snapped tensely. "Get down!"

From its great height the three-headed nightmare had done what she'd feared it might: surged forward in a clumsy pounce, trying to bring down and crush the flying things that were wounding it with its great bulk.

Hawkril and Craer dived away from the hollow, into the trees, and Embra's outflung arm sent the Lady Talasorn over backwards onto her shapely behind and whirling away, head over heels, down a muddy, leaf-cloaked slope into the wider forest.

She had a brief, confused glimpse of the Dwaer flaring into eye-searing brightness, trees toppling, a dragon-head—*Gods, 'tis as big as a small castle!*—striking at someone—Blackgult?—off to her right, and then the dragon screamed again, and all other sounds were swept away . . .

Her left arm hurt. She was lying on it, twisted into a huddled tangle around three leaning tree trunks, and someone was whispering anxiously, "Tash? Tash? Are you—?"

"Alive?" she replied, finding her mouth full of blood. "I'm not sure."

Craer's hand stroked her cheek tenderly. She reached up to hold his fingers and keep them there, leaning into his soothing touch with a contented murmur.

"What happened, lord of my heart?"

"Well, I—*what did you call me?*"

His voice was so swift with excitement that Tshamarra Talasorn felt a thrill of power. "Well," she purred, "lord of my bed, anyway."

He did not—quite—sigh, but the Lady Talasorn heard his disappointment, even over the faint rumble of Hawkril standing some way off, commenting in low tones, "There was a time when the bed would have been all you cared about, Longfingers."

Craer made no reply to that. Instead, he bent closer to Tshamarra and asked, "Can you move? Should I try to lift you? The battle's over."

"One of them, anyway," she said wryly. "I—Lift me. I seem to be wedged . . ."

As her knee was turned, she gasped in pain, and Craer snapped, "Embra, get over here!"

"Not yet, Craer," the Lady of Jewels snapped back. "Just hold her still—I'm busy."

"Graul and bebolt," Hawkril gasped. "How deep—?"

"I'll live," Blackgult said shortly, his voice tight with pain. "Get the beast dead first."

" 'Tis dead, or dying, Father," Embra replied. "See? It dwindles."

"Turn me," Tshamarra hissed to Craer. "I have to see."

The procurer's hands were tender, and therefore slow, but the Lady Talasorn was turned back to face the hollow in time to see the scaled, three-necked lump subside to the size of a cow—and a row of broken-off teeth, just the tips of dragonfangs—melt at the same rate from the punctured and battered breastplate of the Golden Griffon.

Hawkril was holding Blackgult up, though Embra's father was bent over and shaking with pain.

"Ribs, at the very least," the armaragor told his lady. "He's fading."

"Craer!" Embra snapped, without looking, as she strode toward Blackgult with the Dwaer flickering in her hand. Was its radiance more feeble? "Help Hawk. Get him lying down, *gently!*"

"A moment more," Blackgult gasped, holding up a staying hand. *"Look!"*

Such was the snap of command in that last word that the overdukes all turned to gaze at the same thing: the great three-headed dragon melting back into the dirty, much-hacked body of a man, lying sprawled on the lip of the hollow with a look of staring horror frozen forever on his face.

"The plague-magic," Embra said bitterly.

Blackgult nodded. "Some regain their proper shapes," he growled, trembling in Hawkril's hands. "Others do not."

He swayed, and even as Craer let Tshamarra fall back against a tree and sprang toward the man who'd once been his master, Blackgult groaned, bent double, and spewed forth blood of a hue none of them had ever thought to see out of a man. His head shifted horribly, sliding into a longer shape, a snout with teeth that became fangs before their horrified eyes, armor sliding askew as the flesh beneath it shifted and sank, becoming—

"Tash! To me!" Embra cried, the Dwaer flaming. "He'll try to use the Stone—*he's reaching for it!*"

Hawkril flung himself forward into a roll that mashed Blackgult's growing, reaching tentacle to the ground, pinning it among rocks and wet leaf-loam. Tshamarra Talasorn clambered up the tree she'd been leaning against, took two running steps, and collapsed with a scream of pain—and Craer plucked her up, staggering, and ran on, carrying her clumsily to where the Lady Silvertree was beginning to slowly walk in their direction, her eyes and concentration never leaving the man who'd sired her.

The Dwaer flared as she came, and Blackgult threw back his head and roared in pain as a sudden glow of magic washed over him. His armor fell away with a clatter, baring the scaled shoulders beneath. Bones writhed beneath that hide as new limbs burst forth, grew barbs, and expanded, reaching out . . . and out . . .

Hawkril wrestled with the tentacle beneath him, struggled to his feet, and lumbered toward Blackgult—as Embra hissed another spell that sent sparks racing over her father and banished his scales.

Craer fell heavily, pitching Tshamarra to the ground. She crawled over his fallen form and on, clawing her way across the forest. "I'm coming, Embra!" she cried—and caught her breath in horror as a tentacle raced toward her, sliding through the long-fallen leaves like a black, wet tongue.

"Craer!" she called—and her man groaned to his feet behind her, plucked her up by the hips, and staggered toward the Lady Silvertree, who was now enshrouded by the whirling radiance of another spell she was weaving.

As Embra's magic grew in brightness and started to blaze ruby-red, Blackgult roared in fresh agony, and grew many eyes. Grotesque and glistening, they sprouted all over him, of varying sizes but all staring in beseeching pain. The body sporting them slumped, turned a muddy hue, and many sucking mouths or holes opened in it, to the accompaniment of horrible wet sounds.

Embra hurled her spell a scant moment before Craer fell again and sent Tshamarra crashing into her, and as the two sorceresses rolled and tumbled together, the Dwaer spinning up out of Embra's grasp, the thing Blackgult had become roared in triumph or hopefulness, and surged forward like a beached seatusk, seeking to reach the glowing, hovering Stone.

Hawkril struck him, shoulder to monstrous bulk, and they crashed together in a shuddering tangle that sent Blackgult struggling through a nightmarish succession of forms. Jaws appeared, snapped, flowed, and were gone, eyes rose and fell atop tentacles and heads and dorsal ridges, tentacles and claws and talons sprouted and melted back into the ever-flowing flesh—and Craer flung himself into the heart of the amorphous body, both boots first.

The thing that had been Blackgult shuddered and wailed, a high and horrible wet fluting cry that sent its many jaws falling open and tentacled limbs collapsing back into shapelessness, and fell back.

It was still thrashing and roiling on the ground when two frantic hands closed together around the glowing Stone. Two pairs of blazing eyes met, and then turned with one accord to gaze at the ever-changing monster. Mouths murmured incantations in unison, hands shaped spells, and the Dwaer sang.

Radiance after rushing radiance burst over Blackgult and settled, and under their sway the slithering of shapes slowed and then halted, until it seemed like a puddle of flesh lay on the forest floor.

Flesh that slowly became pinkish again, and hairy, as it dwindled. The sorceresses went right on murmuring spells, advancing in careful unison as Hawkril and Craer drew warily back, until they knelt an arm's reach from the quivering flesh.

Slowly Embra extended her hand, the Dwaer in it, out and down to the pool of flesh . . . as if offering it. The incantations continued unbroken as the Stone spun very slowly in a grasp that gave it no such encouragement.

As the armaragor and procurer watched with wary eyes and half-drawn blades, the flesh seemed to shudder, and then bulge upward toward the Dwaer. Like an eyeless worm it rose, wriggling, and grew fingers, thinning itself into a human hand . . . and reaching forth to touch the Dwaer.

The Stone flashed, the pool of flesh seemed to shiver and clench into a wild, whirling variety of shapes . . . and then the hand led down into an arm, attached to a body with a familiar face . . . and Ezendor Blackgult was blinking at them, eyes like two coals in a shaking, sweat-drenched body that was his own. Human once more, he groaned, bent his head as the tears came, and collapsed onto his face, exhausted.

"Get up," Craer snapped, picking up the nearest piece of Blackgult's armor and tapping the sprawled, naked man with an air of disgust. "I don't see why you're weary—*I'm* the one who's been doing all the work!"

14

Riding Through Blood

Sparks raced around her, riding a surging power that left Maelra Bowdragon awed. Rushing magic swept her into its coils, whirling away the dark and narrow storeroom of magics that Uncle Multhas had always thought was his own little secret, in a torrent of air and crackling lightning that left her breathless.

When the chaos fell away, Maelra became aware that she was no longer crouching in the gloom of that hidden Bowdragon storeroom. She was somewhere dim that smelled of damp earth, somewhere she'd never stood before—but that was, yes, familiar. A place she'd visited as a sending: the abode of the Spellmaster of Aglirta . . . and there he was, standing in the shadows watching her.

Shivering with excitement, Maelra met the cold and knowing eyes of Ingryl Ambelter. She'd seen such soft smiles from men before—smiles that lingered on the sleek curves of her body, but always fled when they learned her heritage. She'd never seen one surmounted by such a deadly gaze, though.

Swallowing, she held out her armful of enchanted Bowdragon things—the mirrors and coffers and daggers she'd obediently stolen for this man a moment ago. One slid in her cradling grasp, and she shifted her arms hastily to avoid dropping it. This was real. She was truly here, somewhere underground near the river in Aglirta, far from home . . . and two short strides away from more power than she'd ever felt before. Her skin crawled at its awakened, pulsing presence.

"Come," the Spellmaster said with that same softly dangerous smile, holding out a beckoning hand and cradling the glowing Dwaer-Stone with the other. "There's much to do."

"Ah, aren't you going to . . . uh, yes. Of course," Maelra replied, hearing the faint scrape of a booted foot on stone behind her, and casting a quick glance over her shoulder.

Baron Phelinndar stood regarding her calmly, his armor gleaming and his sword raised—poised to plunge into her back! Yet already he was lowering it, and a Dwaer-Stone was glowing in his other hand.

Maelra whirled back to face Ambelter, to see if these men really possessed *two* Dwaerindim—but the Spellmaster's hand was now empty. Trying to keep her face expressionless but knowing Ambelter had seen her eyes narrow, she swallowed again and said, "Yes, we've much to do."

"My father and all of our horses are just *fine*," Embra said sharply. "Or so the Dwaer showed me, Craer—and believe me, it lets you feel as well as see."

The procurer held up a hand. "Pillory me not, Lady; I was merely pointing out that our mounts all appear . . . ah, restive."

Tshamarra sighed. "Well, wouldn't you be, Craer, if you were a horse?" She waved one slim hand. "Look around us!"

The choice view of Glarond they were enjoying at that moment included at least six clusters of carrion-crows, vultures, and worse. What was left of a corpse presumably lay at the heart of each squawking, pecking group—and more than one plume of smoke was rising from distant barns and farmhouses. The cottage nearest to them had already been burnt out, and now stood blackened, roofless, and deserted. Livestock wandered aimlessly, bawling their displeasure and loneliness from time to time—except when arrows whistling from stands of trees brought them thunderously down, and men raced out to hack at the twitching corpses, cut off legs or large hunks of rump and ribs, and hurried back to the trees again.

The only other living humans the overdukes had seen since leaving the forest had fled from them in terrified disarray, but the five had already learned to keep well away from woodlots and thickets. Evidently the good folk of Glarond were not too witless with fear to aim bows, and not too ammunition-poor to stint on loosing arrows at five mounted strangers.

Arrows hissed out of some trees now, arcing high into the air to thump and thud into the ditch, well short of overduchal horses—or torsos. "Are we this close to brigandry in Aglirta?" Craer snarled in disgust, turning in his saddle to glare at the dark stand of trees the shafts had come from.

"Evidently," Embra sighed. "Remember, Craer, it takes three generations of relative peace and order for folk to trust in kings and laws and such . . . and yon folk have seen barons change with the passing seasons, armies on the march, lawless magic hurled hither and thither, ceaseless talk of new rule in Flowfoam, Serpent-priests whispering in their ears every bebolten year—and now a madness and beast-curse that no one defends them against or tells them truth about. Be glad they've got bows and the wits left to use them!"

"Gah!" the procurer snapped, spurring his mount away. "You speak truth, I know, but I don't have to like it!"

Tshamarra rolled her eyes and called, "Rein in, Lord Idiot! When the *next* three-headed dragon comes, I want you right here at my side, so you can die with the rest of us!"

Craer shot her a disgusted look back over his shoulder—and reined in.

Embra gave Tshamarra a much more respectful glance, and murmured, "Impressive."

Whatever reply the Lady Talasorn may have been planning to make was lost forever in a sudden scream from the trees to her left. She turned to look, lifting her shield as swiftly as any warrior now, and beheld . . . more striding-to-nowhere folk in torn and soiled garb. These Aglirtans were quiet as they walked, but their shudderings and wild stares betrayed plague-madness.

"Don't be letting anyone bite you, I'm thinking," Craer said grimly, half-drawing his sword.

"Let's just keep riding," Hawkril growled. "There's nothing we can do for this many folk—except find the Serpent-priests and put a stop to their plague-spreading."

"While there's someone left alive in Aglirta, you mean?" Craer asked bitterly, his hand still on his sword.

They urged their horses to a faster pace, and the snorting beasts seemed eager to comply; firm hands on the reins were required to slow them from a gallop. More wandering humans shrank away at their approach—save for one man, more oblivious than the rest, who kept plunging into convulsions, rising again to walk normally, and then sinking down into spasms again. As the overdukes rode up, they saw him fail to straighten from his latest writhing, as hair—beast hair—suddenly sprouted on his body.

Craer hissed in disgust and drew his sword, but Embra snapped, "Craer, *stop!* I need this one captured. Hawk?"

"Arrow to your bow, Lady," he rumbled, spurring forward.

"What means he?" Tshamarra asked quickly. "I've heard those words before."

"Oh. Old lovers' saying of the Vale," Embra replied absently, her eyes on Craer turning to spring from the saddle on one side of the man, and Blackgult racing smoothly past to snatch the reins of the procurer's mount, while Hawkril reined in on the other side of the now-crouching, snarling man. "From an old ballad: 'Lady, I'll be the arrow to your bow/Command me lifelong, in all things' . . . and so on."

"Oh," the Lady Talasorn replied, almost wistfully.

Embra shot her a curious glance, and then looked swiftly around in all directions to make sure no one—and no *thing*—was getting ready to attack or pounce. Aside from obedient male overdukes, that is.

The man looked like a wolf, now, his transformation into beast-shape almost complete. And when he lowered his head and snarled threateningly at Hawkril, Craer deftly looped cord—a line he'd been carrying wrapped around his waist, belt-fashion—around the man's legs.

The man-wolf whirled around with a roar, snapping—and Craer shoved his sword broadside-on into its jaws, just as Hawkril caught it by the neck with both hands, straddled its back, and sat on it. The transformed man squirmed and thrashed. But Craer wound his line around all of his paws and then his snout, pulling the cord tight, and Hawkril kept him pinned . . . and it was clear that as long as they kept their positions, the man-wolf wasn't going anywhere.

"Nicely captured," Blackgult said, holding a snorting horse with either hand. He looked at Embra. "Want to practice, I presume?"

"Precisely." The Lady Silvertree held up the Dwaer, and said to Tshamarra, "I want you to ride my mind as I try this."

As the Talasorn sorceress nodded, Embra turned her head. "If it works, and we see another wolf, we'll try it again as you join me, Father. We have to know how to purge the plague, and practice doing it, until forcing folk back to their own shapes isn't a battle against the Dwaer but something we can do readily."

The plague in their captive was subtly different from the last one they'd felt in their own bodies . . . but having seen the man before he was forced out of his own shape helped, the two sorceresses discovered. Their memories of his proper self gave them something to move him toward as the Stone in their shared grasp forced the man-wolf through a dozen or so transformations. The Malady seemed to be watching them, shifting to minimize their success but having no place to hide, and eventually being driven down to . . . nothing.

When he was himself again, the plague-magic broken, the man stared at them in haggard, unshaven horror—and fainted.

Craer caught him by the simple tactic of being under the man as he collapsed. "Well," he snapped, wrestling the man into a sitting position, " 'tis a quieter thanks than some you've received."

Embra gave him a wry smile. "The next wolf we see, we must try this again, to see how we fare without knowing the proper human form we're trying to restore."

Craer rolled his eyes. "Exactly how many wolves am I going to have to cuddle for you?"

"How many fingers have you left to count with?"

Blackgult snorted as he handed Craer back the reins of his horse. "Now *that's* a waste of time, Embra: trying to trade witticisms with Lord Delnbone. I take it the only way of learning how to fight down the plague is the hard way—and through such battles coming to understand the Serpent-magics of the Malady well enough to break them?"

Embra nodded. "It . . . changes, each time I contact it. Except . . . ," she frowned, and added slowly, "when the infections have come from the same source. I think. I'm not sure yet, beyond knowing the differences are there and that the Malady seems to alter itself when assailed. So each battle's different, but one learns what to do—the same way armaragors master their weapons, I guess."

Hawkril swung up into his saddle. "You forgot one small but crucial part of achieving weapon mastery that must prevail through all battleblood practice: staying alive."

They rode on, practicing staying alive as they crossed the wooded ridges that kept this part of Glarond little visited by outlander merchants. It was a country of small farms, rolling hills, and unmarked lanes—but now held a wearying harvest of corpses and fearfully skulking Glarondans, though overduke-seeking arrows became fewer.

The five rode even more warily as their trail descended into broader valleys where more prosperous farms sprawled, but not a single cart or traveler did they meet. It was as if the land had been emptied, everyone rushing off downriver to Sirlptar to some festival or other, leaving their farms and shops and smithies to—

Wolves! As Craer and Hawkril, in the lead, rode around a bend where the trail curved between two hills crowned by gnarled everember trees, three panting farmers sprinted across the road—with a man-sized wolf loping hard on their heels!

Its jaws were agape, the hindmost farmer only just ahead of them as he crashed through a blackthorn bush, stumbled on uneven ground, and then staggered on.

Craer sprang from his saddle, right into the wolf's path. The beast blinked at this obliging apparition, shied aside as if to race around it, causing Craer's riderless horse to rear and then bolt, and then whirled in at this new arrival from one side, biting down—onto the procurer's sword, helpfully slammed flat, edge-on, into its jaws. Its strike bowled Craer over, and he rolled over on his shoulders snarling like a wolf himself, putting his boots into the beast's ribs to keep it from pinning him with its weight.

His toe-blades made it yelp—and then Hawkril was there, bounding from his own saddle to pounce on the beast. Wrapping an arm around its neck, he shoved aside Craer's sword and used his weight to roll the beast over on its back, putting an ungentle knee into those same ribs—the wolf yelped again—and then ramming his armored forearm between its jaws.

"Forefather!" he yelled in pain, as it bit down hard enough to crush his bracer deep into his skin. "This one's a right monster!"

Freed from his own rolling on the road, Craer bounded up and reached a hand in to swat the wolf hard on the end of its nose, breaking its bite and sending it into a helpless flurry of mingled sneezing and growling. Hawkril shifted his grip, getting both hands firmly around the shaggy throat, and bent the struggling body back over his knee . . .

"I can't—" Embra gasped, as Dwaer-light washed over the struggling bodies. "I can't find a man's mind at all, inside that, that . . . thing . . ."

"Daughter, that's a *real* wolf," Blackgult snapped, keeping his own firm hold on the Dwaer, "not a plague-borne monster!"

"*Graul!*" she gasped in horror, staring down at the wrestling bodies in the road as their horses danced and Blackgult held them back from fleeing by main strength. "What'll I—?"

Her father gave vent to an exasperated growl of his own, and did something to the Dwaer that made it burn in Embra's grasp. She caught her breath and hissed in pain, dropping it—and as it spun out of her hand to hang in midair, linked to the Golden Griffon's fingertips only by tiny crackling tongues of energy, something like a flash of white lightning burst well beyond the fray, spitting bolts back toward them.

A moment later, Craer was hurled back between the horses like a small, ragged ball, voice rising in fear as he spat an endless stream of curses. Hawkril crashed into the ditch by the roots of an everember tree, and the wolf was flung the other way.

"What—?" Tshamarra cried, looking wildly around for Craer as the Stone flickered in midair, raggedly lighting a sudden mist of its own spinning.

"Use the Dwaer to quiet the horses," Blackgult ordered her, "before the pack beasts get all the way back to Stornbridge and Craer's mount finds the next barony or tries to leap the Silverflow and the mountains beyond, hmm?"

Tshamarra gaped at him.

"Use it!" he roared into her face—and she shuddered, gulped, and reached out for the Dwaer . . . which obligingly drifted toward her hand.

Embra was already scrambling down from her saddle, the Dwaer forgotten. "Hawk? *Hawk!*"

"That's right," Craer announced sarcastically from behind them all, making Tshamarra gasp in relief and evoking a growl from Blackgult as her Dwaer-guidance wavered, "run to see if the man as big as a horse and covered in armor as thick as a castle door is hurt! Don't bother about the acrobatic and incredibly clever Craer Delnbone, hurled away through the trees in great peril to life and limb! Spare not a thought for the brilliant mind that tricked the Tersept of Launsrar out of four horses and the pay-coach they were hitched to! Or the Seneschal of Mrorn Castle of his beautiful daughter! Or"—the trudging procurer caught sight of Tshamarra's startled look, and added hastily—"well, perhaps we'll not mention her, after all. Perhaps we'll dwell instead on . . ."

"Catching the horses and belting shut our overclever lips for a change," Blackgult snarled, leaning down from his saddle in a jangling of shifting armorplates to shake the procurer down to his fingertips.

Nose to nose they regarded each other for a moment, ere the Golden Griffon let go his tight grip on the procurer's throat, dropping Overduke Delnbone back onto the road with the comment, "Besides, you must have relieved Launsrar of his pay-silver whilst spying on him for *me,* so the chests in that coach should have been mine—and I don't recall seeing one thin coin from them!"

"Father, *stop it!*" Embra screamed from the ditch behind Blackgult, bursting into tears. "You may've killed Hawkril—using lightning when he's all in armor, you *idiot!*—and all you can—"

One great hand rose from the armored form she was draped around and patted her shoulder reassuringly, before lifting to stroke her hair. "M'lady," a familiar voice rumbled, "I live. I—"

"Hawkril!" Embra flung her arms around her man, heedless of the bruises his armor dealt her, and let loose a flood of tears.

"—confess that I can't hear you, just now . . . my ears seem to be all a-roar . . . Is the wolf dead?"

Craer looked up from his examination of the smoking beast in the far ditch, wearing a grin that wouldn't have looked out of place on the face of the wolf itself, and said, "Very." Then the armaragor's words sank in, so he stopped talking, lifted his hand in a salute, and then made the circling, pointing-at-the-ground hand gesture Aglirtan warriors use to denote death.

Hawkril lifted an arm out of Embra's swarming embrace to return the salute, and Craer's eyes, following the movement, found themselves looking straight into an unfamiliar face in the trees beyond. A dark-eyed, intent man, wearing—Serpent-robes!

The procurer's favorite dagger was in his hand in an instant, and out of it in the next, with a second fang coming to his fingertips even before he burst into a racing sprint that took him across the road, made Tshamarra's horse rear in startlement and Embra gape at him, and gained the far bank at a dead run, bouncing from tree to tree in his snarling haste to get to where—

—the Serpent was choking his slow way to the ground, with the hilt of Craer's dagger under his chin and a look of hurt disbelief in his eyes. Craer used his second blade to slash at the man's fingers, spoiling any desperate last spell the priest might have been trying to cast—and then saw a shimmering in the air beyond the tree the priest had been crouching behind.

There was a face in that roiling of the air, but Craer saw only the coldly furious regard of one eye ere the shimmering turned and shrank in on itself, collapsing into—

Nothing but a spark or two, as Craer savagely plunged his blade through the air where it had been, snarling and hacking, hacking, hacking . . .

"Craer?" The voice behind him was Tshamarra's, and it was low but laced with alarm.

The procurer whirled around, dancing to one side out of long habit in case someone was planning to put a shaft or lance through him as he turned. His lady stood alone, the Dwaer spinning above her left shoulder, shaking her head with a wry smile on her face. "Did you see who it was?"

Overduke Delnbone shook his head. "A man, not someone I know. He saw me. Another Serpent-priest, of course, probably this one's superior. That was a talking magic, wasn't it?"

Tshamarra nodded, and then embraced him. As their lips met, his hands tightened on her hips, and she murmured something wordless and held him tighter, lips working against his, until—

"I can't think any of this is calming the horses," Blackgult observed calmly from just behind the Lady Talasorn.

She stiffened, and Craer lifted his mouth from hers to give his onetime lord master a rather cold look. Blackgult crooked an eyebrow—and then grinned like a pranksome lad and turned away.

A startled Craer saw Hawkril smiling at him from the road, and Embra sighing and crooking a beckoning finger. The Dwaer floated to her, and Tshamarra turned swiftly in the procurer's arms, feeling it move—and then relaxed. "Lord Blackgult," she said after a moment, her voice holding a clear warning, "I shall devote some time, as we ride on, to considering what's most suitable to say to you."

"But of course," the Golden Griffon replied with a courteous bow, as he took the reins of his horse and prepared to mount. "I'd expect nothing less—and my as-yet-unspoken reply awaits *you*."

"Oh, thank the Three," Embra observed sarcastically to the cloud-studded sky. " 'Tis wonderful to discover my father, under his armor, fame, and years of swaggering wooing, is just another Craer."

"Just?" Craer demanded indignantly. "*Just?* Lady Embra, I begin to regret deeply that I ever broke into your bedchamber to steal your gowns, I do!"

"No," Hawkril rumbled, "you just regret that we got caught. I don't, though." He grinned at his lady, and added unnecessarily, "I can hear again."

Embra looked at Tshamarra, and the two sorceresses rolled her eyes together.

"Bowdragons have always been masters of magic," Maelra answered the Spellmaster, a trifle stiffly. "We were archmages in Arlund before there *was* an Aglirta, kingless or otherwise."

That earned her his soft smile. "How nice," he purred, in a tone that was anything but. "Yet you'd do well to remember that a tradition of sorcery and mage-lore, while vital to all who work magic, means nothing to the accomplishments of any one practitioner. Do the Wise rule realms, or advise kings daily at court, or dictate policies by their very presence and feared powers?"

He strode across the room, and then turned and snapped, "No. 'Tis archmages who can truthfully claim such accomplishments. 'Twas an archmage that made *this*," he added, lifting the Dwaer, "and now an archmage wields it—alongside a baron."

Those last three words sounded like a hasty addition to Maelra, and no doubt they did to both of her hosts, given the way Ambelter flushed and the Baron Phelinndar strode swiftly to his side, to lay a firm hand on the Dwaer.

"In short, young Bowdragon, many may prance and take airs in their attempts to gather importance and to cow warriors and petty rulers. But those who work magic know better: beyond our ability to guide and harness the forces we call 'magic,' we're none of us special. We're simply masters of greater or lesser amounts of technique, experience—and power."

The Spellmaster made the Dwaer flame, causing Phelinndar to flinch and shrink back, favoring Ambelter with a dark look. "*This* is power, little one," Ambelter continued, ignoring the baron. "With it, we're mighty; but even without it, as men of Aglirta, we've more experience and expertise in the hurling of spells and of their precise consequences and effects than all of your uncles put together. Your sire and his brothers practice magic at leisure, exploring as they will—but the good baron and I confront magic in battle almost daily, and constantly work with it, straining spells to their utmost and reshaping them for new uses. Bowdragons may master magic out of pride, and take the time to hone castings and details we cannot . . . But if we make a single mistake, 'twill mean our deaths—and yet here we are, very much alive."

He took a step toward her. "If our paths are to run together for the nonce, 'tis best that you respect our power properly, so obedience to us will become your watchword, and pride in your heritage be set in its rightful place: a comfort to you, but not a throne you can relax upon, or a mirror you can sneer at yourself in. *You* should rightly take pride only in what you alone have done—and the way to win such pride is to follow our orders, and in that doing come to be someone your uncles will regard with awe."

The Spellmaster glanced at the baron, a silent signal that brought Phelinndar forward until they stood side by side once more, each with a hand on the Dwaer-Stone. "Watch, and taste just a little of the power we wield," Ambelter added, as the Stone flared into brilliance that should have blinded Maelra, but instead somehow surrounded her with white, gleaming light—as if she was enveloped in clear, interlocking gemstones large enough to meet above her head.

She gasped in wonder, narrowing her eyes in case this glory might become a flash to blind her—for she'd truly be an obedient slave to these two men then, if they desired her so—but instead each facet around her kindled an inner flame that built until it became a different scene of somewhere in Asmarand. Countrysides seen from castle ramparts, seacoasts where boats wallowed past on rolling waves, mossy and overgrown ruins in deep forests, dark fastnesses lit by flickering torches, busy markets with cobbled streets . . . all of them windows onto living vistas where birds flew, winds blew, and folk strode and waved and pointed.

She cried out in pleasure, seeking to peer at several scenes at once. But even as she did everything shimmered, the scenes flowing into their constituent hues, and she heard Ingryl Ambelter cry out—with anger and surprise, not pleasure.

"What is it?" Baron Phelinndar snapped, his voice somehow distant and echoing.

Ambelter was closer. Maelra could feel as well as hear his reply as he said, "*Another* Dwaer, very close by! We must—"

Then their converse shifted, plunging into a bright but private thread of thoughts, not voices, that Maelra could not follow. She could still feel, though, through the rushing of shifting radiances and flowing, swirling power—and she beheld, across a dimness that could only be a place where the power of the Dwaer was not present, a rising, rushing arc of power akin to what she was caught up in, but somehow subtly different . . .

That must be the other Dwaer, or rather its power unleashed—and *this,* here beside her, rising in urgency and brightness, must be whatever Ambelter and Phelinndar felt they "must" do with their Dwaer to . . . to . . .

Lash out, in a burst of ruby-red and defiant power that shook Maelra with its might even as it thrilled her . . . clawlike bolts that slashed at that other flood, stabbing across the darkness between like fingers of lightning, seeking to disrupt!

Seeking, and succeeding. With a thrill that left her gasping, Maelra Bowdragon watched that great arc of power split apart, riven asunder to thrust streamers and sprays of energy in all directions. A backlash slammed into the flow around her, thrusting her up above the chaos of wrestling energies. Such *power!* Such . . . By the Three, to be able to ride this, across all Darsar like a roving dragon, slaying wherever it glanced . . .

That other Dwaer-flow was shattered entirely now, curling in all directions with a mighty grandeur, turning, turning . . .

A scrying-whorl burst apart, shedding spinning arms with a fury that rocked the cavern where a lone figure with a surprised and melting face crouched over it. Even as the whorl-blast plucked him from his feet and hurled him back, the Dwaer in his hand spat forth a flood of sparks that became stabbing spears of lightning—bright bolts that raced all over the grotto, glancing back amid showers of shattered stone, to stab through him.

With a scream that was more rage than pain, the ever-shifting figure sprang into the air, using the Dwaer that was searing his hands as a flying steed to take him up above the lancing death. Smokes trailed from his blackened body as he flew, snarling as he fought down his agonies to heal himself and master the roiling energies of his disrupted Stone once more. Whirling across the cavern he came, fighting, fighting . . . and prevailing.

Whoever had struck at him—and 'twas not the Silvertree lass, but some other—would taste the fire of a Dwaer wielded by someone who knew how to use it! The Koglaur threw back a head that sported only a mouth to gasp away pain and draw in deep gulps of the lightning-reeking air, and came to a halt, floating in the air high above the cavern. Smoke curled in the light of the last few lightning bolts, as he sucked them back into the Dwaer in his hands until it quivered, as red as blood and as angry as he was.

He turned his eyeless head as if he could see—or smell, in the sharp smoke-stink—his foe. Turned, stiffened, and acquired a grim smile. Slowly he lifted the Dwaer in both hands.

There were two, both with hands on the same Stone. Well, 'twas time to let them burn! Right about—*now!*

The world flashed and splashed, and Maelra Bowdragon was suddenly back in the Spellmaster's lair, its flagstone floor rocking under her boots as wild lightnings and showers of sparks burst from the Dwaer in Ambelter's hands.

Yes, the Spellmaster's alone—the armored form of Baron Phelinndar hurtled away from that outburst of wild magic with a raw cry of terror and pain.

The very air crackled and flowed, forcing its shuddering through Maelra's body—and suddenly she wanted nothing so much in life as to be far, far away from it, somewhere safe from this dark cave where magic that could blast castles apart could at any moment veer a trifle and make scattered ashes of Maelra Bowdragon . . .

She whirled around, to flee she knew not where, and from behind her came the roar she'd feared and expected: the sound of Ingryl Ambelter's voice raised in anger. Wordless, wet and bubbling anger, as if he was spewing forth soup or wine and trying to snarl at her around it—a sound that lent her even more fear and swiftness.

Panting, she raced three steps before something terribly cold caught her wrist and shocked her into instant immobility, frozen in mid-run with one leg raised high and the other trailing behind.

She'd have toppled but for that icy grip—the one that swung her around to face the Spellmaster's angry face. "Don't you ever *dare!*" he spat—the light of unchecked magic spilling out of his eyes like bright smoke, hiding them from her, and the same roiling radiances spurting from his mouth like liquid flame.

Those bright energies washed over her frozen face, and with a helpless foreboding Maelra felt something more than the tingling of wild Dwaer-power that had already stirred her loins and set every hair on her body standing out like so many whisper-thin spikes. A horrible creeping sensation rose within her, an invading *something* that stole right through her, alive and aware, *looking* at her with cold amusement from within as it came . . .

Unable even to scream, Maelra reeled inwardly, sick and terrified. *So this is what it feels like to be doomed.*

Ambelter must be using his Dwaer to force himself on her, to lurk in her body and spy on her from within . . . Well, so much for her fears that either Ambelter or Phelinndar might rape her; would any physical violation be much more than a dull irritation after *this?*

She stared into Ingryl Ambelter's gloating face, still unable to see anything but flames of wild magic where his eyes and mouth should be—and as she watched, his horrific glee melted into the likeness of a grinning skull, two tiny stars of cold flame twinkling in its eyesockets as it grinned at her.

Those eyes that were no longer eyes *looked* at her, and Maelra felt the amused and fell regard of an old and wise intellect. Then one eye distinctly winked, and the leering skull melted away and was gone, leaving the angry face of the Spellmaster of Aglirta behind it, his dark eyes snapping as he shouted, "Obey me, stupid wench! On your knees, and be glad I don't just break your pretty but useless little neck!"

And Maelra Bowdragon went to her knees, lifting her hands in pleading supplication as if Ambelter was an altar of the Three Gods. Her reverence turned his shouting to glee in an instant, though his eyes still danced with anger, and he recovered himself as the lightnings faded and the room returned to normal.

Then he waved a hand, and the armored, silent men who'd stood around the walls like statues took a pace forward in unison. Maelra stared at them wildly, wondering what new horror was to be visited upon her. She'd thought they *were* statues. Their eyes stared back blankly, out of faces whose flesh was twisted and drooping, like melted and then rehardened wax.

15

Lessons Grimly Learned

*E*mbra Silvertree shook her head to clear it, the Dwaer round and hard and familiar in her hands, the only reassuring thing in all this blood and battle.

It had been two deserted hamlets and the ashes of one burned cart with gnawed-to-the-bone horses still harnessed to it later when they'd stopped to rest. She'd barely reached some handy bushes for privacy when the attack came.

It was sudden and almost blinding, like bright ruby fire inside her head. She gasped, staggered, and then . . . somehow . . . mastered her Stone once more, feeling as winded and bruised as if someone had punched and kicked her repeatedly.

Emerging from the bushes in a sort of weary daze, she watched her fellow overdukes standing by their horses—looking at her expectantly.

Three Above, when did I become Lord Master of this motley band of heroes?

The Three forebore to answer that silent question, and Embra smiled grimly and told her companions, "Glarondar. As fast as we can. If 'tis at the other end of this road, as it always has been, someone there has a Dwaer, and is using it right now. Probably the same someone who just tried to wrest control of this Stone away from me. And before you ask: I'm fine."

"A Serpent!" Craer snarled, leaping into his saddle.

"Ambelter!" Hawkril growled, swinging himself up onto his horse.

"Phelinndar!" Tshamarra insisted, clawing her way up onto her own mount.

"Anyone in Aglirta," Blackgult suggested with a quiet smile, his battered armor clanging as he leaned down a hand from horseback to assist his daughter.

The moment Embra was mounted, Craer spurred his horse into a gallop.

"Ho, there!" Hawkril called. "How fast d'you want to stick your fool head into the *next* Serpent ambush, hey?"

"Might as well be swift, so Embra can slay them the faster and we can get on," Craer called over his shoulder.

"Hear me: Even if we ride these poor beasts until they fall over, 'twill be next morning at the very least before we see Glarondar."

"So we'll steal fresh horses," Craer replied airily. His horse snorted and shied under him, as if in answer to his words—but really to avoid stepping on a dead horse sprawled in the trail, wearing arrows and surrounded by the blood left behind by the scavengers that had torn open its belly and plucked out its eyes. A skull and a few scattered bones beside it bespoke the fate of its rider.

"Well, this one's free for the taking," Hawkril observed. "Hey, Longfingers?"

Craer snarled and dug his boots into the flanks of his weary mount again.

Dwaer-power gripped the Baron of Glarond with viselike fingers.

"Tremblings and protests aren't reassuring to the good folk of Glarondar," Arthroon said firmly. "They much prefer smiles and a show of reverence to the Great Serpent to come. So you, my good and obedient Baron, will give them that."

A sudden surge of pain and a forcible trip to his knees in front of the gently smiling priest reminded the terrified baron that he was utterly under the control of the Dwaer. Now it was forcing him up again, past the ornate window that was displaying nightfall drawing down over Glarondar, to the mirror.

"Smooth out the wrinkles and square the shoulders, there's a good baron," the priest purred, as the magic suddenly let go of Glarond's arms. He gaped at his reflection, and then almost frantically brushed and tugged and smoothed, turning side-on to better judge his appearance.

Lord of the Serpent Belgur Arthroon nodded approvingly, took up his snake-headed staff, and indicated the door. "Open it, bold Baron Glarond, and show your people how devoutly you worship the Serpent."

The baron hastened to obey, as a drum started to beat in the courtyard below.

"Ah, we're just in time for the drinking of the plague-wine," Arthroon observed, prodding baronial shoulders with his fanged staff. "Down to the courtyard, and kneel to the priest serving wine there."

Helplessly, the baron started down the stairs, fixing a smile onto his face before the Dwaer could do it for him. Smiling like a snake, Arthroon followed him down into the rising chants and quickening drumbeats. It sounded as if all Glarondar had come to join in worship—and service—to the Serpent.

All fools, and all doomed. Yet if one was a priest of the Serpent, life was good . . . and could only get better.

The spears came down to bar his way. "Your name, and business in Flow-foam?"

"Suldun Greatsarn, loyal warrior of the King, reporting back to His Majesty under royal command to do so," growled the grim, exhausted man in mud-smeared and battered armor.

"Whether you are or are not a king's warrior, I very much doubt if he'll see you if you try to enter the inner rooms of the palace dressed like that," the guardcaptain told him coldly.

Suldun lifted an eyebrow—and then took a pace away from the guards, back down the steps. Spears swung around to menace him, so he descended below the guards' reach, and took a horn from his belt.

Its call brought a dozen warriors racing down the steps, swords drawn. The shieldsar who led them glared at the guardcaptain. "What're you doing with a royal horn?" he snapped.

The grim officer waved at the bedraggled and helmless figure down the steps. "Nothing, for I have none. *He* sounded it."

The shieldsar's head swung around. "And who are you, brig—oh. My pardon, Greatsarn. Come up! Our orders are to take you straight to the King at any hour!"

Suldun bowed his head and mounted the steps past the guardcaptain's frozen face, gently pushing aside spearpoints to do so.

He was very weary, but the shieldsar's guards practically swept him up in their enthusiasm and haste, rushing him through guarded doors, along back passages, and through more guarded doors, until they arrived quite suddenly at an unmarked door guarded by warriors in glittering plate armor, and stopped.

The shieldsar and the officer commanding this doorguard bowed solemnly to each other, and the shieldsar and his men withdrew. The gleaming officer regarded Suldun expressionlessly for a moment, then opened the latch of the door and waved the bedraggled knight through.

The small, narrow room inside had no other doors and rather sparse furnishings, but was afire with the first rays of sunset spilling their gold through two tall, narrow windows onto a manyshields board on the table between King Castlecloaks and the bard Flaeros Delcamper.

As the door closed behind Greatsarn, both looked up, and Raulin smiled, hooked a third chair out from under the table with his boot, and said heartily, "Sit down, Suldun. Your look at the Vale appears to have been less than leisurely. Tell us!"

Greatsarn waved warningly at the bard and the five glittering-armored guards ranged around the walls of the room, but the king just grinned, propped his elbows among the miniature forest of carved, spired manyshields pieces, and commanded, "Speak freely."

Suldun sighed, and said, "Your Majesty, I know of no soft way to say this: Widespread violence, death, and unrest now rule the kingdom."

There was a sudden stillness in the room, but King Castlecloaks merely nodded and gestured for more, so Greatsarn unhappily added, "The Blood Plague seems everywhere, even in Sirlptar—and so are the Serpent-priests, preaching that they can end the plague if the people support them . . . support them, that is, in slaying you and all your nobles and courtiers. They gather armies, promising immunity from the Malady to all who fight under their banner, and prepare to march on Flowfoam."

"Again," Flaeros sighed. "And who've we left to defend it *this* time?"

A guard coughed. The bard and the king looked up at the sound, in time to see that guard give them a menacing smile—and drive the point of his sword through the throat of another guard.

That startled victim toppled to the floor, gurgling, and all of the other glittering-armored guards grew smiles, drew steel, and advanced on the three aghast men around the manyshields table.

The guard commander looked at his king over the glittering point of his drawn sword and said almost gently, "Not us, kingless—and soon to be lifeless—fools. *We* serve the Serpent."

The dawn mists were racing across the fields like hurrying ghosts when the Overdukes of Aglirta rode into Glarondar.

Folk gave them fearful or sidelong glances as their exhausted horses plodded between outlying inns and cottages along what had become a good wagon road some hours back. A stone gate announced the formal edge of the town, and a confused, sleepy crowd of armed men were milling about in its arch.

"Smiles of the Three," Embra murmured, "someone's armed the farmers and shopkeepers. Craer, guard your tongue!"

Hayforks and scythes waved in hands obviously unused to wielding them. Men in smocks and homespun crowded fearfully together with hireswords in motley armor whom most barons would have termed "brigands" at a glance—and all of them shrank before the curt orders of officious men wearing . . . Serpent-robes!

"Embra," Craer muttered, "I don't think riding right into this waiting wall of Glarondans is a wise—"

A priest shouted an order and pointed at the overdukes. There was a general roar—and a thrum of bowstrings. Blackgult flung out his shield in front of Embra's horse, which promptly reared—as a handful of shafts banged against armor and shields and glanced away.

"Good," Craer said, wheeling his mount, "they're terrible archers. Let's get out of here before—"

Blackgult erupted in a roar and spurred his mount forward, flinging away his shield to stand tall in his stirrups and swing his sword with both hands in great wild slashes of the air.

"Gods, he's gone witless!" the procurer yelped—in the instant before he fell silent in horror and gaped at Tshamarra.

The Lady Talasorn was also upright in her saddle. Unlike Blackgult, she was arched over backwards, and an arrow stood out of her breast—or rather, a serpent as rigid as an arrow. As Embra and Hawkril both snapped curses, she reeled and fell back over the high cantel at the rear of her saddle. Craer screamed and spurred toward her.

Embra got there first. Hooking an arm around Tshamarra to keep her from falling off her horse, she lifted her Dwaer and blasted the serpent-arrow to smoke. The frantic procurer saw its head vanish down to tumbling fangs, which fell from Tshamarra's breast as he reached for her.

"Hawk! Get my father!" the Lady Silvertree shouted, eyes like flames—and something roared out of the Stone that swept the town gate clear of men, Serpent-robed or otherwise. They were flung against nearby buildings moments before the raving Golden Griffon would have ridden straight into their leveled forks and spears, and the brief, wet chorus of their thudding landings was thunderous and sickening.

Ezendor Blackgult crowed in triumph and flourished his blade, while

Hawkril rode hard at him from behind. There was a wet gash on the Golden Griffon's face, purple-edged around his welling blood . . . *Graul*, a serpent-arrow must have sliced into him!

Embra mastered her anger long enough to spray lightnings at bows and faces she could see behind them, on balconies of the tall houses of Glarondar just inside the gate, and then turned her attention to Tshamarra and the gabbling Craer.

The Lady Talasorn's face was purple, and there was froth in her mouth. Craer screamed something wild and wordless at Embra, and she snapped, "Keep her in her saddle and keep her breathing—don't let her choke on that, but *don't* let her bite you! Get going back the way we came!"

Embra almost tossed Tshamarra to the procurer, who made a startled, strangled sound as his stricken lady ended up draped over his head, and turned her attention back to Hawkril and her father.

The armaragor had just clapped a hand onto Blackgult's elbow and spun him around, which brought his sword slicing over Hawkril's head. Hawkril caught hold of it and punched Blackgult hard in his armored gut, forcing the older man to let go his blade and try to be sick, all down the armorplates he was beginning to shed.

The Griffon snarled, or tried to, as Hawkril wrestled their mounts around in a wide turn and got them headed back toward Embra. Blackgult went on roaring and ineffectually beating Hawkril's arm with his fists, but the armaragor caught hold of the baldric-strap that crossed Blackgult's breast under now-missing armorplates, and hauled him onward by main strength.

Embra frowned, reached out with the Dwaer, and put her father to sleep.

He slumped onto Hawkril's arm, and as the two armored men galloped on, the armaragor looked up at Embra to reassure himself that she was the cause of Blackgult's collapse. "What now, Em?"

"I believe 'tis called 'retreat in haste,' " the Lady of Jewels replied, pointing at the dwindling horses of Craer and Tshamarra. "Catch them up as fast as you can, and get them stopped. I must heal Tash *very* swiftly, or we'll lose her."

The armaragor nodded and spurred past, growling, "Why exactly were we in such a hurry to get here?"

Embra sighed and urged her mount after him, spinning a Dwaer-shield against arrows for herself. "Why, indeed?"

. . .

"Turn right, along that lane!" the Lady Silvertree shouted, seeing a farm track branch off into the trees of a large woodlot. "Turn—"

Of course they couldn't hear her. She used the Dwaer to snap the same command into all their ears—and saw the heads of both Tshamarra and her father lift groggily in response. They turned, and she Dwaer-twisted her shield into a great cloud of mist to hide where they'd gone from anyone following, after risking a brief glance over her shoulder. A few horses were just emerging from the gate, bared steel glittering on their riders . . .

"A leisurely overduchal grand promenade down the Vale, to be sure," she murmured bitterly, heading down the lane.

It sprouted smaller side trails as it wound through the trees, a small creek meandering to the right and farms to the left. Down the second trail—Embra used the Dwaer to give directions again—was a larger wood. If a lane entered it, there must be at least a woodcutter's clearing they could use. She told Craer to stop when he found one that didn't have dogs and hostile folk in it, and get Tshamarra down to the ground and lying quiet there, as quick as he could.

A few moments of hard riding later she saw a dim glade, an open place where trees met overhead. Craer and Hawkril were wrestling saddlebags off horses therein like madmen, and then shouting and slapping each beast in turn to make it gallop on and away.

They caught at the head of her own horse as she hauled hard on the reins to bring it to a halt, almost making it sit right back and fall over in its weariness.

"Down, my lady!" Hawkril cried, snatching her down into his arms.

Embra clutched the Dwaer. "Careful!"

"Oho!" he rumbled. "Hear that, Craer? She wants us to start being *careful* now! At last!"

"Too bebolten late," the procurer hissed, his face white with anger and worry. "She's dying, Em! *Do* something!"

The Lady of Jewels ran forward into the green gloom. Blackgult sat muttering on the ground beside a small, still form lying on a heap of wood shavings that stretched to several woodpiles beyond. Tshamarra's breathing was a wet, liquid sound, and her eyes were clouded over and milk-white.

Embra swallowed. "I'll try," was all she could think of to say, as she lifted the Dwaer.

Belgur Arthroon looked up suddenly from his leisurely morning feast, his head arrowing forward like that of a snake. The Baron of Glarond managed—just—not to shiver at the sight.

"A Dwaer!" the Lord of the Serpent snapped, eyes afire. "*Very* near!"

He rose in such haste that most of the table's contents spilled onto the floor, but he spared them not a glance as he pointed at the most capable hireswords the Church of the Serpent had been able to find, hereabouts, and the most dangerous of his underpriests, too—even Fangbrother Khavan, a dog too terrified to be disloyal. "Come!" he ordered them all. "There's something we must seize."

"Uh, Scaled Master?" Khavan stammered. "T-the baron?"

"Stay with him," Arthroon snapped, "and obey him, for his orders will be my own!" He lifted his Dwaer meaningfully and then hurried out, the men he'd beckoned clumping and clattering after him.

As they reached the hall below, he made his first silent urging with the Dwaer, causing the baron to turn to Khavan and say, "I've named Lord Arthroon my successor here in Glarond, should anything happen to me. He's ordered me to tell you to punish me freely, if I disobey you in the smallest way. Of course, if you act against his wishes, I'll order you slain in his name."

The Fangbrother looked surprised, and Arthroon watched him through the baron's eyes long enough to hear him say, "Well, then, Glarond, serve me that roast from the table—and then get down on your belly like a rat and eat up every bit of food that's fallen to the floor. You are forbidden to use your hands when doing so."

"*Yes,* Lord," the baron gasped, whirling toward the roast.

Arthroon shook his head, smiled, and left them to it. By then, his swift strides had carried him to where men were scrambling to ready a horse.

"Leave it, and come," he ordered. "We'll walk—'twon't be far. Out yon gate. Priests of the Serpent, form a ring around me, warriors to the outside."

When they were walking swiftly together, a storm of robes and armored men that split the gaping Glarondans like a bared blade as it streamed toward the gate, he snapped, "Heed, men of the Serpent! Stint not in use of your spells in the fray to come. We must surround our foe, and hurl all the battle-magic we have, upon my signal! No spell is too deadly, and—if you'd like to live to see it—nothing need be saved for the morrow!"

"Lie easy, Tash," Embra murmured, frowning over the glowing Dwaer. Beneath it, Tshamarra's bared breast rose and fell, the venom rising out of the gashes made by the serpent-arrow's fangs, bubbling forth dark and glistening. "Easy, now . . ."

"I–" Tshamarra gasped, eyes still clouded and unseeing. "I'm on fire!"

A sudden convulsion made her jerk and thrash her limbs, and from where he was standing bending over them both Craer burst out, "Embra, can't you *do* something?"

"Yes," Embra told him crisply, "and so can you. Get out of here and stand guard against the Glarondans you *know* are coming after us, and leave me alone to do what I have to do. This isn't easy, you know: I have to understand how the venom works to learn how to drive it out, and then banish what it's done. If I just attack the poison, I'm using the Dwaer only as searing fire–against Tash's blood, and inside her body!"

"Come," Hawkril rumbled firmly, taking his friend by the shoulder. "You go stand guard that way, along that track, and I'll go yonder, where the lane curves by those trees."

The procurer nodded reluctantly, then bent down quickly and kissed Embra's shoulder. "Thank you, Em," he whispered, and was gone.

Embra shook her head, smiled–and then pounced on Tshamarra as the Lady Talasorn convulsed again, moaning and jerking her limbs violently.

Wrestling with the smaller woman, Embra lost her smile swiftly. The Blood Plague and the venom were at war with each other inside Tash, and Dwaer or no Dwaer, Embra hadn't the barest beginnings of any idea how to stop the damage both were doing.

She plucked up the edge of Tash's undone leather bodice and thrust it between the teeth of the Talasorn sorceress to keep her from biting her own tongue. More venom bubbled forth.

Ever so carefully, with the point of her belt-knife, Embra made a small cut on her own forearm, let her blood drip onto the largest wood chip within reach, and then used another sliver of wood to transfer some of the venom from Tshamarra to her blood. As they swirled together with the faintest puff of vapor, she slapped her hand down on her Dwaer, cast a quick glance around to make sure no woodcutter or lurking Serpent-priest was approaching, and then worked a spell that took her down, down . . .

. . . into the hot red pool where the venom was spreading, curling out like smoke into the ruby sea from the first oily ropes of its arrival. Thus the poison changed the blood, and so it spread, changing this, and that . . .

But how was the plague changing both blood and venom? Surfacing from her magic into the relative brightness of the glade and blinking around again to make sure no peril approached, Embra took Tshamarra's own knife, made a similar cut on Tash's arm, used another wood chip to add this new blood to the mix, and went down into the tiny ruby sea again to watch.

Ruby sea and sky, all one, and this purple, heavy hue must be the plague—or rather, what plague did to blood, for around it the rest of Embra's blood was turning the same hue, crumbling into the spreading darkness with silent, frightening speed . . .

With the Dwaer she risked trying to twist the blood-mix, thus—and did something that made the wood chip shudder. Hastily she stopped, and instead strove to fight the darkness by changing it to match some of the blood it hadn't reached yet. The darkness thinned and shrank, and triumphantly she repeated the process, eating away at the still-spreading purple gloom again and again until it was reduced to a tiny mote. No matter how she tried to alter that mote, it remained, spreading forth again and again—until at last, in rising anger, she burned it with a tiny burst of Dwaer-fire . . . and it vanished, leaving only untainted blood behind. Venom and plague were both gone.

She'd done it!

Embra sat back on her heels and snarled wordless triumph at the leaves high overhead. Then she leaned forward to use the Dwaer on her friend—and was startled to see a tiny wisp of flame escaping from Tshamarra's lips, blackening the leather as it hissed past.

Frantically Embra called up the power of the Dwaer and dove "into" Tash, shaking her head. "Sarasper was the healer," she muttered. "I'm more like a chambermaid who only knows where to hurl buckets of water to clean by crude rinsing, and naught else."

There was no one there to hear her but the silent Tshamarra and her father, who'd come awake with the banishing of the plague from the sorceress. He looked sharply up at Embra with eyes that seemed to see nothing, and announced, "Much cleansing is needed before the Vale can be what it was. If the Vale can ever be what it was."

"You," Ingryl Ambelter told Maelra with a smile, "are going to Flowfoam for us." The Spellmaster swayed slightly as Dwaer-magic crackled in the air around him. The melt-faced men leaned forward, as if lured by it.

"I need you to fetch me some bones from *there*," Ambelter explained sweetly, as if to an idiot child, "and bring them back *here*. Oh, and kill the King while doing so, and carry his crown back to us, too."

"Some bones?" Baron Phelinndar frowned. "What magic're *they* for?"

"A traditional weaving," Ambelter replied soothingly. "Part of being Spellmaster. The crown, my dear Baron, is for *you*."

He turned back to Maelra. "Well, my dear? 'Twill be dangerous, but we'll both be with you, via spells, to guide and warn; you needn't be frightened."

Though she knew his reassurances must be false, Maelra's heart leaped with excitement. "When do I start?" she asked eagerly—and saw Phelinndar's eyes narrow.

Ambelter's excitement, however, matched her own. Nodding in satisfaction, he strode forward, put a hand to the bodice of her gown, and tore it down and away from her in one great wrench.

She looked at him with her great dark eyes, trying to read what lay behind his own fierce gaze. His eyes were on hers, not on her bared body. Hurriedly she slipped her arms out of the rag that remained, to stand before him nude but for her boots.

He was not standing and surveying her—though the baron was—but was already whirling away from her to snatch and tug plates of armor from one of the melted-faced men.

Turning back to Maelra with a battered and stained shoulder-archplate in his hands, he regarded her slender hips coolly, nodded, and held it out to her, to put on.

With a rustling of leaves, Craer Delnbone thumped down into the clearing, fresh blood glistening on his sword. He waved at Embra and called cheerfully, "Visitors! See?"

When Embra looked up, he waved his bloody sword and ran back into the trees, heading back to his tree-limb perch to await the arrival of the next hurrying Serpent-band.

"Back to the merry slaughter once more," he murmured, wiping his sword on the moss of the nearest tree trunk.

Embra watched the procurer go, her lips growing thin, and then turned and snapped, "Father!"

Her father was plague-addled; the arrow's venom was working on him differently than on Tash. Thank the Three—that was why he was still alive.

When her call garnered no reaction, she raised her voice and hailed him as Blackgult, and then as the Golden Griffon.

He turned his head. "Yes, my page?"

"*Here,* Father," she commanded briskly. "Help me carry this lady fair—who's delicate, and in some distress—around behind yon woodpile."

"But of course," he replied swiftly, rising to help. "I hope I had no part in bringing her to her present, ah, state?"

Embra sighed. "No, not really. No more so than the rest of Aglirta."

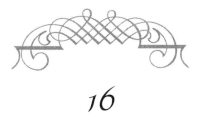

16

Serving the Serpent Well

The Dwaer spun faster, singing and soaring almost a foot higher—
and as if in answer, Tshamarra Talasorn arched and twisted
under Embra's fingers, rising right off the ground.

Embra drew back from the floating, quivering figure, and frowned.
"There's something . . . ," she murmured aloud, eyes narrowing as she
stared at the younger sorceress.

Suddenly quite another something struck Embra hard on the shoulder,
driving her to the ground, chin-first.

It was the boot of a warrior, who'd leaped from atop the woodpile
behind her to snatch the Dwaer out of midair. Clutching the Stone, he
rolled away and up to his feet, whirling around with a grin of triumph—and
as Embra scrambled to her knees, fingers moving to shape a spell that
would have to be fast, other armored men came rushing around both sides
of the woodpile with drawn swords.

Where were Hawk and Craer?

She let her hands fall again as the warriors formed a blade-bristling wall
facing her. In unison they took a slow stride forward, faces bleak.

"Embra Silvertree," the warrior hefting the Dwaer said silkily, "your
father once tortured me. I'm going to enjoy this."

Embra crouched protectively over Tshamarra. The eyes of the Talasorn
sorceress were still closed, but her arms and legs had started to writhe
again, slowly and fitfully, as she settled a little closer to the ground. If she'd
still held the Stone, Embra would have been trying to work gentle healing
on her.

At that grim thought, the Lady Silvertree turned her head to seek her father. Blackgult sat huddled nearby, rocking slightly in seeming obliviousness.

A sudden blaze of Dwaer-light brought her gaze back to—the Stone, glowing brightly in the warrior's hand as he paced menacingly forward, his eyes glittering . . .

"You gave her *enchanted* armor?" Phelinndar's roar echoed around the chamber. *"Why?"*

The Spellmaster of Aglirta quirked an eyebrow. "Enchanted, my dear Baron?"

The nobleman's sword sang out so fast that even Ingryl Ambelter flinched. "Ambelter, I may not be a mage, but I'm *not* a fool. Kindly remember that," Phelinndar snarled. "You give the wench armor twice her size and it fits her perfectly, then it glows when you use the Stone to send her—what does that tell any dolt with eyes, *twice?* 'Tis magical!" The baron rammed his blade back into its scabbard with an angry clank and barked, "So answer my question!"

Ingryl Ambelter drew a deep breath, hefted his Dwaer, and said smugly, "The spells on it prevent anyone from successfully tracing her to us . . . whereas *I* can trace it."

He strode across the chamber with his usual air of amused superiority. "Now, my increasingly angry Baron, you're right to be unamused about all of my boldnesses, so let's sit down and discuss what I've done and why, and what we'll do next. I must introduce you to the Sword of Spells."

"A sword? Something I can wield?" Phelinndar asked eagerly, despite himself.

The Spellmaster shook his head. "Not an actual blade, but rather a series of interwoven spells."

The baron did not trouble to hide his disgust, but Ambelter only smiled thinly and said, "You know magic is the key to power these days, Phelinndar—or you *should,* by now."

"Oh, I know it," the baron snarled, "but nothing's going to make me *like* it."

"Let her down," the warrior ordered curtly, "or—" Warningly he lifted the Dwaer in one hand and his sword in the other.

Embra looked at him, and then back at Tshamarra. Did he really not know . . . ?

"I—I'll have to undo my spell," she said, trying to sound frightened, and discovering that she really was.

Without a Dwaer-Stone, Embra Silvertree was just one unarmored woman confronting thirty-odd angry warriors. She swallowed, and found herself trembling.

He smirked and took another step forward, tossing and cupping the Dwaer like a child playing catch-stone. "You're nothing without this, are you?"

"True," she whispered, from her knees, and he took another step forward. A bare three strides separated them now, but he'd brought his sword down to point at her. He wasn't going to blunder any closer, in case the touch of a sorceress bore any nasty little perils . . .

"S-so, should I–?" Embra asked, nodding her head at Tshamarra, who was moaning and writhing, as if about to awaken . . . writhing on empty air about a handwidth clear of the ground. One of the warriors muttered something to another, and there were grins.

"Keep your hands still!" the warrior snapped, and she froze, eyes fixed on his, clinging to the faint hope that Tshamarra's rousing would alarm him.

It did. "She's waking up, isn't she?"

"Yes," Embra told him anxiously, "and I don't know what she'll do. She went mad, and she's too powerful for me to control, even with the Stone. Her family rules Arlund with sorcery."

"And if you undo your spell?"

"She'll sleep again," Embra lied, keeping her hands very still. The warrior locked eyes with her.

Tshamarra writhed more strongly.

"Do it," he snarled, and Embra nodded, reached out for Tshamarra, and carefully cast a spell that took but two gestures and a very short murmured incantation. It was one of the few she had magic enough left to power . . . O, Three aid me, let this one have no feel at all for using a Dwaer!

She felt the faint creeping sensation of the spell starting to take effect, and launched herself up and over Tshamarra in a single bound, landing and springing again before the watching warriors could do more than shout. Her magic snatched at the warrior's sword, plucking it to one side as if tugged by a gale—and for the scant seconds she needed, he did as any warrior would: he held onto it, fighting fiercely to keep possession of his weapon.

That left his arm pulled across his body and his side turned toward her, as she landed right at his boots—and embraced him.

Time slowed to a thunderous heartbeat. Between one clap and the next,

Embra called on the Dwaer. The moment she touched him, an unsorcerous man with no power to use the Stone to resist her, she could feel its power, reach its power, *seize* its power!

With a shout that echoed in every head around the woodpiles louder than in her own she made the Dwaer fling away metal in all directions, repelling it from herself . . . or rather, from their locked bodies, she and this warrior who hated her so much for something done to him by a dead man most of Aglirta believed to be her father.

Blackgult was hurled away like some sort of armored ball, bouncing with clangorous crashes toward the line of warriors—who were themselves flung back to crash into trees and crumple, blades whirling from numbed fingers to flash away deep into treegloom.

Embra opened her fingers, and the Dwaer flew into them. Then she stepped back from the warrior, lifting him into the air to float frozen in front of her. Only his eyes could still move, and they darted this way and that in wild terror before staring helplessly at her.

"You," Embra told him softly, sounding far more menacing than she felt, "shall be my shield."

As if her words had been a signal, the air was suddenly full of large, dark arrows, stabbing at her in a hail—snake-arrows!

Gaping fangs first, the enchanted-rigid serpents came hissing at her from three sides, and the sorceress had no choice but to use her living shield to drive aside many of them, running right behind it so the snakes aimed at her unprotected flank would also miss.

Serpent-priests were running out of the trees now, on all sides of her but the woodpile. Embra called on the Dwaer, seeking to fell them all by flinging broken hiresword bodies at their ankles, but something met the force of her Dwaer-thrust, blunted it, and forced it to a halt everywhere on her right.

Behind her, some priests had fallen, and others were fighting for balance or crouching to hurl spells before they dared advance farther. Embra spared them no more attention—not when she had eleven, no, twelve Serpent-priests giving her various cold grins as they strode toward her, defying her Dwaer with . . . what could only be the power of another Dwaer!

Somewhere nearby, probably in the trees just behind these smiling Brothers of the Serpent, someone was using another Stone . . .

She must find out who, and get it, and to do that she had to avoid being slain by these oh-so-enthusiastic Serpents. They were lifting their hands to shape spells even now, or brandishing cruel fang-knives, their eyes all fixed on Embra Silvertree.

So she gave them flame, the easiest thing to call forth from a Dwaer: a wall of roaring, streaming fire that hid those laughing men from her and set the branches of trees overhead crackling. Biting her lip, Embra lowered her wall and thrust it hard away from her, hoping to trap men within it.

Screams told her she'd succeeded, but there weren't as many cries as she'd hoped. Either they were swift-footed indeed, or the wielder of the rival Dwaer was—

Yes! Her flames parted and rolled back like curtains, letting cold laughter through. It was coming from a man standing behind the no-longer-grinning priests—and so was the telltale glow of awakened Dwaer-power.

"So death comes for you at last, Embra Silvertree," the richly robed Lord of the Serpent drawled, the power of the Stone glimmering in his hand carrying his lazy voice clearly to all ears through the snarling flames and the cries of the wounded. "The doom you so richly deserve, and have cheated for so long, visited rightfully on you at last in the divine name of the Great Serpent. *I* am the instrument of that doom, and I am—Belgur Arthroon, Lord of the Serpent!"

"Your pomposity," Embra muttered, as she lifted her Dwaer with hands that became flaming claws, "almost matches that of Ingryl Ambelter. Almost."

And flames streamed from her fingers, tugging at her own wall of fire, lifting it . . . lifting . . . until the smoldering priests and warriors coughed and staggered free of fire, the flames shimmering above them like a bed-canopy, a billowing carpet of fire that suddenly—*fell,* full upon their heads in a wash of bright-flowing flames!

Through the fresh screams and thrashings, the Lord of the Serpent snarled something, whirled his Dwaer around his head as if it was a hurl-hammer—and the air throbbed, there was a blinding flash of white light, and *something* rolled out in all directions, a great rush of power that broke over Embra, leaving her tingling and breathless, and raced on through the woods, moaning with a strange fury that disturbed not a single leaf.

Armor flickered and pulsed wildly among the men facing her, and Embra felt her Stone tremble in her hand, its own flashes mirroring the dying spell-glows. Her flames were gone, banished with all magic in that great outpouring of Dwaer-power, but most of the Serpent-priests and warriors stood in shuddering silence, seemingly dazed.

Across that unnatural hush, Embra heard Belgur Arthroon's shout of triumph die away uncertainly as he stared at the dull Stone in his grasp. Had he destroyed it? Or drained all its power for a time?

The dead warrior floating in front of Embra thumped to the ground, the rigid serpent-arrows crumbling to ash as he fell. He crashed down atop

Tshamarra—who awakened from her spell-slumber in a snarling whirlwind of biting and kicking as she rolled onto the dead man, clawing with her hands for a strangling grip on his throat.

"Easy, Tash!" Embra hissed. "He's dead! Dead of snake-venom!"

The Talasorn sorceress stared up at her, rage ebbing in those dark eyes. Then she turned her head to look where Embra was staring: across the body-strewn, much-trampled glade at the Lord of the Serpent.

Belgur Arthroon was spitting curses at the Dwaer-Stone in his hands, and it was spitting tiny lightnings right back at him—but little else. Shaking his head, he let it fall at his feet, glared at the Lady Silvertree, and raised both hands to cast a spell at her.

"He *ruined* a Dwaer-Stone?" Tshamarra gasped. "Is that possible?"

Embra shook her head. "No. He misused it foolishly, breaking all magics within reach." She raised her own Dwaer, and a soft light kindled in it. "Which leaves me free to . . ."

She fell silent, and Tshamarra turned again to see what Embra was gazing at. Arthroon's hands were lifted to cup and hold the glow of his gathering magic, and his eyes were alight with triumph as he chanted the last few words of an incantation both women recognized. It would bring into being a sphere of raging lightnings . . . a sphere he'd doubtless hurl at them both.

Something else was rising behind the Lord of the Serpent, something darker and taller, gleaming in the gathering spell-glow. A figure in armor . . . Ezendor Blackgult, awakened from his mind-slumber. As he rose, the Golden Griffon swept his sword up in a thrust that began at his knees, and sliced the air upward with the full weight of his swordarm behind it.

The point of that blade burst through Belgur Arthroon's neck from behind and slid out of the priest's mouth like a long, rigid, bloody tongue.

The stricken Serpent-lord stared wide-eyed at Embra, choking on the last words of his incantation. His spell collapsed into fading fires that splashed into his palms and then flowed down to lick the ground and die away entirely. Blackgult pulled back his blade to thrust again, but the Lord of the Serpent said nothing more as he sank to the waiting loam in a last, reluctant kneeling.

Embra slashed out with her Dwaer, sending thin bolts stabbing like lances into warriors who were beginning their own charges toward Blackgult. Her father grinned, waved at her, and whirled to hack down the next priest.

Embra turned to face where she knew none but Serpents stood, and blasted that clump of men, hurling them back into the trees. Then she turned swiftly to make sure no one was coming up behind her, kept turning when she saw no foe until she came around to face the Serpent-men on the far right—and blasted them, too.

Her Dwaer flickered in the wake of that magic, its radiance visibly fading. Tash gasped at the sight. Embra gave her a grim look. "We'd best get that second Stone," she snapped, and the Lady Talasorn nodded and set off across the clearing.

In the heart of a fray of hacking, snarling men, Blackgult was slaying his third priest. Something rolled under a boot, and Tshamarra darted at it with a wordless cry.

Embra nodded. That was the Dwaer, dull and dark, and . . . that was a priest, fallen in the thrusting and jostling, reaching for it!

She raised her own Stone to give those reaching fingers a desperate blast—and something like a silver fang flashed down out of the leaves overhead to quiver deep in sundered flesh, pinning the screaming priest's hand to a root.

"That's my Longfingers!" Tshamarra shouted delightedly, running hard with Embra right behind her. Another priest abandoned attempts to weave a spell through the warriors jostling to get at Blackgult, and dived to snatch at the fallen Stone—and Craer swung down from a bough, kicking aside a priest's head to get a clear view, and threw a second dagger that flashed down under the fallen Dwaer just as the priest's hands were about to close on it—and sent the Stone bounding right past Tshamarra's elbow to where . . . Embra could snatch it up.

A blinding flash rocked the clearing, and two balls of lightning sprang away from each other, one of them trailing Embra and her scream of pain. Those lightnings faded in her hands as she crashed to earth, to become her Dwaer . . . and the others dwindled back into Arthroon's fallen Stone and crashed at the feet of a Serpent hiresword.

That warrior bent to catch it up—and Blackgult thrust his sword past the man he was fighting, into the hiresword's backside.

With a startled groan the warrior fell forward—and was almost beheaded by Hawkril as the armaragor burst out of the fray, sweeping aside Serpent-sworn bodies with his busy blade. He raced toward Embra, roaring her name.

Tshamarra whirled to follow him, as Craer bounded past her with an affectionate slap, to bury a dagger hilt-deep in the back of the warrior fighting Blackgult. That man collapsed with a soundless cry, and Blackgult burst over him and got a hand on the errant Stone.

Both Dwaerindim flared into blinding brightness again, though the one clutched to Embra's breast did so only momentarily, as Hawkril cursed helplessly above her, and Tshamarra looked wildly from one Stone to another.

The one between Blackgult's fingers spun momentarily into the air, spitting lightnings that hurled the Golden Griffon and at least two hitherto-eager priests away, and swept Craer off his feet, tumbling him over the body of the warrior he'd just slain.

As the Stone fell, another Serpent-warrior blundered forward and scooped it up—only to snatch his hand back and let it fall, roaring in pain. Craer daggered him from behind, and he fell on his face beside the Stone. It flickered on the trodden ground like a baleful eye, untouched by anyone, as a wounded hiresword rose up behind Hawkril, blade in hand—and Tshamarra flung herself at the back of the man's knees, stabbing with her dagger.

He fell, shouting, and twisted around to slash at her. She parried that blade desperately, teeth clenched, and then stabbed him again, in the face this time. Again, and then again, until she rose grimly, panting and bloody-handed, from a hiresword who'd slay for the Serpent no more.

She was tottering to her feet in a strange quiet. Beneath Hawkril's guard, Embra was dazedly moaning her way back to consciousness, her Dwaer flickering on her breast. Blackgult was slowly moving around the glade, stabbing wounded men, and Craer was racing about doing the same thing. Tshamarra had the impression that many men had fled into the deep woods; as she peered around, half-afraid she'd end up staring into the eyes of some archer or triumphant priest finishing a spell, Craer came toward her, dragging a priest by means of a strangling cord around the man's throat. There was a bloody dagger in the procurer's hand, more blood all down one side of his face, and a fierce grin beneath it.

"Over here," he snarled, hauling hard at the feebly struggling Serpent-priest. The man looked hurt, and almost fell as Craer tugged him forward. The Serpent halted, swaying, in front of Arthroon's fallen stone. "Take it up!" the procurer snapped.

"Craer!" Tshamarra gasped, "what are—?"

With desperate speed the priest snatched up the Stone—and as he roared in pain and the Stone flared, Craer stabbed the man and then rushed the staggering, dying body over to the woodcutter's chopping block.

"Hawk!" the procurer cried, holding the priest's sagging arm across the block. Hawkril took three swift strides and brought his warsword down.

Still clutching the Dwaer, a severed hand bounced into the leaves underfoot. Craer picked up the gory appendage and flourished it triumphantly. "I've always said you'd need a hand in life, sooner or later!"

"Craer!" Embra's protest was weak, but no less disgusted.

"Aye, I know not which is worse," Hawkril rumbled. "The man's deeds, or his jests."

"Put it away," Embra commanded, "but keep it safe. Some trap has been laid on it, to let only that dead Serpent-lord wield it. 'Tis something I can no doubt break with my Dwaer, but I'll need time to study how."

"Perhaps," Blackgult offered, joining them, " 'tis blood-consecrated to folk who have Serpent-venom in their veins."

Tshamarra displayed a bloody hand to her fellow overdukes, and tried to smile. "That would be me. That warrior cut me."

Embra gave her a look. "Tash, I'm not sure trying to touch it now would be a good idea. You need Dwaer-healing again, before that venom . . . which reminds me: Father, should I be healing you in all the haste I can manage, before you fall over dead?"

The Golden Griffon shook his head. "When that Serpent-lord broke his spells, the plague left me. He must have been the source of the spell on the serpent-arrow that struck me. When I cut him down, my mind cleared, too."

The Lady Silvertree stared at him. "So if we slay a plague source, we cure all the creatures it's infected, too!"

"Perhaps," her father agreed. "Or perhaps not, if they've been forced into beast-shape already." He gave her a mirthless smile. "We'll just have to see."

"Hey, now," Craer said with a frown. "*You* have a Dwaer, Em, and sorcery of your own to overmatch half the Vale. Tash has mighty magic, too; what if she could wield a Stone, too? We'd be . . ." He broke off as Embra spread her hands in a silent gesture of acceptance.

Tshamarra came to him a little unsteadily. Silently Craer held out the severed hand, and she reached down for it with slow care, not touching the dead, dripping flesh that until recently had been part of a priest of the Serpent.

As her fingers closed gingerly on the Dwaer, there was a flash, a snarl of lightnings lashing forth from the Stone amid a spitting of sparks—and the blur of the Lady Talasorn being flung across the glade.

She crashed headlong into the armored form of Hawkril, who bent hastily to cradle her and so keep her neck from breaking, but found himself plucked from his feet and hurled into a tree.

"Hawk!" Embra shouted, wobbling her way to her own feet and rushing to him. Craer was right behind her; as he ran, he tore a cloak from the shoulders of a body and whipped it around the severed hand holding the Serpent-Dwaer, forming an improvised sack.

"Hawk?" the Lady Silvertree gasped, going to her knees beside the two tumbled bodies. The armaragor opened his eyes, winced, and then groaned. "No doubt I'll live," he said slowly, moving a shoulder slowly and wincing again, "but . . ."

"Lie down again," Embra commanded, and turned to Craer. "Take Tash off him. Gently, to let her lie right here."

"You'll be healing?" the procurer asked unnecessarily, as Embra's Dwaer rolled up into the air, glowing, and it started to sing.

"I trust," Embra replied, not looking up as the glow grew and the keening song of the Stone rose, "you'll put the other Stone safely in a saddlebag or suchlike, and keep it well away from me for this next little while."

Craer nodded, and trotted across the glade to do just that. A flitting movement caught his eye as he went, and he stopped above the saddlebag and looked back at the boughs where it had been with apparent casualness. When he was finished stowing and buckling, he brought the saddlebag most of the way back to Embra, set it down, and went to her.

"Lady Silvertree," he murmured in her ear, as he reached down to take Tshamarra's hand, "at least six bats are watching us, from two trees back behind me. Just above the crooked bough with the two dead side branches."

Embra nodded. "I know what that means, yes." She whirled suddenly, the Dwaer flashing–and lightning tore through the leaves of the crooked bough. Two sizzling, squeaking black forms fell to earth, rocked, and lay still, and the others raced away through the woods, swooping and darting. Embra sent one more bolt after them, but although leaves in plenty flared up and crackled to ash, no more bats fell. Four at least had gotten away.

"Is our Master of Bats out and free, do you think?" Craer asked gravely.

Embra lifted her shoulders in a shrug. "It scarcely matters whether he's still chained to that cell wall or not. He's free to spy and work magic afar, and that brings us the same danger."

Craer nodded. "And Tash?" He risked another glance down at the still, pale form in front of him. The fingers in his felt like ice.

Embra smiled. "She'll be fine, and Hawk too. They'll awaken in a moment."

"I," the armaragor announced heavily, "am awake now. And viewing the prospect of fighting our way through every last house and back alley of

Serpent-ruled Glarond with increasing lack of enthusiasm. Craer and I must have slain over a score of men each, fighting our way back to you here."

"Given this sudden surfeit of bats," Blackgult agreed, joining them with a dark, smoking bat corpse in his palm, "I agree. 'Tis time to talk to the Master of Bats again. Even if he's fled Flowfoam, we must confer with Raulin about the Serpent-spawned unrest and whelming to arms, up and down Aglirta—and then perhaps take our King into hiding for his own safety."

Hawkril frowned. "Where?"

"Well, there're always the ruins of Indraevyn," Craer said wryly. "Or a certain Silent House."

King Castlecloaks hauled hard on a cord that rang a servants' bell, but the advancing guards only sneered.

"You really think some bearer of wine trays can smite us down?" one asked mockingly. "*Before* your bodies lie butchered here? 'Tis time to *die,* Your Majesty!"

Raulin and Flaeros had already drawn their belt-daggers and retreated, Greatsarn taking a stand before them with his sword drawn. As all three backed into the farthest corner of the chamber, the bard caught up the manyshields board and swung it like a man about to send a shield spinning edgewise across the room. The spired playing pieces bounced and rolled under the boots of the guards, but caused no slips, stumbles, or falls—only wider sneers.

"Fools," one guard said scornfully.

"Corpses," another corrected, gliding forward with his steel raised to strike.

Suldun Greatsarn swallowed and hefted his sword, knowing he must slay without being slain, at least until all but two of the traitors were down . . . and not knowing how by all graces of the Three he was going to manage that, against warriors so skilled, fresh, and careful. They advanced in a slowly tightening web, not allowing any gap a swift swordsman could use to strike, nor making any mistake that might leave a royal path to the door—even if the guards outside that door could be trusted. The boy king *was* going to die here this day, plunging all Aglirta back into bloodshed or the softly gloating tyranny of the Serpent . . .

And then a section of solid stone wall hard by Flaeros Delcamper swung open, striking the bard's shoulder a numbing blow. An unfamiliar man bustled out of it, calmly turning aside a startled Delcamper dagger-thrust with a hand somehow hard enough to parry steel, and murmured, "Flee!" to the three startled men backed into the corner.

Even as the king, his loyal warrior, and the bard gaped at the newcomer and the rectangle of dank, waiting darkness behind him, the guards charged forward with a roar—but the newly arrived man seemed to *flow* past Great-sarn, growing taller, and barred their way with hands that became hissing serpent-heads.

As the traitors hesitated, those heads melted back into human hands again, but the face above them had changed, becoming dark-eyed and scaled. A forked tongue undulated in its fanged mouth as it hissed, "Ssssso! Disssobeying ordersss *again*?"

The guards halted, lowering blades in bewilderment, as Greatsarn almost hurled the two younger men into the passage and then followed them. Barely had he ducked out of the room than its door swung open, revealing a page and a courtier—who promptly screamed at the sight of the drawn swords, and fled.

"Wh—who are you?" a guard snarled.

"The Sssupreme Ssserpent," the towering figure told them coldly. The warriors traded looks, growing pale, and then let their swords menace the floor as they backed away.

Without taking his eyes from them, the Supreme Serpent reached out an arm and swung the door of the secret passage closed. Putting his back to it, he leaned on it, folded his arms, and said, "Now, sssupposse you tell me jussst how many of you are here on Flowfoam, who givesss orders to who, and sssuchlike."

The guards exchanged doubtful looks.

"I'm waiting," the Serpent-priest added softly, and all of the warriors hastily began to speak at once.

17

An Array of Grim Faces

Darkness shimmered, gave birth to swirling glows, and then silently replaced them with a dark-eyed young lass in armor. Maelra Bowdragon looked around herself in wary awe, smelling cold, dank stone, old dust, and something more—a reek of death, or perhaps recent fear. This part of the cellars of Flowfoam Castle looked shattered: a webwork of cracks, not all of them small, wandered across the walls, floor, and ceiling. Yet silence reigned, the air was stale, and dust lay thick and undisturbed.

I'm here, she thought. *No one seems near. 'Tis very dark.*

"Your armor," a thin, cold voice erupted from the steel curving over her breast, startling Maelra for one shivering moment, "allows you to see where there's no light. Concentrate on remembered brightness—sunlight or fire or lamp glow."

Maelra did so, and the gloom seemed to roll back before her eyes, though her surroundings grew no brighter. She could now see that she stood in a stone-lined alcove off a passage, only paces from a round, waist-high wall that was probably a well—or had once been, for it was now cracked, and no odor of water or cool breeze came to her.

I can see, she announced silently. *There's a well.*

"Good," the Spellmaster's voice said, almost smugly. "Go out into the passage and turn left. The passage will turn right shortly. Follow it, around its next bend—to the left, soon after the first. Stop and tell me when you reach the third bend."

I proceed, Maelra reported calmly, and did as directed, hearing only the faint scrape of her boots on the dusty stones. The cellars seemed deserted and lifeless, but when she reached that third bend, and saw a door in the wall to her right and the passage turning away from it to her left, there was a high, faint singing in the air. She stepped back from the bend, and it faded, but returned as she advanced again. She reported this, and Ingryl's reply sounded approving.

"That's a ward. You must be very careful. The Serpent himself prowled the cellars since my departure, undoing some spells and drinking others. Most will have returned, over time, for I doubt he took the time or trouble to break them properly. Therefore, much remains that can slay or entrap you if you fail to heed my instructions precisely. Do you understand?"

Oh, yes, Maelra thought, and if he felt the faint sarcasm that seeped into that sending, Ambelter gave no sign of it.

"Don't step forward. Kneel where you are, and pass either bracer you wear over all the flagstones around you, one stone at a time—close to the stones, but taking care not to touch them. Note which ones glow, and what symbols appear on them."

Maelra did so, and reported back what she found. The Spellmaster's voice, when it came again, sounded irritated. "Someone has wrought changes. Step forward *only* onto the flagstone that did not glow. Then explore the stones around it with your bracers again."

Again Maelra did as she was bid. This time, two stones—also to the right—failed to glow, and Ambelter directed her to them. Repeating this process once more brought her to the threshold of the closed, unmarked stone door.

"Undo the neck-strap of your breastplate, and let it fall forward into your hand. Let it touch no stone, nor fall to the floor." When Maelra did so, finding the air very cool on her skin—a surprising amount of sweat had built up under the metal—a glowing line of light slowly appeared on it, curving as she watched into the shape of something that resembled a triple fishhook. "You see the rune?"

Yes, Spellmaster, Maelra replied, managing to keep the tremble of rising excitement out of her mind-voice, if not completely out of her hands. The breastplate shook in her grasp.

"Good. Hold the plate with your right hand so it doesn't touch the door, and use one finger—it matters not which, but only one—of your left hand to trace that rune on the door. Touch the door *only* as part of the rune-tracing, and pull your hand back when you're done. The door will glow where you touch it."

It did, and when Maelra completed the rune, the singing in the air around her abruptly ceased. Then, with no more sound than a whisper, the door opened by itself, gliding inward.

"Don't step into the room yet," the Spellmaster said sharply. "Touch the doorframe and say this word: '*Narathma*.'"

Maelra did so. The stone doorframe briefly awakened to a cold blue glow, and then faded into darkness again. She tried to use that light to peer into the room beyond, but gained only the impression of a fairly small chamber with a stone ceiling about the same height as the one above her in the passage.

"Now bend down—don't let the breastplate touch stone—and pass one of your bracers over the threshold and as much of the floor within as you can easily reach."

No glows, Maelra reported, doing so.

"Step into the room, and then stop. Touch nothing, including the door and the doorframe. Look around—with your eyes only—and tell me what you see."

Sagging shelves, stones fallen from the ceiling, smashed and opened coffers on the shelves, a few books whose pages look to have melted away, some empty niches cut into the wall—and a trestle table with an open casket in it. I can see bones, within.

"Approach the casket, but step back at once if you hear a singing or see a glow."

No such, Spellmaster. I'm beside the casket. There's a human skeleton in it, a few bones crumbled away, but largely intact. Not disarranged. There's a sort of wooden frame built over them, inside the casket.

"Good. Are you afraid of bones?"

These are just bones.

"Pass a bracer over the casket—do any of them move? Any glows? Are the eyesockets of the skull still dark?"

All is dark and still.

"Good. Step back from the casket and strip off all your armor. Get bare—take off everything."

Wondering privately what stripping, here in the dusty, chill darkness, had to do with "bringing back" these or any bones, Maelra did so. As she did off the last piece of armor, darkness returned in a rush, leaving her blind.

Spellmaster, I'm bare—but I can no longer see.

" 'Tis of no matter. You know where the casket lies? You can find it without blundering into it? Do so."

Done.

"Climb up onto that frame, and lie there, facedown. Try to avoid putting your hands and feet down among the bones."

Maelra started to do so—and then froze, teetering on the brink of falling back into the darkness. *Ambelter, the bones are glowing!*

"So they will. Have no fear. I myself have done what you are doing, without any harm at all. Get onto that frame."

Swallowing in the darkness—how could one at once be so cold and yet sweating so fiercely that one's skin was slick?—the young Bowdragon sorceress did so, tingling with excitement as she lowered herself onto the latticework of cold, dusty boards. The fell glow from the skeleton beneath her was bright enough to light up the room around her now . . . and as she steadied herself just above it, though its eyesockets remained empty and dark, it seemed to be *looking* at her. Maelra swallowed again, the frame creaking as sweat rolled down her nose and she hurriedly swiped it away to avoid letting it fall onto the bones beneath.

Done, Spellmaster.

"You'll have noticed that the frame keeps you from crushing the bones, but allows you to reach them. They're the remains of Gadaster Mulkyn, once a mighty mage, and you must not pull one bone apart from another. To have the power to slay the King and hurl aside his guards and courtiers, you must do as I say: Reach down with both of your arms, and your mouth, and embrace the bones as if they were a living man and he your lover."

Maelra lay above the skeleton, staring down into its dark and empty gaze and eternal grin, and wondered what would truly happen when she touched it. What was Ambelter keeping from her?

"Be not afraid, lass! You'll feel power passing into you, naught else. Maelra Bowdragon, I command you—"

My, but the Spellmaster suddenly seemed more fearful than she did! With a shrug and a smile, Maelra Bowdragon reached down and embraced the unknown.

Power! Magic more than she'd ever felt before slammed into her, so sudden and clear and cold that Maelra arched up and back from it, shrieking soundlessly at the ceiling at the same time as she unthinkingly kicked at the frame, seeking to grind her pelvis down into the heart of what was flowing into her.

The skeleton shot bolt upright, passing like a ghost *through* the boards, and suddenly was embracing her, cold bones sliding hard and smooth over her trembling flesh, grinning right into her face with eyes that had kindled into two arctic stars floating in darkness, dry bony jaws parting as if to bite or kiss her . . . and then, just as she sought to try to shove it away and stream and struggle, the bones softly sighed into dust, and a wall of ruby fury rolled into Maelra's head. A voice that left her quivering in cowering silence in a small corner of her own mind announced gloatingly: *HELLO, RASH YOUNGLING. I AM GADASTER MULKYN, AND THIS BODY WILL DO JUST FINE.*

In a cavern where many men with melted faces stood silently, staring at nothing, Ingryl Ambelter gasped in horror as his mind-spying was severed as if by the slice of a knife. Gadaster was aware, and as powerful as if Ingryl Ambelter had never slain or bound or spell-drained him! He'd poured himself into the young wench, now, and—

"Claws of the Dark One," the Spellmaster gasped, hands shaking, and then mastered trembling fingers enough to shape a quick, imperious gesture with one hand, his Dwaer flaring into full life in the other. The armor was his only hope! If Gadaster was dust and this Maelra's body now his, he could be slain!

The body that had been Maelra Bowdragon knelt upright in the casket, head almost scraping the ceiling, and murmured two words she'd never known before. Then, quite suddenly, she was gone and something changed, all over the walls—scant instants before the discarded pieces of armor on the floor glowed with Dwaer-light and then burst with a violent roar, shredding the casket and shelves and everything else in the chamber in a frantic whirlwind of shrapnel that shrieked and rang off floor, ceiling, and walls with force enough to shatter stone blocks and send many deadly shards slicing down into the slow, drifting dust.

The cellars of Flowfoam shook briefly around the shattered, long-hidden room, and then, slowly, grew still once more.

Ingryl Ambelter muttered anxious words over his Dwaer, and peered into the roiling whirlwind. Did he dare send light to follow his farscrying?

He dared not fail to do so.

He must know if this oldest, yet most unlooked for peril had been destroyed at its birthing . . . or was coming for him, even now . . . ?

He must know, must see what had befallen in the chamber where he'd kept his most secret and darkest magics for so long . . .

With both hands clutching his Dwaer in a clawlike grasp, Ingryl Ambelter stared into it, trying to wrap its power around him in a shield, and gazed through it at—ruin. Coffers, shelves, and casket were all but small and twisted shards among the dust. Nothing was left. The glow of fresh magic hung in the air, reverberating in waves of silent brightness . . . a violent casting, just before his own . . . and there was another enchantment crawling all over the walls. Crawling and dripping from the ceiling . . . blood. The walls were adrip with blood!

His eyes narrowed. A splendid wench, to be sure, tallish and yet supple, but—so much blood in her? And not a single hair, of all that long mane of hers, left behind?

A ruse, or so he must assume. Knowing his old master, it could very well be.

In a sudden pale, shaking fury, Ingryl slammed a spell into his Dwaer that would sever his scrying and slap down anyone trying to ride the spell-link to him.

Sweating, he sagged back into his chair and whispered, "Horns and kisses of the Great Lady, sap-spittle of the Forefather . . . bebolten dung-slung talons of the Dark One!" Staring unseeing at the Melted who stood in what was left of the armor he'd stripped from them, looking unseeingly back at him, the Spellmaster went on swearing.

It lasted a long time, but the Baron Phelinndar waited until Ambelter's curses died away into half-heard hisses before he said grimly, "I told you, wizard, that this was a fool's plan from the start. Your towering arrogance always gets us—"

"Be still or be dead!" Ingryl Ambelter snarled, plucking up the Dwaer as if to hurl it into Phelinndar's face.

Then he halted, and the two men sat in the cavern staring across a table at each other in hard-breathing silence, rage and fear warring in both their gazes.

The Dwaer-glow faded and left them looking at the beautiful lawns and gardens of Flowfoam—and two low, grassy mounds right in front of them.

Hawkril and Blackgult looked down at the graves of Sarasper and Brightpennant, but Embra's head snapped around to give Craer a questioning look. The procurer peeked into the saddlebag clutched in his hands, and announced, "Still there. The Dwaer looks whole—and dark."

Embra nodded, and said merely, "The cells."

They hurried into the palace, the grim glow of the Stone Embra held all the warrant they needed to make guards hasten aside at their approach, and descended into darkness.

Both swords and the Dwaer were held ready as a certain door scraped open—but in the damp, dark chamber beyond, a certain sorcerer still hung chained to the wall.

"How much have you seen?" Embra asked softly, without greeting. "Enough to keep your sanity, I trust?"

The Master of Bats laughed bitterly. "Many say I lost that years ago—just as you did, little darling of jewels, under your father's hands and his mages' teachings. His kisses were sweet, I trust?"

Embra's lips tightened. "You heard my first question?"

The sorcerer gave her a glare. "Of *course* I've been watching," he said mockingly. "What else is there for me to do? All folk of Aglirta should see their overdukes at work, and marvel thereby. I thank you for the entertainment."

Craer bowed with full court flourishes, but Blackgult said grimly, "Make us tire overmuch of bandying words with you, Huldaerus, and we'll simply slay you. Aglirta already has more unscrupulous mages than it can hold; we don't need you."

"Ah, but you do," the chained wizard replied. "Who else has the leisure"—he rattled his chains—"to watch what's happening, and see all? Have you looked upstairs yet?"

"Why?" Embra's voice was sharp. "What's afoot in the palace?"

"Faceless and Serpents everywhere—even with your pet imported bard to harp him on his way, your boy king can scarce avoid treading on his foes as they glide and slither down every passage. You really should be more attentive to your duties, and spend less time gallivanting about the Vale. Is it not written that 'The Serpent has many heads, and shall arise again and again'?"

"Old books say much," Embra replied, "and most of it is witless fancy—as even a casual reader can tell when so many works contradict themselves from page to page, let alone standing against the tellings in other books. Is it not also written, Huldaerus, that there's no Serpent at all, but merely men who seize the mantle for their own purposes?"

The Master of Bats grinned. "Ah, well now. You've come to waste my time in an interesting manner at last."

"Think not," Tshamarra Talasorn said suddenly, "to prolong our stay or inflate your own importance, mage, by wasting *our* time overmuch. I know spells that can make your imprisonment an eternity of itching, or gut-sickness, or stabbing pains, or make you burn so keenly that you plead with your jailer to douse you in icy water, or slay you and so end your torment."

The chained wizard regarded her thoughtfully, and she answered his unspoken question. "No, I'm not Vale-born, nor given to cruelty. Yet for mages who've offered me any menace—as you did to these my friends, in past strivings in ruined Indraevyn—I cleave to the sensible advice of my family: Destroy, as soon and as harshly as possible. Those who work magic must be rightful and useful in their deeds, or others will cleanse all lands of their presence. By working tyranny with your sorcery, you endanger us all."

"So all must be burned away save you, maid of steel?" the Master of Bats asked quietly. "Which of us will then be the tyrant?"

"Bandy not words with me," the Lady Talasorn replied calmly, "but speak plainly and to the point. Darsar needs all the skilled mages it can rear—I'd rather gain you as a friend, sir, when this is all over, than reap your bones now."

The chained man looked at her. "Well, then, I'll lay aside my anger—on one condition: That you tell a few tavernmasters in Sirlptar, or wandering traders from other lands, if any still be in the Vale with this plague rampant, that I'm chained down here . . . so that if you're all slain in the game of Serpent and Dragon, someone will know where I am, and come looking."

"That, Lord," Craer said, "has already been done. As Lord Blackgult told you when we put you here, we've almost as little liking for this as you do. The King sent word of your disposition with his envoys to the Delcampers, and his messengers to the court trade agents in Sirlptar, at our suggestion. These folk were in turn instructed to inform certain local sages."

"Truth," Embra confirmed, the Dwaer flaring in her hand.

The chained wizard gazed at it longingly for a moment, then sighed and said, "So speak plainly, and I'll do so too. You've come to me because you caught sight of my bats, and wanted to be sure I was still imprisoned. Be assured that I am: This is no spellspun shell or seeming chained here before you, but myself. I've only recently managed to send forth my little spies—your man Thannaso is most attentive—but I know where to look and whose shoulder to peer over, and have seen much. Let me say just this: Many of those old prophecies seem to be coming true. In the words of the great Haundrakh, 'Fate at last catches up.' "

"The Lady Embra and I have both read all of those writings," Blackgult said calmly, holding up a hand to silence his fellow overdukes, "but dismissed their various fates as impossible. In the history unfolding before us, Aglirta has broken from them with the death of the Serpent—and he *is* dead, for we were there, and felt, and saw."

The Master of Bats bowed his head. "I don't claim otherwise, but the Lady was right in pointing out old Aumthur's contention that many men in turn wear the mantle. Like most mages, I thirst most for finding new spells when I seize old tomes—but once protected by the proper magics, I take care to read all, and I've come to believe Maumanthar's view: The Serpent and the Dragon aren't one person each, but rather creatures of the Arrada."

"A moment," Hawkril rumbled. "We came here to seek plain answers, and now snarling's abated and we speak politely—yet I hear nothing plain. I'm no mage, and scarce care who Aumthur and Maumanthar were, if they're safely dead, but *what* is the Arrada?"

Tshamarra opened her mouth to reply, then closed it again and waved at Embra.

The Lady Silvertree raised her brows and turned to the chained man on the wall, lifting her hand in a "will you?" gesture.

Huldaerus smiled crookedly. "The Arrada's the underlying magic of Darsar. Magic is no god-gift, despite what priests say, but the natural forces of all living things in Asmarand—whereas sorcery is ways we've learned to harness and control these powers."

He fell silent, but both Embra and her father waved at him to continue. Arkle Huldaerus grew a real smile, just for a moment, and continued, "These forces swirl and contend constantly, but also rise and fall in cycles, battling each other chiefly in two contending musterings: one of dark savagery—the Serpent—and one of bright cleansing—the Dragon. Sometimes one is victorious and sometimes the other."

The procurer and the armaragor were listening intently. The chained wizard looked from one of them to the other, and added, "All thinking beings—beasts and swordswingers and cobblers, not just wizards and priests—can work to sway these musterings, strengthening one side or the other. Neither side is necessarily 'good' or 'bad,' mind, but to most folk the Dragon appeals more. We all prefer places and things dear to us to be just as we want them, and things we hold precious to be clean, and unwithered, and at orderly peace."

"Oh?" Craer asked skeptically. "And how do I manage this swaying of the battle, against no foe I can see to put a dagger into?"

The Master of Bats grinned. "That's a deriding I've heard many times before—a dismissal I'm sure Maumanthar heard often enough to grow right tired of. We do this by praying to the Three, and to lesser gods, the spirits that dwell in certain dells and pools and caverns. Of the Three, the Dark One is allied to the Serpent, the Lady to the Dragon, and Forefather Oak to the overall Arrada, the great balance or All."

"So," Hawkril rumbled, " 'tis inevitable: There'll be a new Serpent."

"I believe there's one already," the imprisoned wizard murmured.

"Who?" Blackgult asked sharply, but Arkle Huldaerus just shrugged in his chains.

The Golden Griffon's eyes narrowed, and he took a threatening stride forward, but the Master of Bats smiled and shook his head. "Truly, I know not. My bats see things only where I dare to send them."

It was the turn of Embra to narrow and sharpen her gaze. "Will there also be a new Dragon?"

The chained mage shrugged. "Of course. A useful ally—*if* you can find whoever it is, and meet their price or treat them properly."

"Life is just full of ifs, isn't it?" Tshamarra asked softly.

Chains rattled as the manacled man shrugged again. "*If* you freed me," he said slowly, "I could perhaps help."

"Or not," the Talasorn sorceress said sharply.

The Master of Bats grinned rather unpleasantly. "Or not," he agreed. "Reap as you've sown, Overdukes."

Even as the words left his lips, a din arose outside the cell. Echoes, as always down in the Flowfoam cellars: the much-grown sounds of stumbling, frantically running feet, fast approaching through the dark passages.

The overdukes whirled around, lifting weapons, as the chained wizard watched with interest.

They were in time to see a crownless, ragged-cloaked Raulin Castle-cloaks sprint past the open doorway, lit by bobbing torches clutched by two hard-eyed warriors who pursued him, swords drawn. At their heels ran another man, who sported no human face at all, but rather the emerald-green, shiny-scaled head of a serpent!

"Claws of the Lady!" Craer snapped, hurling himself through the door with the rest of the overdukes in frantic, shoulder-bruising pursuit. A bat swooped past their heads, but none of them bothered to strike at it as they pelted down the passage after the flickering, dwindling torchlight.

"Tash!" Craer gasped back over his shoulder, at the lithe woman running along not far behind. "Can't you . . . fly?"

His lady shook her head, and panted, "Takes too long . . . to cast . . . without Dwaer . . . become hurled arrow . . . No way to fight or parry when reach . . ."

"So what by all the Three-engloried splendor is magic good for?" the procurer snapped.

"Oh," Blackgult called, "saving kingdoms, felling the Great Serpent—little things like that."

The sounds of their voices made the snake-headed priest glance back, a forked tongue darting from between his lips as he hissed in anger and surprise. He slowed, and threw up his hands to cast a spell—and Embra stopped, pointed the Dwaer at him as if it was a sword, and let fly with a bright needle of force that lit up the passage blindingly bright for a moment.

The other overdukes cried out, but kept running—and by the time Craer could see again, he was stumbling over the thrashing, headless corpse of what had recently been a Serpent-priest.

"Graul and bebolt!" he snarled, veering to find a wall and claw himself to a halt until his gaze cleared. "Why can't you blast down those two warriors, Em? Hey?"

"They're safely around a corner," the Lady Silvertree replied, as she joined him, guiding her fellow overdukes together. "Or I'd not even have dared cook this snake. Such bolts don't bow to royalty." The Dwaer had protected her against the flash of its own strike, and Blackgult had anticipated her deed and clapped a hand over his eyes, but the others were still blinking blearily at the near darkness around them.

Embra sighed, made the Dwaer glow gently, and ignored the bats—a trio now, at least—flapping around her. "Come *on*," she said. "Run, and I'll try to touch and heal as we go. We've got to catch them before they get to a—"

Even as she spoke, she saw that there was a well room ahead, with six passages leading out of it. When she let her Dwaer go out and brought blinding darkness down on them all, she could see no torch-glow ahead, anywhere.

The Lady of Jewels cursed as coarsely as any warrior, and then reached out with her Dwaer and started banishing the hurt she'd done to the overdukes stumbling blindly around her.

Then, shaking her head, she led them on, the Dwaer leaping again to golden life. Craer bounded into the lead, Hawkril running to join him, and Blackgult fell back behind the two sorceresses.

When they reached the well—Craer glancing down into its dank darkness, just to make sure—Embra doused her magical radiance once more. Nothing; the darkness was utter, unbroken.

"Claws of the bloody, blood-spitting Dark One," she began softly. "To lose them now, when—"

"Em!" the procurer snapped, hearing a tiny shriek close by his ear. "Give us light!"

With a sigh, the sorceress did so—and found five bats circling her head. As soon as she stared at them, they flew away across the chamber, and through a certain archway. Without hesitation she ran after them, murmuring, "My thanks, wizard. Remind me to free you much sooner than I was intending to. Perhaps even before we've both died of old age."

A bat screamed in her ear, then whirled away to join its fellows. Embra Silvertree gave it a savage grin as she hurled herself around a corner, down a few broad, unexpected steps, and on along the unfamiliar, winding passage.

It ran for a long way without doors or side chambers, during which time a determinedly sprinting Craer caught up to Embra, gave her a reproachful look, and took up his former station ahead of her, with Hawkril moving to join him . . . all at a dead run.

They'd just started to really gasp for breath, and slow with weariness, when the passage suddenly descended sharply, hooked to the right, and opened into—a large cavern that shouldn't exist.

Embra stared, slowing in bewilderment now as much as exhaustion. She'd been bound to all of Flowfoam by the Living Castle enchantments of the Dark Three, unfinished as they were, and . . . and this place was not part of them. It should not be here, it—

—presently held crates upon crates of what looked suspiciously like a ready armory of weapons, and two warriors racing around them, after a staggering, panting-to-exhaustion king!

Running out of curses, Embra stopped, held up her Dwaer in a grip so hard her fingers turned white around its rising glow—and hurled a paralyzing spell upon all three distant running figures.

The air around her flashed, and then flowed crazily . . . and Embra felt her own limbs tightening and stiffening.

Shuddering, she forced herself to hold tight to the Dwaer, and used her last breath to snarl one of the oldest spells she knew, calling on the Stone to power it.

The Dwaer flashed strangely, and she could suddenly move freely again. Around her, an explosion of gasps told her that her fellow overdukes had also been freed from paralysis.

Something had hurled her magic back at her. Something had stood against the ravening power of a Dwaer-Stone, in a defiance she'd begun to think was impossible unless the gods themselves—

Another Dwaer. Eyes narrowing, Embra looked at the saddlebag on

Craer's back. It was ahead of her, directly between her and the fleeing king—and his would-be slayers, too.

She ran on, trying to keep the procurer in view as he ducked and dodged around and over the crates, hurling daggers at the warriors ahead—until at last he ran across an open space, and she could snatch the two breaths she needed.

Holding up her Dwaer, Embra gasped out an enchantment—and her Stone blazed up brightly.

Craer staggered in mid-run as something tugged sharply upward at his saddlebag—and then burst right through its leather, spinning up into the air and blazing as brightly as Embra's own Stone.

Something flashed and crackled back and forth between the two Dwaerindim, like a double-ended arrow sent flashing from one deadly bow to another and back again.

Still running, Craer looked up at the sudden explosion of light over his head—and promptly sprang up onto the nearest crate, leaping high and . . .

. . . closing his fingers around the stump of the severed priest's hand holding the Stone. Craer's weight dragged it down, the sheer flowing force of magic passing between the two Dwaerindim making his entire body shudder, and landed hard on the crate, falling forward to the floor and rolling to his feet still running . . .

Just as Hawkril's warsword stabbed desperately out—and a scant swordlength in front of its tip, the two running warriors both snarled in triumph, and together drove their blades through the body of the fleeing king.

18

The Sword of Spells

olmur Bowdragon straightened with a sigh that sounded suspiciously like a sob. His arms trembled as the spell-flame dancing amid the three Bowdragon brothers wobbled, sputtered—and died, in a spitting of sparks.

Multhas sat back, his face gray with effort and despair. Ithim fell to the tiles, weeping bitterly.

In the searching linkage they'd forged, the three brothers had grimly found the faintest trace of their missing Maelra—but just now, as they'd closed in on her, those faint, distant traces had been chopped off, as if by a knife. There could be little doubt that they'd just felt Maelra Bowdragon die.

Another of their bright young gone—the last one who'd had power enough to impress anyone with sorcery. Dolmur clutched the arms of his chair as if his fingers were talons that could pierce and crumble wood, and stared up at the high ceiling above, feeling sick and empty. How soon would it be before the dome above him, and all others in Arlund, resounded to the stride of some conquering mage?

Unless they bred again, to some sorceress who was a very Dragon of sorcery, the Bowdragons were doomed. Cathaleira, Jhavarr, and now Maelra—the brightest children had all gone to Aglirta, and had all been slain.

Sobbings and snivelings rose from outside the circle: the lesser, still-living children, probably as much afraid that they'd be expected to venture to their deaths next, as they were grieving Maelra.

Dolmur ignored his writhing, facedown youngest brother for the moment, and asked Multhas flatly, "What's your wish that we do now?"

He'd expected the ever aggressive Multhas to explode into either hot or icy rage, but surprisingly, his bearded, usually blustering kinsman just shook his head, empty-faced, and whispered, "Nothing. Not another drop of Bowdragon blood must be given to Serpent-ridden, plague-riddled Aglirta. Let us build a spell-wall, turn our backs on it, and try to forget. Nothing will bring our dead back."

"No," Dolmur told him, as flatly as before. "We must know what happened to her. The time for revenge may not be now, but we must *know*. Or that 'not knowing,' and her loss, will haunt us and change us forever."

The patriarch lifted his gaze from the dark, despairing eyes of Multhas to regard the younger Bowdragons around the circle, and ordered, "Get your most powerful magics together, and meet me back here, as swiftly as you are able."

The younglings stared at him in awe—or was it terror?—until he let a frown settle onto his face. Then they hastened to obey, the youngest fleeing for the doors like storm-driven rags, and the eldest reaching out to drag away the ashen Multhas and the weeping Ithim.

The blade-transfixed young man staggered in the Dwaer-light, turning agonizedly toward his slayers—in time to see Hawkril furiously hack both warriors to the ground, torches bouncing and rolling. He swayed, face twisted in pain, as Craer ran toward him and Embra called, "Craer! Get away! I can't heal him if your Stone's too close!"

"Overdukes!" the dying man cried. "Get to your King!" And then he fell on his face and rolled over, bluish blood gouting from his mouth and nose.

Reaching him, Embra stared down at . . . features that were melting from Raulin's into . . . blank facelessness. A Koglaur!

She looked up at her fellow overdukes, as they gathered around her in this deepest cellar of Flowfoam. They stared down at the corpse, traded astonished looks—and then turned and raced back to the passage that had brought them to this hidden place.

Bats circled and swooped around Embra's head as she hastened, emitting tiny, chill chuckles of mirth. She ignored them—but knew full well, as she ran, that in his cell the Master of Bats was hanging in his chains, coldly laughing.

Raised in exasperation, Baron Phelinndar's voice sounded like the building-to-a-scream growl of a great hunting cat on the prowl. "You think we've *still* got time for spell-frippery, with this Gadaster bone-wizard on the loose, looking for you?"

Ingryl Ambelter stepped around a motionless Melted with a sigh meant to warn the baron that his patience wasn't infinite, and placed the long-locked coffer carefully on the table.

He silently bade the dust-covered undead to step back and make more room here in the center of the cavern, and then turned to the simmering Phelinndar. "We need this more than ever if Mulkyn survives," he said coldly. "And if he hasn't, we should proceed as we've planned, so as not to end up striving against a triumphant Church of the Serpent *after* they've secured their rule over the Vale, when they'll have leisure enough to send priest after priest after hiresword army at us."

He beckoned a single Melted forward, and made the shambling, grotesquely twisted thing hold out its hands. Brushing dust from each gray-and-yellow palm, he put into them small items he'd need once he began spellweaving, produced a key from empty air with a murmured word, and unlocked the coffer.

"More than that," the Spellmaster added, eyeing the glowering baron, "I keep my promises, and you were most insistent—were you not?—that I fully inform you of my plans and magics."

He gestured grandly at the table. "So, now, observe or not, as you prefer, as I begin the long and exacting process of interweaving a Sword of Spells that will give me—us—control not only of the mind of someone but their powers."

"Such as Embra Silvertree?" Baron Phelinndar growled, hands clutching the hilt of his sword, where they always went when he was in need of comfort.

Ambelter nodded. "Or Gadaster Mulkyn, or Dolmur Bowdragon, or even this outlander Talasorn wench who seems to have been made an Overduke of Aglirta when our backs were turned. I have, however, some-one other than all of these in mind."

"Oh?" the baron asked, but the Spellmaster had already started to chant a spell, raising his arms out in front of him as if to proffer a chalice or bowl that wasn't there to someone taller than he, who also wasn't present.

The air between his empty hands shimmered restlessly as the incantation rose in volume and urgency, was briefly shot through with sparks, darkened as if a long evening shadow was falling across it . . . and then thinned to emptiness once more.

Ingryl Ambelter let his hands fall, and then nodded as if satisfied. He seemed to be able to see something Phelinndar could not; all that the casting had achieved, as far as the baron could tell, was to create a certain singing tension in the air that had not been present before.

"Who?" he asked roughly, persisting. "Three take you, Ambelter—have we an agreement, or have we not?"

"We do," the Spellmaster replied curtly. "Patience, please. I'll tell you when I'm done. This series of castings is exacting and precise, and I must keep many things in my mind as I work—or all will be ruined. Rest assured that when I'm done, my intended victim won't have been chosen by the magics; we'll have ample time to debate then."

The two men stared at each other across a cavern that now throbbed and thrummed with magic, an ever-growing din of power that crackled around Ingryl Ambelter as the baron watched—crackled ever more hungrily, though the Spellmaster stood calm and expressionless.

Phelinndar wondered if he was watching a weapon being built before his eyes that could slay him with careless ease—or if Ingryl himself was becoming that weapon. Either way, he stood in peril if he fought the wizard now. Staring into Ambelter's eyes, he nodded slowly.

Ingryl gave him a mirthless smile and then turned to his table and launched into an incantation.

The baron glowered at the mage's back, then sighed, turned away, and found his chair. If he was going to be blasted to ashes before the day ended, there was nothing he could do to prevent it, or to successfully flee and hide . . . so he might as well wait in comfort.

The Dwaer-Stone was glowing on a little table in a far corner of the cavern, away from Ingryl's spellweavings—but throbbing in time to those building spells. Phelinndar glanced at it, and then walked over and scooped it up. If Ambelter had put some sort of warning spell on it, to alert him if someone other than he touched it, well that was just too bad. Let all his spells be wasted, and let him rage.

If Ingryl was going to have his Sword of Spells, his forgotten and taken-for-granted baronial sidekick was going to have what was his, too: the Dwaer. Phelinndar sat down, swung his booted feet up onto the Melted who'd been made to kneel into a footrest some days ago, drew his sword and laid it ready in his lap—just in case—and hefted the Stone in his hand.

The glows of spell building upon spell rose brightly around the distant Spellmaster. Watching them rise and feeling the matching thrum of rising power in the Stone in his hand, the baron began tossing the Dwaer a handspan into the air and then catching it, tossing it again, and then catching it. A lump of rock that wizards would kill for. Truly, Darsar was strange.

The heart of the cavern was now filled with pulsing, humming lines of glowing magical force that floated immobile in midair, forming a man-sized cage. The baron had seen it built, spell upon spell, watching with increasing alarm, both hands clutching the Dwaer.

If only he knew how to use the thing! Oh, he could hurl blasts of burning or smiting force from it, and use it to spit out mists or light or make him fly . . . But a wizard could cast any spell he could think of, using the Stone to power it—and Orlin Andamus Phelinndar was beginning to fear two things: that Ambelter could from afar make the Stone blast anyone holding it—including foolish barons—and that this thrumming cage was meant to hold, and somehow torment, no-longer-needed barons. All around him the Melted were swaying forward with each throb of the spell-cage, rocking back between so as to stay in one place without toppling . . . and the air itself was beginning to feel thick and *flowing*, building to . . . what?

Ambelter seemed finished casting spells for the moment. He'd turned back to the table and was removing some small items from his coffer. The baron peered, but couldn't see what they were from such a distance, with the wizard's body half-blocking his view.

He rose, Dwaer in one hand and ready sword in the other, and strode forward, as softly as he could. Halfway across the cavern, as he threaded his way among the motionless Melted, he came to a wary halt as the Spellmaster swung around and displayed what he held. There was a crooked smile on Ingryl Ambelter's face.

"No, good Baron, I'm not thinking of turning on you. Nor should you think to do the same to me—anything you unleash from the Dwaer will be caught by this Sword of Spells and hurled back whence it came, whether I know what you're trying or not. But see!"

He held out his hands. In one was a lock of dark hair—human hair—and in the other was something small and shriveled.

"Skin and hair from the man I hope this Sword of Spells will strike, and possess for us. They'll make certain my pounce pins the right person."

Phelinndar swallowed, and then waved his sword. "Do it," he said shortly.

Ambelter bowed as courtiers do when receiving orders, turned back to the cage, and put the wrinkled, crumbling scrap of skin in a brightness where two lines met, and the hair in another such moot. Both were only empty air, but both held their newfound burdens as if they were ledges or tabletops.

The baron stared at the floating relics and shuddered. This magic could just as easily be used on him—or any man. "And this fortunate dupe is?"

"Ezendor Blackgult," Ambelter said softly. "Baron, sometime regent, and the man I hate most in all Aglirta. I must influence him before the spell I wove on the Dwaer they seized from the snake-lovers wears weak, or they break it. Once he bears a Dwaer, he'll be able to protect himself so I'll not be able to drive this spell-sword of mine home, no matter how stealthy my approach."

Phelinndar shook his head. "I only hope this plot works better than your last."

The Spellmaster gave the baron a cold look above the spell-glows, and then sighed. "As do I," he snapped, turning back to the throbbing cage. "As do I."

The Master of Bats *had* been laughing—though his mirth had broken off when Craer snatched two bats out of the air with sure hands while drawing level with the open door of the wizard's cell, broke a wing of each before they could bite him, flung them through the doorway, then kicked the door closed with a *boom* that echoed down the passage.

The rest of the overdukes just kept running, panting past without slowing as that door slammed; they knew Craer would be past them to his usual place at the fore in a few breaths. Up the steps they went, bursting past guards who turned with frowns and lowered glaives in case this clatter of haste meant prisoners loosed, into brightly lit Flowfoam Palace.

"Hold, in the name of the King!" a doorguard bellowed immediately.

"Make way, in the name of the King!" Craer called back, not slowing.

The guard lowered his glaive with a snarl, but the procurer stepped to the left, and then abruptly dodged right and ducked to the floor, under it.

The guard hadn't even managed to frame a curse ere Craer was up again, tugging at the glaive's shaft. His jerk sent the guard staggering forward, off-balance—and into the waiting arms of Hawkril, who tossed the man aside like a doll. Guard struck wall with a loud clang of armor, and it was the guard who bounced, fell, and groaned in pain.

His fellow doorguard flung down his glaive and ran for an alarm-gong. Embra snapped, *"Craer!"* in exasperation, and called on the Dwaer to shove the man aside—only to be sent staggering with a shriek of frustration as the other Dwaer-Stone sent her magic right back at her.

Craer whirled and flung a dagger—which flashed like silver fire across the passage and struck the running doorguard's neck, hilt-first, driving the man to the floor in a daze.

The procurer flung open the nearest door, and found himself peering down a narrow flight of stairs that led, judging by smell, to a jakes. He nodded approvingly, dragged the moaning guard to the doorway—and then administered a solid kick to the man's backside. With another groan and a few descending thuds the man disappeared, and Hawkril came striding with the first doorguard and tossed the man gently after the first.

Craer then slammed the door, assumed a casually lounging pose against it, and asked mildly, "Yes, Lady Silvertree? Can I be of service to you in some small way?"

Embra shook her head. "I've been wondering that for over a season now, and not found an answer. Perhaps if 'twere the fashion in Aglirta to hire jesters . . ."

Tshamarra snorted. "Well said, Lady! Craer, stop playing the fool and snatch us a courtier or senior guard who'll know where Raulin is and take us to him. *Now!* Get on with it!"

The procurer gave her a pained look. "You know, Lady Talasorn, I do believe that's just what I've been doing for most of this day? Running here, there, and everywhere with the rest of you overdukes puffing along like a lot of fat, flutter-feathered bustards *behind* me!" He turned with a grand gesture of tragic dismissal. "But enough. Wounded by your words, I go!"

And he sprinted off down the passage to where the next pair of guards were waiting, peering warily over leveled glaives and wondering what had befallen their comrades.

"Make way!" Craer called this time, as he ran. "Overdukes of the King command you!"

The guards lifted their glaives, but one of them snapped, "Wherefore?"

"We hunt Serpents!" the procurer snapped back. "Where's the King?"

Their suspicious frowns told Craer all he needed to know, but by then Hawkril had lumbered into view, and the guards gave way before his more familiar—and formidable—figure. One of them even offered, "Ah, Lords, we know not!"

The overdukes ran on through Flowfoam Palace, brushing past startled-looking envoys and courtiers they'd never seen before, in search of someone they knew. The palace was busy in some areas but curiously empty in others, and guards' challenges were fewer than they should have been.

Blackgult was shaking his head in puzzlement by the time they reached and then left behind the guarded but deserted throne room. As they ran down another passage, he growled, "Something's not right. Huldaerus must be chortling. Have the Serpents—?"

He never finished that question. They came to a high, many-balconied gallery where guards should have been looking down on other guards standing beside desks where scribes and Clerks of the Royal Person mounted a last line of defense against uninvited visitors trying to burst in and "just see the King for a moment." The hurrying Overdukes of Aglirta found no scribes or clerks, and no torches blazing along the dark balcony above—but instead literally ran right into a frightened ring of guards.

The armsmen whirled around with shouts of alarm, swords flashing. Craer and Hawkril parried, yelling, "Turn your blades! Overdukes of Aglirta command you!"

Then they saw what the guards had been menacing, and gasped: "Horns of the Lady!" in ragged unison.

The guards were clustered warily around a snarling, already wounded beast; the massed points of their glittering blades had been keeping it against the passage wall. The monster was a chaos of talons, scaly serpentine arms, tusks and fur, an undulating thing with the head of a boar and the build of a bull—and it was wearing torn scraps of armor that looked as if, before being torn or burst apart, it had been a match for what the guards were wearing.

The monster roared and charged. As the guards shouted in fear and leveled their blades against it, Hawkril ran to meet it, swinging his warsword in a great slash that caught in those snarling jaws and drove the beast back to cower against the wall once more.

Talons clawed the air as the beast drooled blood and growled, but it made no move to rush forward again, now that the unbroken ring of steel had returned.

Blackgult eyed the dangling, clanging fragments of metal it wore and asked, "This was one of your fellows, hey? How did he—?"

A guard shook his head. "Just groaned and hunkered down—and then started to . . . *change*. He screamed a lot, but we didn't want to . . . I mean . . ."

"Plague," Tshamarra said grimly. "Embra, can you—?"

"If Craer gets himself well away from me, perhaps. Every plague-healing's just a little different from those before," Embra replied sourly, peering at the wounded beast. "Three Above, hasn't Aglirta suffered *enough*?"

One of the guards staring at her started to tremble so violently that his fellows turned to look—whereupon foam burst from his mouth, his eyes started to weep blood, and he burst into a wild, lilting scream and swung his blade wildly—nay, blindly—in all directions.

As his fellow guards drew back from their newly stricken fellow and the beast saw room to move and started to growl its way forward again, something hissed down amongst them. It was swiftly followed by more somethings: strangely thick arrows tipped with gaping fangs!

"Serpent-arrows!" Hawkril bellowed, chopping at them with his warsword as Craer cursed and dodged ahead, seeking to get under the place where the deadly hail of snakes was coming from—yon balcony!

"Three *spit*!" Tshamarra raged, ducking behind a screaming guard whose face had sprouted a snake. "Is there no end to this?"

Beside her, Embra sobbed out her own curse as she tore away a snake that had bitten her arm, and flung it as far as she could, reeling. Her arm was burning already, and she just hoped Craer was far enough away . . .

Crouching over her glowing Stone as more snakes rained down around her, striking many of the guards, Embra called on it to purge her of poison. It flared up in a brilliance so bright and sudden that she knew the other Dwaer was too close—even before its power shocked into her from behind, meeting the healing magic within her, and left her writhing, blinded, and gasping for breath on the floor.

"Em!" Hawkril roared, as if from a great distance—though she knew somehow that he was standing over her, shielding her with his own body. "Lady mine, are you well?"

"Now that," she snarled through her tears, shuddering, "was a *stupid* question." A fresh wave of pain made her whimper and twist uncontrollably, and then it ebbed and she could claw her way to her feet, enough to cling to him and scream, "Craer! Get away! *Get away!*"

"Gone!" came an answering shout, echoing from another room. Embra hissed in pain, gathered her strength, held the Dwaer to her breast—and tried again.

This time the Stone erupted in flames, bright tongues of magic that scorched nothing and chilled Embra to the bone. She lost her hold on Hawkril and fell to her knees, shrieking and clutching herself in rocking agony—and the flames that were not flames rose up in a bright blaze that lit the high gallery as bright as day.

"There!" a guard snarled, pointing up at the balcony. Blackgult crouched down behind Hawkril as the armaragor followed the guard's pointing arm.

Grinning down on them from on high were at least seven Serpent-priests with bows, and in their midst was a palace servant, a lass with a decanter of wine in her hand. As the priests reached for fresh arrows—war-shafts, this time; they seemed to have run out of enspelled snakes—she unstoppered it and poured it down on the heads of some of the guards struggling with the beast, laughing. "A little more plague, sirs?"

Embra was curled up in a ball, rocking and moaning gently, her body aglow with strange, crawling magic. Just above her, Blackgult was nearing the end of a careful, one-handed spellcasting, his other hand thrust into his daughter's lap, where her Dwaer was.

Hawk cursed at the sight of the laughing wench, and lumbered forward into a charge—but was met by a fiercer charge, as the beast that had been a guard burst over its wounded fellow armsmen, and struck Hawkril with a crash. As they struggled, talons raking and a warsword rising and falling in the midst of coils and tentacles, the Serpent-priests bent their bows and drew back arrows to their ears—arrows that were aimed at the Lady of Jewels and her father.

And Blackgult finished his spell with a brittle smile.

There was a sudden grinding rumble from overhead, a tremor that shook the room. On the balcony, priests were sent staggering, and more than one arrow flashed harmlessly away to crack against the far wall, shiver, and tumble in shards and slivers to the floor. The servant girl screamed—and went on screaming as the ceiling above the balcony split apart, in rents that ran as fast as the fingers of an anguished opening fist . . .

. . . and crashed down on the balcony, breaking it off the wall with a noise like angry thunder and shattering it in a huge heap of rolling stones on the floor below. Blackgult plucked up Embra and dragged her back from sliding, tumbling stones just in time.

Dust rose in a roiling cloud, out of which loomed a blood-spattered Hawkril, the shorn-off, pulped remnant of a tentacle still clinging to his shoulder—and a retching, softly sobbing bundle in his hand that proved to be Tshamarra.

Someone else came staggering out of the dust behind him, and Blackgult grabbed for his sword and discovered he'd lost it in the tumult.

The new arrival coughed, wiped a hand across his face to reveal himself as one of the guards, and held up the cracked, dust-caked upper half of the decanter the servant girl had been waving so mockingly.

"She must have been plying us with plague-laced wine these last two days," he gasped, "that grauling Serpent-worshipper!"

"If she's been doing that all over the palace," Hawkril growled, reaching for his dazed lady, "Raulin could be dead already!"

"Too high a price to pay for ridding Aglirta of excess courtiers," Craer agreed with a twisted smile, appearing out of the murk.

He turned to Blackgult. "Nicely done. I was almost up to them when the top of the stair broke. Let's find the next way up; 'tis the far side of yon cross-passage, I recall."

"Yes," Blackgult agreed. "Yell when you reach it. Then perhaps Embra can get herself healed without Dwaer-magic tearing her insides out, hey?"

The procurer gave him a reproachful look. "I ran as fast as I could."

"And you will again—right now. Why, you'll be getting good at it, soon!"

Craer's reply was a very rude gesture—but he obediently hastened, and Blackgult was puffing too severely to join in his signal shout when they reached the stair they'd been seeking: a flight of marble steps strewn with dead bodies and witless, drooling men.

Craer glanced up it, waved a hand at all the slaughter and ruin, and said to the onetime Regent of all Aglirta, "Would *you* store a king up yonder, amid all this?"

"Get going," Blackgult told him grimly, "and we'll see, won't we?"

"Who knocks?" a voice asked suspiciously, from the other side of the door. The small, slender man flattened against the wall as far away from the door as he could get and just reach the edge of the door with his fingertips called back, "Craer Delnbone, Overduke of Aglirta. I've another overduke—Blackgult by name—with me."

There was a period of silence, then the voice declared with flat and very unwelcoming finality, "Any man can claim to be an overduke."

"Ah," Craer replied almost delightedly, "but can they correctly mimic my arch overduchal knock? The maid-enchanting lilt of my voice? The stunning beauty of my hand you're staring at through yon spyhole you so fondly believe I don't notice? Come to think of it, who else would come knocking—instead of using a spell or an ax on your door, or stuffing snakes under it to hiss their welcome for them, hey?"

They heard faint laughter from behind the door, then an order, a voice raised in tones of objection, the snap of another order, and then the sounds of a doorbar being lifted and bolts being thrown.

In a rattle of chain, the door opened just wide enough for a guard in full armor, with the visor of his helm down, to peer out. "Who else stands with you?"

Craer preened like a maiden, and then ran his hands over his hips like a strumpet. "Aren't we enough?"

Blackgult rolled his eyes. "Let us in, Greatsarn, before he gets worse. And *believe* me, he gets worse."

The guard withdrew, the door was opened just wide enough for both overdukes to slip through—and slammed shut behind them by guards who hastily fumbled the bolts and bars back into place.

"Imprisoning yourself to save some foe the trouble?" Craer demanded of the young, smiling man sitting at a table at the back of the room. "Raulin, d'you mind telling me just who this most puissant enemy is?"

If Flaeros Delcamper or any of the handful of old, trusted warriors in the stout-walled upper room—the stub of a long-vanished turret, sporting but the one door, a roof-hatch, and two narrow archers' windows—were shocked at hearing the King of Aglirta addressed so abruptly by only his first name, none of them showed it.

"Anyone and everyone," Raulin Castlecloaks replied with a sigh, slapping the table in weary exasperation. "I hope you brought food. We're starving up here, and hardly dare mount more armed expeditions to the kitchens. It cost us Ilger and his three underguard trainees two days back."

"No, Raulin," Blackgult told him darkly, "as a matter of fact we didn't, but if you stay here, I'll fetch the rest of your wayward overdukes, and we'll scour the kitchens for you. Embra might even be able to purge any poisons in whatever provender we find there. I take it the Serpents don't quite openly rule the palace yet?"

"Well," the young king replied ruefully, "not this chamber of it, at least."

Blackgult rolled his eyes again. "Remind me to leave you alone in Flowfoam Palace less often, lad. At least you had enough sense to choose a room a handful of willing swords have some chance of defending—but that's about it."

"Lord Blackgult," the bard from Ragalar said quietly, "might I remind you that you address your King? More respectful words would be advisable."

"No, Lord Delcamper, you may not remind me of such matters," the Golden Griffon told him flatly. "I'm getting too old to have time left for such foolishness—but not yet so age-enfeebled as to become respectful of anyone. That way lies ruin for all Aglirta, just now, no matter whose backside warms the throne."

The king pretended to be shocked, but as Flaeros Delcamper started to sputter with indignation, Raulin burst into whoops of laughter—the rather wild laughter of someone seizing on mirth after too long with nothing to laugh at—and told the room, "May the Band of Four live forever!"

Craer grinned. "Well, that's one more sharp difference of opinion between you and the Snake-lovers, to be sure. I—"

His face changed, and he clutched at the saddlebag slung over his shoulder. It was rising, the worn leather shifting, and as he caught at it, a sudden glow spilled from under its flaps.

"What have you there?" a guard growled, hefting his blade.

"A Dwaer-Stone, and its doings right now tell me another Dwaer's being used close by."

"Somewhere on Flowfoam?" Flaeros asked sharply.

"Somewhere within a few chambers of right here," Blackgult answered. "Have you a spyhole, or the like, looking in this direction?" He waved at the barred, bolted, and chained door behind him.

"No," Raulin replied. "Why?"

The Golden Griffon smiled. "I'm fairly sure the Lady Silvertree is coming up the same steps we did, but I'd rather not fling the door wide to see if that's so—just in case I end up welcoming someone *else* who can casually flatten overdukes and palaces alike with a Dwaer."

"There's no need," Embra's voice said crisply from the empty air beside him, causing Craer's saddlebag to tremble wildly and light to flare from it as if a whirling inferno of flame spun within. "The enchantments of my childhood are still useful for some things—and finding known sources of mighty magic is one of them. We're all here; open the door."

Blackgult turned to do so, and Greatsarn moved to help him, but a guard barred their way, sword raised, and said coldly, "I don't recall hearing the King give his permission regarding any use of this door—'tis barred for a *reason,* y'know."

"Either we open it," Blackgult told the armsman, reaching for the first doorbolt as if there wasn't a swordtip in his face, "or she'll blast it down and all of us with it. Unless, of course, she gets irritated."

The sword drew back a little. "And if she is, what then?"

The Golden Griffon shot two bolts and reached for a third. "Then," he told the guard, "she'll do something much worse."

The guard regarded Blackgult expressionlessly for a moment, as the oldest Overduke of Aglirta went on tossing aside bars, lifting pins, and unhooking chains, and then silently stepped back, taking his sword with him.

"No," Blackgult said to the king not much later, as they watched one of Tshamarra's spells cook a roast from the kitchens without need of hearthfire or spit, "I'd best remain here on Flowfoam with you, to defend and advise.

Tshamarra can take my place in the Four whilst they go forth to strike down Serpent-priests the length of the Vale—and, I suppose, the usual mercenary warlords or nobles who're taking advantage of the plague to set themselves up as war leaders against you."

King Castlecloaks spread his hands. "I never wanted this crown, you know. Any of you would be so much better as Aglirta's king—even if you sat there hating it. But you're also the realm's best defenders; no matter what's unfolding, I can never see a better way forward than what you propose. So you'll get no argument from me. I'm right glad to have you here, Old Lion, while the rest of you hunt the Serpents. What now?"

"What must come first, Raulin," Embra said from across the room, "is the breaking of the spells laid on the second Dwaer, so my father can wield it. Then we go hunting . . . and I believe our first quarry should be the missing Baron Phelinndar, or whoever's taken his Dwaer from him. We must assume the Serpents have the fourth, and I'd prefer that we be able to muster three against their one when they make their usual bid to openly and grandly snatch Aglirta."

Raulin nodded. "You'll break these spells, of course?"

"If we're not actually fighting Serpent-priests and I can spare the time and attention to work freely, it shouldn't take long. Here on Flowfoam, I can call on the Living Castle enchantments to source more power, protecting me as I strip away the trap-spells. Tash and my father can help me."

"Right after we've all eaten," Blackgult said. "We'll find one of the cellars, and leave Craer and Hawkril to entertain—ahem—guard you."

Flaeros Delcamper rolled his eyes. "You play manyshields, I hope?"

"Not unless you're wagering," Craer said brightly, "and I don't see enough wealth lying about this room to wager with. You wouldn't happen to have any outlying castles filled with beautiful maidens, would you?"

"Lord Delnbone," Tshamarra said softly, and the procurer winced.

"Then again," he continued swiftly, "we could tell you airy tales of our exploits to pass the time and inspire any bards present to compose ballads to our gallantry, and—"

"Annoy all of you thoroughly," the Lady Talasorn added, causing King Castlecloaks to struggle on the edge of exploding mirth again.

Flaeros sighed and began to arrange pieces on the manyshields board. "While you begin the feast," he said, "Raulin and I will try to get in a game or two before you start ruining our play with your no doubt helpful suggestions."

"Lord Delcamper," Craer said slyly, "might I remind you that you describe the King of Aglirta, in a room full of his subjects? More formal titles would be advisable."

Several of the guards snickered.

Tshamarra sighed. "You see? 'Tis starting already."

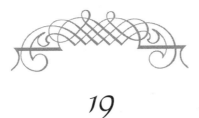

19

True Faces Revealed

The younger Bowdragons stared around in awe at the copper-sheathed walls reaching so high overhead, and at the polished marble floor studded with countless curving runes and intricately graven inset floorstones. Even those who tried to pretend they weren't impressed kept looking down at the carved stone faces of their long-dead ancestors set here and there into the floor, each effigy marking a vertical burial beneath. The glittering eye-gems of those faces seemed to stare accusingly up at the living Bowdragons. The youngest, though they'd all taken the chairs he'd indicated for each one, leaned toward each other in their seats, as if seeking to huddle together. The air was rich with magic, drifting and coiling . . . and waiting.

It was a room in Arlund most of them had never seen before. Years had passed since a Bowdragon had perished and left behind a body that could be buried here.

Dolmur had not bothered to share his reasons for bringing them down to this deep and hidden place. Buried magics and enchantments yet lingering around Bowdragon bones could augment the sorcery of the living—and if things were to go bad this day, he wanted his family to face what befell together, not weep at more vanished and lost kin.

He looked up from his chair now, less at his two brothers than at their offspring; so many young and frightened faces. Armed with magic and ready for war.

Yet not ready. These who were left were not the bold and warlike.

They'd never be ruthless sorcerer-lords or wandering archmages of power. The Bowdragons were doomed already.

" 'Tis time," he said calmly. Well, if 'twas in his power, 'twould be a more dignified doom than most. "Remember, obey my commands absolutely. We'll use our magic to farscry Aglirta and learn who slew Maelra, not repeat the mistakes of our departed ones, and blunder into that land lashing out at every ruler and mage we see."

They stared at him in silence, waiting . . . nervously rather than eagerly, looking more like warriors being sent into battle than mages about to taste the power of a true meld for the first time.

"All rings and coronets on? If not, don them now."

He waited through the resulting brief flurry of movement, noted that everyone seemed to be seated comfortably, and lifted his hand.

In answer to a spell he'd cast and left waiting more than twenty summers earlier, certain floorstones flipped back, and staves of power slowly rose into view beside each chair.

More than one Bowdragon gasped at their beauty and obvious power. Within a humming halo of blue flame, each metal shaft stood upright with no hand to hold it, entwined about with intricately sculpted arms and flourishes of metal that bore enchanted gems and glowing runes. Each was topped with an open claw, a long-nailed hand that looked human, and partly was.

"Each of you now take up your scepter," he said quietly, "and hold it out until the hand atop your staff can grasp it. Let the hand do so."

Some of the scepters were extended with reluctance, a few even with trembling fear—but extended they all were, after a few moments that seemed an eternity. The seated Bowdragons then stared at him and each other in mounting wonder as the thrumming power reached into and through them, and they started to share thoughts and sight . . .

Someone gasped, and Dolmur said swiftly and firmly, "The meld begins. Sit still, all of you, from now on. It can be death to arise suddenly, at the wrong time, whatever happens. Remember: Obey me absolutely, or you may doom not only yourself but all the rest of us."

Ithim and Multhas had done this before, but the shuddering power was making the younglings visibly excited, eager at last, as Dolmur swiftly wove the spell that called on the power of the staves to spy from afar. "First," he announced, his voice now echoing in their minds as well as in their ears, "we'll gaze upon Flowfoam, observing any wizards there who serve the King of Aglirta . . ."

. . .

The room shook, hurling Blackgult and Tshamarra into the air like rag dolls, and a web of crackling lightnings burst out of the untamed Dwaer as it shot from its cage and skidded along the floor, rending flagstones in its wake.

Eyes swimming, Embra used her Dwaer to drink in those lightnings—and slowly, like fisherfolk dragging laden nets out of the Silverflow, she managed to drag the second, enspelled-against-her Stone closer.

When it hung in front of her, spitting angry sparks and smokes, she drew in a deep breath, cloaked herself in all the power she could summon, and—clasped her hand around it, whilst still firmly gripping her own Stone.

And thereby learned what true pain was.

Tshamarra, lying dazed and winded on shattered and jumbled rock that had been a smooth, unbroken floor not long ago, thought she'd never heard such a loud and powerful howl of agony, not even from clawbears of the peaks burned alive by Talasorn spells.

Raking tangled hair out of her eyes, she stared at Embra—who stood rigid in Dwaer-glow, arms outstretched and with a warring Stone in either one.

The eyes of the Lady of Jewels were like raging flames, and lightnings seemed to be tumbling from her mouth. Tumbling . . . and slowly dying away.

Embra swayed, uttered a weak but very unladylike curse, and then stumbled forward, looking wearily down the room to Blackgult. "Please come and get this, Father," she gasped, "for I fear I'll fall on my face if I have to walk all the way to where you stand. I . . . gods, I *still* hurt. Dwaer-healed, yes, but my body doesn't quite believe it yet."

She shook her head. "Don't any of you *ever* try that. The pain . . ."

The Golden Griffon chuckled. "I knew you'd do it, lass. Did I not set out to sire someone fit to rule the realm, all those years ago? A sorceress to shame all others?"

"You sound like Craer," the Lady Talasorn muttered, as she hastened to Embra.

The Lady Silvertree sighed. "Ah, to have been born a man," she said lightly, "and so always know exactly where my feet and all Darsar beneath them are headed, even before I stop to think."

Tshamarra drew back as Embra dropped the newly tamed Stone into her father's hands, threw up her hands, and gasped, "Lady, how can you speak so of the Lord Blackgult, your own father?" There was a twinkle in her dark eyes, and the corners of her lips twitched.

Twitched, then curved, and then burst into merry laughter. Embra joined in as they embraced in giddy mirth, rocking briefly breast-to-breast as men often did. By unspoken agreement, however, as their laughter died into chuckles and they drew apart again, they refrained from slapping each other heartily on backs and shoulders, and snarling praises back and forth like tossed fruit.

That was about the time they noticed that Ezendor Blackgult was standing as still as a statue, staring down silently at the Stone in his hands—and that it was twinkling gently, casting up tiny moving reflections onto his motionless face.

"Father?" Embra asked hesitantly.

"Lord Blackgult," Tshamarra snapped, "attend us!"

The Golden Griffon's head slowly lifted, and he blinked. "Aye, I hear and heed." He shook himself, and then smiled. "Gods, girl, but I was scared you'd been blown or burned apart right in front of me."

He shook himself again, and was suddenly the brisk, sardonic Blackgult of old. "So, shall we raid the kitchens and pantries properly this time, and get you and your men a good night's sleep or tumble, as you prefer, before you set out down the Vale again? Hey?"

The Lady Talasorn spread her hands. "Seeing as we have privacy here, why don't you two use the Stones together now, to seek the other two Dwaer?"

Embra and Blackgult exchanged glances, lifted eyebrows . . . then nodded. They went to opposite ends of the chamber, and Embra waved Tshamarra behind her so the Talasorn sorceress wasn't standing between the two Dwaerindim.

The air between the Stones started to sing almost immediately, and that singing somehow carried Embra's murmur clearly to the ears of the others. "Feel it, Father? Power's taken *thus,* and received thus. Try . . . yes, 'tis easy, see? Now let me do the scrying, and feed me power when I call for it . . . yes, yes, that's it . . . now! Give me power *now!*"

The singing rose into a whistling snarl and then climbed into a shriek that made Tshamarra wince and cover her ears—as Embra suddenly cried: *"More!"*

A breath later, Blackgult called, "There! Over there! I saw . . ."

The singing died, and Embra nodded. "Yes, definitely another Dwaer. Close by the river, but underground—*just* underground, perhaps in a cellar. There was other magic around it, something stirring . . ."

Blackgult said nothing, and it was a moment before Tshamarra glanced in his direction and saw him standing hunched over, trembling. She'd seen a man stand like that years ago, after a sword had thrust through his guts and then been snatched out again. He'd stood swaying thus for some time, feeling his death filling him, ere toppling . . .

"Embra," she said quietly, laying a hand on her friend's arm. The Lady of Jewels followed her gaze, and watched her father slowly straighten and then look down at the Stone in his hand with a certain surprise. She exchanged glances with Tshamarra, and then strode down the room, the Lady Talasorn right behind her.

"Father," she asked firmly, taking Blackgult's chin in her hand and staring into his eyes, "how fare you?"

He gave her the wry, crooked smile he used so often these days. "As well as can be expected after a defeat that cost me my army, friends, wealth, and barony, and left me hated by thousands of folk who still seek my death; a short but harried career of outlawry; aging right out of the days when women clawed each other to share my bed; the cares of regency; personally battling the Great Serpent a time or two . . . and being mind-blasted. I get along."

Embra gave him a frown. "Your list is not unfamiliar—but tell me more about this 'mind-blasted.' "

Blackgult glanced at her and then at Tshamarra, and for a flickering moment his eyes seemed to glow green. "Once, in battle, I used a Dwaer to snatch myself away from the midair blast that killed Jhavarr Bowdragon. Calling on the Stone to speed me out of being torn apart, I was trapped in linkage to it when the blast broke over me and, ah, *twisted* the Dwaer. I can remember, sometimes, what I once was—but there are always mists now, clinging and hiding. My memory—even my thinking—comes and goes, despite the Dwaer-healing since."

His gaze flicked up to Embra, thrust into her like a cool swordthrust, and then dropped away again. " 'Tis gone," he added quietly. "None can restore it, for none can see what was there before. I am . . . *worn down*. Feeling old. For the first time I see in myself feebleness, and failure, and forgetting."

Blackgult lifted one hand, regarded it, and then let the newly tamed Dwaer settle into it. "More and more," he said, hefting the Stone, "this seems a toy for younger folk—and the long sleep more and more welcoming." He sighed, looked away, and then back at Embra and Tshamarra. "Yet I know my duty," he told both sorceresses. "The King shall not stand unguarded."

There was a strange, tender look in Embra's eyes as she lifted her hand and touched his cheek with a gentle finger. "Thank you," she whispered. "I truly have a father—a sire finer than others in Aglirta can dream of having."

Her arms went around Blackgult, and she kissed him. Blackgult put his own arms around her as delicately as if she was a slender crystal carving—and they rocked together gently. Tshamarra heard a soft, broken sound that made her frown, and glide closer, and then come to a sudden stop.

Ezendor Blackgult was sobbing. When he could speak again, he murmured, "Oh, my precious one. Live, child, and make Aglirta brighter."

His arms tightened around his daughter, and he added quietly, his voice steady now, "Oh, lass, I am so proud of you!"

Embra started to weep, then. Tshamarra Talasorn watched for a moment, her eyes very bright, smiled . . . and then quietly withdrew to the door, slipped out, and was gone.

The cage of shimmering force spun silently in the cavern air before them like a knife rolling slowly across a tilting table. Spell-lights winked and glowed like tiny stars as it turned—and Ingryl Ambelter smiled. "Behold," the Spellmaster exulted, "the Sword of Spells."

"Truly finished, this time?" the man standing behind him asked, cradling a softly glowing Dwear-Stone against his armored breast.

The wizard turned to face the baron. " 'Twas done before," he said smoothly, "when I said 'twas, but now I've tested it on a man I happened to know, yonder down by the river, and snuffed out his mind like a candle. Wherefore we know it works."

Ambelter took two restless strides across the chamber, ducked around a dust-covered, impassive Melted, and whirled to face Phelinndar again.

"Now," he gloated, "we can begin—slowly and softly at first, like a boy hunting frogs with a spear. Subtly I'll turn Blackgult to my will."

"*Our* will," Baron Phelinndar reminded him coldly. "Or had you forgotten me already, *friend* Ambelter?"

Fury flashed across the Spellmaster's face, just for a moment—though that was quite long enough for even a Baron of Aglirta to recognize it, as he was sure he was meant to—ere the wizard masked it with the smooth reply, "Of course not, Phelinndar. I merely meant that I, as the one of us who knew him best and knows magic better than he does, will be able to subtly guide him more than you could, and so should be the one influencing him."

The Sword of Spells spun a little closer as Ambelter added warningly,

"If Blackgult becomes aware of what we're doing, our danger will be much greater than mere loss of control of a key man of Aglirta."

"Of course," the baron agreed quietly, inclining his head politely and oh-so-subtly lifting the Dwaer as he did so. *I must destroy Ingryl Ambelter even sooner than I'd thought,* he told himself silently as he turned away, *or perish at his hands—leaving Aglirta itself his next victim.*

Maelra Bowdragon screamed, but no one heard her.

Again she shrieked, raging in helpless fury inside her own skull. Gadaster grinned savagely all around her embattled awareness, showing her that he'd heard her—as he made her body slay her kin.

Fire flashed back in savage reflection from the burnished copper banners soaring on all sides to the ceiling as she—as Gadaster Mulkyn, in coldly firm control of her body—spell-cloaked her in a semblance of her favorite clinging black gown, and then transported her to the heart of Uncle Dolmur's weaving, in the deep chamber in Arlund she'd only seen once before.

Mists swirled and cleared around the edges of her gaze. Barely had Bowdragon eyes lifted to recognize her, and excited smiles appeared, when the cold, ruthless thing that had once been Spellmaster of Silvertree took control of all the roused Bowdragon magic with a few deft weavings that Maelra could not even follow, let alone understand.

Frantically she tried to scream warnings, tried to wave at those of her blood to flee or guard themselves, but Gadaster's cold, silent laughter cloaked her in his mockery as he made her smile and spread her hands in thanks and welcome instead. Then he sent the whelmed power of Dolmur's weaving down her arms and out of her fingertips, lashing her own kin with death as they sat with their scepters.

The howling storm of magic that dashed the youngest to whirling bones in their seats forced staff after beautiful enchanted staff to explode, in blasts that shook the room and brought more raw power whirling up into Maelra.

Gadaster roared with soundless, triumphant mirth in her head as she watched Multhas Bowdragon struggle to his feet in the raging storm of her hurled magic, disbelief and rage twisting his face as the runes on his robes burst into flames, one after another, their magic spent vainly trying to protect him.

As their eyes met, hatred kindled in his gaze, though she struggled to plead apologies, tried vainly to weep—and stared back at him in anguish, trying to tell him, to make him see she wasn't . . . wasn't . . .

Gadaster guided her limbs and lips through swift, cruel castings that blasted her older cousins where they sat. Uncle Multhas stared at their dyings in shock and rage, and then back at her with his own lips snarling a spell that would surely slay her, would tear her apart limb from bloody limb before his eyes.

So this was Gadaster's cruel trick: She'd slay her family and be slain doing so! Maelra tried to show Multhas with her eyes that she had no willing part in all of this, tried to scream her innocence—and managed only to make a sort of feeble mewing as he leveled his hands to guide the magic that would rend her.

Something flashed and winked off to one side, and Gadaster forced her to turn her head and see what it was. Green, winking sparks danced where Uncle Dolmur and Ithim her father had been—somehow, Dolmur had managed to whisk them away!

She exulted, seizing on the only good thing she could in all of this slaughter, as the death-spell cast by Uncle Multhas failed right in front of her eyes, and Gadaster made her send back a deadly magic that would make the flesh melt slowly off his bones.

Uncle Multhas stared in horror at the bare, glistening bones of his fingers . . . and then watched them fall away, one by one, as the creeping sorcery that was taking his life climbed up both of his arms . . .

Multhas looked at Maelra in terror, trying to plead for mercy, and saw the same pleading look in her own eyes, directed back at him. The sorcery gnawed at him with frightening speed.

He died bewildered and despairing. Around his crumbling, toppling form enchanted item after enchanted Bowdragon item burst or melted, surrendering flames of magic that swirled up to join Gadaster's ever hungry, ever-growing spellstorm.

Maelra hung at its glowing heart, trying to whimper and lose her gaze in the flames, and so not see what Gadaster did to her loved ones and their power—but the cold, commanding presence in her head prevented her missing a single moment.

The last Maelra saw, ere she threw herself into his laughter and let the chill, laughing darkness overwhelm her, were many tiny plumes of spellsmoke rising from the eye-gems of the stone faces in the floor, as the last spells of her ancestors were drained away . . .

And then, mercifully, the darkness took her.

"My Maelra," Ithim Bowdragon whispered, staring unseeing into the darkness.

"She was," Dolmur agreed gravely, "and she was not. 'Tis best, brother, if you believe we're the last living Bowdragons, and she's lost to us."

"I–Kill me, brother, if you have any love left for me at all," Ithim said brokenly. "I've nothing left to live for. All our family thrown down and swept away. All gone, all dark . . ."

"No, Ithim," the eldest Bowdragon replied in a voice of cold, heavy iron, "there's much for us both still to do. We have a family to refound, and revenge to prosecute for all our lost and fallen. *You* have the greatest revenge of all."

"I do?"

"Vow with me," Dolmur Bowdragon commanded, as they floated together in the dark refuge where he'd spellsnatched them. "Vow this: That we shall never die, nor rest, until we hunt down and fittingly slay whoever was riding Maelra, to make her attack us all as she did."

Ithim's voice rose. "I felt our foe—cold and gleeful, more a master of magic even than you! Yes, of course my Maelra could not have grown so in sorcery, in such a short time." His voice changed, becoming a wavering, conspiratorial whisper. "So strong . . . Dolmur, do you think we can do this?"

"Ithim," the patriarch of the Bowdragons whispered back, "I think we *must* do this—or the Three Watching Gods will not have lost just one over-proud human family this day, but all Darsar!"

He waved a hand, and a few sparks kindled in the darkness as he added, with more bitterness than Ithim had ever heard in Dolmur's voice before, "And what will they do for amusement then?"

"So of course," Overduke Delnbone was saying airily, "I had no choice but to accept her surrender—minus her cloak. She protested, as women do, say-ing the night was too cold to be running arou–"

"Craer," Embra Silvertree said into his ear, though she was to be seen nowhere in the room, " 'twould be a very good idea to fall abruptly silent right now. *Right* now. I very much doubt your lady will want to hear all about the time you chased an unclad Naevrele Lashantra down three streets in Sirlptar . . . especially as she happens to be Tshamarra's cousin."

"Ooop," the procurer remarked brightly, as Flaeros, the king, and Sul-dun Greatsarn all broke into grins—and across the room there sounded the rhythm of sharp raps upon the door that announced the arrival of the two Lady Overdukes.

"Well, I'm afraid I'll have to finish this little tale some other time," Craer gushed hastily, catching up his saddlebag. "Hawk and I have a noble audience with some heaping platters in the kitchens."

Greatsarn waved a hand. "Oh? And the saddlebag?"

Overduke Delnbone straightened, assuming a look of dew-washed innocence, and replied, "I didn't say just how many platters, now, did I?"

"Craer," Embra Silvertree said into his ear, in person this time. "Get out. Get out now, while you still can."

The procurer whirled around with a flourish—but the soft breast he'd been intending to run into wasn't there. Instead, he found himself staring into a pitying smile. It belonged to Embra, who'd spun away in unison with him, to fetch up facing him just out of reach. She gave him a sigh and the words, "Procurers are *so* predictable."

Craer was still trying to think of a dignified answer to that observation, with the delighted laughter of all the men in the room ringing in his ears and a scornful Tshamarra Talasorn giving him a hard stare, when Hawkril strode past, smoothly took hold of his ear, and swept him out the door.

"Finest shalarn," the cellarer told the towering armaragor eagerly, almost panting with fear. "Brought straight from far Sarinda."

"Man, 'tis *green*," the warrior growled, holding the bottle in one hand with surprising gentleness—considering the iron strength and increasing tightness of the grip he had on the cellarer's belt with the other.

The castle officer's legs dangled well clear of the ground, kicking slightly. He was busy deeply regretting his earlier swift rudeness—but how was he to know these two ruffians had the king's leave to raid the palace kitchens, let alone the royal winecellar!

"Ah, well, ah-ha-ha, so 'tis," he offered hastily, fervently wishing he'd donned his older, looser truss that morning, as the armaragor's grip made all his hidden underbelts—and their buckles—dig ever deeper into soft, private areas of his anatomy. "A very splendid emerald green, ah-ha, *yes!*"

"Deep green and aromatic, you say?" the armaragor asked skeptically, giving the wine another critical stare. "Well, then, *you* drink some, whilst I watch!"

He rammed the cellarer down into a chair and thumped the bottle down in front of him. Well behind the quivering official, the four guards summoned earlier by the Lord High Cellarer to scourge and then expel the two intruders chuckled openly.

They shall all boil in oil, screaming for mercy, the cellarer vowed silently, as he gulped eagerly. "Why, I couldn't! Friend warrior, this is some of the most expensi—"

"I'm not your friend," Hawkril growled, thrusting his face close to the red and quivering visage just beyond the bottle, "I'm an Overduke of Aglirta, and I'm giving you a command. Consider how quickly you'll obey—for your alacrity may have some bearing on two things: how much longer you're cellarer of Flowfoam, and the remaining length of your *life*!"

"Hawk, I know he was extremely insulting, but let him live, hey? Empty yon bottle over his head, make him fetch a dozen different ones for each of us, and let's be gone from here," Craer muttered, from behind the hulking armaragor.

Hawkril swung around to give the procurer a surprised look. Craer was sitting at a kitchen table, looking at his bowl of soup as eagerly as if a friend had just drowned in it. "You feel as restless as I do?" he asked.

The procurer didn't look up, but he did nod. Emphatically.

Hawkril turned back to the cellarer. "Fetch those two dozen bottles—in a pair of carrybaskets, mind. If you do so swiftly, I won't have to come looking for you, will I?"

For the first time in his life, the Lord High Cellarer of Flowfoam Castle set about obeying an order at a run.

Their stroll ended up where they'd both known it would, though neither had said a word in that regard: at the graves of Sarasper and Brightpennant. Several empty bottles had been discarded in their wake, and the huge haunch of boar in Hawkril's hand had been literally whittled down—with two very sharp belt-knives—to a short end of meat around a long, bare bone.

"So, have you decided what it is that overdukes do yet, besides bully servants?" the shorter stroller asked his taller companion.

"Chase wenches and steal things, if they're also procurers," came the dry reply, and then, in a different voice, "No. Nor have I looked ahead, to beyond battles against Serpents and nobles. I've never thought any of us will live to see time enough to wonder. If ever we drive down the Snakelovers, and somehow hammer loyalty into the nobles, 'twill be our turn to do the same to the merchants of Sirlptar next."

Craer opened another bottle, poured a goodly amount on one grave and then the other, saluted the fallen ones quietly by name, and then asked, "So what's been riding you, these last few days? Between fights to the death and a certain Lady of Jewels, I mean?"

Hawkril let out a long, reluctant sigh and said slowly, "Fear. Fear for her. Something's going to happen to Embra. Something bad. I can feel it."

He looked sidelong at Craer, expecting the usual wry quip or light-heartedly tasteless comment, but his old friend wore no smile. Lifting his eyes to meet Hawkril's gaze, the procurer nodded soberly. "I've dreamed of such things, too—different horrors, different grim fates, but all of them dark."

They stared at each other in silence for a long, long breath, and then in unison, without another word spoken, turned to look south across the river.

On the ever-rushing waters below, a larger, grander barge than most—one of the most splendid for hire in Sirlptar—was drawing up to the Flow-foam docks.

"Of course it's not wise," the King of Aglirta told his guards angrily, "but I'm going to do it anyway. The Three damn me if I'm going to cower in a corner of my palace forever, neglecting my realm around me. *These* idiots made me King, and I'm not going to sit there in front of them shirking every last royal duty!"

The idiots so forcefully indicated were the overdukes who walked so closely and watchfully around him, only a faint shimmering of the air indicating that two of them were using the Dwaer-Stones held ready under their court cloaks to shield the young king.

Blackgult—who'd brought word up from the docks to the bard Flaeros Delcamper, and so also to all in the room with him—strode before King Castlecloaks, and Embra Silvertree walked behind him, with the sorceress Tshamarra Talasorn flanking the monarch on one side, and Flaeros walking beside him on the other. The royal guards in their full armor, Suldun Great-sarn watchfully at the rear, stalked along in a tight ring around this royal party—making the steps down to the docks quite crowded.

"I see the Delcampers stint not," Tshamarra remarked, surveying the boat that awaited below.

"The best is always cheaper in the long run," Flaeros replied, as they came out onto the broad sweep of the docks, and the guards there lifted their weapons in salute and stepped back.

The voyagers, all in Delcamper livery, were drawn up to greet the king: a dozen servants, with the swordcaptain of their travel escort of six house warriors at their head. He saluted Flaeros, bowed to King Castlecloaks, and then smoothly stood aside before anyone could speak, revealing who'd been standing behind him: an old, small woman leaning on a silver-handled cane.

"Your Majesty," Flaeros said with a broad smile, "may I present again to you the Lady of Chambers who has served so many of my family so well, for far more years than I've been alive—and is more truly noble than any dozen Delcampers: the Lady Natha Orele."

The king grinned and extended his hand in time to stop the aged Lady of Chambers from trying to kneel to him. "No, please—no one should kneel to me unless I'm passing sentence on them," he said firmly. "Flaeros, be informal, hey?"

The bard grinned and joyfully swept the old woman into an embrace. "Am I mortifying you enough, Orele?" he asked, when he'd finished kissing her.

"Tolerably, Lord," was the dry reply—which so delighted Raulin Castlecloaks that he took a turn at embracing a Lady of Chambers.

"Now *that* was foolish," she chided him. "I could be a murderous priestess of the Serpent!"

Raulin grinned. "Well, are you?"

"Not this morning, dear," she said gently. "But let us all start this formidable climb, the sooner to have something to drink, hey? I'll be putting us to work right briskly, by the look of you two. Has the palace run short of servants, or is there some crazed current fashion for sleeping in your armor?"

As the king chuckled and stepped back to offer her his arm, the shimmering of air that surrounded him fell upon her for a second time, and she turned and looked straight at the Overduke Blackgult, who stood watchfully to one side, one hand on his sword-hilt and the other on his Dwaer-Stone.

"Well, who's this?" she asked quietly, peering.

"Overduke Ezendor Blackgult," Flaeros said helpfully. "He used to be Regent of Aglirta—and is still famous throughout Asmarand as the Golden Griffon. You've met before, remember?"

"Ah, yes," Lady Orele murmured, her gaze locked with Blackgult's. They measured each other in wary silence for a long moment, unmoving, and then the overduke bowed his head gravely and turned away.

"There is one who took ship with us in Sirlptar," the swordcaptain murmured, "who's not of Ragalar. A warrior of Aglirta sworn to the King's service, I believe, one Tesmer by name."

Raulin whirled around to peer at the dock. "Tesmer? Where is he?"

"Still on the barge," Blackgult said, pointing. "Wounded, by the looks of him."

The king frowned. "Flaeros, please take the Lady Orele to the rooms prepared for her, with the rest of your household, who are all most royally welcome. We must meet Tesmer without delay."

If Blackgult had not thrust out a firm hand to bar his way, Raulin would have been on the barge in the next instant. Greatsarn gave the king a reproachful look as the Golden Griffon and two of the guards went onto the barge instead, raised the trusted king's warrior from the chair he'd been seated in, and brought him onto the dock.

Tesmer was pale, and bore enough of his clothing torn up and tied in strips around one of his legs to make it thrice the thickness of the other, but he struggled to kneel until Blackgult firmly sat him down on a dock bench and held him there. Raulin sat beside him and said, "None of that nonsense. How fare you? What befell?"

"A sword slash only, Your Majesty," was the grim reply. "Light blood-spill, given where I've been and what I've seen." He glanced up at the ring of faces behind the king, guards and two sorceresses, and hesitated.

"I have no secrets from any here," Raulin said quickly. "Speak freely."

Tesmer sighed, sat back, and said, "Majesty, I'll be blunt. The Blood Plague has spread, an unknown sword has slain the Tersept of Bladelock in his bed, and the Baron of Adeln killed by the Serpents. Small armies commanded by the Baron of Glarond and the Tersept of Ironstone clashed with great loss of life and no clear victor. I've spoken with many of our eyes downvale, and it seems Serpent-priests are everywhere, bullying and making trouble—but none as yet seems eager to whelm a force of swords to directly attack Flowfoam."

"I was wondering when you'd get to the good news," Raulin said in dry tones. "My thanks, Tesmer. We'll take you to the healers and then the kitchens, and we can talk more of this much later: I'll send for you. Don't worry about falling asleep—if my messenger finds you snoring, we'll talk on the morrow."

"Thank you, Your Majesty," the warrior replied quietly, letting his shoulders slump for the first time. "A good bed will be a rare treat."

"As many a goodwife says, when her husband is beyond hearing," the Lady Talasorn murmured, causing Tesmer to look up in astonished amusement, and several guards to chuckle.

The king shook his head, arching his eyebrows. "You make wedded life sound so jolly, Lady Overduke."

"Good," the sorceress replied with a smile. "Even young kings should be fairly warned."

Embra chanced to look at her father. He gave her a savage grin, and she rolled her eyes in eloquent reply.

"Ah, yes," Tesmer muttered, so quietly that only the Lady of Jewels could hear. "I'm home all right. Back among the halfwit jesters, hey, hey."

She found that very funny, but managed not to sputter too loudly in her mirth. Overdukes are, after all, heroes of the realm.

"You'll be able to find your room again?" the steward asked anxiously.

Tesmer smiled his thanks. "I've done guard duty over these chambers before, as it happens," he said quietly, "and the kitchens, too. I'll be all right."

The steward bowed and hurried away, glad not to have given offense and in some haste to pay court to the far prettier Ragalan chambermaids who'd arrived this day. The trusted king's warrior watched him go, and when he was out of sight, turned to the stairs that led to the kitchens.

For someone who'd once guarded both the kitchens and the apartments he'd just come from, Tesmer's next actions were curious indeed. Passing a landing whose door opened into the bustle of the pantries, he continued down the stairs into darker depths. When he reached the deep darkness of the cellars, he did not pause to light a torch from the rack kept ready by the brazier, but strode away into the endless night, soft-footed and almost silent.

A pantry hatch promptly opened in the ceiling above. It let two things down into the darkness: a sack-seeking hook that was destined to find nothing because it was reaching down the wrong hatch, and a brief shaft of light.

That radiance happened to fall straight upon the warrior. He glanced up, but no one was looking down. The wielder of the fetch-hook had turned to listen to someone loudly and profanely informing him of his error.

Which was a good thing, because the familiar features of Tesmer had twisted on one side into quite a different face, with a longer nose, a sharper jaw, and lighter hair. The change was swift, and had already spread to the other side of the warrior's face when the closing hatch took the light with it again—and the changed man strolled deeper into Flowfoam's nigh-deserted cellars.

Perhaps, as King Castlecloaks had once remarked, the palace cellars were never quite deserted enough.

20

Dreams Bright and Dark

The baron took another cautious step closer to the snoring woman, and the air flickered warningly again. Flickered, and then—another step—flared into a wall of raging flames. Phelinndar stepped back hastily from that crackling heat and studied the blistered edge of the hand he'd thrown up in front of his face.

The pain, as he flexed his fingers, told him the flames had been quite real. He stepped around a dusty, motionless Melted and tried to come at the seated sleeper from another direction. Again the flames came.

He stepped back and cried, "Oh, gods, Ambelter, they're *here*! The King and all the Overdukes, come to slay us with Dwaerindim!"

His shout echoed around the cavern, but the fat, ragged woman the baron knew to be Ingryl Ambelter did not move. The snores became, if anything, a trifle louder.

Well, the wizard had certainly seemed exhausted by his spellweavings. That last spell he'd raised looked somewhat like the shieldings he customarily cast around himself when he wanted to sleep—though he'd never used a shielding that made him look like anyone else before.

Still, 'twas wise: someone spell-spying from afar would see some old woman, not the much-hated Spellmaster of Aglirta. Those flames would dissuade hungry beasts or lurking brigands—and no doubt the shielding would rouse Ingryl to full wakefulness if treacherous barons or anyone else hurled weapons at the slumbrous wizard, or spells, or tried to blast Ambelter with a Dwaer-Stone.

Phelinndar walked as far away from the sleeping mage as he could, the

Dwaer cradled comfortably in his hand. Of course the Spellmaster dare not link his shieldings to this Stone; that would leave him defenseless against anyone using a Dwaer, such as—again—treacherous barons named Orlin Andamus Phelinndar.

Which in turn left Phelinndar free to use this Stone in his hand just as he liked. In truth, 'twas no wonder the Spellmaster was finally snoring in the hands of the gods. Most men would have fallen on their faces days earlier—but he'd not sleep forever, so . . .

Hunched into a corner that he was fairly sure—or at least hoped—held no stored magic items, the baron tried to ignore the stink of his ever more chafing armor, held the Dwaer up in front of his face, and tried to look *into* it.

The Stone grew warm almost immediately, and glowed, ever so slightly . . . and then white warmth was all around Phelinndar, and he was falling gently through it, through mists and drifts of cloud, toward some unseen place ahead where the light was brighter . . .

Brighter and more blue, a light that leaped with arcing, flowing energy, like lightning bolts sprayed from an invisible storm to stab all around him . . .

If only he knew how to *use* this lump of rock that wizards so lusted after, to hurl castle-shattering spells as they did!

A sword was a sword—oh, there were skills to learn to use it well, but any fool could pick one up and see which end was sharp and which end one gripped, and could swing and jab and slash empty air or some defenseless tree and in five breaths know how to use it to—clumsily, aye, but surely—slay!

But magic, now . . . magic was like swinging a snake instead of a sword, and wondering when it would turn and fang the hand that held it.

Baron Phelinndar was suddenly sweating so hard that drops were falling from the end of his nose. He snarled silently at those whirling lightnings. All he wanted was to speak with an old friend and arrange a place to run to, if he ever broke purpose with the Spellmaster snoring yonder—and somehow managed to live.

Hulgor was the man he needed. Good old Hulgor, who'd demand his price but be true to the bargain, once struck. They'd made many a coin together when Baron Orlin Andamus Phelinndar had been only Orlin Breselt, Tersept of Downdaggers. That first chance meeting in Sirl town had won him his only trustworthy trading partner—sharp when making deals, but true to every last coin and letter once they were sealed. That florid face was probably age-blotched by now, the sword-gray hair going white . . .

The Dwaer-mists grew suddenly darker, rolling to frame a gap or window of empty white light that grew larger, brighter, and then shot through with colors. Green, mostly . . . yes, 'twas showing him someone clad in green: a man in a richly embroidered dark green doublet . . . a man now turning away, a golden flagon as large as a chamberpot in his hand.

Hulgor! Yes, 'twas Hulgor Delcamper to be sure—and by the looks of him, as large, florid, quick-tempered, brawling, and wine-loving as ever! Hulgor's hair was almost entirely white, and his skin was wrinkled, but there were no blotches or staggerings, nor anything about him that told the world "old" or "infirm" or "unsteady." His fierce brown eyes were still hawk-alert.

Hulgor strode through a doorway and was gone. Phelinndar furiously desired to keep Hulgor in sight, glaring down at the mists and blue lightnings and shifting windows of light. There was a brief whirling of Dwaer-mists, and then he was seeing Hulgor in another room, large and richly paneled and lit with many candles.

Those flames flickered in many-spired silver candelabra fashioned like castles with many turrets—castles that looked to be about three feet high, as they rose up from long, mirror-smooth wooden tables. Hulgor looked restless, and stumped down this dining hall glaring at portraits of women who looked just as irritated to be up on the walls as he did to be looking at them. This must be Varandaur, the great Delcamper family castle that faced the stone city of Ragalar across a bay. Wasn't a Delcamper a friend to the boy king? A bard?

Flaeros, that was his name. He must be nephew to Hulgor. Hmm. Perhaps Varandaur would not prove so safe a bolt-hole after all . . .

Well, 'twasn't as if this particular baron had a great array of folk he could trust, to call on. Phelinndar sighed. In fact, 'twas Hulgor or no one, if one spread blunt truth bare before the gods.

"Hulgor," he hissed, willing the old noble to hear him. "Hulgor!"

The man in green stiffened and then shot a dark, suspicious glance over his shoulder. Then he turned to follow it, and stalked down the room, peering in all directions.

"Hulgor!" Phelinndar whisper-shouted, trying to will himself into the old man's way. The Delcamper man came to an abrupt stop, as if he'd seen something in front of him, and stared at Phelinndar—or through him.

Hear me, the baron willed, *and see me. Let me hear you.* Hulgor's lips were moving—angrily, by the looks of them—but Phelinndar could hear nothing. Nothing but softly swirling mists, like distant waves lapping on a beach.

Three look down! Bebolt this grauling Stone, anyway, and all such things! Why should mages swagger around hurling doom with them, and all the rest of Asmarand have to bow and cringe or die? Why couldn't a baron—

"Downdaggers!" Hulgor Delcamper growled in astonishment, stealing a quick glance at his flagon as if thinking the wine might have brought him this vision.

"Yes!" Phelinndar shouted. "It works! It works!"

The old man in green winced. "Magic! I forgot you're a baron now, Downdaggers. I suppose some spell-bauble came with your keep and blazon and all. What's afoot?"

"Plenty, Hulgor, and I need your help. I've got something powerful that the Spellmaster of Silvertree—the worst of the Dark Three, remember?— very much wants. I'm living in his lair right now, wondering how much longer he'll put up with me."

"Run," Hulgor suggested, taking a quick swig of wine.

"Not yet, but soon—and I need somewhere to run to."

Old Delcamper eyes narrowed. "So you want me to imperil the ancestral seat of my family for you, hey, and court Spellmasters as foes? You'd be thinking of coins and gems and the like to make such colossal idiocy worth my while, now, wouldn't you?"

The baron winced. "I'm a poor man, Hulgor . . ."

"The old gambits are the good ones, hey?" The old noble grinned. "Well, so am I. As my teeth fall from my head and my body hunches and my skin sags, young lasses no longer leap lustfully upon me as they once did, and I've heard of a spell that'll fix all that. I'll need a Sirl thousandweight in gold to get it, mind you . . ."

Phelinndar gave a little crow of laughter. "Hulgor, what're you drinking?"

"Something my sisters brought back from their last shopping voyage, south," the noble growled. "The one we're all still paying for. Better make that *two* thousandweights . . ."

"Two Sirl thousands? Hulgor, you must be mad!"

They were both grinning, now, and Hulgor almost rubbed his hands as he sampled his flagon again, sighed in pleasure, and said, "Pity you can't taste this, old friend. But of course in decadent Aglirta every last baron must have cellars of stuff almost as good, just lying there to be sold to passing barge traders for, say, *three* Sirl thousandweights . . ."

.   .   .

"Four once more," Craer murmured, looking around the room. "Your turn in the Band of Four, my lady."

"I know." Tshamarra's voice was low. "I'll try not to fail you."

Embra shook her head. "Don't let your sly-tongued lord upset you, Tash; you earned your welcome long ago. My father's better placed guarding the King—and running Aglirta for all of us. We need your spells and your . . . ah, fire."

Tshamarra smiled. "Thanks. I think."

Craer put an arm around her—and for once, she didn't slap it away. Thus emboldened, he asked, "Em, why exactly are we here? An empty chamber, quite secluded . . . is this another of your rend-the-sky-with-spells sessions?"

The Lady of Jewels smiled as she guided Hawkril to stand in a particular spot in the large, bare, and dusty hall. "Ah, so perceptive, Lord Longfingers. 'Tis time to try another Dwaer-tracing. We're back to one Stone, yes, but here, with the doors barred to keep out guards and the like, we can also use any spells Tash and I cast—and the Living Castle enchantments."

"Do yon locks and bars keep out Koglaur and bats?" Craer's voice was skeptical.

"Craer Delnbone, *will* you stop crying gloom for once? I can't think of any other way to avoid rambling around the Vale just waiting for trouble to find us, so . . ."

"Well said," Hawkril rumbled. "Raise your magic."

Embra nodded, laid a hand on his forehead, and carefully announced, *"Lamarantha!"*

Hawkril acquired a frown. "What're you doing, my lady? This feels . . . strange."

She stared into his eyes. "Did you hear the word I just spoke? Can you recall it? *Don't* say it aloud! You remember it?"

The mountainous armaragor nodded. "Aye."

"Can you hold it in your mind?"

He nodded again.

"Good. Say that word later, when I wave my hand at you thus, hey?"

"And doing so will—?"

"Unleash the spell I just stored in you. It's what you feel in your head right now."

" 'Tis *moving* . . . like a worm come up after rain, questing back and forth," the armaragor complained.

"Good. Mages know that feeling well."

"Hmmph. No wonder your tempers are often short."

Craer chuckled and shot a swift, warning look at Tshamarra. "Don't you be trying that on me, now!"

"No." The Lady Talasorn's smile was sweet. "We've something else in mind for you."

Craer took a swift, suspicious step back, away from them all. "And what would that be, precisely?"

Something curved and bright and familiar suddenly glowed in the air right in front of his nose—and then fell. Without thinking he caught it . . . and found himself staring down at the Dwaer, bright and slightly warm in his hands.

"Look into it, and feel its flows," Embra called from across the chamber.

The procurer gave her a wild look. "You tricked me!"

"And will again. Yet you'll wed yon Stone soon enough, and want to have it always in your hand; the hard task will be yielding it up to me again." The Lady of Jewels reached into her bodice and held up a small pendant. "See you this?"

Craer glanced and then grinned. "Closely seen already, Lady; 'tis a professional weakness we procurers have. A few tiny belzorels, the central stone some mountain rock or other, polished smooth—of no great worth, probably a family jewel."

"Indeed, and yet worn because it bears a minor enchantment against maggots and crawling worms and mites, to keep my hair free of such things—and to be drained in a moment for a spell, should I have need. Now look you into the Dwaer, and try to feel and see this pendant through it. Other magics here in this chamber will have their own glows, but try to find just this one."

Obediently, Craer stared into the Stone. Silence hung around him for some breaths ere he murmured, "*Well,* now. A procurer could get *very* used to having such as this. I see it."

"Good. I'm casting a spell that will make this pendant seem as a Dwaer to you, just for a moment. It won't *feel* like a Dwaer, but 'twill have the right radiance to your scrutiny."

"Aha," Craer commented, a moment later. "Distinctive."

"Yes. Remember it; that's what you need to be seeking. Now I'll need to do something more to you. Sit on the floor, cradle the Stone in your lap with one hand, and sit on your other hand, fingers spread on the floor. Don't move it when you start to feel power flowing up into it."

"Magic?"

"Yes, from Flowfoam itself: my Living Castle enchantments."

"Impressive," Tshamarra remarked, as Craer settled himself. "And my part?"

"When I wave to Hawkril and he unleashes his spell, ensnare it with one of your own. Both magics will lose their original effects and become raw, entwined power. Will that force into me, and I'll feed it to Craer. He won't have long to seek, but will have quite an impressive thrust of magic behind him—which may cause him some discomfort. As long as he holds the link together, all should be well."

Embra gave Craer a wry smile, and added, "Until we find another Dwaer, that is. When that happens, try to picture—in your mind—your eyes flying to it, and then look down as you speed straight toward it; you'll see the countryside where you're headed. *Don't* try to see who's holding the Dwaer and what's right around them, for that will surely alert them. We'll need you to hold the link to that other Dwaer, unless you see more than one, or anyone strikes at you with their Dwaer. In both cases, turn away, and throw mists between you and them."

Craer raised skeptical eyebrows. " 'Throw mists'? I do that . . . how?"

Embra smiled. "Try 'flying' your eyes toward me now—and when you reach me, veer away and mentally throw up some mist, by plucking at the mists that will seem to be all around you. Try it."

After a moment, the procurer grinned. "Easily done. I've just smoothed the mists away again."

Embra nodded. "I felt you do so. We're ready. So here's my scheme: If we find one Stone, we jump to it and do battle. When we get there, Craer, I'll need you to get our Dwaer to where Tash or I can touch it as fast as you know how. If we see multiple Stones, we trace where they are and then stop to decide whither we go. In all cases, of course, ignore the Dwaer my father's holding."

She looked at Hawkril, who nodded, and glanced at Craer. The procurer also nodded, wiped sweat from his brow that hadn't been there a few breaths before, and turned his head to look at Tshamarra, mouthing some silent words that might have been "I love you." She gave him a fond smile, and then turned to Embra and inclined her head once.

Four overdukes drew in deep breaths together, and Embra closed her eyes and flung up her hand in a wave to Hawkril. He said his remembered word, Tshamarra hissed a swift incantation, Embra quivered—and the Stone in Craer's hands suddenly glowed like an evening star.

Craer found himself hanging in glowing mists, lit from behind him by a growing radiance that was cradled in Blackgult's reassuring presence. He turned his attention away from it, looking out into the endless mists else-where, and—*there*! Over there!

He could feel Hawkril's ragged wonder, Tshamarra's cool calm, and Embra's strength and slight pain at the power roiling through her. They were with him, were aware of what he'd found, were flying with him . . .

. . . to a cavern, in damp Aglirtan earth and stone nigh the Silverflow, where a Dwaer was awake and alive in the hands of someone unaware of them, someone whose attention was bent elsewhere, someone against a wall far from a glowing web of magic, a shielding around a lazily turning cage of force-lines . . .

Craer forced himself to stop looking at those fascinating flows of power—Three Above, no wonder mages grew so hungry for power; 'twas the greatest ecstasy imaginable!—and back at the Dwaer. It was in the hands of an armored man, no mage . . . Phelinndar!

He was conscious of Embra taking power from him now, of the flow that had been racing up through the numbed hand he was sitting on now reversing to drain back the other way. Even as he wavered in confusion, not wanting to lose any of that thrilling force, he felt her mind-voice: *Hold to him, Craer. Hold to him!*

Determinedly he did so, clawing his attention away from the fascinating beginnings of Embra's weaving of a magic that would snatch them all from Flowfoam to the cavern he was seeing. He thrust his attention at the renegade baron, clinging to the edges of the awakened power of that other Dwaer. Something bright arose behind him as Embra did her work, caught him up as it surged forward in a mighty wave, and then threw them all through the mists, Darsar brightening and sharpening around them as they were suddenly—

—elsewhere, crashing into the midst of that glowing cage of magic, the shielding vanishing around them in a howl of flame. Embra had flung the Four together, breast to breast, and she slapped Craer's Stone and clawed at the humming cage of magic around them at the same time, shattering it in an instant.

Craer staggered in the thrall of magic clashing and roiling around him, pain and glory and savage fire all grappling in and *through* him, and cried with mocking enthusiasm: "For Aglirta! For glory! The Four are upon you! Obligingly surrender, or die!"

The snoring woman shot bolt upright with a shriek of surprise and dismay. The shielding that should have seared intruders to bones was gone, the Sword of Spells collapsed into whirling sparks around her, and—a Dwaer glowed not a dozen paces away, in the hands of *Embra Silvertree*!

The Band of Four, all of them, here in his lair!

Ingryl Ambelter lashed out with his mind in a fury, goading the Melted into the best lurching, shuffling semblance of a charge they could muster. Clumsy clay they might be, but in this crowded room they were so numerous that they'd hamper his attackers as if the walls themselves were reaching out to grasp and bludgeon and blunder into the way. And that should give him time to—

The Dwaer flashed, and a Melted in front of him, along with most of the table he'd been seated at, vanished in a roar of flame and a shrieking spray of splinters that lanced out in all directions like deadly arrows. Snarling, the old woman that was Ingryl Ambelter threw himself to the floor behind the ruin of the table—and into a drifting, flickering cloud of dying magic that had been his Sword of Spells ere the Dwaer had shattered it and drained much of its power.

He hissed a few swift words, and what was left flowed back into him, filling the disguised Spellmaster with more power than his body had ever held before. Like cool fire it flooded him, setting his fingers and teeth to tingling.

Gasping, he spent some of it on a shielding that would drain the next Dwaer-blast to come his way, and a mere trifle more on unseen eyes that soared to the ceiling of the cavern and showed him every cranny of it.

The Band of Four were wrestling with the Melted, that beast of an armaragor hacking at unliving limbs like a woodcutter, and the procurer doing his usual dance of leaps, twirls, and magpie grabs at anything that glowed or looked valuable. Phelinndar was crumpled into the farthest corner, trying to do something with the Dwaer, his face twisted into the grimace of the unpracticed and nongifted mind-struggling with greater enchantments. He was . . . trying to communicate with someone afar!

The baron's look of horror told the Spellmaster that he hadn't been expecting the Overdukes of Aglirta to make an appearance here, but his blunderings could quite well have summoned them! Well, by the Dark One, Phelinndar would die in a few moments—*Graul,* but he should have been slain days ago!

Embra's Dwaer flashed, and a dozen advancing Melted were shredded by a ravening light that cleared quite a space in front of her, their bones bouncing and crumbling into dust. Dark One look down! If she were to do that thrice more, she'd be facing a certain Spellmaster directly, and—

Gods! The other one, the little she-sorceress, had just hurled a handful of conjured fire into Phelinndar's face, and was making a grab for his Dwaer!

Desperately, Ambelter hurled most of the magic he'd just drunk along the lingering threads of the mind-lock he'd cast on Phelinndar days ago, seeking only to flood the Dwaer with fire, and—yes!

The Stone burst into flames as the wench laid hands on it, searing her. She threw back her head and shrieked, falling away from the Dwaer with her hands and bodice ablaze. The baron whimpered, his own hands burned to stumps of ash—but the Stone fell into his armored lap.

Phelinndar shuddered in mewing agony as Ingryl Ambelter let fall his disguise and used the last of his borrowed magic to hurl himself across the chamber like a darting hawk.

The armaragor didn't even see Ingryl, but that great warsword flashed perilously close to the diving wizard as Hawkril reeled back from hewing down a Melted, and swung his steel around in a great arc to hurl himself forward into another. Craer was ducking under a lurching undead warrior, and darting toward a scattering of small, glowing trinkets that had fallen from a shattered shelf, and Tshamarra's scream was lost to the ears of everyone in the great roar of Embra's Dwaer hurling back rank after rank of Melted, as it built into a great lash of flaming force that would be turned on the Spellmaster next, unless he—

—touched the Dwaer, scooping it up heedless of the pain, twisting its hot blaze of fury into the magic he needed, a shield to do this, a Dwaer-maze ready to do that, and a lance of his own, to stab at—

The Lady of Jewels was swifter. She spun away from the staggering horrors of twisted flesh confronting her, and lashed out with her Dwaer at the triumphantly blazing figure behind her, who held a still-flaming Stone in his hands. If she could smite him before he could raise the magics he sought . . .

Ingryl Ambelter grinned like a wolf as his shield did its work, thrusting aside all of the Embra's fury into—the Baron Phelinndar.

Orlin Andamus Phelinndar's eyes snapped open. He stared despairingly into the Spellmaster's cruelly smiling gaze for one last, dying moment ere baronial eyeballs popped into sizzling ruin, fire raged around inside that skull, and armor surged and buckled from the force of the bubbling, smoking fury beneath. And then the bones that had been Baron Phelinndar slid in a tumbled, smoking heap down the wall, trailing blackened armor, and Ingryl Ambelter spun around to face Embra with the Dwaer in his hands—and struck back.

In a chamber of gleaming tables and castle candelabras in distant Ragalar, Hulgor Delcamper blinked, growled, and stiffened, feeling a sharpness in the air and an echo of power bursting and surging, as all sight of oily Orlin

Downdaggers was swept away, probably forever. The old noble brought his flagon up ready like a mace in one hand and snatched out his belt-knife with the other, tensing for a battle that . . . did not come, as the air fell silent, and breath after ragged, anxious breath passed.

The Spellmaster had no hope of blasting the lass down, Dwaer to Dwaer—not with her alert and angry, and all her armed and ready friends close around her, but his lance of magic was ready, and all he had to do was . . . *this.*

Into the ragged fire of her Dwaer the fury of his own Stone crashed, and as the opposing powers of the Dwaerindim clawed and roiled, his lance leaped over, and through—and struck home.

"No!" Embra howled, recognizing him even as she wrestled his attack aside. "Ambelter, you snake, get you *gone* from my *mind!*"

In a fury she threw him out, and fought to shape the fire of her Dwaer into a blade to strike back at him—but his own Dwaer was already flashing, whirling the Spellmaster away in a vanishing that left a singing, shimmering Dwaer-maze in his wake.

"Longfingers!" Hawkril roared, as he hacked down another Melted and all the rest suddenly froze where they stood like so many statues. "What magic's that?"

Craer found his feet, disgust on his face as the baubles he'd been snatching up crumbled into dust between his fingers, and said sourly, "A wildfield, or some such: it banishes you anywhere if you enter. I'd say that whatever mage just escaped us left it behind him so that we can't use a spell to trace him, even with a Dwaer."

He turned his head, and saw Tshamarra writhing in soundless agony, tendrils of smoke streaming from her. Embra Silvertree was on her knees not far away, clutching a wand and a flickering Dwaer to her breast as if they were wounded children. Her face was wet with tears, and she was trembling.

The armaragor and the procurer sprinted across the cavern like men possessed.

"Embra!" Craer howled, long before he reached his stricken lady. "I need your healing here!"

Lady Silvertree did not reply. Hawkril fell to his knees as he skidded to a halt, and put his arms around her as gently as a feather seeking the earth. "Lass," he rumbled, "how fare you?"

"He . . . touched my mind," the Lady of Jewels whispered. "Trying to enslave me through the old enchantments. Ingryl Ambelter, the Spellmaster of Silvertree Castle, lives yet—and he's stronger than ever."

Arkle Huldaerus came awake out of a vengeful dream as magic thrummed through him, washing over him with only a hint of its full fury. He blinked up into a young, beautiful, and unfamiliar face bent close to his, and thus lit clearly in the spark-shot glow of the magic she was hurling at his chains, and shook his head. Surely he was still asleep, and dreaming?

No, Master of Bats, this is no dream.

The mind-voice was so strong and cold and cruel that Huldaerus was stunned, too awed to even breathe.

A chain parted, and he fell a few feet down the wall, fetching up at the end of the remaining chain with a jerk. Manacled and swaying helplessly, he dared not even cower. How could one so young have such power? Such fell wisdom?

Oh, of course, how foolish of him. 'Twas a spellspun disguise, it must be. Long, raven-dark hair falling in smooth splendor over a clinging black gown. Slender hips, great dark eyes—a semblance that would make more than one man swallow at the sight of her.

The Master of Bats swallowed now, as the last chain was severed in a burst of calmly wielded magical fire, and he fell to the floor of his prison cell. The landing was hard, but bats fluttered up from his boots and sleeves as he bounced and winced, and he smiled up at them.

The young sorceress waved a casual hand, and unseen magic snatched Huldaerus briskly to his feet, steadying him when his long-unused legs wobbled. He clung to the wall, drawing in deep, shuddering breaths, and when he trusted himself to stand, turned to face his unknown rescuer and gave her a smile. She'd freed him, and still stood here, so it followed that she wanted something of him.

"Arkle Huldaerus, at your service, Lady," he said, his voice starting out rough but sounding pleasant enough after a few words. "And you are—?"

The sorceress smiled, something dancing in her eyes that made the heart of the Master of Bats, lonely recluse that he was, leap in sudden hope. Wisps of magic stirred about her, cloaking her in a soft halo of spell-glow, and he dared to let his smile widen, and his hand extend in friendsh—

Magic slammed him back against the wall so hard that one shoulder shattered audibly, and a rib gave way below it. Huldaerus writhed, pinned helplessly, as that same thrusting force casually crushed one of his bats after another, as a bored vintner might squash grapes, plucking each out of the dark air and whisking it to within a handlength of his nose before slaying it.

As the small, brittle, and very dead lumps pattered wetly to the stones, each weakening and sickening him with its fall, he became aware through tears of pain that the darkly beautiful face looking into his had changed.

Framed by that long, magnificent hair now was a human skull, grinning at him with eyes that were two glittering lights of old and mighty mockery. They were the last thing to remain, as the lithe body and then the bone-face melted away from around them—and then one of them winked, and they vanished, too.

Arkle Huldaerus leaned against the wall in utter darkness, spitting blood onto the unseen stones at his feet, and felt his manacle-free wrists in slow disbelief. Any moment now he'd awaken properly, and find himself back on that cold and endlessly patient wall . . .

But when at last he stumbled away from where he'd been chained, letting his fingers trail along the stones, and felt his way to the cold, unseen metal of the cell door, the Master of Bats knew the visitation and his freeing had truly happened.

An unknown, deadly beauty of a sorceress had freed him, made it clear she could casually slay him whenever she pleased, and departed. Someone who'd found him here, alone and enfeebled, and so could find him again whenever she desired.

Arkle Huldaerus shuddered, suddenly feeling the cold, and leaned against the door. He had to get far away from Aglirta, and stay there this time.

If he was even going to be allowed a "this time."

Tshamarra Talasorn drew in a sudden, shuddering breath. Her hands quivered as if she'd been about to snatch them away from Embra and the icy healing mists of the Dwaer. Yet she bit her lip, tears streaming down her cheeks, and kept on holding her hands out—just as steadfastly as Craer was holding her, his arms wrapped around her shoulders comfortingly, his cheek against hers. Her breath caught again, and Embra glanced up from her work.

"Almost done," the Lady of Jewels murmured. "Can you move them?"

Tshamarra wriggled her fingers cautiously, and nodded, trying to smile.

"How do they feel?"

"Tight—as if the skin doesn't fit. They're . . . Forgive me, Em, but they're too long and thin and graceful—like yours. I'm shorter, see?"

Embra studied Tshamarra's hands critically, put one of her own next to them, nodded, and did something that made the Lady Talasorn stiffen and sob—and then held their hands together for comparison again.

This time the smaller sorceress nodded in emphatic thanks, and Embra clapped her on the shoulder, rose to let Craer comfort her, and strode back to the embrace of *her* comforting man.

Hawkril was as large and reassuring as always, his strength enfolding her like a castle wall with a warm hearth in it, and Embra leaned against him and relaxed, just for a moment.

The grotesquely deformed zombies had begun to wander mindlessly around the cavern again, and after one of them lumbered slack-jawed toward them, Embra sighed, murmured, "Excuse me, love," into Hawk's chest, whirled away from him—and blasted the Melted to a smoldering heap of ashes.

Then she shrugged, the Dwaer shining in her hand like an eager full moon, and dealt the same fate to Melted after Melted. "These should have been destroyed with their maker," she muttered, "but I'll be grauled by corpse-worms before I'll let Ingryl Ambelter command them a day longer!"

Craer looked up. "Now *there's* an image."

Embra sighed, turned with hands on hips, and gave him a glare. "Could you leave me in peace to think just for *once,* Craer? If this was Ambelter's lair, there could be traps in plenty all around us—and useful magic, maps, all sorts of valuable things, too."

"Oh? What *sort* of valuable things?"

"No, not more baubles that'll fall to dust in your hands, Lord Delnbone. I was thinking of coins—wizards need to buy things occasionally just like other folk, you know—and gems, which can be used to store dozens of spells."

"*Well,* now," the procurer said eagerly, "why didn't you—?"

"Because I was busy putting Tash's hands back together, and didn't want to have to wipe spatters of pulverized Craer off my face and garments, that's why."

Hawkril took a few steps into the room, his warsword in his hand out of sheer habit. Ashes swirled and eddied around his boots with every step. "You blasted them all?" His voice held both hope and disappointment.

"I hope so," Embra replied, "but he's always liked to cage things; we may find beasts and half-crazed mages and the Three know what else. Please wait, love, until we can do this together."

"The Band of Four once more, hey?" Craer asked, helping Tshamarra to her feet. The Talasorn sorceress was still flexing her fingers in wonder, as if not quite able to believe they were hers. She looked up at her lord sharply.

"Never ridicule that term, or our fellowship," she said in a voice that was low, calm—and as firm as iron. "Never."

Maps proved to be few, written schemes nonexistent, spellbooks gone. There were a few half-finished spells whose natures were obvious to Embra and Tshamarra at a glance, a handful of old enchanted things recovered from tombs and caches (buckles and heraldic cloak-pins for the most part, loot that Craer and Hawkril examined rather dubiously, but that made Tshamarra ooh and aah), and no captives.

Embra used the Dwaer to twist the unfinished spells into traps of minor nastiness for Ingryl—or anyone else—who might come poking around the lair, and then called on it to whisk the Four back to Flowfoam.

A few breaths after their departure some of the ashes boiled up into the shape of a dark and ghostly figure—out of which stepped a slender, dark-gowned girl with a long fall of hair and a skull for a face. Gadaster grinned around at the cavern for a few moments, paused to be amused by the puling traps, and then made Maelra's body weave a soundless spell, and—vanish.

The ashes swirled, and then seemed almost relieved to settle down again.

21

Arrivals and Departures in Violence

The old lady sighed. "I can see why it is that Aglirta is truly the Kingless Land."

Flaeros cast a quick glance at the closest guard, one of an impassive pair by the doors, and hissed, "Lady, this may not be our King, but he is still a King! Insult him not so!"

Lady Natha Orele sighed again, and turned to face the other young man sitting before her—the one who was wearing a crown. "I do not insult Your Majesty," she said firmly, "I do Your Majesty the courtesy of speaking truth—something your courtiers seem to have in very short supply, I might add."

" 'Tis a disease at court, Lady," King Castlecloaks replied gravely. "Yet tell me: Why think you Aglirta is truly kingless?"

"With Snowsar and with you, 'tis always rush to fight this and strain to withstand that—and never to snatch time enough to make the little decisions that shape life in the realm, assuming you do win your ways and there is still an Aglirta on the morrow. In short, you play warcaptain, and have time for little else . . . and so do not rule, and so enjoy not the trust and loyalty of your people. Without that, you are nothing, no matter how many crowns, coins, and lances you command. Of course the task before you is—as it has been too often these past few seasons—to rid Aglirta of the Serpents. But have you given any thought to *after* that?"

"Why, uh"—the king coughed—"no."

"Ah. Thank you. Some truth handed back to me. Very good," the aged Lady of Chambers said briskly. "Now I'll pass from truth to my opinion.

Hear it, think on it, but follow it not if you think I'm wrong—and believe me, I can be *very* wrong. If I were King . . ."

"Yes?" Raulin reached up as if to take the crown from his head and hand it to her.

"Don't," she said sharply. "I would do a poor job, and Aglirtans would never accept me—some old, wrinkled, outlander woman? *Really!* But hearken, King Castlecloaks: Were I you, I'd do away with all barons. Keep the rank of tersept, and yourself move often and—this is crucial—*unpredictably* from castle to castle, up and down the Vale. Meet your subjects directly, see to their needs, and work with the clergy of the Three to keep worship of the Serpent outlawed henceforth. Make sure each and every person sees some reward, and complaints are answered, and so on. The people will see that you serve them, and *you* reward them—rather than regarding you as some distant, decadent figure who ignores them while their local baron struts and exploits and oppresses and occasionally rewards. In short, they'll see you as needful, and as theirs."

Raulin Castlecloaks regarded her with shining eyes. "Before the Three, I swear to do so! As soon as the realm is rid of the plague and the Serpents!"

"Mind you do," the old woman told him sharply. "Darsar is full of rulers who will do great things and keep high promises as soon as something else is taken care of. But they do lots of taking care, and yet there's always a something else in their laps preventing them from rising to seize those great things they promise."

Raulin sighed, and nodded. "I can see how easy 'twould be to fall into such ways. Flaeros, you must be my reminder, and hold me to all my promises."

The bard lifted his eyebrows. "Me, Your Majesty? You really think any one man can do all that?"

There was a moment of startled silence, and then Raulin and Orele both burst out laughing. The guards turned their heads, surprised, as the king and the two Ragalan outlanders chortled and guffawed together like younglings at a revel. Then the armsmen hastily resumed their expressionless, statuelike poses as the three rose and parted, the old woman withdrawing to her inner chambers and the two young men striding toward them.

"Bed for me," Raulin was saying, as the guards flung the door wide for them.

Flaeros nodded. "A good idea. My bit of floor calls to me." The guards followed the two, exchanging looks that were not—quite—smiles. Since his arrival, the bard had been sleeping with the guards who stood watch and slumbered across the door to the king's chamber, to prevent any more attempted regicides.

Despite their brisk pace, both young men yawned more than once on their walk through the passages. Neither they nor their guards glanced into every dark alcove they passed.

Most of those spaces were empty, but in one of them the eldest Overduke of Aglirta stood with his hand solemnly clapped over the mouth of a buxom chambermaid—to still the gasps she'd made as his other hand wandered beneath the unlaced, hip-high sideslit of her gown.

When the guards were past, she bit one of his fingers gently, and purred, "Ah, but 'tis good to have you back to your old self, Griffon. Now play fair; let me do a little . . . exploring with my fingers, too."

"Gladly," Blackgult muttered. "The battlements, Indalue, or somewhere warmer?"

"Your bedchamber, I think," she whispered, before running her tongue along the edge of his hand. "You thrust me back against far too much cold, hard stone last time. Besides, I've thought of a new use for bedposts."

"O-ho? If 'tis truly new, 'twill be worth seeing," the man once considered the most handsome—and lusty—lord in all the kingdom murmured, as he glanced out of the alcove.

The passage was deserted, and he let Indalue lead him out into it toward his bedchamber. They went quickly, hand-in-hand, chuckling like younglings.

Craer came awake suddenly. Something was wrong. Tshamarra was writhing beside him, moaning in dismay and pain. Before he could raise a hand she rolled over atop him. She was slick with sweat, her smooth skin drenched.

"Tash! I'm here! What's wrong?"

The Lady Talasorn sobbed and clawed at him. "Craer! Help me!"

"I'm *here,* Lady! What is it? What were you dreaming?"

The sorceress shook her head wildly. "No dream . . . I never dream unless spells lie on my mind . . . and I've none left." She convulsed in his arms, so violently that he was almost thrust from the bed.

"I'm burning up," she gasped. "Flames, flames everywhere!"

Craer held her, trying to comfort her by murmuring empty reassurances and stroking her shoulder, but she swore at him, trembling and panting, and turned in his arms to hiss furiously, "I'm *not* dream-addled, my lord! I'm . . . I'm . . ."

"Pleased to see me," Craer suggested, kissing her. She tried to protest, tried to pull her head away, but his hands were busy, and in a few moments she was pulling at him hungrily. Craer chuckled inwardly; the old distractions were the sure ones.

And then, as his lady arched atop him in their shared passion, his inward laughter chilled in an instant. Above him in the darkness, a tiny wisp of flame had darted out of her gasping mouth.

"So what," Blackgult asked, as Indalue bit his shoulder again, "is all this about bedposts? Hey?"

"Not . . . *yet* . . ." the woman beneath him growled—and then he felt a sudden burning across his back. It came again, and he heard the whirring that brought it this time. The Golden Griffon thrust out a hand in the darkness, caught the knotted rope-cord she wore as a belt around his palm, and jerked, pulling her into a tangled ball ere he broke her grip on it.

"So," he murmured triumphantly, "we flog our horse onward, do we?"

He sat up and gently flicked the tasseled end of her cord down across the breasts he could not quite see. Indalue hissed and arched under him.

"Yes," she whispered, " 'tis almost time for the bedposts." The cord fell again, and she twisted and bit at his knee. He brought the cord down harder, and she growled, "Yesss!"

And then she screamed.

"What—?" Blackgult asked sharply, hearing the horror in her cry.

"*Move,* Lord!" she cried, thrusting upward so furiously she almost bucked him off the bed. "Behind you!"

Blackgult threw himself forward into the darkness, over the side of the bed and into a scrabbling, skidding landing on the floor. His sword . . .

Indalue screamed again as his hands found the hilt they were seeking. He whirled around on his knees, and saw—a glowing, grinning skull bending over the bed, framed by long hair. It was reaching for the pillows with hands that glowed—slender, girlish hands—and under them was . . . his Dwaer!

Indalue clawed at those hands, and the skull-headed intruder hissed and dug fingers like talons into the chambermaid's face.

Into, Blackgult saw as he scrambled up faster than anything he'd ever done in his life, and whipped back his sword to throw—for living flesh shrank away like mist before sun where those glowing talons touched, and Indalue's shrieks rose into raw, frantic terror.

Blackgult threw his blade right into that skull-face—what mattered it if he hit Indalue as it whirled? She was doomed already—and sprang for the pillows.

He had to get the Stone—and he did, clawing single-mindedly for it in the darkness, and so never seeing his blade strike something unseen around the head and shoulders of the intruder and go clanging away into the shadows, trailing sparks . . . or clumps and tresses of hair fall from the bare, lolling skull that had been Indalue's lovely head moments before, as his bedmate sagged back in death.

The skull-faced sorceress let go of the corpse and reached for Blackgult, but he bent his will furiously upon the Dwaer—and sent forth a wall of green flame that thrust the intruder back across the room in an ungainly stagger, carrying footstools and sidetables with it in a crashing fury.

A tapestry on the far wall caught alight and blazed up, green flames racing, and by its light Blackgult saw his newfound foe's hands raised to shape intricate gestures of spellweaving—a magic he did not know—so he used the Dwaer to snatch a great mirror off the wall and smash it, edge-on, into those hands.

Its shattering was deafening, and crowned by a scream of pain and dismay that must have come from the skull-face. Blackgult tried to lash it with Dwaer-force again, but a yellow haze was creeping around the edges of his vision now, and he suddenly found it hard to keep his feet.

He wrestled with the Stone, seeking to stand strong, but a spell came across the room and slammed into him, shattering the bedposts like kindling—and smashing open the doors of the room behind him.

There was a moment of whirling yellow haze and red fury, and Blackgult found himself lying numbly near the wall, with more yellow mists rising before his eyes. The Dwaer was still in his hands—he thought—and he could hear shouts and the poundings of running feet. Somehow he snarled his way to his feet again and padded wildly forward, shaking his head to try to clear it. Where was the skull-sorceress? Where . . . ?

Purple fire blinded him. Cold laughter came from behind it, as pain burst into Blackgult's side and flung him against a wall as if he was a toy, the Stone tumbling away, his fingers smashed like twigs . . .

And then everything was yellow, and he forgot all pain as rage made him strong. He saw the grinning skull across the room, and went for it . . .

. . .

Hawkril thrust an evening cloak around Embra's shoulders as he stamped his feet into his boots. Drawing his warsword, he threw down the scabbard and ran.

Dwaer cradled in her hands and the cloak slipping down her bare shoulders, Embra sprinted after him. Gods, but Hawk was fast! Those boots were all he wore, and he dodged and ran along the passages like a furious wind.

Somewhere ahead of them the palace shook again, and there was a brief, bright flash of light. A spell-duel was going on in one of the bedchambers! That almost had to mean at least one of the Four was involved.

A deeper, booming blast nearly hurled Embra off her feet as she skidded around a corner, and was followed by a smaller, splintering crash.

They were very close now, and through all the tumult of spell-blasts and things breaking and the shouts of guards she could hear the slobbering snarls of a marauding beast. Then she heard Hawkril's voice raised in a great bellow: "*Away!* Away, monster, or die!"

Embra raced barefoot around a corner, startling an onrushing guard, and burst into a room that no longer had a door, and was now busily spilling smoke and firelight out into the passage.

Her father was bounding about a room that was all splintered, burning furniture, naked and snarling. There was foam around his mouth, his eyes were wild, and he carried his Dwaer carelessly in one hand, as if he'd forgotten what it was.

Stalking ever closer to Blackgult as he ran, trying to corner him, was a young sorceress whose face was a glowing skull. A dead chambermaid lay sprawled on the floor amid the splayed and splintered wreckage of Blackgult's great bed, and guards lay here and there about the room, moaning and kicking feebly. Just two of them still had weapons up—and they were hunched against a wall, pale fear ruling their faces.

As Hawkril charged the skull-sorceress, a spell ripped out of her hands at him. The armaragor dived one way and Blackgult bounded in the other direction, whirling the glowing Dwaer around his head like a trophy.

The sorceress ran toward the Golden Griffon, and the guards launched themselves from the wall in a desperate charge at her. On the other side of the room, Hawkril shouted in pain as the spell tore into the walls above him, hurling shards and slivers of wall panels and furniture in all directions.

Embra let fly with her own Dwaer, straight at that skull-head. The fingers of the sorceress were sprouting sudden shafts of crackling light, and where they thrust, guards were screaming and staggering. One man blundered into Embra's striking magic and was flung away, torn and dying.

Blackgult slew another guard bare-handed, wrenching a helmed head around until the neck below it cracked.

Embra's thrust of Dwaer-fire slammed into the crackling spell of the sorceress, and the room rocked with an ear-ringing blast. Blackgult was hurled aside, his Dwaer flying from his hands to bounce off in another direction, and the sorceress was sent staggering backwards.

Bare but for his boots, a moaning Hawkril slowly found his feet, splinters sticking out of his side and back like blades. He stalked across the room toward the sorceress, who crouched, awaiting him, and began to weave a new spell.

Tight-lipped, Embra sent another Dwaer-blast at her. Its fury made the discarded Stone flare up into bright radiance, and the skull-face turned to regard the glow of the fallen Dwaer.

Desperately, the Lady of Jewels called on her Stone to snatch her to a particular flagstone of the floor just beside the other Dwaer. She dared not seek it directly, for fear of her magic going wild or Blackgult's Stone being driven away by her magic. The skull-sorceress was running hard, and diving for the Stone.

Blackgult roared, another guard in his hands, and whirled the man around his head. Strangling and helpless, the guard let go of his sword—and it spun right into Hawkril, sinking deep. The armaragor went to his knees in gasping pain, as Embra screamed: "Hawk!" . . . and her magic whisked her away.

She landed on the spot she'd chosen—and a heavy, armored body, stinking with fear, smashed into hers, slammed her to the floor, and rolled away, whimpering in terror. Blackgult had thrown the guard in just the wrong direction, at just the wrong time.

Gasping for breath, Embra rolled over, fumbling for her Dwaer—and looked up into the triumphant grin of the skull-sorceress, who was rising with a glowing Stone in her own hands.

Raging, Blackgult ran at the sorceress, his hands lifted into claws—and as his arms closed around her, she spun and blasted him with the Dwaer, the Stone in her grasp actually thumping into his chest.

The Golden Griffon's hairy, broken body was flung up at the ceiling like a child's doll—and Embra Silvertree called on the Living Castle enchantments to pull open the floor beneath the skull-sorceress.

Her foe fell a few feet into the hitherto-solid stone floor, off-balance and startled—and Embra slashed at the sorceress with all the power she could quickly snatch out of her Dwaer.

Something splintered, a scream burst from skeletal jaws—and Embra's magic struck the far wall of the bedchamber, shattering it in a long, stone-splitting crack, and rebounded back into the skull-sorceress from the other side.

The sorceress screamed again, sudden flames of twisted magic roaring up her limbs as she shuddered in agony. Embra's attack had disrupted a Dwaer-magic her foe had been shaping—and the skull-sorceress was caught in the roiling result.

Embra promptly thrust upward with the Living Castle enchantments, and the floor spat the skull-sorceress violently at the ceiling.

As the shoulder of the sorceress slammed into the stone overhead, the Dwaer fell from her spasming hands. She grabbed at it, once, hopelessly, and Embra used her Dwaer to make her own snatch at the Stone.

A mistake. Magic exploded between the two Dwaerindim in a thick white arc of snarling lightning that numbed Embra's arm and sent Black-gult's Stone ripping across the chamber, trailing sparks and flames of magic. In a far corner it spun itself crazily into a burst of magic that hurt the eyes . . . and was gone.

"Graul!" Embra spat. "Transported the Three alone know where!" She whirled and blasted the falling skull-sorceress again . . . but this time that cold grin seemed to hold triumph, and all the fury she sent at her foe was snared in a spinning that ended in another burst of magic.

The ruined bedchamber suddenly held one less mysterious skull-headed sorceress.

"Graul," Embra panted again bitterly, holding her Dwaer close as if its familiar curves and hardness could console. She felt in need of comfort just now. "Gone, and Father's Stone too, and now we have a new foe and don't even know wh–"

She bit her lip and called on her Dwaer to try to trace the vanished Stone, as it had done before. In the heart of all this spell-chaos, 'twasn't likely . . . Yet, if it hadn't gone far, there was a chance . . . just a chance . . .

There was a bestial snarl from behind her, and someone slammed roughly into Embra and clawed at her throat, tearing the cloak away.

She backed into her attacker, hard, and those hands didn't manage to close on her throat. She blasted him away as gently as she could, and turned to face—

Her father, of course. Blackgult crouched naked, wild-eyed and panting, clawlike hands reaching for her. With a roar he gathered himself and came at her again—and with a sigh, Embra dodged aside and spun a cage for him out of Dwaer-fire.

He howled in pain as its bars of fire burned him, and hurled himself against them again and howled all the more. Embra stared at him helplessly as he went on hurling himself into pain—and then, as guards flooded into the room with many torches and a gaping Raulin and Flaeros, she sat down on the floor, bare as she was, and started to cry.

Screams split the night in an otherwise pleasant bedchamber in Varandaur. Two shrieks, either side of him, ear-shatteringly close. Hulgor Delcamper came awake bewildered and bolt upright in bed, half-deafened by the frightened cries of . . . oh, aye: the two chambermaids he'd bedded for the night, Nuelara and . . . and the other one.

They were staring at the same thing he was. Hulgor Delcamper blinked at a stone—a rounded, palm-sized lump of fieldstone like any of the thousands of such he'd seen up in the high meadows. But none of them had ever shown the slightest signs of doing what this one was: blazing with white light, and chiming and humming, too, as it floated in the air above his bed, spinning slowly.

Hulgor found wits enough to curse—though he still couldn't remember the name of the lovely lass on his right—and scrambled across her to snatch up his sword.

Shaking it out of its scabbard as Nuelara fled and the other lass clung to him, whimpering, the old Delcamper noble shook the chambermaid away, stood up on his bed—and jabbed at the thing.

He struck home, with a roar of satisfaction—and then the Stone roared, too.

His blade was ringingly torn apart in twisted, tumbling shards—as a numb-armed, cursing Hulgor Delcamper was flung across the room.

His landing smashed flat a stool he'd never much liked, and sent his carefully laid out clothes for the morrow tumbling to the floor. He struggled up out of the tangled wreckage with a snarl and stalked back across the room, bare-handed.

The Stone still hung above his bed, glowing softly and tinkling gently right where it had been when he'd awakened. Like a prowling cat Hulgor slunk up onto the bed, stepped all around the floating rock in a slow, padding circle . . . and then, very slowly as he swallowed with a very dry throat, reached out for it . . .

Silence fell in the shattered house of Morauntauvar of Sirlptar, with its ceiling gone to starshot night sky overhead. Then the Spellmaster of All Aglirta heard the tiny, fitful crackle of flames rising from his slain foe's body.

This had all gone wrong. Sirlptar's self-styled mightiest wizard was dead, but magic Ambelter should have won here was mostly destroyed. Seething, the Spellmaster started to search, pulling his shielding-spell tightly around him.

He'd found an unscorched book of spells and some sort of enchanted orb ere the air flashed behind him, and he whirled around to find—four Serpent-priests, their hands raised in gestures of parley. Standing with them were the seven sleepy, hastily roused mages of Sirlptar that Ingryl had expected to see—for it was Sirl custom to make revenge pacts with other mages. One of them was rather angrily specifying quite a large sum of money to a priest—so these wizards must be hasty, last-moment hires.

"Spellmaster of Silvertree," one of the priests called. "Hear us in peace, we ask thee!"

"Spellmaster of All Aglirta," Ingryl Ambelter corrected coldly. "Swiftly give me good cause *why* to listen, if you would live."

"We've unfinished business with Morauntauvar of Sirlptar," the priest replied, "but after farscrying his demise at your hands, 'tis our judgment that you are the more powerful and capable mage, and have the perfect temperament we seek. Are you interested in undertaking the task Morauntauvar had agreed to?"

The Spellmaster of All Aglirta regarded the Serpent-priests coldly, his Dwaer glowing ready in his hands. "That would depend very much," he replied politely, "on what that task was."

The priest turned and murmured something to the priest beside him, who in turn uttered a brief incantation—and vanished, along with the Sirl wizards, leaving just a trio of Serpent-priests.

The Spellmaster frowned, and used the Dwaer to visibly strengthen his shielding. If they reappeared on all sides of him . . . or on the floor below, and blasted in unison upward . . .

"Certain ambitious Brethren of the Serpent," the priest said quickly, "had just hired Morauntauvar to aid them with his spells in their coming bid for the throne of Aglirta."

Ingryl Ambelter lifted an eyebrow. "Well, now . . . say more. Please."

22

The Many Uses of Dwaerindim

"By the Three," Craer said thankfully, stumbling sleepily into the waiting bath, "but I could get used to being an overduke!"

Tshamarra smiled up at him from the scented waters. "Servants have their uses." She offered him a goblet from a tray beside her, shielding it with a hand against his splashings. "Warm mulled Arl-wine?"

Craer made a face, and then changed his mind and snared the goblet. "I'd better accept. The way our lives have been unfolding this last while, safe food and drink is best snatched whenever offered by opportunity—or pretty sorceresses who aren't wearing any clothes." He paused, just before reaching the dregs. "This wine *is* safe, isn't it?"

Tshamarra shrugged. "I'm still alive." She sat up and rolled over, dripping—a delightful sight that Craer stopped to appreciate—and cast a rather sly look back over her shoulder at him. "Seeing as you're up and you've been watered, how about washing my back?"

"Was that an artful way of asking something else, Lady?" Craer asked the ceiling, as he set his goblet down carefully.

"Lord Delnbone, surely you've learned by now that when I want something of you I ask for it—directly. My back?"

With a sigh, Craer reached for the bowl of scented lave-oil and the scraper, and set to work.

Tshamarra almost purred. "There's an itch there, just a little high—ahhh, yes. That's it. Just keep—"

"Morning," Hawkril Anharu rumbled, from above. Something in his tone made them both jerk their heads up to stare at him.

"I need you now," the armaragor told Tshamarra. "Hurry!"

Wordlessly she extended her hand, bare as she was, for him to haul her up out of the bath. Craer swiped oil from her as she went and followed hastily in her wake, snatching the warmed robes the servants had left ready to dry himself with, and stamping his feet back into his boots as he came.

"Could Aglirta just possibly arrange to need rescuing next time *after* we're dressed?" he asked Hawkril, as they hurried to the door and out, scattering servants and guards. The armaragor had already caught up Craer's leathers and dagger-belts and Tshamarra's boots and breeches, but the procurer hastily snatched a few more items—including something to adorn his lady's upper half besides the sharp edge of her own tongue.

" 'Tisn't Aglirta," Hawkril growled, " 'tis Embra. Em and her father."

Craer winced. "This isn't going to be one of those bad jokes, is it?"

"I don't know what it's going to be," the armaragor snarled, as they hurried down passages together. "That's why I came for you."

Craer put a robe over his lady's shoulders, and they both rubbed themselves as dry as they could as they hastened around corners, past grim-looking guards, and through archways where more guards waited.

"This is *not* filling me with carefree joy," Craer observed, as the crowd of courtiers and palace armsmen following them grew. They passed a room where the smells of fresh food wafted forth, and Tshamarra threw her lord a look that at once bade him firmly to behave himself, and at the same time told him that she knew what he was feeling, and felt much the same.

Flaeros Delcamper and six guards stood in front of the closed doors of Blackgult's chamber. They stepped aside wordlessly as the three overdukes strode up—and Tshamarra swept off her wet robe and unconcernedly laid it in the bard's hands.

Flaeros barely had time to stare at her bared flesh, drop his jaw, and flush furiously ere Craer took off his robe, too—and cast it over the bard's head.

"Keep these closed behind us," Hawkril told the guards, as he shouldered his way through the doors. Craer and Tshamarra followed—and halted with identical anxious gasps.

Blackgult's chamber was burn-scarred, riven, and strewn with heaped, broken furniture. The dead chambermaid's blood had dried, but she still lay sprawled and skull-headed in the wreckage. The center of the room was filled with a humming, glowing, slowly turning cage of magic, greatly grown from what Embra had Stone-spun to imprison her crazed father the night before.

Blackgult hung awake at its heart of the force-cage, the Dwaer glowing like a sleepless star to his right, and Embra—disheveled and fast asleep, her hair dangling around her—hung in a lesser cage beside her Stone. Both Blackgult and his daughter were wrapped in nightrobes that looked to have been thrown over them rather than donned. Blackgult gave them a brief, intent look as they entered, and then cast his eyes down at the floor below.

"She's been here all night," Hawkril growled, as Craer and Tshamarra hastily dressed. "Trying to heal him—'mind mend,' she called it. Yon cage has been growing all the while. At first it was thrusting out new bars at her bidding, but she fell asleep sometime in the night—after I did, for I didn't see slumber take her—and then I think *he* was commanding it, at least sometimes."

"You sat guard against the doors, sword in your lap, didn't you?" Tshamarra asked softly, tugging her last garment—a silk jerkin—into place.

"Of course, Lady. 'Twas needful."

There was a gentle chiming as the slowly, silently rolling cage changed again, some of its bars shifting to join other bars in brief flashes of magic, opening up some of the barriers around Blackgult and drawing him in closer . . . closer to the glowing Stone.

Craer's eyes narrowed. "Who's causing that?"

Hawkril shrugged. "She's asleep, and I dare not try to wake her—so I'd say 'tis the Griffon. It's been proceeding like this since I awakened and fetched you. He *was* right over yonder, up nigh the wall."

Tshamarra frowned. "So unless Embra's dream-guiding this, or the Stone itself is doing it, or someone unknown is influencing the Dwaer from afar, Blackgult is bringing himself somehow closer to the Stone."

She chewed on her lip for a moment, and then added reluctantly, "There's a spell that might . . ."

Hawkril shot her a glance. "Do it."

Craer held up a hand in a "stay all for a moment" gesture. "What befell the Griffon? Do we know?"

The armaragor shook his head. "Plague come again to bring rage upon him, or some doing of the Dwaer or the skull-sorceress . . . Em knows not. She did this to hold him until she could go into his wits and find out, so as to heal."

"I heard him tell Embra about being mind-blasted in a Dwaer-battle," Tshamarra said quietly. "His memory and reason have been coming and going, all this time since. Yet just yestereve I heard an old servant here say the Lord Blackgult now seemed like his old, old self, years younger and smiling again." She shrugged and waved at the chiming, shifting cage. "So if he's doing that, what do we do?"

Craer glanced at her and then called: "Blackgult! Lord Blackgult!" The caged man did not look up, or give any other indication that he'd heard. The procurer frowned, and then shouted: "Old Slyhips!"

Hawkril gave Craer a swift, sidelong look. That had been a name none of Blackgult's troops had dared to use to his face, for fear of being personally beaten before dismissal—a beating that usually involved jaw-breaking, or the removal of teeth, or both.

Again, the Golden Griffon seemed not to have heard.

Craer, Tshamarra, and Hawkril looked at each other grimly as the cage chimed and changed again. Blackgult was definitely being brought closer to the center . . . where the Dwaer was.

Hawkril gazed up at his longtime lord. The Golden Griffon, for years considered the most desirable, dashing—and dangerous—man in the kingdom. For much of that time Hawkril Anharu had been his most trusted armaragor.

And now, trust was . . . Hawk sighed, absently tapped the pommel of his sword for a breath or two as he thought hard, and then turned to Tshamarra. "You had a spell?"

The Lady Talasorn nodded. "A way to touch your lady's mind. 'Twill make sure she's unharmed, see if Blackgult or anyone has her in spell-thrall, and wake her if we deem awakening best. It should also tell us if she's still in control of this cage. Whatever we find, the touch of my magic should do her no harm."

Hawkril waved at Embra. "Do it."

"Wake her, too?"

Hawkril eyed the cage as it contracted yet again, set his jaw, and nodded. "Aye. Do that too."

The Lady Talasorn drew the bell-cut sleeves of her jerkin back to her elbows, struck a dramatic pose designed to keep them there, and carefully cast a spell. The cage flickered, the Dwaer flashed with momentary bright fire, and something almost visible sped from it to Tshamarra's fingertips. There it winked silently in a brief, half-seen explosion of phantom sparks, and was gone.

And Tshamarra reeled, winced in pain, and sank to her knees, holding her head.

"Tash?" Craer's hands were cradling her shoulders with falcon-swift speed. She shuddered, groaned, and then sagged into his arms. The procurer shot a look of alarm up at Hawkril, who shrugged helplessly and bent over the stricken sorceress.

"Lady?" he rumbled.

Tshamarra clenched her teeth in a spasm of agony, and then threw back her head, opened her eyes again, and gasped, "Full Dwaer-thrust . . . my own magic, back at me . . . Woa-*ho,* that hurt!"

And then the cage sang. A high, splendid chord of bell-like tones echoed back from the cracked and scorched walls, making all three over-dukes look up.

Ezendor Blackgult grinned down at them in savage triumph, dark fire in his eyes—and the Dwaer in his hands. He hung now at the heart of the cage, its glowing bars falling away from him like so many severed strands of spiderweb.

"Griffon?"

"Blackgult?"

He answered their anxious hails with a wordless snarl of triumph and waved the Dwaer as if it was a ball he intended to hurl. Echoing its move-ments, the cage swirled around him. Then its glowing bars of magic streamed at the slumbrous form of the Lady Silvertree like the boldly reach-ing tentacles of the great glistening sea-beasts who were wont to snatch and drag sailors and their ships down beneath the waves.

The bright strands fell around Embra in a tangle, a net of entwined and fused force that shocked her awake. She was still gasping and shaking her head to clear it when the Dwaer flashed again—and was gone, Blackgult with it!

Embra screamed, and reached vainly for the empty air where it had been, shaking her head now in denial.

Tshamarra peered up at her, face still twisted in pain. "Em? How can I free you from that? I . . . I don't know if I can work magic, just now . . ."

The Lady of Jewels bent her head, drew in a deep, shuddering breath, and then said slowly, "No. Save yourself the pain. I can . . . Hawk, are you there?"

"Lady," the armaragor growled, shoving forward against the collapsed cage of glowing magic until its power brought him to a halt, flaring warn-ingly, "I am. How can I help?"

"Use a rope or something, and drag me down through all this, until I can touch the floor—or a wall. Then keep back. Whatever you do, *don't* try to charge through what's left of my cage to reach me."

The armaragor frowned for a moment, and then spun around and charged across the room, slipping and sliding over rubble, to snatch up fallen tapestries. Some of them still sported great gilded and tasseled pull-cords, and he sliced these from them with grunts of satisfaction, tossing them back over his shoulder to where Craer could scurry and catch each one up, knotting them together with swift skill.

The two men returned in a surprisingly short time with the heavy rope in their hands, and tossed it up into the cage . . . where, despite Craer's shrewd throw, it tangled in dozens of glowing strands of force—strands that hung motionless, no matter how hard the two men tugged. Tshamarra staggered to her feet as she watched them struggle, bewilderment on her face.

"A stone," Embra called. "Knot it around a stone, and throw it over me, so it falls onto me."

"But Em—"

"After what I've been through this night, and the burning these strands are dealing me now," the Lady Silvertree said patiently, "getting hit in the face with a rock will seem like a child's caress. Truly. Now *tie* the grauling thing around a *stone!*"

In sudden haste the procurer and the armaragor complied, and then Craer swallowed, swung the rope a few times—and threw, hard and high.

The stone struck a strand of glowing magic, tumbled, struck another strand and bounded sideways, ricocheted over a third—and hit Embra on the shoulder hard enough to make her gasp and shudder, but not hard enough to stop her from wrapping both hands around the rope and clinging to it. Her fellow overdukes waited until she mastered her pain enough to straighten up out of her trembling crouch, wrap the rope around herself several times, and then tuck the stone under her arm and give them a weary nod.

Then they pulled, slowly and steadily, while Embra wriggled and contorted and reached, slipping between strands and under strands and through gaps in the tangle. Once they had to let the line slack so she could climb back up two strands that met in a trench no one could have passed, but she made her wincing, struggling way through the bars of her own cage until at last she touched the floor.

There she drew in a deep breath, looked up, and cried, "Let go, and get you back!"

The three overdukes scrambled hastily to the door—and behind them, the strands of magic writhed and flared into flames, in a humming inferno that became too bright to look at in half a breath.

Heat blistered the three as they huddled against the door, and Craer murmured, "So, Hawk, how does it feel to sleep with enough fury to do *that?*"

The armaragor gave his old friend a look. "Probably the same as you feel, abed with as much bright magic."

The Lady Talasorn managed a smile. "My, you've the tongue of a courting bard in you, Hawk!"

"Oh? I'll make him take it back out right quickly, when I find it," was the growled reply—and Tash had to look twice before she was sure that he was joking, and dared to laugh.

The fire died away as swiftly as it had flared. Craer spun around and grabbed Hawkril to stop him charging to Embra—but failed. As the armaragor's determined progress towed him across still-hot, creaking flagstones, he called, "So what was all *that*, Lady Em?"

All traces of the cage were gone. Embra Silvertree stood tall, all signs of pain fallen away. She held out her arms for Hawkril, but gave Craer a look of distaste. " 'Lady Em'? Procurer, *how* much longer d'you want to live?"

"Sorry," Craer replied. His voice was contrite without a trace of mockery, startling all of his companions into looking at him. "What did you do just now—the fire, and all?"

Embra smiled at him from the depths of Hawkril's embrace. "When I can touch any stone of the palace, I can call on the Living Castle enchantments. I used them to drink the magic of the cage." Her smile faded. "So now we must rob a few rooms of enchanted things to power the spells Tash and I will need—to fight without a Dwaer, and bring us back home if need be. Oh, and I must get boots and a sash, at least, for this nightrobe. Then the castle enchantments will serve again to source the best seeking spell we can manage—and we must hope by the Three that my father's crazed enough to keep his Dwaer in use, and our magic finds him. We fling ourselves to him, and . . ."

"Risk our necks again," Craer concluded mockingly. "My, what a change!"

In a dark, deep stone chamber, fingers longer and more sinuous than a human's slid around the edges of a stone block, and tugged.

The stone grated out, and the owner of those wormlike fingers reached into the revealed cavity behind it and drew forth a small sack. The sinuous fingers grasped four objects through the rough canvas, carefully holding them apart from each other, as if they were as fragile as eggs.

The sack was set down with great care, and the fingers lengthened and curved like snakes into its open end.

Four times they slid inside, each time emerging with something spherical and setting it gently on the floor. When the snakelike fingers withdrew for the last time, four rock crystal spheres glowed faintly on the floor. Each had one flat side, graven with a rune. Those symbols were the sources of the glows.

The wormlike fingers touched one rune as a long, convoluted, and harsh word was uttered—and from that sphere sprang a whirling, shimmering cloud of colors. The fingers turned the orb over onto its flat side—and the shimmerings instantly became a sharp, bright, three-dimensional image of a young, imperious-looking man in robes.

The owner of the fingers bent its head to regard the image—though its face was a featureless mask of flesh, without visible eyes. Yet it walked very slowly around the image as if studying it, stopped, and then started to move again, more slowly, almost creeping around the seeming of the robed man.

As the faceless creature moved, its body shifted and flowed, becoming more and more like the robed image. When the likeness was exact, a robed man slowly circled a bright, stationary duplicate of himself, making sure of every last detail. Then he straightened to match the pose of the image, walked a few experimental steps in a stride very unlike the sinuous, padding gait of his earlier, faceless form, and announced: "I am Jhavarr Bowdragon."

The dark chamber seemed unimpressed. The Koglaur chuckled, collected the four spheres—the image promptly vanished, restoring complete darkness to the room—and returned them to their hiding place, putting the block of stone back into position.

Then the false Jhavarr Bowdragon went a little way along the wall and drew out another stone block, with appreciably more difficulty this time. Behind it was a little wooden box, from which the transformed Koglaur drew forth a lump of stone that glowed, just for a moment, at his touch.

"Everyone bent on conquering all Darsar should have a Dwaer," the false Jhavarr Bowdragon murmured, cradling the Stone almost lovingly as he carefully restored the box and its concealing wall-block.

Then he held up the Dwaer, made it flash in earnest, and left that secret place.

The man who was not Jhavarr took his next step on the cold stone floor of a different dark cavern. Only one step, ere he stopped, let the Dwaer illuminate his face, and asked the darkness calmly, "Father? Uncle Dolmur?"

His words fell into silence, but it seemed to the Koglaur that it was an intently listening silence rather than a lonely, empty one, so he announced,

"I am Jhavarr Bowdragon, son of Ithim, much changed from what I was . . . and I seek my kin. Father? Dolmur? Are you there?"

"You do *not* sound like Jhavarr," said a deep voice from directly behind the Koglaur. Despite himself, he flinched and spun around.

Dolmur Bowdragon stood facing him—or rather, floated upright, dusty-booted feet planted on empty air a few inches clear of the ground.

The false Jhavarr sighed. "I know. Much of my remembrances are gone forever. I was caught in a Dwaer spell-blast while fighting Blackgult, the Regent of Aglirta, and . . . it took me months to recall my own name, let alone my lineage and that I could work sorcery at all. Uncle, does my father yet live?"

"He does," Dolmur replied gravely, and lifted a hand. As it swept up, weeping could be heard: a storm of helpless sobs coming from a man behind the Bowdragon patriarch, that the darkness was yielding up at the same pace as Dolmur's rising hand.

"My son!" Ithim whispered, when he could manage words.

"Father!" Jhavarr stepped forward eagerly—but came to a swift halt when Dolmur raised his other hand in warning.

"You've sought your kin and found them," the senior Bowdragon said calmly. "What now?"

Jhavarr met Dolmur's eyes, looked away, and swallowed. "I—I need your aid, your sorcery, your wisdom. Both of you." His voice shook with sudden fury. "I crave vengeance for what was done to me, on Blackgult and all Aglirta, whoever kings it there and every last mage of power of that land. Let them all be scoured from Darsar."

"Yes, yes!" Ithim cried. "Of course!" He struggled against Dolmur's restraining magic, seeking to reach and embrace his son, until the patriarch let his hand fall and freed his brother to rush forward.

As Jhavarr rocked in his father's embrace, Dolmur smiled grimly. "I suspect this undertaking will be the death of us all. Yet let us do it. If the Bowdragons are to fall, we should take at least one kingdom with us."

He floated forward. "If our refuge is so easily found, our sorcery may be less puissant than you hope . . . so let us set to work crafting battle plans, and spells to go with them. I refuse to rush into my death fray unprepared to deal the worst I am capable of. I suppose one might call this Bowdragon pride."

Jhavarr smiled eagerly. "So Aglirta is doomed?"

The eldest Bowdragon's answering smile was somewhat fainter. "Well, now. Perhaps we should say rather, 'Aglirta as we know it.'"

.   .   .

The mists that always attended teleportation fell away from their eyes. The Band of Four crouched, weapons ready, a smooth, hard floor underfoot—and found themselves staring down the length of a palatial, lofty-ceilinged bedchamber, its walls all white plaster relief carvings and gleaming closed doors. The towering bed was unmade, its linens and overfur slumped onto the floor. A frightened feminine face stared at them for a moment around the edge of a door beside it, and then vanished.

Tshamarra raised a hand to send a spell arrowing after she who'd fled, but let it fall again without making any futile casting. Her fellow overdukes were already spreading out and trotting forward—toward a desk where a man who was neither young nor slender was sitting naked, a large decanter of drink in his hand, staring at . . . a hand-sized, faintly glowing rock that lay on the polished wood in front of him.

Fear and bewilderment were in that man's stare as he put the decanter to his lips and quaffed deeply. He seemed not to hear the overdukes until Craer was less than a handful of racing strides away.

Then he looked up with a growl, snatched a dagger from the bench beside him with surprising speed, and sprang to meet the intruders, bare as he was.

Gray-white hair covered much of that unlovely, paunchy body, below a face reddening with rage as well as drink. Its owner glared at his four unexpected visitors with no trace of fear as he brandished his blade, dodged aside from Craer's racing attack, and whirled with that same swiftness to slam himself into the speeding procurer and send Craer crashing through the bench rather than letting his outstretched hand snatch the Stone from the table.

The naked man snarled a word—and there was suddenly a dagger poised above Craer's throat, and three more knives floating point-first before the eyes of the rest of the Four.

"Who are you?" the man demanded. "Speak, or I'll start slaying!"

"We're the Overdukes of Aglirta," Hawkril rumbled. "Come here seeking yon Stone. We know you not, nor mean harm to you; please accept our apologies for this intrusion. What is this place?"

The naked man took another swig from his decanter. "This is Varandaur castle, nigh Ragalar, seat of the Delcampers, and this is my bedchamber in it. I am Hulgor Delcamper—one of the many aging wastrel uncles Flaeros has doubtless told you about. He spoke well of you Band of Four." His eyes ranged across them, and then he spun around, went back to his desk, set down the decanter, and laid a hand on the Dwaer sitting there. "You want this. Why?"

" 'Tis one of the most powerful things of magic in all Darsar, and we need it to defend the Vale against the priests of the Serpent," Embra replied. "We lost ours in a battle not long ago, and hoped to recover it. How came you by this one?"

Hulgor shrugged. "It appeared in the air, just here—not long ago, as you say." He picked up the Stone and hefted it. "I'm not one for magic—yon floating knives are a casting laid ready here by a hired mage, not any doing of mine—and have been sitting here wondering how to get rid of it before slaying mages came for me." He grinned. "Fair greeting, slaying mages. I'd like to bargain with you."

"Speak," Tshamarra said softly.

Hulgor leered at her as if she was the one standing naked and not he, and said, "I've a restlessness in me. I've wanted to go and see how young Flaeros is getting on, and visit Flowfoam—I saw it once, years back—but I hate sea voyages and spewing my guts over the rail for days, into storms that hurl it all right back over me. If you offer me no violence, and take me there with you, I'll give you this lump of rock that's so important to mages."

The Four looked at each other. Then Embra, a disbelieving smile tugging at her lips, nodded at the naked noble. "Agreed. By the realm we all serve, I swear this."

Hulgor Delcamper looked at them all, one after another, and received murmured agreements as he went. He gave Craer an extra glare, and received a sheepish smile and spread hands in return.

Hulgor grinned at that. Then he nodded to them all, strode forward as if he was a grandly robed ruler and not an aging, sagging, hairily naked man, and put the Stone carefully into Embra's hand.

Doors burst open with a sound like thunder, and liveried guards burst into the room, glaives and swords glittering, with the chambermaid who'd fled at their arrival at the head of one group. Her scream and pointing arm was ignored in the general roar of competing cries: "Hold! Surrender! Down arms!"

Embra rolled her eyes, Hulgor grinned at her, and the Dwaer flashed in her hand.

Guards sprinting across the polished floor skidded to astonished halts, and Nuelara screamed again. Hulgor Delcamper and the four armed intruders were gone, vanished as if they'd never been.

The guards stared helplessly . . . at a gently rocking decanter on a table, and four dark daggers floating in midair.

No one was there to stare back.

.   .   .

"The Three must hold this place sacred to them, for some special purpose," Ezendor Blackgult muttered, as he stood on a crumbling balcony of the sprawling ruins of the Silvertree Palace known to all Aglirta as the Silent House. The burial ground below him was an overgrown maze of trees, shrubs, and leaning tombs.

Then red and black rage rose in him again, choking-strong. Blackgult went to his knees and mindlessly clawed at the stones of a nearby stair for a few frantic breaths, ere he remembered his own name and went boiling up those same steps, to come out on the battlements.

Shuddering, he fought down the madness and stared grimly out across the Vale, to where the long green isle of Flowfoam lay in its quiet splendor out in the Silverflow.

Plague-rage, oh yes, burning strongest where he'd been bitten . . . poor Indalue must have been infected, and never knew it.

"So here I am at last," he told the uncaring wind bitterly. "Back in the Silent House, the haunted graveyard of half the mages and adventurers Aglirta has ever birthed—wrestling with the Blood Plague."

The rage rose again, and he started striding along the battlements, half-shouting, "If I could hold to my wits long enough, and remember a tenth of what I should be able to, I could heal myself with this!"

The rage passed like a spasm, and Blackgult held up the Dwaer he'd seized not long ago, regarded it regretfully, and whispered, "But I can't."

He walked aimlessly along the battlements, ignoring scattered human and beast bones and the black gorcraw vultures that flapped heavily away at his approach—to land again just out of reach, and watch him balefully . . . patiently.

Anger rose again, sudden and hot. "A weapon, yes—blast this, savage that, burn the other! Destroying's always easy . . . But crafting, mending, healing—why, gods, *why* do you make *those* so hard, hey? Afraid we struggling beasts will achieve something, and rob you of your entertainment?"

The wind snatched those bitter words away, but brought back no reply. Cold-faced, Ezendor Blackgult found a stair and started down. He'd seized this Stone from his own *daughter*!

To leave her defenseless while he died here, driven mad by the Blood Plague. Gods, to be laid low by the sneering Serpents at last! No! *No!*

He was roaring that aloud, he realized dimly, hammering the crumbling stonework with the Stone that could not shatter, screaming and raking the old stone blocks as if his bleeding fingers were talons that could rend . . .

Gasping, he found himself at the bottom of the stairs, in much pain. Evidently he'd fallen, and now had fresh bruises to add to the sickening plague-surging in his guts. He rolled over, sat up with a growl, and glared at the Dwaer.

Well, if die he must, adorned with this bauble half ambitious Darsar sought, he'd die *using* it, by the Horns of the Lady!

First, let it be revealed who else was in the Silent House beneath him, just now—what creatures were breathing, which ones were moving, who was making noise . . . and who was working magic.

Aha! Scuttling things, gliding snakes, lurching skeletons mindlessly guarding this chamber or that . . . an ancient, sighing awareness that was more of a seeing shadow than anything else . . . and a large group of frightened men in armor, busily looting an inner chamber under the snapped orders of no less than *nine* Serpent-priests!

Well, now. The Silent House did have a deadly reputation to maintain . . .

Ezendor Blackgult smiled like a prowling wolf, clutched the Dwaer to his breast in both hands as if it was a newborn babe, and set off into the darkness at a run, letting the rage build, but using the Dwaer to cling to scene after scene of the House ahead of him, and thereby hold to his wits . . . the Three willing . . .

"This, Lord Sir?" the warrior asked timidly, lifting a crumbling shoulder blade and the dangling brown bones of an upper arm. Two slim metal bracelets slid down them, green with verdigris but still displaying either runes or graven script.

"Yes! Take care, mind!" the Brother of the Serpent snapped, pointing an imperious finger into the open coffer the warriors had brought. "Wrap them twice around in those linens, so they'll directly touch nothing else we put in there!"

His glare promised the warrior death or maiming if there was any inadequacy in the wrapping, ere he spun around to shout, "You, there! Elmargh, or whatever your name is! Pry out the block just above yon carving—*pry,* I said, not smite!"

Ilmark of Sirlptar hid his grimace well. He'd been skilled at tapping out old mortar when this bellowing priest was spewing up mother's milk, and was doing this just as deftly now. Another two gentle taps, and an entire line of mortar fell away, allowing him to slide the flat blade of his mattock in under the wall block. Carefully he rocked it, letting the block break the rest of the mortar—and then, ever so slowly, he slid . . . it . . . out.

A large, dark space was revealed behind the block, and the priest of the Serpent fairly crowed in triumph.

"The Great Serpent rises in me!" he cried, throwing his arms wide and nearly knocking teeth from the mouths of the lesser priests on either side of him. "He has made me wise! Stand aside, warrior, and let me see what treasure awaits!"

He snatched a lantern from the nearest priest and strode forward, barely noticing the alacrity with which the warriors faded out of the way and back toward the mouth of the chamber. The other priests crowded forward behind him, murmuring, "Careful, Masterpriest Thraunt!" and, "What can you see, great Thraunt?"

Masterpriest Thraunt raised the lantern and peered carefully into the cavity in the wall, sudden wariness afflicting him. The Silent House was said to be riddled with traps, and he'd heard more than a few grisly tales of overbold treasure seekers who'd found their deaths instead of riches . . .

After a moment of tense peering, he could breathe again.

A few breaths later, he relaxed. There were no signs of guardian creatures, enchanted or otherwise—no spiders spell-slept to awaken when intruders disturbed their niche, nor crawling bone-things held together and given horrible unlife by spells. Nothing awaited above to slam down, or behind to fire or thrust out. Just a small statuette of an armored prince with a sword—as tall as his own head, and seemingly carved of a single, massive ruby.

There was lettering around its base, script of an archaic, elaborate flowing style little used in these more hasty days, but words he could read: *Blood of Silvertree Know Better.*

Hmmph. Well, they hadn't had they? They'd come to this their palace and died, in their dozens, all struck down by the Doom of the Silvertrees! Perhaps this hidden statuette bore the anchor-spell of that ancient Silvertree curse.

He whirled around and snapped, "One of those cloths, and be quick about it!"

The priests wavered, and then one of them turned to call a warrior. Thraunt was quick to roar, "No! One of *you*: the Holy of the Serpent!"

The priests all looked at him with fear or perhaps respect in their eyes, and then stooped and scurried and elbowed each other in a way that brought fleeting, swiftly suppressed grins onto the faces of the watching warriors. Thraunt resolved to deal with those insolent idiots later, after . . .

The cloth was laid into his waiting hand. He gave the priest who'd proffered it a brittle smile that warned that no praise would be forthcoming for something that should have been foreseen and done with no need for order, offering no delay to a superior—then turned and gingerly lifted the statuette, holding it only through the cloth.

It was hard, and smooth, and heavy, and did not feel as if it held hidden secrets in its innards, or bore a lurking surface enchantment. Thraunt turned it, marveling at the beautiful carving—solid ruby, all right—and then set down the lantern and with both hands reverently laid it in the coffer.

There was a murmur from the priests as they got their first proper look at it, and as the warriors started to lean for their own look, without quite daring to step forward from the edges of the room, Masterpriest Thraunt looked up at the holy men of the Serpent and said softly, "Let this not out of your sight for even a moment. Two of you must watch it at all times, for if it goes missing"—he flicked his gaze meaningfully in the direction of the warriors—"all of you shall make a *very* firm, perhaps final, answer for it."

They nodded, slowly, reluctantly, and silently. He kept on staring until he had seen each priest's nod—and only then did Masterpriest Thraunt flip the ends of the cloth over the ruby carving, straighten up with a satisfied sigh, and turn to see . . . dark wisps of vapor curling out of the niche in the wall!

He almost kicked the coffer flying in his haste to get back and away from that ancient trap—for what else could it be?—and stumbled, falling into the waiting hands of only two of the warriors, for the rest had fled in a wordless rush, and were now somewhere down the long passage they'd arrived by.

The pair of warriors roughly but skillfully thrust Thraunt upright, and he turned in time to see that fool of a novice, Ornaugh, choke, clutch his throat, and make a peculiar, desperate whimpering sound—before he fell over on his face, clawing at his neck.

He'd been unable to swallow, Thraunt realized—in his few moments of thought left before the other priests burst into and over him and out the doorway. The last two warriors sprinted in their wake, leaving the Masterpriest battered and winded on the floor, with a peculiar prickling sensation in his nose and throat . . .

No! By the Serpent, *no!* Masterpriest Thraunt was up and on his feet and through that door as fast as he could run, coughing around a tongue grown strangely thick, and trying to keep up with the bobbing lanterns of his craven fellow priests before they left him in utter darkness, here—

There was a bright burst of light from ahead, around the corner of the passage they'd just taken, and an echoing roar that sounded oddly like . . .

There was a second blast, and the tattered remnants of what had been Ilmark of Sirlptar, or Elmargh, or whatever his name was, came bouncing and whirling into view, all of the limbs rolling to a stop separately.

Spell-blasts! That was it! Just like those he'd seen in a courtyard in Sirlptar, when first observing a casting of the fireburst spell that the Brotherhood called "Fire of the Serpent." Someone—a traitor? a rival priest?—had blasted everyone under his command as they'd run along the narrow passage.

"Great Serpent!" Thraunt gasped, the words half a prayer and half a curse, and trotted forward warily, readying the best spell he knew: a "Wrath of the Serpent," the stinging cloud of flying, biting snakes that even anointed priests of the Serpent feared . . .

There was another blast, a short, choked-off scream, and more remains bounced and rolled to a dusty, grisly halt ahead. Thraunt slowed, wondering how long he should wait in silent hiding before venturing around that corner.

This was no trap, for traps do not howl and scream wild laughter, then sob and snarl and hoot and howl again. This sounded like someone gone plague-mad. Perhaps a mage, come here to loot, who'd been caught by the fangs of one of the guardian snakes he'd dropped to guard their way out of the ruins . . .

Well, if so, all he need do was wait, and this foe would die raving, and leave the way clear. Thraunt knew he was not a patient man, but when the clear alternative is being blown apart . . .

Around the corner came hissing shouts, and then snapped orders and the clang of blades—far more blades than his warriors bore, even if none of them had fallen. Wild roars followed, mixed with loudly declaimed gibberish this time.

Other priests had planned treasure-snatching expeditions into the Silent House, and although there'd been agreement to allow each foray one day before the next went in, Thraunt had known at the time just how feeble that agreement was . . . This must be another, larger Serpent party; he could hear spells being hissed and chanted that could only be the weavings of anointed Brothers of the Serpent. Could they have slain his command?

Yet why then all the hooting and howling? And why the sudden, fear-filled shouts? Surely they'd lurk silent, and creep forward hoping to take him or others in these haunted ruins unawares . . .

More blasts, rocking the ceiling and the floor beneath his feet this time, and the spell-chants suddenly ceased. Thraunt crept forward, not daring to stay where he was any longer for fear of the throat-prickling gas behind him—but he was still three long strides shy of the bend in the passage when a tall man wearing only a nightrobe stalked around the corner, leering and lurching. Tall and handsome and somehow familiar, he carried a glowing rock in his hands and was crooning to it wordlessly, as if it was a baby he was comforting.

He barked with laughter when he saw Thraunt, and the stone flashed—and Masterpriest Thraunt, in the last few seconds of life as a Dwaer-blast raced toward him, understood that what the man held was not merely an enchanted lump of stone but one of *the* Stones.

And then he experienced his first Dwaer-blast, and his last—and all Darsar went away, just like that.

Blackgult laughed loud and long, holding the Stone high in triumph and letting it spew little stinging lightnings down his arm, cascading snarling sparks across the floor. With these fires he'd slain at least four dozen Serpent-spawn—three different bands of them, by the Horned Lady!

Well, they'd come seeking treasure . . . and unfortunately for them, they'd found it!

Ezendor Blackgult chuckled gleefully as he strode into a dusty, long-ruined chamber of lofty size, somewhere in the westerly wings and turrets of the Silent House. Ah, but at least he'd not be dying alone. He'd butchered a respectable host of Snake-lovers this day! Why, ther—

Light flashed in the gloom before him, three bright and expanding spheres of radiance. Out of each stepped a tall, slender, robed man—two strangers, and a younger companion one he'd seen before. Seen, and thought dead forever, in the skies above a battlefield here in Aglirta: Jhavarr Bowdragon . . . and judging by the faces of the elder pair, he'd brought his kin.

"Ezendor Blackgult," the oldest wizard greeted him coldly, as the other two launched without hesitation into complicated spellweavings—bindings to keep him in this chamber, by the sounds of their incantations. "I am Dolmur Bowdragon. This is my brother Ithim—and I believe you've already met Jhavarr. Bowdragons never forget . . . and Bowdragons pay all debts."

The Golden Griffon threw back his head and cackled. "So," he added joyfully, completing Dolmur's threat, "prepare to die! Aha-ha-ha-ha!"

And with that laughter still echoing off the ceiling above him, Blackgult blasted it with the Dwaer and brought that end of the room crashing down atop his three newfound foes.

Two of them ran, desperately, breaking off their spellcasting. But the one who'd called himself Dolmur calmly spread his hands, and the great chunks of ceiling thundered down onto . . . something unseen, that sent them tumbling and rolling aside.

And then bursting apart, into powder, under a Dwaer-blast! One of the three—Jhavarr, it must be, for it had come from his side—had a Dwaer!

Blackgult roared out his rage and excitement. There was a way of forcing a blast from one Dwaer to another, now . . . *yes!*

Exultantly he did what he'd read in a dusty old tome in the palace library. It hurt the wielder, aye, but what cared he for that? He was dead anyway! Let a richer harvest be reaped, and old Blackgult go down to greet the Three with three dead Bowdragons to his credit. *Yes!*

The blast, when it came, swept away Dolmur's spell and took all three Bowdragons by surprise. Ithim screamed as the two older Bowdragons were flung away like rags, bones splintering audibly. Jhavarr, holding his Dwaer, was caught in the blast-glow, frozen in pain and rooted to the spot by the sheer power racing through him, his face twisted in dismay . . . and as the magic roared on, his slender body slowly changed, melting away from the likeness of Jhavarr Bowdragon into . . . bony facelessness. A Koglaur!

The two torn and bleeding Bowdragons saw the transformation too.

"Duped!" Dolmur snarled. "We've been tricked to our dooms!"

Ithim screamed again in fear and despair—and he was still screaming when Dolmur did something that abruptly snatched them elsewhere, leaving the Koglaur alone to shudder as Blackgult sent another Dwaer-blast through him.

"Skill and savagery, that's the way!" the Golden Griffon called jovially. "You faceless, sneaking rogue, you!"

The Koglaur turned his smooth, eyeless face toward Blackgult, and the Griffon felt the weight of coldly seething scrutiny. Then, abruptly, the Faceless One vanished, leaving the chamber dark and lonely once more. Inconsiderately, he'd neglected to leave his Dwaer behind him.

"Ah, well," Blackgult told the walls around him, "Victorious, the Golden Griffon can get on with dying in peace, then."

Or perhaps . . . just perhaps . . . He held up the Dwaer and cast a careful shielding-spell, three-layered and intricate. Blackgult was shaking with weariness when he was done, and dark anger was rising in his belly again, so he made haste to work a last, healing magic, and let go of the Dwaer.

It drifted away from his upflung arm, and gathered speed as it went, curving along the inside of his shield-spell. Blackgult tore off his robe and laid it out as a bed as near to the center of the shield-sphere as he could quickly judge. He laid himself down hastily, closed his eyes, and pictured the Dwaer whirling around above him in a steady orbit, clinging to images of its speeding glow as the anger surged.

If he was to live, he had to rest. In trance, if he'd recalled Sarasper's instructions aright, the Dwaer just might be able to purge the Blood Plague from his body. "Well, now," he muttered, sinking down into the dark warmth where the rage rolled and snarled, "to be rid of the plague and healed hearty again . . . wouldn't *that* enrage a few Serpent-priests? They might even do something foolish and violent . . . But then again, how would the rest of us tell?"

Chuckling, he let the darkness take him.

23

Great Serpent Rising

*I*ngryl Ambelter smiled politely at the dozen or so elder Serpent-priests facing him as the underpriests who'd brought him here scuttled hastily out and closed the doors. Protective magics sang almost audibly in the air; every one of these old men must have shield-spells active. The room was small and bare: stone benches faced the oratory floor he was standing on, amid two large pillars. There was but the one visible door—and, rearing out from the wall to his left, a stone statue of a snake poised to strike.

The Spellmaster gave it a long glance to make sure it was sculpted stone and not a spell-frozen snake of monstrous size, and then regarded the priests again. "You know who I am. And you would be—?"

One of the oldest men spoke, without rising from his bench. "All of us hold the rank of 'Lord of the Serpent,' most exalted in our Brotherhood beneath the Great Serpent himself. We are not all the Lords, but rather the oldest and largest faction among rival groups of Lords who hold differing views on who the Great Serpent is, and how we shall find him."

Ingryl nodded. "Forgive my ignorance, but beneath you in the ranks of the Church are . . . what titles?"

Another priest spoke. "Beneath us are a handful of Masterpriests, below them a very much larger mustering of senior clergy who are styled 'Priest of the Serpent,' then again a smaller whelming of priests called Scaled Masters, and then the great bulk of the Brethren, who are all 'Brothers of the Serpent.' Below them are Fangbrothers—such as those who conducted you here—and beneath them come lesser ranks of no account, down to the novices. Under every Great Serpent the titles and standings have changed somewhat."

"And you are all, if I understand things correctly, truly wizards, using spells known to mages everywhere as well as Serpent-related magics held secret by the Church?"

"Yes. The Great Serpent has access to a great web of spells known as the Thrael, the legacy of the original archmage who founded the faith and became the first Great Serpent."

Ambelter nodded. "And you need me to–?"

The priest who'd first made answer held up a hand. "Let us first describe our situation, Spellmaster of All Aglirta. I am called Caronthom 'Fangmaster,' and serve as First Voice in our councils. This"–he indicated the second priest who'd spoken–"is Raunthur the Wise. The reports returned to council tell us that the Church has now successfully infested all Aglirta with the Blood Plague that turns men to beasts we can command, or drives them to slaying rage. We know and can provide antidotes to the effects of the venom, and so keep people 'untainted' if we choose. Through the use–and withholding–of this 'Grace of the Serpent,' and through fear, we now effectively rule every town and hamlet of the Vale, behind the backs of many tersepts and barons. Others bow to us directly."

"Have the rival Serpent-lords aided you in this, or do they work against you?"

"They are actively and enthusiastically part of the Church. Our disagreements are over the identity and coming of the Great Serpent, and how and where we should seek him, not over the rightful goals of the faith."

Ingryl Ambelter nodded. "Is the priest called Yedren part of your faction, or a rival?"

"Not one of us," Raunthur said gently. "I believe the term 'rival' is a trifle strong."

The wizard nodded. "Rathtaen? Ormsivur? Of you, then, or not?"

"Not."

"Harsadrin? Thelvaun?"

Caronthom arched an eyebrow, and waved one hand. "You seem well acquainted with us. Well, then . . ."

A glowing map of the Vale appeared on the floor all around the Spellmaster. Ambelter hastily stepped back out of it to see better as the Fangmaster pointed to spot after spot on the map.

"The most important Lords of the Serpent who stand against us, besides those you've named, are Naumun in Sirlptar, and Lethsais, over here in Telbonter. I would also describe Hlektaur in Dranmaer and

Boazshyn of Ool as less friendly to our approach than to the one advocated by Yedren—which is to pick a brainless novice from our ranks and make him Serpent over us all, controlled by we of the inner council through a great web of blood-spells."

"And why is that not a good notion?" Ambelter asked, his eyes on the winding Silverflow. The magic of the map made its waters seem to endlessly move.

"We contend that one so feeble of mind in the first place and so addled with spells in the second can have no hope of mastering the Thrael, and thus be useless in whelming and commanding the true power of the Church."

"And who are the Lords who lean to your views, or whom you know to be part of your faction?"

"Our two Lords in Ibryn," Caronthom replied, "Maskalos and Cheldraem. Also Rauldron of Tselgara, Old Nael in Rithrym—so called because his son, Nael, is also of our Brethren, though but a Fangbrother as yet—and Pheltarth in Adelnwater."

"Kelhandros in Sart," Raunthur added, and the Fangmaster nodded at this amendment.

"An impressive list of wizards," Ambelter commented. "So how can my spells make a difference, one way or another? If you have all these masters of magic among you, and rule the Vale already, what do you need me for?"

"To help us find the Great Serpent, assist us in disputes with our ah, rival Lords, and to help us openly conquer the kingdom. We must rule in Flowfoam."

The Spellmaster looked up from the map. "It seems to me that you could just walk in at any time and sit on the throne. Neither Flowfoam nor the wider Vale holds much of anyone who could or would stand against you."

The Fangmaster gave Ambelter a considering look. "Well, not so. Despite our best efforts, Aglirta still has barons and tersepts ruled more by ambition than by fear of us—and some of these have already invited outlander hireswords into the realm to fight for them. More than a few wealthy Sirl merchants are also watching what unfolds in Aglirta, and gathering mercenaries for their own forays into the Vale."

Raunthur the Wise nodded. "We can't get terrified farmers and villagers to rise in arms in any numbers or effectiveness. If we move openly to take Flowfoam, we'll be forced to hire outlanders to forge an army of our own."

"And so? A shortage of coins has never seemed to be among your problems."

"No," Caronthom agreed, "we've hired armies before and could do so again—but we dare not begin whelming until the new Great Serpent has been found, or we face the danger of becoming the victims of our hirelings. Some brute of an outlander warlord will crown himself King of Aglirta—and we'll have achieved nothing but to rouse the whole realm, weaken it, and empty our coffers."

Ingryl Ambelter nodded. "That's more wisdom than I've heard in many a year. So how will I know if I've found your Great Serpent for you? How do *you* tell when you've found him?"

Raunthur the Wise shook his head with a smile, remembering. "There's a . . . feeling. Any Priest of the Serpent knows, the moment they're in the same room as the chosen one. We can *feel* the power of the Dark One, flowing from him."

Ingryl Ambelter nodded again. "Well, that seems clear enough. I accept, with thanks." He smiled—and the Dwaer beneath his robes erupted in a bright blast of force that stabbed out at the shieldings of Caronthom and Raunthur.

In an instant they flared to a blinding brightness, and the Dwaer-bolts sped on to the shieldings of the other priests, leaping from one to another. Some of the Serpent-lords tried to weave magics of their own, in the space of a scant breath, or rose to flee; but when their shields were struck, those magics were rooted to the spot, and then—one after another, like mushrooms frying in a pan—popped and died to shrunken darkness, leaving nothing of themselves or the men they'd held behind but a little sizzling wetness. So passed most of the Lords of the Serpent.

The slaying was done in less than four breaths. The Spellmaster of All Aglirta smiled around at the last drifting smokes, used the Dwaer to suck in every vestige of heat and spilled power, cast another long look at the Serpent-statue, just to be sure, and calmly strode to the door.

It was trembling and straining under a magic cast by some of the boldest priests outside. Ambelter smiled tightly. Before leaving the ruined house in Sirlptar, he'd knotted his thieves' sack into a bulky neck scarf that looked more like a bib than anything else, to cover the Dwaer. He adjusted it now so that the Dwaer was completely hidden beneath it again, carefully put one hand on the Stone beneath its concealment, and banished the scry-seal spell on the doors—apparently with an airy wave of his other hand.

Several priests almost tumbled into the room. His hand never leaving the hidden Dwaer, the Spellmaster stepped back and let them all flood in.

They stared around at the empty room, still echoing with power and sharp with the smell of fiery death, and then looked at him in dawning terror and anger. But before any of them could yell or hurl anything, he said coolly, "The most senior Lords of the Church have charged me with a great task, and then taken themselves into seclusion with a very powerful magic. I have been set in office over you until the Great Serpent himself commands otherwise."

He turned to the man he judged the most dangerous, and added, "My first orders to you are to go and summon to me here Maskalos and Cheldraem from Ibryn. They are to meet with me without delay." Without pause he pointed at the next man and ordered, "Bring here also Naumun of Sirlptar."

Continuing to turn, he pointed at the next priest and commanded, "Escort to me Lethsais, from Telbonter."

The next priest was trembling with fear or rage, and Ambelter spoke to him gently. "Bring me the Lord of the Serpent Yedren." He continued naming the Lords he'd been told of, and issuing firm orders for them to be brought to this chamber.

"And who are you to give such orders?" a Masterpriest demanded furiously. "I see no Caronthom assuring us that we are to obey you—nor countermanding the orders he earlier gave to *me,* which were to watch you carefully, wizard, for signs of evil deeds or intent toward our Church. I can only—"

The Dwaer flashed under the concealing scarf, just for a moment, and the flagstones beneath the shouting Masterpriest moved, rippling like living things. They drew back into huge serpent-jaws, jutting up into fangs with a yawning mouth between—a mouth inhabited by the now frantically spell-weaving Masterpriest, whose booted feet seemed to be stuck in the heart of the opening maw.

As the other priests watched in pale-faced silence, the mouth widened almost lazily—and then closed with a snap, snatching the shouting man down into the floor. Stones rippled again and then lay flat and seemingly solid once more.

"I'd hoped to avoid unpleasantness," the Spellmaster said quietly, "but the authority given to me *was* absolute. Go and fetch some other priests, one of you; I'm sure you know as well as I do that I haven't assigned devout faithful to fetch all of the Lords of the Serpent yet, and now I'm short one fool of a Masterpriest. He was going to bring Kelhandros here from Sart, so now I'll need someone else for that task. And mind you bring them without delay, Brothers; the urgency is such that the Church cannot wait. Go now, all of you. The only one I expect to see again without his assigned Lord of the Serpent is the one fetching me more Brethren to serve me as summoners."

The scramble for the lone door was as frantic as it was fearful, and Ingryl Ambelter barely had time to smile before he was using the Dwaer to draw the door firmly closed behind the last fleeing priest.

He spell-sealed that door for time he needed to conjure a floating mirror in the air before him, work a very complex and exacting magic on himself, study his reflected result critically, and make a few adjustments.

When he banished the mirror, unsealed the door, and turned to face it once more, a stealthily invisible shielding-spell gathering strength around him, the Spellmaster of All Aglirta sported a green-scaled snake's head in place of his own. He flashed his yellow eyes with a smile, tasted the air with his flickering forked scarlet tongue, and waited for the new group of priests to appear.

If he served all of the Lords of the Serpent the same deadly fate, priest after priest, he could hardly help but become the Great Serpent in truth. Well, he'd always been good at crafting magics against poisons and venoms—and it was a better way than many of gaining the throne of Aglirta.

The mists fell away, and the world around them had changed. They stood in a high-vaulted, arch-windowed chamber hung with rich tapestries, a floor of gleamingly smooth marble beneath their feet. Guards in bright-polished silver armor whirled around to face them, glaives flashing in their hands as they dipped. Their wielders gasped, straightened again, and bowed their heads. The nearest one said swiftly: "Fair greeting, Lord and Lady Overdukes."

"Fair greeting, Braeros," the Lady Silvertree replied gravely, for all the world as if she wore naught but a nightrobe, sash, and boots every day, and customarily went about the world collecting unlovely and aging naked men. "Where bides the King?"

"In the Southern Sunchamber, Lady," the guard replied swiftly, "with the Lord and Lady Delcamper."

Embra nodded her thanks and the overdukes hastened to the southern doors of the room, with Hulgor padding along barefoot in their midst frowning and asking Flowfoam around him, "*Lady* Delcamper? Has the lad married, then? Why, the scamp! To manage a courtship without laying a hint of it amongst us, his dearest kin . . ."

As they trotted along a passage, crossed a larger, grander one, and mounted a broad flight of stairs, servants and courtiers alike cast swift, startled glances at the unclad stranger among the four hurrying overdukes, and then as quickly looked away again and continued about their business.

Craer took silent note of those few who froze and then hastily ducked away in a different direction than they'd been proceeding—and as they turned on a landing of Axehelve Stair, he laid a hand on the arm of the duty page of that stair, and murmured, "Suitable garb for this noble lord who accompanies us, with a dresser and a screen, to the Southern Sunchamber, before I draw twenty breaths more."

The page bowed and raced off down the steps as the overdukes proceeded, passing several pairs of stern and watchful guards, and entered the Sunchamber.

A small ring of guards faced outward in a corner of that large, bright, and mostly empty hall. Within the ring of sentinels, three folk sat at one end of a table that had chairs for six, talking earnestly: King Raulin Castlecloaks of Aglirta, and—

"Flaeros, you young rogue!" Hulgor roared, lumbering forward with his arms flung wide. The guards lowered their glaives menacingly, even as Hawkril bellowed, "Blades aside and rest easy, all!" and the bard stood up and gasped, "Uncle Hulgor!"

The guards glanced away from the onrushing, naked graybeard to their king, and Raulin grinned and waved a hand to indicate agreement with Hawkril's shouted order. The guards drew aside, revealing—

"*Orele,* graul you! Gel, I *thought* the maids'd been a trifle more on both the lazy and frisky side this last while! Well, by all the watching stars and gods—"

And then Flaeros and his uncle slammed together in an unruly bear hug, and Hulgor's words were lost in roaring laughter. The older Delcamper shook Flaeros, ruffled his hair, and then scooped him off his feet and carried him like a featherweight child's doll to where the Lady Orele waited demurely—and swept her up into the same jovial embrace.

Crushed against his overweight nakedness, the wrinkled Lady of Chambers clung to her cane as the guards watched, some of them grinning openly, and gasped, "Don't crush *all* of my ribs, you great bear!"

Hulgor bellowed laughter into her face, making her wince visibly, and then held Orele out dangling at the full stretch of his arm. "Well, now, Old Wrinkles, ye still look as slyly beautiful as ever, under all that starch and sharp tongue! Why, graul me if—"

"*Lord* Hulgor," the aging servant said primly, "at your age you should be *very* aware that 'tis less than seemly for men of your station and present lack of dress to go about accosting servants of any gender, particularly mine. Have you misplaced your dresser? Or left some wench in such rude haste that your garments remain strewn about her bedchamber, perhaps?"

"Uh, the Lord's dresser," the breathless page announced from behind them all, judging this the proper moment to interject. Craer thanked him with a grin, and guards chuckled as Hulgor let go of Flaeros and snatched Orele up in both hands to bring her close for a kiss.

"Ah, now, Sweethips, 'tis not like that at all! Why, not a—"

Lady Orele was shorter and far more slender than the Lord Hulgor, but her present position in midair placed her feet at a most effective height for dealing with accosting lords. She made use of that situation now, abruptly.

The Lord Hulgor announced his reaction to Flowfoam with a strangled "Eeep!" and a hasty, staggering return of the Lady Orele to the ground. It was accomplished with as much care as a pain-wracked, doubled-over man of advancing years can manage, and Orele acknowledged his effort with a curtsy before telling him severely, "As I've said before on several occasions, my lord, I am not to be addressed by that love-name in public. Nor as 'Wrinkles,' 'Old Boot,' or some others you should recall." Then she whirled around to turn her back on him, ere calmly resuming her seat.

Flaeros gazed at her, shaking his head slightly, before turning to the king and saying, "Your Majesty, may I present the Lord Hulgor Delcamper?"

The wincing, naked man glanced up from his pain and gasped, "Ah, yes, ye'd be Raulin. Charmed."

The king took Hulgor's hand and chuckled. "Likewise. Be welcome in Flowfoam, and at all our councils. Nice fashion statement, but one I hope few of my courtiers will adopt." He hesitated, and then added with a grin, "Save perhaps the Lady Factor of Sart, Florimele, and—"

"Not now, Raulin," Embra Silvertree told him warningly. "You know such public revelations will only lead to trouble. Florimele's mind is far less lovely than her skin, believe me." She turned and gave Craer a hard look. "And before you say something clever, Lord Delnbone, 'tis none of your business and irrelevant anyway, so ask not how much experience I've had of either." She turned her head again. "Lord Hulgor, is our bargain fulfilled?"

Dressers were swarming around Hulgor Delcamper, and his face was still creased with pain, but he managed a nod, a smile, and the words, " 'Tis indeed."

Embra nodded, and turned to her three companions. "Then, Over-dukes, we've an unfinished task and a Stone to accomplish it with." She drew off her boots, thrust them through her sash, and stroked her bare feet across the marble floor, nodding as she felt the old Living Castle enchantments stirring. Then she held up the Dwaer. "Let's try again to trace the Dwaer my father holds."

Hawkril promptly turned to the page and growled, "Proper garments for the Lady Silvertree, here in haste!"

"A moment," the Lady Talasorn added, as the lad rose out of a florid bow to race for the doors. "Bring also, from the chambers I share with the Lord Craer, the belt with three pouches on it. Open none of them, mind, unless painful death beckons you strongly this morn."

The page nodded and ran out. Several courtiers tried to crowd in as the door opened, but the guards were watching the king and Hawkril for signals, and received the same gesture from both. Accordingly, they swept the room clear again and closed the doors, despite shrill protests.

Silence fell in the Sunchamber, and the Four became aware that they had an interested audience. Embra was already trembling in near trance, calling on the Flowfoam enchantments and the Dwaer whilst trying not to "hear" either, but the other overdukes gazed at everyone crowded into the room until Craer waved a dismissive hand and said, "Now, now, there's not really going to be much to see. This is *real* magic, not—"

"Craer," Tshamarra warned silkily, and the procurer shut his mouth softly, without saying another word. The guards goggled at him as if the Three themselves had appeared in glowing splendor to work a miracle before their very eyes . . . because, of course, that was more or less what had happened.

At which point Embra opened her eyes again and murmured, "I've found Overduke Blackgult and that Dwaer—in the Silent House."

The other overdukes looked at her, and Hawkril rumbled, "I find myself unsurprised."

Embra nodded and sighed. "Somehow I knew we'd end up back there before long."

Craer shrugged. "We should fix it up and make it *our* palace."

She wrinkled her nose. "Haven't you forgotten that it drives Silvertrees mad?"

Craer grinned at her. "It's already done its worst to you, I'd say."

They stuck out their tongues at each other in unison.

The Sunchamber doors crashed open. The Four whirled around, the guards swung down their glaives . . . and relaxed again as the red-faced, panting page and two chambermaids came trotting across the room, bearing clothes.

Embra unconcernedly undid her sash, letting her boots fall, and tossed her robe to the floor. The page stared, swallowed, and then twisted around as he skidded to a stop in front of her, so that she beheld his back, and he was facing the chambermaid who held a heap of lacy and frilly things. The page tentatively dug into them with trembling hands, mumbling, "Wasn't sure . . . just which . . ."

The Lady Silvertree patted his shoulder and then bent past him, brushing against him very distractingly. "None of these," she said, brushing aside most of the diaphanous silk. "These are for Lord Hawkril's entertainment, not rough travel."

The armaragor rumbled wordless embarrassment behind her as Embra plucked up a scrap of silk and then a pair of leather breeches, placing the former as a breechclout and sliding the latter on over them. She selected a plain cotton shirt, a broad cummerbund belt of stiff leather, and then a leather warrior's jack, good boots, gloves, and a half-cloak. "My thanks. Hawk, buckle me up, will you? And bring one of those cloaks—my liking for unadorned stone floors as beds wanes and wanes."

"Ah, I was—" a voice hailed them, from across the chamber, but Orele and Embra snapped: "No!" in unintentional unison.

The Lady Silvertree added, "Lord Hulgor, please take no offense when I say that getting guests bloodily killed holds no attractiveness for we of Aglirta. We go now to a haunted place of much magic, where we'll face traps, poison, monsters, and perhaps a hostile madman with one of *these*." She held up the Dwaer, and added softly, "Forgive me for saying this, Lord Delcamper, but you'd not last six breaths."

Hulgor sat back with a sigh. "No offense taken—graul you, Lady. Bring me back the tale of what befell, mind!"

"We will," Embra promised, and turned to survey the rest of the Four. "Ready?"

"As much as always," Tshamarra replied with a sigh. "Take us."

The Lady of Jewels smiled grimly, waved a hand, the Dwaer flashed, and the mists rose.

Mists curled and sank away, and the Band of Four blinked in the gloom of a great chamber, as Embra's Dwaer flashed and another Stone winked back in reply, from not far away.

It was whirling in an endless loop around a man lying unclad and asleep upon a robe on the dusty stone floor: Blackgult, looking much as they'd seen him last. At every flash of Dwaerindim, the air around the orbiting Stone glowed momentarily, outlining a great curving barrier like a sphere of armor.

"He's in trance, probably healing himself," Embra said quietly, "and that's a shield-spell around him, a powerful one. We'd best wait for him to awaken, and hope."

"Hope that he's healed?"

"Hope that what awakens is still Ezendor Blackgult, and not something else," the Lady Silvertree replied grimly, advancing to where she could peer all around the large chamber. "Find the doors, all of them. We'd best mount a guard."

"Embra," Craer said warningly, pointing. A snake had reared up in the dust just inside one open doorway, regarding them with glittering eyes. Unhesitatingly, Embra blasted it to oily smoke with a Dwaer-bolt. Black-gult's Stone and shielding both flared into answering light, but seemed otherwise unaffected.

"Just a snake, or Serpent-work?" Tshamarra asked, as Craer and Hawkril advanced on that door, blades ready in their hands.

"Serpent-work," the Lady of Jewels replied shortly. "That was a spy, spell-linked back to someone else; I hope I gave him a searing headache. Come, Tash, let's spell-seal these other doors."

The armaragor peered through the open archway. "No door left here, not for years. Dark and empty passage, opens out fairly soon . . . and we forgot torches."

"So we did," Embra said with a sigh, turning away from the door she and Tshamarra had just sealed, tracing it with glowing fingertips in unison with the Stone held between them. "We'll have to conjure up a door, then, and—"

Whatever else she was going to say was lost forever in a sudden hissing flood. Dozens of serpent-arrows came streaking along the passage and through the doorless arch in a deadly storm. They sizzled to ashes where they struck Blackgult's shielding, but otherwise broke from their racing flights in midchamber to whirl into separate strikes at the Four, darting like wasps.

The Dwaer flashed in Embra and Tshamarra's shared grasp, and from both sorceresses a gigantic cloak of flame snarled up—and fell over the hissing missiles.

Flaming snakes writhed and tumbled in all directions, falling as embers and whirling scraps of ash, but many of the rigid serpents still swooped and soared. Craer sprang high to slash one to ribbons in midair with two daggers, and Hawkril waited warily, warsword raised, to hack down any snake-shaft that darted through the pursuing claws of Dwaer-flame.

Only one did, and his slash struck it aside just enough for him to grasp its body and fling it to the floor. The armaragor stamped on its head, hard, and whirled away from the feebly wriggling remains—just as the door Embra and Tshamarra had sealed burst with a roar of dust, rubble and searing magic.

Serpent-priests came leaping through that fog. With a shout of glee Craer sprang to meet them, his blade flashing and Hawkril right behind him. A half-seen priest stopped and raised a bow. Before he could fire a serpent Embra sent a Dwaer-blast into his face—and then whirled to fire another, larger bolt at something large, bony, and bestial that was crawling slowly in through the doorway.

It quivered, seemed to shudder soundlessly . . . and kept coming, as large as a one-horse cart, its low body covered with angled plates of bone.

Tshamarra cursed softly and backed away from the advancing bulk. "What *is* it?"

"Hawk!" Embra called sharply. "Back here, please! I like not the look of—"

Another monstrous *something* loomed up out of the drifting dust of the felled door, gliding through the ranks of Serpent-priests, and a soft green glow of magic wafted out from it, washing over the procurer and a priest he was busily slaying.

They stiffened and groaned in unison. Then the Serpent-man toppled, trailing blood, and Craer ducked away, falling heavily amid the rubble and losing the gory dagger he'd just used. On his hands and knees he scrambled clumsily but hastily back to Embra.

A Serpent-priest ran after the procurer, but Hawkril plucked up a fallen stone and hurled it hard, taking the man in the face and hurling him back into a hard landing on the floor.

Craer slithered to Embra's feet, his voice a raw gasp. "Whatever that is, its magic numbs . . . weakens . . . Three Above, it *still* hurts . . ."

Tshamarra hastily snatched the Dwaer from Embra and bent down to touch Craer's shoulder with it.

The Lady of Jewels eyed both advancing monsters, and frowned. "Hawk," she asked quietly, "what are these beasts?"

"Fearsome monsters, Lady," Craer offered brightly, shaking still-numbed hands as he smiled his thanks up at the Lady Talasorn. Embra didn't even bother to sigh.

The armaragor pointed at the bone-plated, crablike creature advancing slowly toward them from the archway. Serpent-priests could be seen advancing in its wake, keeping well back. "Yon's a dargauth, moving about as fast as such things can move. 'Tis like a gigantic scorpion without a stinging tail. Those two pincer-claws up front are what it slays with; they can easily crush warriors, armor and all. See the dark syrup dripping from its barbs? Smeared on . . . poison, methinks."

"Plague-taint," Tshamarra murmured. "Let's blast it."

Embra nodded, and they directed the full fury of the Dwaer on the crablike dargauth as they backed away, eyeing the other monster now. Blackgult's circling Stone flashed at each orbit, tugging at the fire the sorceresses of the Four were sending.

"Over *here,* Ladies!" Craer snapped.

Embra whirled, stabbing out with one hand, and brought the Dwaer-fire with her. It washed over a handful of spellweaving Serpent-priests, setting the clinging dust cloud aflame, and seemed to struggle with a fresh gout of the soft green glow spewed by the larger, gliding monster.

Craer shook his head. "The Snake-lovers certainly seem to have made the Silent House their home. Hawk, this beast would be–?"

"A sarath of the swamps. They must have used spells to tame it, but yon green light is magic of its own, that slows prey and foes, even puts small creatures to sleep or freezes them where they stand. The spell-bolts come from somewhere amid those spines along its back, but it feeds like a score of eels: with many little fanged sucking maws on its belly. We're food to it–and it can smother, too. I've only ever seen one before."

"Charming," Tshamarra remarked, as they backed away to the very tingling edge of Blackgult's Dwaer-barrier. "Any chance of getting these two horrors to fight each other?"

"Not while the priests are controlling them," Embra replied grimly. "I'll not be surprised if both these beasts turn out to be humans twisted by the plague."

"We haven't swords enough to fight both," Hawkril rumbled. "Any swift sorcery?"

"Little time for *that,* either," Tshamarra snapped, watching the beasts close in. Neither the scuttling thing nor the gliding one were moving with any haste, but they were both perhaps four running strides distant now, no more, with grinning Serpent-priests behind them.

The Dwaer flashed in Embra's hand. "Close together! Hurry!"

The Lady Talasorn looked a silent question at the taller sorceress, who replied, "I'm shielding us, just as my father did himself. I'll try to link to his barrier. If I manage it, I can bring it forward to enclose us, leaving us protected by his Stone, and free ours to smite again."

The air glowed around them, a faint, pearly radiance that visibly threw back a gout of the sarath's green glow. Both monsters clawed at the air as if it was thickening around them.

Suddenly the sarath climbed the air in front of the overdukes, whirling up on its side to drift along in front of them, underbelly raised to gnaw hungrily at nothing with its dozens of lampreylike mouths.

"Well," Craer offered, studying those questing jaws narrowly, "this certainly beats getting drenched in beast-blood and wondering if you're unwittingly hacking up all the tasty bits. I—"

There was a sudden flash and roar from behind them, and the room rocked. The Four found themselves whirling through the air, away over the sarath and the rubble of the shattered door, the air around them gleaming like a great shell of armor.

Amid frantic Serpent-shouts, a strange, bubbling cry arose from behind them, liquid and slobbering and agonized. The overdukes crashed into the far wall of the chamber, drifting to slow stops against creaking, dust-spewing stone as their shared shielding-spell smote the wall and stuck there, held by a great thrusting force. With one accord, they struggled to turn around and see what was happening behind them. "Has the Griffon—?" Craer gasped, his words echoing with a strange, soft distortion.

The monsters were both torn, splattered heaps against the chamber walls, broken-bodied priests strewn among them. Beyond, in the leaping heart of Dwaer-fire . . .

Blackgult lay sprawled and bare, just as before—but awake now, staring fixedly at nothing above him, and screaming. His raw cry went on and on, neither rising nor falling, and its mindless anguish made all of the Four wince or shudder.

If the Golden Griffon's mind was still his own, he would surely have been staring at the slender young woman who floated just above him, barefoot and clad in a clinging black gown. Her hand was on Blackgult's Dwaer, and her eyes were on the Four.

Great flashing dark eyes, gloating openly as she smiled. She was beautiful, long raven-dark hair swirling around her as if with a life of its own as she sneered at Embra's attempts to wrestle the shielding into some sort of lance, to stab at her. The Lady of Jewels struggled against the force pinning the overdukes against the wall, snarling . . . and as she slowly forced the flickering shield forward, Hawkril and Craer raised their weapons and advanced with it. Three strides, four . . .

The Stone flashed in the hands of the stranger—and abruptly she was gone, the force that pinned the Four vanishing with her. Blackgult's screams ended in midbellow as the overdukes tumbled to the floor.

"Graul it, doesn't Darsar have *enough* mysterious and beautiful sorceresses?" Hawkril growled.

Craer grinned. "Ah, Hawk, there're never enough, you know! Why, I—"

Tshamarra caught hold of his arm with one hand and dealt him a stinging slap across the face with the other.

Then they were driven abruptly apart by the passage of a whirlwind between them: Embra, running hard toward Blackgult with their Dwaer glowing fitfully in her hands. "Father? *Father!*"

Boazshyn of Ool was fast. He managed to conjure the clawed and fanged beginnings of a spell before the Dwaer swept him away—but he died as surely as had tall and patrician Lord of the Serpent Yedren, who'd spread empty hands and said flatly, "I cannot fight you, mage, and I will not. But neither will I bow or plead to a wizard, particularly one of Silvertree's Dark Three."

Ingryl Ambelter grinned as the oily smoke that had been Boazshyn drifted away, and regarded his own tingling fingers. This was succeeding beyond his wildest hopes—if he drank the lives of these fools with the Dwaer, some measure of their power passed into him! Busily slaying Serpent-priests just might be in truth the road to truly taking the mantle of the Great Serpent.

Power . . . *this* was power, more than he'd ever felt before. Power in and of him, not Dwaer-flow . . . might of his own. He could feel the flows of natural energies around him now, faint but ceaseless. His adopted serpent-head felt . . . *right,* as if it had always been part of him. Yes, increasingly so, it felt fitting and proper.

There came another respectful knock at the door. "Lord Ambelter," announced the by now familiar voice of the tremulous priest he'd made doorguard, "to you have come the priests Rauldron of Tselgara, Maskalos and Cheldraem of Ibryn, Pheltarth of Adelnwater, and Old Nael of Rithrym. They await your pleasure without."

"Rauldron may enter," Ambelter called, making his voice loud, imperious, and grandly welcoming. "We shall speak alone, ere you admit the others."

The doorpriest knew by now to close the door firmly between each arrival, and keep the other priests well back from it. Long-laid and powerful enchantments made scrying into this chamber difficult; no one would be casually eavesdropping from outside. Wherefore Rauldron, like all of the others before him, was doomed.

The Spellmaster of All Aglirta smiled as the doors opened to admit a slightly frowning priest. Handsome, dark-haired, and keen-featured, with eyes that darted everywhere. Yet empty-handed, and alone. Ambelter's smile broadened. This was truly like skewering flatfish from a feast platter . . .

"Welcome, Lord Rauldron," he began, gesturing toward the front bench. "Though unfamiliar to you, I have been charged with a most sacred mission by Caronthom 'Fangmaster' and Raunthur the Wise. It involves you and all of the other important priests of our faith, and—"

The doors were closing. Ambelter strode to the bench, deliberately exposing his well-shielded back to his guest. When he was seated, Rauldron should be in just the right spot for an easy Dwaer-drain. Why, he was getting quite deft at this . . .

The fire snatched the Spellmaster off his feet, shredding his shieldings as if they were nothing more than mist, and flung him headlong into the bench with bone-shattering force.

Luckily, Ingryl's own hand was already on his Dwaer, and his hastily spun shield drove the bench before him, shattering it into great shards as it smashed into the next bench, and that one in turn to the next.

In the grinding heart of their destruction, Ingryl Ambelter whirled, his rage and Dwaer-fire rising together.

Lord of the Serpent Rauldron grinned at him, the glowing web of his next Dwaer-weaving already flashing out toward the Spellmaster—and for just a moment, it seemed to Ingryl that he was looking into two mocking, glittering lights in the empty eyesockets of a skull rather than the flat, brown eyes of the priest.

And then his foe's Dwaer-attack fell on him with the crushing force of a hammer, stabbing through his crackling, flaming shieldings in a dozen places.

The Spellmaster shrieked in fear and spun frantic Dwaer-fire around himself, whirling it in a spiral that—*yes,* thank the Three!—caught up the bolts reaching for him and whisked them around and around him to augment his own armor.

Ambelter's own slashing counterbolt went hopelessly awry, twisted by the maelstrom of magic around him, and cracked its way along the front wall of the room, slamming the door open and scorching its way into the far corner, where it clawed mightily at the stones and spent itself.

His foe lashed him with a Dwaer-spell that rent his whirlwind as if it was nothing—a nothing that flashed blindingly and rocked the chamber again with the shrill shriek of its dying. The Spellmaster flung himself aside and spun himself a better shield, hurling another bolt at his foe—or so he desired Gadaster to think.

In truth, this bolt was but a shell of the one he'd hurled before. It took the same flashing path as its predecessor, as the man who was not Rauldron strode forward, weaving another Dwaer-spell, but veered out the open door while just a small and snarling offshoot raced on to the corner.

The other priests were in the audience chamber outside, eyeing each other in open fear as the battle raged in front of them—and Ambelter's draining bolt fell on them like the clutching fingers of a desperate man, splitting to strike every man there.

One of them had time to hurl a magic back into the chamber, a net of fanged serpent-mouths that Gadaster casually destroyed. He sent back a flood of lightning, and as the priests stood rooted, struggling against Ambelter's draining magic, that river of lightning struck them all at the knees, hurled them to the stone floor, and slew them. Ambelter's drain-tendrils greedily took their lives.

Even as Gadaster struck at him again and the Spellmaster was forced to retreat, his shieldings faltering and failing in showers of sparks and blossoming darkness, Ingryl Ambelter felt new energies—the stolen vitality of the priests on the threshold—come raging into him, followed by something else.

Something large, and deep, and dark. Something that made him tremble at its very touch. More power than he'd ever tasted before, shuddering into him, making him strong, and cold, and . . . and . . .

INGRYL AMBELTER, a god whispered in his head.

"Y-yes?"

YOU KNOW ME, AS ALL MEN KNOW ME.

"Yes, Dark One!"

YOU HAVE SEIZED POWER ENOUGH. I AM PLEASED. BE NOW THE "GREAT SERPENT," IF IT AMUSES YOU TO BE SO.

And the Thrael opened out around him, thrumming and vast and—thrilling. In the heart of clashing Dwaer-fire, even as Gadaster's attack stabbed into him and agonies that should have slain him surged through him, Ingryl Ambelter beheld . . . and gasped. So *this* was what he'd been missing! Not just Stones of trapped and frozen power, but a living web of magic, with awareness of its own, great—

AMUSE ME.

And suddenly that great weight of darkness was gone from his mind, without even bothering to utter, "Or else."

Ingryl Ambelter rose out of what he now realized had been an awestruck daze, and gathered his newfound power around himself. So *this* is what it was, to be a Great Serpent!

With a bellow of exulting laughter, the Spellmaster of All Aglirta hurled a bolt that should easily destroy his former master, Dwaer and all!

A flash was born beyond his spread fingertips, and then a mighty roar arose and went on and on, as the far wall of the scorched chamber vanished, the ceiling fell into his bolt and suffered the same fate, and sunlight flooded in to show him room after passage after great chamber of the building beyond vanishing into rubble and emptiness, the sheared-off edges slowly collapsing inward with ground-shaking thunder.

The sunlight also flashed back from something small and bright and whirling, that hung in the air much closer to him. At a spot where Gadaster—in the Bowdragon maid's stolen body—might well have been.

Ingryl peered at it, and then nodded grimly. Gadaster had teleported away and left behind a shimmering wildfield—just as he himself had done when fleeing his lair, to keep the cursed Band of Four from following. Should he try to use his Dwaer to trace and follow, he'd be whirled away to a random elsewhere.

Ah, but what if he called on the Thrael instead?

Shimmering in his mind, it waited, but Ingryl saw in a moment both its lure—he could spend oblivious days racing along its flows, examining this new magic, and that—and its unsuitability.

No doubt he could trace his foe's teleport, given hours of looking or lucky anticipation of where Gadaster might be headed, so that he looked first in just the right place . . . But what, during those hours, would his onetime master be doing? Teleporting again almost immediately, for one thing . . .

Bah! What need had he now, to concern himself with such trifles? Let the skull-wizard strut around in his stolen wench-body! Ingryl Ambelter might have had to worry about a walking skeleton with wiles and a Dwaer, but the Great Serpent could laugh at the worst Gadaster Mulkyn could do!

Ambelter's own Dwaer blazed with a fierce, triumphant flame in his hand, and he laughed as he looked down at it, half-drunk on the dark, whispering power raging in him. It would always rage there, making him as restless and as mighty as he was now . . .

Letting him do—*this!*

He gave in to the whispering urgings and grew, transforming himself, towering up over what was left of the riven temple walls, becoming serpentine and giant, a Great Serpent in truth.

Wavering higher, as tall as the highest keep he'd ever stood upon, Ingryl Ambelter gazed down the Vale, opened great fanged jaws, and roared in triumph.

His roar came out as a thunderous hiss, as he swayed back and forth, gloating. The Silverflow made its own coiling way across the land below him, the Thrael reached out like a glittering net around him, and . . . the Thrael!

The moment he thought of it, its fascination snared him again, and he dwindled, the gigantic serpent-body forgotten. The Great Serpent shuddered down out of sight, towering into the sky no longer.

Lost in the wonder of the Thrael, Ingryl Ambelter stood naked amid the shreds of his torn robes, his Dwaer-Stone blazing in his hand, and never noticed the surviving Serpent-priests, all around him in the ruins, going to their knees and then to their faces on the stone floor, in silent, awestruck reverence.

24

Shapechangers and Secrets

Glowing mists flickered and ebbed . . . and the Band of Four stood in the Throne Chamber of Flowfoam Palace, the barefoot body of Ezendor Blackgult cradled in Hawkril's hands.

Guards stiffened and reached for blades, but the Lady Silvertree sternly bade them stand back, a Dwaer-Stone flickering warningly in her hand.

They obeyed, one veteran daring to ask, "Ah, the Lord Blackgult . . . how is he?"

"Exhausted, no more," Embra replied curtly, knowing the truth to be very far from that. Blackgult now seemed free of the Blood Plague, but the Dwaer-clash had harmed his mind once more. Awake, he saw them sometimes and at other times did not, and his mumblings were as wildly irrelevant as a drunk crying out in his nightmares.

The Four were most of the way to the royal apartments when doors ahead of them boomed open, and palace guards in full armor strode in, strung bows in their hands.

King Raulin Castlecloaks strode along at their rear—and at the sight of the Four he pointed at them and cried furiously, "*There* they are! All loyal to Aglirta, slay the traitors!"

Craer promptly sprinted away, angling off to the right so that any archer missing him would be sending a shaft into the knot of guards around the throne. Embra stared at the king in disbelief—and then sent Dwaer-magic slapping at the guards and their arrows alike.

Tshamarra sprang to Embra's side, to where she could touch the Stone, and Hawkril growled and hunkered down to shield Blackgult, reaching for his warsword—as the guards let loose a hail of arrows.

Embra's magic should have frozen those shafts in midair and stilled the shouting men who'd sent them . . . and for a moment did just that, plunging the chamber into silence—ere something flashed at King Raulin's throat, and Embra's magic was dashed down.

Arrows sped for them once more, and Embra snarled and called on the Dwaer to boost her snatching at the Living Castle enchantments. Here in the Throne Chamber her ties were very strong—and the ceiling obeyed her will, great chunks slamming down to shatter the gleaming marble floor, and smashing arrows to the ground.

Tshamarra's first spell barely touched the king, as his Dwaer flashed again—but just for a moment, Raulin's face drooped, melting flesh falling impossibly away from his teeth, and Embra cried, "A Koglaur! A Faceless One impersonates our King!"

Two Dwaers flashed as one, and wrestled. Some guards looked back at Raulin Castlecloaks in astonishment, but others obediently charged the overdukes—and as Hawkril rose to meet them, he felt a tug at his sword-belt. Blackgult had snatched out the armaragor's best dagger and was running with him, racing to greet the foremost guards with bared steel.

Embra clenched her teeth and called on the Living Castle enchantments again. The floor rose, rippling in a great wave that snatched guardsmen—and Hawkril—off their feet, and sent Blackgult and the false king both staggering.

A bolt from the Koglaur's Dwaer smote Embra, scorching her arm. Tshamarra had momentarily weakened Embra's Stone to source a spell, a magic that now pelted the Koglaur with fragments of riven marble floor, seeking to drive the Dwaer from his hands.

The Faceless flung himself down to cradle his Stone as his borrowed shape started to slip, fingers subsiding into pale, squidlike tentacles ere they could be smashed by the rocks slamming into them.

Blackgult shambled and mumbled his way forward in lurching haste, barefoot and fire-eyed, and fearful guards ducked away from him.

Grimly Embra called on the Living Castle enchantments again, rending the floor to plunge the Koglaur into one of the long-empty strongrooms beneath the Throne Chamber—and Tshamarra cast a spell that rained down more shards of stone on his head.

The Faceless One blasted those stones to dust with his Dwaer, and then used it to collapse more of the floor, giving him a rough ramp up and out of the pit Embra had dumped him into. He swarmed up that rubble slope as a many-legged thing—and found himself facing a snarling Ezendor Blackgult.

The Golden Griffon pounced on the Koglaur savagely, stabbing and slashing in a frenzy. When the bloody, shuddering Faceless slapped tentacles over Blackgult's face, seeking to smother him or break his neck, Tshamarra shouted a magic that snatched both Craer and Hawkril to the shapeshifter, and they sliced and sawed tentacles as fast as it could spin them.

Craer struck hard through a cagelike web of sliding flesh at the Koglaur's glimmering Dwaer—and its tentacles slapped back the three battling overdukes in a sudden convulsion.

As Craer skidded away on his shoulders, gasping out a curse, Blackgult and Hawkril roared in unison and waded back into the ropy, many-armed body. Embra murmured a swift spell that plucked a sword out of a startled guard's grasp and put it into her father's free hand.

The Koglaur reared up over the two overdukes, growing great dark necks swimming with many-eyed jaws. Guards all over the room shouted in horror at the rising monster, and loosed arrows at those swooping, snapping heads. Scales sprouted on them—too late to save some, but swiftly enough to send many arrows rattling harmlessly away.

Two heads bit down on Blackgult's weapons, squalling in pain as they closed around sharp, slashing steel. A third head darted between, fangs gaping wide to tear out his chest—but Tshamarra sent lightning down its revealed throat, and the head convulsed and shrank back, shuddering and spewing smoke.

Ceiling stones broke free and plummeted at other heads as Embra called on the palace enchantments again, her Dwaer flashing—and in the air above the battling men and monsters, the air sang and shimmered as the two Stones wrestled for supremacy.

Drenched in ichor, Craer and Hawkril struggled through a chaos of writhing tentacles and gouting gore, trying to hew to the Koglaur's heart before the shapeshifter could change again. Tshamarra sent fire racing along the limbs they'd sliced, trying to force the Faceless to leave the damaged parts of its body behind, and so be weakened.

Blackgult roared in pain as the blood-drooling jaws crushed or bit away his hands—and other tentacles dived at his feet, scooping up the maimed overduke and hurling him across the hall at his daughter.

Intent on guiding Dwaer-flows and the Living Castle enchantments, Embra barely saw him—and lost control of both when Ezendor Blackgult crashed into her and sent them both skidding across the cracked marble.

With a roar of triumph, the many-headed monster called on its Dwaer—and lightning leaped from it, stabbing out to arc from blade to blade to armor on all of its embattled sides. Guards and overdukes staggered, howled, reeled and fell—and doors behind the Koglaur boomed open.

The shapeshifter barely had time to flail two heads around to see who'd arrived before Hulgor Delcamper charged into it, driving his blade hilt-deep through pale, yielding flesh and bellowing, "For the glory of the Delcampers!"

Flaeros and the king were right behind him, swords in their hands, and the Koglaur stiffened and then surged its entire bulk back to *lean* toward the king.

Nigh crushed beneath it, Hulgor held onto his sword, and snatched a dagger from his belt to stab and hew, snarling—and on the Koglaur's other flank, a numbed but determined Craer Delnbone raced up a neck, fresh daggers in both hands, heading for Dwaer-glow—

And the Koglaur screamed, a rush of glowing blue blood drenching Hulgor Delcamper. The Stone bobbing not far in front of Craer's nose flashed—and the room was suddenly empty of many-headed shapeshifting monsters.

Craer landed hard on his behind, nose to nose with Hulgor. King Castlecloaks shot glances around his ruined throne room and snapped, "Down arms, all!"

Embra looked up from the sprawled, senseless body of her father, a healing glow already brightening around them, as the other overdukes trudged to join her.

"How is he?" Hawkril muttered.

Embra shrugged, and then shook her head. "Hands, he'll have back swiftly. His wits, now . . ."

As Hulgor, Flaeros, and the king joined them, the Four exchanged weary looks. Waving a hand at Raulin in greeting, Craer peered at his fellow overdukes. "Suppose we try to list just who's carrying a Dwaer, now, hey? I confess I've rather lost track of Aglirta-threatening perils in all this hurly-fray."

Embra sighed. Hawkril put an arm around her shoulders and said with a trace of dark humor, "Well, a certain shapeshifting monster has one."

Tshamarra nodded. "Another was last seen in the grasp of the not-as-dead-as-we'd-hoped Spellmaster."

"Embra has the third," Craer put in, "and the fourth—Blackgult's—was snatched by a young sorceress of some beauty . . . assuming, mind you, that she wasn't this same shapeshifter whose blood is all over us."

Embra sighed again. "So we know who has two of them, the Faceless and us . . . and possibly who holds the other two."

Tshamarra smiled bitterly. "And those three foes all want us dead and Aglirta destroyed."

Craer grinned. "As usual."

"Do you want the Four dead and Aglirta destroyed?" the Master of Bats asked sharply, a glowing scepter raised menacingly in his hand.

Dolmur Blackdragon shook his head. Carefully holding empty hands where Huldaerus could see them, the tall, scorched wizard limped forward, wincing in pain, and turned to regard his brother.

Ithim was in worse shape, and moved more slowly. They traded grim glances and then looked at the Master of Bats again and shook their heads in unison.

"Good," Arkle Huldaerus told them, lowering his scepter. "Then you may stay."

His own walk held more than a hint of a limp as he turned and waved with the scepter for them to follow him through the archway ahead. "More damage has been done to Darsar by fools trying to lay waste to Aglirta than by all the other wars and mage duels I can recall, put together. If you promise not to strike at me or steal magic, I'll show you where I scry the Vale from—and we can sit and watch the fates of those at Flowfoam. Some wine, perhaps?"

Dolmur Blackdragon smiled. "Have you any Sarnen blackjewel?"

The trap-filled, dank, and yet dusty gloom of the Silent House terrified most folk of the Vale, yet it seemed as comforting a lair as any, just now.

For years the rogue Koglaur had used it, slaying fellow Faceless and ambitious Aglirtans beyond counting—but it had never walked these dark, familiar halls in such pain before.

Or staggered through them as it was doing now, a trail of dark blue blood spotting the stones behind it. It shifted shape every few steps in a vain, hissing attempt to leave pain behind.

The Dwaer glowed in its cradling hands, healing . . . but slowly, too slowly. The swift way would knit slashed flesh in ways that would leave forever stiff knots and joints, resistant to shifting shape . . . So, patience and pain.

Aye, patience and pain were its lot, this next while. There was a hidden door just ahead, and then it could either lie still in the tunnel or shift to a wriggling shape and so ascend into the tall, riven turret called the Cracked Crown. There the only annoyances would be squawking, pecking, defecating birds, and—

The Dwaer suddenly flared up with bright, furious force. The Koglaur barely had time to be astonished before the Dwaer-fire was so strong that it was hurled away, roaring at the fresh pain of crisped hands.

The shapeshifter was wallowing on cold and dusty flagstones and staring at the smoke streaming from its blackened claws when a slender human female of dark hair and darker gown stepped from behind a crumbling hanging and plucked the Koglaur's floating, blazing Dwaer out of midair.

She smiled down at the twisting, shuddering Faceless with a Dwaer-Stone in either hand, and said sweetly, "*You* should have been dead centuries ago. You and all your ilk."

Two Dwaerindim kindled into humming brightness as one—and lashed out.

The Koglaur was old, cunning, and still deadly swift. It snarled an ancient incantation that made the sorceress frown and step back in wary alarm—and even as Dwaer-blasts bit into its shuddering, flowing flesh, spell-glows of a strange hue raced back along those twin bolts and washed over the Stones.

The Dwaer glowed and tingled strangely for a moment, causing Gadaster Mulkyn to murmur in wordless alarm . . . and then returned to their former state, their blasts steadying and gathering strength.

The slender sorceress showed no hint of carelessness or mercy, and soon the Koglaur ceased to shriek and shudder. Then Gadaster made a Dwaer raise a spiraling wind. That breeze snatched up the ashes that had been the Koglaur, moaned as it flung them at the ceiling—and then died away, leaving nothing at all on the flagstones where the shapeshifter had been.

"Three above," Hawkril gasped, staring at the bedchamber ceiling. "What *was* that?" He was naked and drenched with sweat, burning inside as if he was on fire. Embra was lying half atop him, down his left side, and she'd been raking him with her nails—causing the pain that had awakened him. And no wonder; her touch *burned.* Wherever their skin met, it felt like a searing Hawkril remembered from long, long ago . . . from the first time he'd curiously plucked a blazing brand out of a fire.

"Fire and flames," Embra whispered reluctantly, rolling away from him.

Her curves were as glistening-wet as his own, and she flung her limbs wide, gasping, "I was swimming in it! Flames, bursting up everywhere, consuming everything, yet burning on . . ."

The Dwaer at her throat glowed steadily, as if nothing was wrong. Its power was awake, of course, spinning the humming web of force that held the moaning, mumbling Blackgult on his bed across the room.

The Griffon stirred, writhing and kicking back his bed furs just as Embra and Hawk had done. Peering at him, they saw sweat glistening to match their own.

As her father started to roar, Embra put fingers to her Dwaer, licking sweat off her lips as it started to drip, and concentrated.

"Craer and Tash?" Hawkril rumbled.

She nodded and acquired the intent look that meant she was mind-speaking with someone. The armaragor could tell from her expression that she was soothing the person she was in contact with . . . Tshamarra, probably. Then Embra lifted her head to meet his gaze, smiling at the tenderness she saw there.

"They've shared the same dream. Warning from the gods, urgent sending, or break-sleep mischief, I know not—nor do I care overmuch. If any of us see snake- or dragon-heads in our dreams, of course . . ."

"It'll mean there's a Great Serpent again," Hawkril growled, "and a new Dragon's aborning."

Embra nodded grimly, and then touched her Dwaer again as Blackgult started to shout incoherently and struggle against the web that held him. As the magic brightened around her father, constraining and then quieting him, she sat back against the headboard with a sigh. "Well, *this* Lady of Jewels isn't going to get much sleep tonight, that's for sure."

Flaeros Delcamper came awake shouting, striking out with his fists into the night. "Fire!" he cried, seeing again those erupting flames, springing up out of the darkness all around him, to singe and then sear . . .

"Fire! Everything was burning up!"

"Easy, lad," Hulgor growled, laying a hand on his kinsman—and then snatching it back with an oath. "Ye gods, the lad's hot! A fever, belike!"

Anxious faces crowded around, lit by a lantern held in a royal hand. King Castlecloaks stared down at the twisting, sweating bard and then around at guards and servants. The two Delcamper maids were blushing as they surveyed all the bared male flesh around them, for only the guards wore anything—full armor, complete with the swords they'd now drawn.

"Put those away," Hulgor said disgustedly, though the swordpoints moved not an inch until the king nodded to support the old noble's order. "The lad needs a healer, not a sword through his guts!" He peered at Raulin. "Ye *do* have a healer?"

The king swallowed and then smiled weakly. "Ah, yes. Somewhere. I'm not quite sure just where in the palace anyone has their chambers, right now, actuall—"

"Never mind," Hulgor growled. "Kings, kings—what good are they? *Lad!*" This last bark was directed not at Raulin but rather at Flaeros Delcamper, now fully awake and staring up at the circle of faces in awe, fear, and—as he recognized some faces as female—mounting embarrassment. The bard snatched at the sweat-soaked linens beneath him.

"Ah, ye're awake—just like all the rest of us, thanks!" Hulgor growled. "Lad, where does Orele sleep? Hey?"

"You were purposely not told that, my lord," a palace servant said severely, "upon her instructions, and—"

"Take us there now," King Raulin snapped. The servant paled, stammered assent, and hurried off, taking up and unhooding a night lantern.

Hulgor scooped up Flaeros and carried the naked bard to the door, slung over his shoulder like a sack of grain. The younger Delcamper stammered protests, face flaming, and then thought the better of it and went along for the ride, watching his own sweat stream steadily down onto the floor below.

"Gods, lad, but you're hot," Hulgor growled. " 'Tis like carrying a slab of boar that's still cooking!"

The king and the guards strode along with Hulgor, close behind the lantern-bearing servant, but it seemed that some of the other Delcamper maids had taken a swifter route—for when they reached the small, plain door of Orele's chambers, it stood open. Lamplight was spilling out into the passage, and the Lady herself, in an ankle-length black nightrobe, sat in a chair facing them, her cane in her hand.

"Hulgor, set Flaeros on the bed," she said crisply, by way of greeting. "You'll find a nightshirt laid ready for him. Get the king a chair, send everyone out, and then lock and bar the door. *Everyone.* I'm not in the habit of regicide, and all of these guards whose hygiene seems so poor would be best deployed well away from my keyhole—but making sure no one else tarries by it."

"Let all be done as the Lady Orele commands," the king said firmly, before anyone could raise protest—and, in a remarkably short time, it was.

"Wrinkles," Hulgor said gruffly, "the lad came awake shouting—"

Orele held up a hand. "I know. You were right to bring him here. Go to yonder board and get everyone a drink. Anything His Majesty fancies we will of course sip first, to show him 'tis safe. Go, Old Ram!"

Hulgor opened his mouth to protest, flushed, grinned, and went.

"You had a dream," Orele told the bard, "that I know all about. Worry not about the heat and the sweat—that will pass. You're neither ill nor crazed."

Flaeros smiled in relief, sitting up. "L-lady Orele, forgive this abrupt asking, but . . . well, I've long suspected you of being one of the Wise . . ."

The old woman smiled. "Well, you're not *completely* stone-headed, I see. Your suspicions are correct."

The bard and the king both leaned forward, grinning at her with identical expressions of eager excitement, two young lads entranced by all the tales of—

Lady Natha Orele raised one bony hand and said severely, "Before you ask, I neither kiss nor mate with toads, rarely flog myself in the moonlight, and have never cast any magics to make anyone sicken or die. On the other hand, I often dance naked out of doors by night, harvest useful herbs whenever I can, and keep secrets well. No, I can't fly, with or without a broomstick. I don't drink blood save when I prick myself, and don't cast love-spells for anyone—even by royal command."

She lifted both eyebrows, together. "Does that take care of your first flood of foolish questions, and buy me time enough to speak of what exactly befell you this night, Flaeros?"

"Uh, ah," the king asked awkwardly, "just one asking: Are there many Wise? Have you seen any in Aglirta, since your arrival?"

Orele regarded him severely. "Are there many skilled singers in your kingdom, Majesty? Can you tell who they are at a glance?"

She let silence fall, and after it had stretched long enough for a tightly grinning Hulgor to steer a glass into every hand but the king's, Raulin said, "Oh. I see. Yes, of course. My apologies, Lady—say on about Flaeros." Then he cocked his head and added, "Any chance of seeing you dance? Later, I mean?"

The old woman sipped her wine, shook her head, and told the glass severely, "*Men.* Kings little better than the rest, I see. It'll be dawn before we're done, so find something to wet your royal throat, Raulin. Hulgor's tried a bit of everything already, so if he doesn't fall over in the next few breaths, 'tis all safe."

The old noble chuckled. "Ye *can* see out of the back of your head, Swee—hem, Natha."

"Trick of the Wise," the old lady said darkly, and then drained her glass in a swig like a man in a hurry to leave a tavern, handed it to the astonished king, and clapped her hands lightly together. "Enough empty tongue-wagging! You dreamt of fire, Flaeros, and came awake shouting. This is not unusual, and probably happened to scores of folk the world over this night—most of them in the Vale."

"Lady," King Castlecloaks said politely, "I believe you've now established that you are eloquent, learned, and can be very mysterious. Can you also speak plainly, and Reveal All?"

Lady Orele grinned at him. Surprisingly, she still had all of her teeth. "The Wise *never* Reveal All, Majesty; you know that. Or should. Let's test your learning: What know you of the Arrada?"

Raulin Castlecloaks sighed. "Beyond the fact that it's a grand name for all the magic of Darsar, which is the gathered lore of our ways of harnessing the energies of all that lives, nothing at all."

The old woman sat back, regarding him with new respect. "Well said, Majesty—very well said. I'd say you have learning enough. The son of a bard, you—and a bard yourself, Lord Flaeros, so you know this too, hmm?"

"I do," Flaeros agreed. "Like Raul—the King, I know very little more than what the Arrada is—and that it flows in cycles."

"Ah!" Orele said, leaning forward again. "Hulgor," she said, "get this King a drink."

Hulgor and Raulin both blinked at her. Ignoring them, she said serenely, "Two creatures manifest at either end of the flows of the Arrada: the Serpent and the Dragon. Now tell me, which one is associated with fire?"

Flaeros stared at the old woman as if she'd suddenly grown three serpent-heads, with a golden crown gleaming on each one. "The Dragon," he whispered.

Orele nodded and raised her glass. King Raulin and the bard both stared at it. Though they'd both seen her drain it to the dregs but a few moments ago, and she'd sent Hulgor away to fill another glass for the king, the old woman's glass was brimful once more.

She smiled at them over it. "Whenever there's a Serpent—*the* Serpent, called by those who worship it the Great Serpent, and usually a human wizard twisted to evil—there must also be a Dragon. When one arises, there comes the other. In the words of the bard Tanathavur—you should know this, Lord Flaeros—'I burned in the night of fire, at the awakening of the Dragon.' You *do* know what became of Tanathavur, don't you?"

"He became the Dragon," Flaeros murmured, wide-eyed, "and was slain in the skies above the Silverflow by the wizard Garaunt, who rode the Winged Serpent!"

Hulgor thrust a glass into the king's hand, another into the trembling fingers of Flaeros—who hastily drained it—and then set two glasses in front of himself and deliberately quaffed them both.

All three men stared at each other as Orele sighed, "An astonishing display of greed, Hulgor. 'Twas always your besetting fault."

"Does that mean . . ." Flaeros whispered, his voice dwindling into a squeak. He tried again. "Does that mean I'll become the Dragon?"

"Not necessarily," the old woman with the cane told him, drinking deeply—and setting down a glass that was just as full as before. "The Arrada visits many suitable folk, ere flowering in one. If no one else in all the Vale saw flames in their dreams hot enough to awaken them, then you might want to set your affairs in order accordingly, but I think that's highly unlikely. Majesty, if you were to issue a royal decree in the morning that any waking dreams suffered this night must be reported . . ."

"I shall," Raulin said, pale-faced. "This is . . ."

"Unsettling," Orele told him. "You were going to say 'exciting,' and discovered that the word was unsuitable. Unsettling is nearer the mark."

King Castlecloaks gave the old woman a respectful look. "Not for nothing are you deemed one of the Wise. Have you any advice for me?"

"Get yourself a wife," Lady Orele said promptly, "but make sure you choose the right one. Bed her well, and sire at least two heirs. Give one to me, to raise far away and in secret." A smile touched her lips. "You see why I wanted no one near the keyhole?"

Raulin Castlecloaks stared at her, his eyes large and dark, and shivered suddenly.

"Secrets, secrets," the Delcamper chambermaid Faerla whispered, her fingers laid carefully across the keyhole of the door that connected their room with Lady Orele's.

Lameira nodded, so close in the darkness that their foreheads almost touched. She was close enough to see Faerla's disapproving expression as her irrepressible friend added mournfully, "Life used to be so simple."

25

A Dragon Over Flowfoam

"I trust," Ingryl Ambelter said mildly in the flickering firelight, "you all understand my orders? And the fate awaiting anyone who disobeys them?"

There was a moment of silence, and then the answer came as a thunderous, ragged murmur: "Yes, Great Serpent."

The snake-headed man looked down at them from his newly shaped, emerald-scaled height (Ingryl Ambelter had discovered he rather liked being head-and-shoulders taller than everyone around him) and hissed, "Good. *Very* good. Now, my Lords of the Serpent, heed me further. Rather than try to whelm armies and march them on Flowfoam, you are to round up all Aglirtans you've managed to infect with Blood Plague, but who you've thus far kept from beast-shape or falling into madness, and give them weapons. I shall do the rest. You shall know my question as to your readiness, when it comes, and I shall expect only one answer."

He let silence hang in the still-shattered chamber for a tightly-smiling moment, and then snapped, "Now go and do this! *Hasten!*"

Men in robes far more elaborate than his own streamed past the flickering braziers to the door—all but a dozen senior priests, who stepped back from the throng to stand along one wall together. When the doors had been closed behind their departing Brethren, they stepped forward in a small group to face the Great Serpent. Each had mind-heard his personal orders to remain, and so knew without a doubt that this wizard commanded the Thrael, and thereby was the rightful Serpent.

Ingryl's eyes seemed to meet all of theirs at once. "Is everyone armed sufficiently? The doorpriests can bring you blades if you wish."

There was a general silence. Priests cast glances at each other, but no one stepped forward or spoke.

The Great Serpent nodded. "Good. You deem yourselves ready, then?"

There were nods and murmurs of "Yes, Highest."

"You know what to do, and that the Brotherhood depends on you this day. Fail us all not."

Ingryl Ambelter threw up his hands, arms spread wide dramatically, and sent them all elsewhere. The Thrael allowed him to command the Dwaer without even touching it directly. Such *power* . . .

As the glow where the dozen had stood faded, Ingryl Ambelter turned away to stroll and smile.

Well, now. Spellmaster of All Aglirta *and* Great Serpent of all Darsar. Not too shabby . . . not shabby at all. The Thrael showed him that his meal was almost ready, and that none of the priests preparing it had dared to introduce taints or poisons. He'd best get to the eating; there was a busy day ahead.

With the Dwaer he'd soon be jumping up and down the Vale, from beacon fire to beacon fire. At each blaze one of the hastening priests—teleporting each other right now to their towns and villages, in a glow of bustling magic so strong that it was almost painful, through the Thrael—would be waiting, with a whelming of armed Aglirtans.

The Dwaer would transport those groups to Flowfoam. When they appeared on the isle, the dozen priests he'd just sent ahead—into hiding in the palace gardens—would quell the magic that stopped plague-madness. The arriving Aglirtans, warriors or ploughmen, would go berserk.

"And so let king and overdukes and all be overwhelmed in loyal subjects, and hewn down," Ingryl Ambelter told the star-scattered sky above him, visible through the riven ceiling. Then he burst into laughter.

The sound brought one of the doorpriests to peer timidly in through the doors. He saw the lone, laughing man grow the beginnings of a tail and rise taller, towering to twice the height of tall armaragors and even more . . . But as the Great Serpent mastered his mirth, his stature diminished again, and the stump of a tail faded away.

"Cease your useless spying," he told the doorpriest without turning, "and bring me some wine. I shall be in the Hall of Coils."

There was a wink of Dwaer-flash, and the room was empty even before the frightened doorpriest could begin to stammer acknowledgment of the order.

·   ·   ·

The center of the Hall of Coils was a great pit whose sides were concentric rings of shallow steps, and its walls were adorned with huge snakes, the carved stone heads and coils standing out in some places almost ten feet from the wall. Huge gems enspelled to glow served as the gleaming eyes of those forever frozen serpents, and the tiles underfoot were painted in scenes of triumphs of the faith. Decades of dedicated work, in this room alone. No wonder this place was hidden high in the mountains, where an Aglirtan army would have to fly to come against it in strength.

Ingryl Ambelter smiled again. The Great Serpent. As empty as all titles—but the Thrael, now . . . worth the dark weight of a fell god's attention, to taste such power. With its web, even now, he could . . .

"Most Holy Lord?"

He could sip wine knowing it was safe, that's what he could do. Ambelter turned with a smile, took the decanter from the trembling priest, and waved away the goblet and platter with the words, "My thanks. Begone, and keep all others from this chamber."

He did not have to turn around to know when the door opened and closed—or to know that he was alone, without anyone lurking to peer through the scores of spyholes in the walls, floor, and ceiling of the vast room. My, but he'd have slain his way to the top of the Church of the Serpent long ago if he'd known what the Thrael was truly like.

The wine was good—and Ambelter used the Thrael to snatch ready morsels from the platters in the kitchens as he strolled, not waiting for scurrying priests to let things get cold as they raced down long passages and up the many stairs. Yes, this was a life much preferable to the lurking loneliness of an archmage in hiding in a cave, surrounded by the unlovely bodies of stolen dead men held in shuffling servitude by spells.

Soon he'd be lording it in Flowfoam, at the very heart of the great garden that was Aglirta—and using his priests like poisoned daggers to seek out and slay mages in Sirlptar. When he ruled that city, it would be time to take down everyone else in Darsar whose sorcery was strong, his own most capable priests included. Oh, yes, he'd make the Dark One proud of him, and taste the flesh of every woman he fancied in all the world, along the way . . .

Sated and gloating, Ingryl Ambelter licked sauce from his fingers, drained the last of the decanter, and strolled onto the balcony that opened off the end of the hall.

Under the stars the Vale lay below, long and lushly green and sinuous—and Ingryl smiled down upon it as a flame flared up on a hill not far off. The first beacon fire.

He tossed the decanter over the wide stone balcony rail, and used the Thrael to enjoy every shriek of its splintering destruction on the rocks far, far below. Hefting the Dwaer in his hand, he sprang up onto the rail.

Teetering on the edge of a killing fall, Ingryl Ambelter laughed at all Darsar—and jumped. The Dwaer flashed, and he was gone.

Darkness shimmered in the Hall of Coils, just inside the archway that led onto the balcony, and parted like a veil to let a slender, darkly beautiful maid in a gown step out. Bare bone gleamed in the spell-glows as the head turned, long black hair melting away to nothingness to expose a skull floating above those black-clad shoulders.

The skull-headed sorceress moved in silence, clutching a lump of stone to her breast as she glided forward on bare feet. The splendors of the hall seemed to hold little interest for her; she went straight out onto the balcony.

In the night below, down the Vale, many fires were now rising.

"So that's your game, is it?" Gadaster Mulkyn murmured. "Well, two can play at that. Flowfoam, ho!" The Dwaer flashed—and the balcony was empty.

"Claws of the Dark One," the king gasped, "is there no end to them?"

"Raulin," Hawkril growled, "get you *down*! A hurled blade could take your throat out in a trice in all this. Get back to guard Orele and let us fight without having to worry about you!"

Before the king could reply, several guards took him by the shoulders and ran him toward the rear, royal doors. Embra's Dwaer flashed on the far side of the chamber, momentarily making the darkened room full of howling, hacking men as bright as noonday. The flood of berserk Aglirtans seemed endless, stretching out the doors and down the passages for as far as the eye could see—and it mattered not how much they fought among themselves, if their numbers never ended. The palace guards were growing weary and being overwhelmed, one by one, overborne and hacked viciously by foes who cared nothing for their own safety, and blundered forward rather than being wary of blades. Only in the narrowest passages were their bodies now heaped high enough to block the way—but Flowfoam Palace was a warren of grand chambers, and it would take days to choke up all of its entrances with the dead.

The floor was slick with gore, in some places puddled inches deep, and still they came: a howling, madly hacking flood of men and maids armed with hayforks, belt-knives, and anything else that could crush or stab or slash. They gave battle to each other and anyone else they saw, wild-eyed and reckless. Courtiers had fallen like trampled weeds before them—if any such were left, they'd fled to cower in the deepest, darkest corners of the palace cellars and dungeons. The guards had died a little more slowly—but fallen they had, one after another, and still the seemingly endless flood of Aglirtans continued. Room by room, the defenders of the palace had been forced to give way.

By the faint gray glow stealing in through the windows, it was almost dawn. Gasping and leaning on their swords, the guards saw the king hustled out of the great throne room. Three Above, that they'd been forced to retreat this far!

At least, in the wake of Embra's latest Dwaer-blast and furious grunting and hacking on all of their parts, they'd found time for a rest at last, with the room momentarily empty of madly attacking, still-living Aglirtans.

"We must bar those doors!" one of the younger guards shouted excitedly, pointing around the Throne Chamber with his sword at the many grand and gilded entrances. His blade was notched and dripping blood that was not his own.

"No, no!" Hawkril snarled at him. "This room's a deathtrap for us, with our few blades. We fall back. Up the Wyvern Stair! We'll make our stand in the Hall of Shields, that has its own kitchens and apartments behind it, and only one back door to guard: that stair down to the cellars!"

"*What* stair down to the cellars?" the guardsman bellowed back, even as he nodded and waved a weary arm to beckon what was left of his command to rally around.

"The secret stair you've now been told about, obviously," Hulgor Delcamper roared, wiping away enough Aglirtan blood to let the guard see his toothy grin. In the same movement he lurched around to peer through his gore-matted hair at Hawkril and shouted, "Gods, man, but you sure know how to lay on battles here! I thought I'd been reduced to tussling over pillows and gown fastenings with chambermaids for the rest of my fading days, but *this,* now! Ho, yes!"

"Fun for you, Lord," a guard said sourly, "but death for us—and for Aglirta."

"Hey, now," Hawkril told the man, as they watched a terrified-looking, gasping courtier run in through one of the rear royal doors, with a pair of guards. " 'Tis the Serpent-sown plague that's done this—and we've fought down the Serpents twice before, these last few seasons, as others did many times in older years . . . and there's still an Aglirta for the Snake-lovers to come and attack, isn't there?"

A guard chuckled. "Well said."

Others around him, however, shook their heads wearily, and one of them muttered bitterly, "Not that we'll live to see more of it."

The doors boomed open, and a blood-drenched titan of a man in full armor came staggering in. The guards whirled around and raised their weapons, but the arriving warrior thrust back the visor of his helm and grinned at them.

"Your magic worked, Daughter!" Ezendor Blackgult roared. "I'm myself once more! Now, which of you idiots let all this rabble into the palace? They've been falling off my sword all the way from the South Armory." Espying the pale-faced and trembling courtier who'd just arrived, he barked, "You! *Next* time, dolt, leave my armor where I can get it, instead of prettying it up to prop in some palace passage. Though seemingly hundreds of plague-crazed Vale folk are trying to violently change my health, I'm not quite dead yet!"

The courtier stammered something incoherent and tried to pluck at the Lady Silvertree's sleeve—only to spring back with a shriek, as the glittering point of a warsword stabbed at him.

The hulking armaragor on the other end of it gave the courtier a cold look and snarled, "Unhand my lady, or die!"

"Ah-uh-uh," the courtier blurted, backing away until he ran into the flat of a guard's sword, held horizontally as a none-too-friendly barrier. "I come from Overduke Craer! He needs the Lady Embra, at once!"

"Oh he does, does he?" the Lady of Jewels sighed. "What's he gotten himself into this time? A little plundering of palace vaults gone wrong? A chambermaid not quite so willing as he'd thought?"

Several of the guards chuckled, but the courtier gabbled, "W-wouldn't say, Lady. Called through his bedchamber door . . . something about the Lady Talasorn . . ."

"Hulgor, stay with Hawk," Embra snapped, striding toward the door the courtier had come in by and plucking that startled dandy by the sleeve, to drag him along with her. "Lorivar, bring two of your best and accompany us."

A guard who until that moment hadn't known the Lady Silvertree even knew his name flushed with pleasure and surprise, and snapped, "At once, Lady!"

Embra thanked him with a tight smile, not slowing. Looking back at them as she made for the doors, she snapped, "Let there be no dispute: Follow the Lord Anharu's orders, and fall back to the Hall of Shields! Mind you bring the King and the Lady Orele as you go!" She held up the Dwaer, and added, "One thing this bauble tells me: The palace is still full of the plague-mad, and they're slaying everyone they meet!"

"Well, that's nothing new," one of the oldest guards growled. "The whole Vale's always been full of mad folk who kill everyone they mislike the look of. They've just brought their ways here to the palace, that's all."

"Nay," another guard muttered, "that's where ye're wrong. Such folk have never left the palace—begging your pardon, Lords—down all the years *I've* been alive in Aglirta."

Some of the guards glanced swiftly at Hawkril, expecting an explosion at these near-treasonous words, but the huge armaragor merely grinned and grunted, "May there be many more, loyal sword. Many more for us all."

"Not much chance of that, I'm thinking," the youngest guard whispered, leaning on his sword and watching drops of other people's blood drip from his drenched hair down into the puddle at his feet—but his words were very faint, and only he heard them, in all the gasping for air of that weary fellowship of mad slayers.

"Who comes?" snapped the voice from inside, as a blade thrust warningly forth through the gap between the double doors.

"The Lady Silvertree, Lady Overduke of Aglirta," Embra snapped. "Now open up, or I'll blast these doors down!"

"How do I know—" the guard within started to say, but a deeper, older voice beside him snarled, "Idiot! Help me with the bar!"

"But—" the guard offered, as the bar rattled. Embra shook her head in weary exasperation as the courtier beside her cried, "Open up! It's *dangerous* out here!"

The door swung wide, and the older of the two guards within grinned at the courtier and said, "Lad, 'tis dangerous in here, too. Thank the Three you've come, Lady!"

He led them through forechamber and feasting room, into the bedchamber proper—where a white-faced Craer met them at the door, daggers in both hands. "The Lady Embra *only*," he snapped. "The rest of you, close the door on us and eat and drink whatever you like here, until we call for you."

Embra sighed. "You're missing the battle, Craer."

"Oh no I'm not," the procurer retorted, thrusting aside tapestries to reveal the bed itself.

It lay bared, down to scorched straw, with the smoldering remnants of its furs and linens kicked to the floor around it—and the reason why hovering above it.

Tshamarra Talasorn lay on her back in midair, arching and writhing, stark naked and as glistening with sweat as if she'd been oiled by servants. She was staring at nothing, in obvious pain, and at her every gasping breath, wisps of fire gouted from her lips.

"Do something," Craer hissed fearfully. "I think she's dying! Could it be Serpent-magic, do you think?"

Embra frowned. "Fire isn't the way of the Serpents," she murmured. "But . . . Ambelter, perhaps? Or another wizard working mischief while we're beset with the plague-ridden?" She stepped forward and held up her Dwaer. "It can't be a spell-trap . . . not with active magic at work."

She glanced at Craer, smiling without mirth. "Breathing fire isn't something Tash usually does when you're alone together, is it?"

Craer gave her a dark look.

"Right," Embra replied brightly. "I'll try a general purging of any magic that's at work on her. There're enough of the mattress ropes left to keep her from harm if she falls, I think . . ."

The Dwaer flashed in her hand. The lone lamp in the bedchamber went dark, the flames spewing from Tshamarra's mouth dimmed . . . and then something raced out of the floating sorceress.

Something that smashed into Craer and Embra so fast that they barely had time to gasp as they were plucked off their feet and flung violently backwards. They burst through the tapestries together, their shoulders slamming into the door in thunderous, numbing unison, and did not even have time to look at each other ere something _else_ surged after the unleashed magic that had hurled them away.

That surge broke over them, Embra's Dwaer ringing like a bell and ramming itself between her breasts, pinning her to the wall in a manner that would have been painful if she hadn't been lost in rapture.

She moaned as if in love-pleasure, writhing and clawing the air, and even Craer, whose mastery of magic was nonexistent, could feel the thrilling power that was making her tremble so, as they hung together in its thrall well clear of the floor.

The center of that welling force was Tshamarra, who was moaning even louder than Embra—almost singing. Her bared body was glowing, becoming as bright as fire. The whole room shook around her, the tapestries and bed falling into scraps that were whirled away to its corners.

Outside in the feasting room, guards shouted in alarm, calling Craer's name, but their voices were almost lost in the gathering, thrumming roar of whatever was rushing out of Tshamarra.

"Gods," Craer cried desperately, "let it not consume her, whatever it is. Let her live! Let her *live!*"

Embra barely heard him. She found it hard and slow work to even understand his words, so enthralled was she with the surging power. This was far greater even than the flow of two Dwaer-Stones, which she'd never forget the feel of, and still 'twas increasing, rising, rising . . .

Such power is true glory to those who work sorcery. Embra moaned and drooled and shuddered, never wanting it to end. She was singing, high and heart-full and wordlessly, lost in the ecstasy . . .

And the woman in the center of the room burst into raging flames, whirling and clawing the air and becoming too bright to see.

Craer screamed her name and hacked at the air with his dagger, seeking somehow to cut the force holding him against the wall, and struggle to where he could reach his beloved . . . in vain.

Tshamarra was flying sinuously now; amid the flames he thought he could see something like a tail, and perhaps wings . . . she whirled, as if she was looking at him, and then whirled away again, to the window, and—out!

Blazing shutters fell away in embers to the floor, and the room was suddenly darker. Outside, something huge and awesome roared exultation at the stars.

"O, Lady, protect her," Craer prayed, and burst into tears. As if in answer to his words, the room flared into sudden brightness again—as beside him, Embra burst into flames, too.

Craer stared at the Lady of Jewels in bewildered horror as she sped toward the window, flying in a halo of fire, her clothes darkening and crumbling to ashes as she went. She was singing, still lost in pleasure, and Craer saw shimmering scales grow all over her magnificent body as she soared across the chamber. Just before she reached the window, her radiance and her flight faltered together, and she sank down to cling to the charred and smoking windowsill, gazing up into the night outside, and gasped, "Yes. Oh, yes. Oh, Tash . . ."

"What?" Craer sobbed, feeling the force that was holding him weakening, but still unable to move away from the wall. "What's happened to—?"

Embra sighed—and fell, her flames winking out. The Dwaer flashed, and she twisted in midair in its glow and came gliding desperately back toward Craer. At the same time, the unseen force holding him abruptly faded, and he hit the ground running.

Embra was coming at him like an arrow, arms spread wide, and Craer hastily flung his knife away and moved to meet her, just . . . so!

The procurer could move like a cat when he had to. His grasp was deft and precise, catching her shoulders, slowing her as he bent over backwards, and then kicking up from the ground just enough to bring them crashing to the floor together, Craer underneath. They skidded along on his leather-clad shoulders and back until they came to a gentle stop together.

Trembling, Embra sagged into his grasp. "She lives, Craer. Aglirta has a new Dragon."

Overduke Delnbone stared into her tear-filled eyes—and then shook his head in furious denial.

"No!" he snarled. "She'll be killed, slain as Sarasper was! And turned into a great beast like he was! I'll . . . *I'll never hold her again!*"

The Dwaer seemed to have become welded between Embra's breasts. She sat up as he howled, plucked it forth into her hand, touched it to Craer's forehead, and murmured something.

And the procurer was snatched from dark anguish into a sort of wondering, slightly melancholy calm.

Sitting astride him, Embra smiled down at him. Almost idly he watched the golden scales fade away, one by one, from her beautiful body. Gods above, she was right under his nose and bared to his gaze at last: soft, sleek, and . . . very warm.

The Lady of Jewels laid herself down into his embrace again, and wrapped her arms around him. "She'll be all right, Craer," she said soothingly. "The Dragon has always had the power to shift shape between its own former form and its dragon-body. She's more powerful than the Serpent, now—and she can't forget you. Right now, your love is everything to her."

She stroked Craer's forehead, and he suddenly became aware that her breasts were brushing against him as she moved.

Embarrassed, he shifted his hands awkwardly, and discovered he was shaking as well as blushing. "I . . . I always dreamed of holding you thus," he muttered, "but now . . . I'm almost scared."

Embra laughed fondly. "Don't be, Longfingers," she breathed, and kissed him.

Craer snapped his head back in shock, almost shoving her away. Embra's breath was *hot*. Sweet, spicy . . . and laced with tiny flames!

The Great Serpent hefted his Dwaer. "Go!" he said sternly, and let its flash send a last band of Aglirtans, Serpent-priests and all, off to Flowfoam.

He was suddenly alone with the beacon fire, here on a dark hill some-where in Aglirta.

Ingryl Ambelter looked up at the stars, and then at dawn coming over the far mountains in the east, beyond the vast Loaurimm . . . the peaks that spawned the mighty Silverflow. He smiled. Soon it would all be his—every last tree, castle, gem, and lass of it. Soon . . .

"That should do it," he said aloud, calling on the Stone to spin himself a scrying-whorl. "There's no need to risk myself on Flowfoam—I'll watch from here."

"Oh, but there is," an old, familiar voice said coldly and firmly, as the air parted in Dwaer-shimmering. *Gadaster!*

Even as Ambelter stared at the skull-headed sorceress and snatched for control of his Stone, letting the whorl collapse into a crackling whirlwind of scorching flames, the slender arms that had belonged to Maelra Bowdragon lifted two Dwaerindim, one in either hand—and sent bolts racing at him.

Ambelter clawed desperately at the Thrael, calling up its full force in such frantic haste that Serpent-priests screamed and fainted up and down the Vale.

Desperately he dragged power out of his Dwaer, into the Thrael, to wrap himself in a great shield—

But the bolts slammed not into the Great Serpent but into his Stone.

It flashed, ringing like a bell—and vanished from the hilltop, taking a startled Spellmaster with it.

Ithim Bowdragon clawed blindly at the Master of Bats, his eyes fixed on the scrying-globes. "That's my Maelra!" he screamed. "I must go to her! I must—"

Dolmur cast a calming spell on Ithim even before their host could shake himself free of Ithim's hands.

The younger of the two old Bowdragon wizards blinked—and then sud-denly seemed to remember that he was in the tower of the Master of Bats, and stood within the power of that fell sorcerer, whose bats were whirling around the chamber in a great angry cloud, even now.

"Your daughter?" Bats settled thickly on the shoulders of Arkle Hul-daerus, their eyes glaring in unison at Ithim, as their master said derisively, "She holds *two* Dwaer-Stones in her hands. Whatever you were hoping to do, don't bother! She needs aid from no one—and there's nothing all three of us and everything in this tower can do against what she wields." He turned back to the flickering globes. "Just watch."

． ． ．

The Dragon soared above the palace, vast and scaled and terrible. Whirling in the air on wings of bright flame, it clawed at the glittering stars and roared in delight.

This was power! Gods, *this* was . . . beyond belief.

Tshamarra Talasorn basked in the screams from Flowfoam beneath her, the puny Serpent-spells crackling up at her to stab too short, and fall away. She lashed her tail, exulting in her sheer might as she banked and soared and slid in rolling curves through the air . . .

Gods, if Craer could see her now! He—

Craer.

In a trice she turned and roared down out of the sky, claws spread, jaws opening. These fools below were endangering her beloved, menacing her friends, threatening Aglirta . . .

She struck savagely, smashing through bodies until she came to a ragged stop in the gardens. There she bit and tore, slashed with her tail, and spat flame until none were left but the burning, broken dead, and men who screamed as they fled. Then the Dragon bounded into the air, turned, and plunged down again, slashing out with a claw as she raced low over a garden meadow, transforming frantically running men into torn, tumbling meat.

Again she swooped, diving over a turret to pounce on shouting Serpent-priests, snapping with her jaws and bouncing once on her belly, grinding men beneath her. Bones snapped like twigs, screams fell silent, and she bounded aloft again.

More Aglirtans were hastening from the other end of the isle, howling and hacking mindlessly at each other as they came, running before the whips of Serpent-priests. Tshamarra crashed down into them, pouncing ruthlessly, and savaged everyone she could reach with claws and flame. Strange burning sensations slid down her throat—the plague, she realized dimly, twisting and fading under her own powers . . . and then she was alone with the dead again, and her bloodlust was fading.

Gods, what power! Yet she'd been slaying helpless commoners. The Dragon shook herself, licked her talons clean, and then peered about, seeking Serpent-priests.

There—robed men, weaving spells against her through a palace window! She thrust talons through the casements, clawing away the stone pillars between windows when some of the men ducked back out of reach, and tore open the outer wall of the room. One slash of her scaled arm crushed the rest of the screaming Serpent-priests against the walls, and they fell and lay still.

Horns of the Lady, she could slay snake-mages almost by looking at them!

Tshamarra went in search of more, prowling around the palace like a great scaled cat, peering and thrusting aside greenery. Dozens of men bolted from such cowering cover when she exposed them. Most she let run, but those who wore Serpent-robes she bit or cooked with the fire she could spew.

When no Snake-worshippers remained alive on the docks and terraces, and in the wooded gardens, the Dragon turned again to the palace, looking in every window. Many times she spat fire into its inner rooms, and heard men shriek and sizzle as they died.

As her slaying went on and the dawn sky brightened upriver, a jangling began to sing and echo in Tshamarra's head—strange high discord that she heard in her mind, its echoes rolling as if across vast distances, but not in her ears. With every death she dealt it grew louder, its tones more frantic. It sounded like a knife sawing through taut harpstrings of metal—a sound she'd heard once when a drunken bard had taken out his fury on a rival's prized instrument—and it grew wilder as her blood-toll mounted.

Then there came a time when the flash of a spell rocked a tower of the palace—and the Dragon peered in at its windows and found five Serpent-priests striding through the smoking bodies of the guards they'd slain, and studying the door of a small, secure chamber. Tshamarra Talasorn recognized that door. Behind it lay a room where some of Embra's enchanted gowns hung, girt about with small magics that kept off the dust.

She snarled fire in at the men—and at the same time thrust one claw in through another window, not caring if she shattered the wall around it, only that her scales blocked the door they'd come in by.

The Priests of the Serpent cursed and wailed and shaped spells in a desperate frenzy—and the Dragon breathed fire in at them until there was nothing left outside that charred wardrobe door but ashes.

And as they died, the jangling sound rose to a sudden shriek—and something snapped. With a wailing of many despairing voices, it all rushed away into nothingness . . .

And the Thrael was no more.

All over the Vale, Priests of the Serpent stiffened, screamed, and their heads burst into flame. Most froze where they stood, and burned like torches.

Fangbrother Maurivan was one of them, crumpling to his knees on a hill above Stornbridge with the throat of a vainly struggling Mistress of the Pantry Klaedra clutched in one clawlike hand—while he wrenched at her string of coins with the other. Blazing, he toppled over onto her, and they both burned.

Up and down the Silverflow folk of Aglirta cried out, fell to their knees in soaking sweats, and starting sobbing and trembling as the Blood Plague left them forever, leaving behind only the memories of what the Serpent-priests had done to them . . . and the revulsion.

In the sky above Flowfoam the jangling, singing sound burst forth, audible to all, and bringing with it a great gash in the air—a rift of dark fire and a bright shimmering flash rising out of it . . . a flood of short-lived radiance that vomited forth the whirling body of a man.

That spreadeagled form spun wildly, trailing black flames, and grew with horrible speed, welling up into something serpentine and monstrous, with a great flat many-fanged head . . . and the Great Serpent reared up, hissing, behind the Dragon as it glided around a tower of the palace—and pounced.

Long, dark fangs struck deep into a golden-scaled tail. Tshamarra whirled around in startled pain, and with a hiss of triumph, the dark, looming snake threw coils of its great body around her wings.

26

Doom, Death, and Dragons

Many boats were on the Silverflow that unfolding morning, crowded with tersepts, their gleaming-armored guards, and with frightened but determined Aglirtans clutching whatever weapons they'd been able to find. All were rowing hard for Flowfoam.

From boat to boat men eyed each other uneasily, but no one dared to break into battle until they knew what lay ahead on the Isle of the King.

The royal island was close now, rising from the broad, rushing river in its usual lush green, girt about with the weathered walls of what for years had been Castle Silvertree.

As the Dragon whirled briefly into view above those gray turrets, there were shouts and curses on the boats, and a brief faltering of oars. Tersepts snapped orders, horns blared, and as swiftly as it had paused, the hurrying journey resumed, boats cleaving the water with men peering warily at the sky ahead and making sure their weapons were at hand.

Then the sky spat forth something that the rowers watched become the Serpent. There were more shouts, and a general lifting of oars to drift, as nigh everyone afloat stared up into the brightening sky.

The Serpent reared up, dark and huge and terrible—and then struck, its sinuous length arrowing savagely down.

The men on the boats barely had time to gasp or cry out before the Dragon was struggling in the heart of coils—clawing its way aloft, still trapped in tightening grip of the gigantic snake, to hang almost overhead as the Serpent bit and bit again.

Men looked up from the water at the nightmare splitting the sky, and moaned or cursed or screamed in terror. Many raised shouts of "Go back! Turn back! We must get gone!"

"No!" a white-haired tersept roared, in a voice that rang out as loud as any war-horn. "Aglirta is _ours_—not some Dragon's or Serpent's or the plaything of wizards! How can we flee now, and dare to call the Vale our own? _Row on!_"

"Well said!" a ragged mountain of a blacksmith bellowed from another boat. Tersepts were, well, tersepts, but many men knew and respected Lorgauth the Smith, and there were other, grimmer sounds of agreement from many boats, all around. A few vessels rested oars and started to drift back downstream, but most of the rowers on the river pulled hard on their oars, heading for the Flowfoam docks.

A dragon-wing beat vainly at the air. Two great scaled bodies rolled in the sky, fangs struck, a gout of flame spewed vainly—and the warring Serpent and Dragon crashed down onto the palace together, rolling and biting like two maddened cats.

A roof collapsed under them with a groan, stones crashing down in a deadly rain inside, and pillars toppled.

The two struggling monsters clawed, bit, and lashed their tails, smashing walls and driving balconies and even entire turrets down to ruin. The Serpent struck and struck again, biting the Dragon repeatedly as they slithered and arched and spat, crushing galleries and great chambers.

And the Dragon burned.

Tshamarra wept as liquid fire rushed through her, boiling along her veins . . . a venom that ravaged her as deeply as her destruction of the Thrael had torn asunder the Great Serpent's powers . . . even as it snatched Ingryl Ambelter back from helplessness in the maze of enchanted mists Gadaster had flung him into.

At last the Serpent had a foe he could see and strike at—a foe he hated and feared—and strike at it he did, again and again. Fangs pierced deep into golden scales, smoking blood sluicing out in their wake, until Tshamarra Talasorn's world became a red-gold whirl of pain, lit by gloating Serpent-eyes and flashing fangs . . .

Dimly she knew her strength was leaving her. She was draped back over a wall, shedding scales as she slid down into the Throne Chamber of Aglirta—open to the sky now once more, and full of running, shouting folk. The pain was like a red river within her, a river of her shed blood, and the flames snarling along it were the Serpent's dark venom, gnawing its way through her . . .

. . .

The western wall of the Hall of Shields cracked and fell away. The armed folk barricaded grimly therein found themselves suddenly staring down into the roofless, riven Throne Chamber.

That once splendid hall was a wasteland of death and rubble. Courtiers, servants, guards, and Serpent-priests alike lay dead in their blood, or were fleeing wildly from the rearing Great Serpent and the Dragon struggling feebly beneath it. Beyond their fray, most of the western end of the palace lay in ruins, little more than crushed heaps of rubble.

"Horns of the Lady," King Raulin Castlecloaks gasped in horror, staring up at the sky and the triumphant Serpent rising to fill it. Beside him, Hulgor Delcamper said something worse.

As they watched—and Craer Delnbone sobbed in despair, beside them—the body of the Serpent started to dwindle.

"Come on!" Ezendor Blackgult roared, darkly magnificent in his borrowed black palace armor, as he waved his warsword above his head. "Band of Four, *to me!*"

The Golden Griffon did not wait for a reply, but raced to where a once secret stair had become little better than a slide, descending steeply into the Throne Chamber.

Hawkril, a fully armored giant once more, sprang after him. Craer stumbled in their wake, weeping openly.

Embra Silvertree strode after him, tall and sleek in battle leathers like those Craer wore. After a few strides she turned to look back at Hulgor, Flaeros, and Lorivar. "Guard the King," she told them grimly, and waved a hand at the Serpent below. "Our duty lies yonder."

"But, Lady Embra—!"

That protest burst from the lips of King Raulin Castlecloaks, standing uncertainly in the midst of the handful of loyal men. He fell silent, opening his mouth helplessly, and reached out to her with one hand . . . not knowing what else to say.

The smile Embra gave him was a trifle sad. "Be of good cheer, Majesty," she said calmly. "There's no better way to spend one's time—one's life—than fighting for Aglirta . . . and who knows? We may live to see another sunset. Remember, lad: 'Tis not when you die . . . 'tis *how* you die."

She nodded to the pale-faced and trembling Raulin, cradled her Dwaer firmly in both hands, turned, took two running steps, and sprang off the edge of the stair, flying down into the battle below.

. . .

The Serpent bit down again, roaring with triumphant, bubbling laughter—but its fangs struck only fallen stone: the Dragon was a small, slender, and half-fainting human sorceress once more, lying crumpled between two fallen pillars.

Overduke Blackgult raced in under those fangs like an impatient black flame to defend her, catching her up into the crook of his arm. "Now, little one," he muttered, "I was once something of a bold dabbler in sorcery . . . I think I can still fly us out of here. You can join the King, yonder, and watch the rest of us die heroically, hey?"

"*Blackgult!*" Hawkril roared from nearby, the crashings of armored footfalls heralding his frantic rush. He wasn't going to reach them in time, before the Serpent—

—Bit down, a fang twice the height of Blackgult plunging down so close beside his hip that he could easily have nudged it with an elbow. The Golden Griffon swung himself around to shield Tash's limp body from the stinging rain of venom that accompanied the Serpent's bite, and coolly finished his incantation.

The gigantic snake snatched its head back aloft, trailing rubble and spilling him sideways . . . and Blackgult swung around to cradle the woman in his arms from a hard fall onto rubble, a fall that never came. His awakening magic sent him gliding along the ground, no more than a handspan above a tumbled heap of fallen stone blocks. He grinned tightly and bent his will to lofting them higher, curving around and up—

"Blackgult!" Hawkril roared again, planting himself with his warsword held pointing right up into the sky, preparing to meet that descending maw.

The warning drove the Golden Griffon to fling himself sideways, curled around the sorceress. The huge snake's shadow fell over them as he spun away, laughing at the success of his magic—and straightened out in a glide that brought them rushing to meet Craer.

The procurer reached for Tshamarra, his eyes blazing. Blackgult put her gently into her man's arms and flew up and past them, curling back around to face—

The Great Serpent's strike was at Hawkril. The armaragor leaped aside at the last moment, into a little hollow in the rubble, and the snake's huge head glanced off rubble and followed, turning to pursue the warrior.

Blackgult flew right at the head, tugging out his blade once more, aiming for those triple eyes. *Three* eyes? No, just two, but with something circular gleaming between them, embedded in serpent-scales . . .

Flashing with hatred, those orbs swiveled to regard Blackgult. The moment their gazes met, he knew who was glaring at him.

Ingryl Ambelter, the self-styled Spellmaster of All Aglirta, was the Great Serpent!

And a mighty wizard still. The embedded thing—a Dwaer, of course!—flashed, and bolts of strange green flame lanced out of those eyes at Blackgult.

There was no time to counterspell, or dodge. The green fire clawed and swirled, streaming icily around him.

The Golden Griffon tried to twist up and out of its reach, but his sword crumbled away to nothing in his hands, his gauntlets and breastplate and shoulder-plates started to follow . . .

Cursing, Ezendor Blackgult soared up and away, trying to dart free of the spell. More of his armor fell from him as he went, tumbling . . .

He swooped, curved, looped and swooped again. One green bolt faded, but the other curved after him, reaching . . . reaching . . .

He turned his racing flight into a dive at the Dwaer, arcing over the huge snake-head to come at it from behind its eyes, so that as it swept up and turned to regard him again, he—landed hard in the scaled ridges just above the embedded Stone, and slapped his hand down on the Dwaer.

Magic stormed into him, at first at his imperious calling—and then, driven with fury, by the Great Serpent beneath him, even as it twisted its head to scrape down along a ragged edge of broken wall, and rid itself of this unwanted rider.

But Ezendor Blackgult had used Dwaerindim in battle far more than his foe, and his mind had melded with the strange flows of power in more than one Stone—so he was able, despite Ambelter's great might, to both withstand the flood of magic that was intended to burn him to mindlessness and spin himself a shield to keep him from harm against the stones.

The Great Serpent roared in fury, and flailed its head back and forth, battering this remnant of wall and then that—and Blackgult clung with his fingertips to the Dwaer, using its own power to keep himself glued to it, and drank in all the magic he could.

He was burning, now, the pain rising in him white-hot and choking, even as it numbed his limbs and made the world recede behind mists of white fire . . .

Grimly, Blackgult hung on, forcing himself to stand against the pain. He would need every last bit of power, if he was to have any hope of—

Ambelter finished a spell, and the Dwaer erupted in fury. The Golden Griffon snatched himself away from it, most of one hand seared to ash, and flew as he'd never flown before, racing across the ruined Throne Chamber like a bolt of lightning.

Craer met him with two drawn daggers and a snarl. "Get *back*! She's done enough—"

"Aye," Blackgult agreed, using a mere wisp of power to stun the procurer for the instant he needed to burst past, "she has. Wherefore it falls to me to do *this*."

He landed, aglow from head to foot and almost a head taller than he should have been, bent in a crackling of energies—and kissed Tshamarra Talasorn full on the mouth.

She lay on her back in what was left of a doorway, with the signs of Craer's frantic digging to get her down and into a cellar chamber below all around her, and though her eyes were open, they were dark.

They flashed as he came down on her, and she started to shudder. Blackgult pulled his head back, almost as if he was sucking something out of her, and then broke free, cradling her around the shoulders to keep her head from crashing back onto the rubble, to gasp, "Pray forgive me, Lady, but *someone* has to be the Dragon."

And he sprang up into the air right in front of Craer's enraged and astonished face, fresh pain raging in him.

He was not the one chosen by the Arrada. Ezendor Blackgult no longer had the power of mind and body to properly be the Dragon. Yet he must be. Aglirta was in need.

"As always!" he finished that thought wryly, though it came out as a great roar. Up into dragonshape he spun, expanding in size almost as much as in agony. He clawed the air and spat fire helplessly, wracked with pain, before he ever got near the Great Serpent.

Hawkril had driven his warsword deep between two scales as Ambelter had rid himself of Blackgult, and was now leaping for his life about the Throne Chamber as the maddened Serpent pounced at him, biting and missing and biting again. Embra Silvertree was hurling Dwaer-bolt after Dwaer-bolt at its eyes, trying to make it miss . . . and, thus far, succeeding. To and fro it went between the two overdukes, arching as it tried to reach over the rubble—and Blackgult fell on it from behind in a savage fury, knowing he hadn't long to live with the Dragon-powers shuddering through him.

"Unworthy, I am," he breathed, though it came out as a long tongue of fire that seared serpent-scales and sent Ambelter writhing away. "Such a pity . . ."

Then the pain was so great that he could only snarl—when he wasn't biting and clawing for all he was worth.

Venom and blood spewed forth together, smoking, and Blackgult dug his fangs in deep and fed fire through them.

The Great Serpent squalled and convulsed, thrashing wildly and sending palace stones flying, in a great rain that pelted down into the Silverflow.

His tail came around in a great whipping blow that slammed the trembling Dragon to the ground. Blackgult groaned, already lost in pain, and Ambelter flung coils around him just as he'd done to Tshamarra. At the same time, he burrowed his great flat serpent-head in through a gap in the rubble into some dark cellar chamber or other, and called on the Dwaer to help him shape an old, old spell. It worked, and as the Great Serpent tightened his coils around the Dragon, his forked tongue twisted into a grotesquely overlong human arm—an arm that reached out to slap the stones.

The Living Castle enchantments were strong here, and the Spellmaster used the Dwaer to make his call upon them mightier than he'd ever been able to before—and halfway across the rubble-strewn battlefield that had been the Throne Chamber before the coming of this dawn Embra Silvertree was dragged to her knees, sobbing and struggling.

The old enchantments were blood-bound to her, and as seductive as the Dark Three had been able to make them then, with full power over her young body and an almost whimsical shared ruthlessness. Embra fought those spells as best she could, but she might as well have tried to stop all winds from blowing across Darsar. She was unable to use the Dwaer, to see, even to breathe . . .

The king and the men and maids watching with him saw the Lady of Jewels fall on her face, senseless. Her Dwaer rolled away from her limp hand.

Hawkril was still a good dozen running paces away from it when the head of the Great Serpent soared back up into view, and then darted down again—and a hand reached out of its wide-fanged mouth, where its forked tongue should have been, and snatched up the fallen Dwaer.

Then the head turned almost gloatingly around to glare at the Dragon, trapped in its coils—and from it beams of ravening magic shot out from *two* Dwaer, lancing deep into the gold-scaled creature.

Stabbed and burned, and then stabbed and burned again, as the trembling, riven Dragon screamed in agony.

Screamed, and then started to dwindle, just as Tshamarra had done.

.　　.　　.

"Oh, gods, no," Hulgor Delcamper growled, as he stood shielding the young and white-faced King of Aglirta with a sword in either hand. "It'll not be long now. Die well, everyone!"

The watchers in the shattered hall saw the Great Serpent rear its head once more in hissing triumph. A shimmering blossomed in the air behind and above that head, becoming a hole surrounded by dark fire—and out of that hole appeared a lone human woman, floating upright in midair. Her head was a skull that in turn seemed to float above her shoulders—and she held a twinkling Dwaer-Stone in each of her spread hands.

"A Sword of Spells has two edges, overbold apprentice!" Gadaster Mulkyn hissed, as the Dwaer flared in unison.

Not to strike at the Great Serpent with ravening bolts of magic, but to awaken the last traces of the mind-link Ingryl had used for years to drain Gadaster's life. With cold glee the skull-headed mage forced his will upon Ingryl Ambelter's mind.

The Spellmaster wrestled against him, a dark and furious mind-struggle that lasted an eternity but no time at all . . . and lost. Calmly and carefully, Gadaster forced Ambelter to work certain magics.

"You wanted the Dwaer *so* much, didn't you?" he said, directly into Ambelter's trapped mind. "And now, lucky lad, you at last have what you've schemed so energetically for. A pity 'twill destroy you and your precious kingdom and probably most of Flowfoam, too. Let the conjunction begin!"

And four Dwaerindim blazed up blinding white, tearing free of scaled skin and grasping hands alike to soar up into the air together in a great floating ring.

As the Stones rose, so too certain folk all over the palace were jerked upright and into full awareness: Embra Silvertree and a handful of surviving Lords of the Serpent. Wherever they were, they stared up at the stones, quivering in helpless thrall.

Many other folk within sight of Flowfoam did much the same—not ensnared by the rushing magic, but awed by the sheer power singing in the air above them, and the rushing hues and images they could now see in the blinding shared radiance of the Stones. Faces of kings and wizards and warriors dead and dust for centuries whirled before all eyes in a flashing parade that—shivered, suddenly, as something darker and more solid burst into their midst.

Something like a dark flame, leaping from Dwaer to Dwaer as it struggled, growing arms and wings and talons and biting heads that all vanished again with the passing moments, thrusting up shape after shape as it fought toward freedom. Arched, wracked, and tattered with pain in the heart of all the flowing magic, it thrust a smooth and faceless head out of the chaos to regard Gadaster Mulkyn, glaring without eyes down at the skull-headed sorceress. The rogue Koglaur!

That moment of malevolence broke the flow of leaping forces into wildly stabbing bolts of lightning that splashed down onto Flowfoam and raced along through its riven chambers like crackling snakes. Men and women screamed, bodies were hurled into the air, and the Great Serpent turned with all the speed of any swift-striking snake and spat a desperate thrust of dark power at Gadaster—not mind to mind, but as another crackling bolt of force, this one of shining black.

The skull-headed sorceress writhed in the heart of it as blackness whirled around her in a great fist, stabbing through her repeatedly—and from the skull burst forth a cold, high, wailing scream of despair, that seemed almost to plead as it rose and grew fainter and fainter, fading away as the Great Serpent shuddered in the pain echoing back across the old link between them.

The screaming skull slowly melted away, revealing in its place the tearful face of a frightened living woman, her long black hair swirling around her as she frantically wove a very swift spell. Her body her own once more, Maelra Bowdragon teleported herself away from the air above Flowfoam Palace, vanishing in a silent instant.

And so passed Gadaster Mulkyn, first Spellmaster of Silvertree, dead a second time, his sentience shattered. "Or is it?" Embra Silvertree whispered, still trembling in Dwaer-thrall. "Is he truly gone this time, or fled into Ambelter or somewhere else?"

The Great Serpent roared in exultation, stretching its great scaled neck up once more—and breaking the thrall that held Embra as it caused the four Dwaerindim to break their ring and whirl around its neck in a new orbit. The Koglaur fell away from them, a torn and writhing scrap of darkness, and fell wetly onto tumbled stones far below.

Amidst that rubble the freed Lady of Jewels collapsed, gasping, but scrambled to stare up again, not wanting to miss a moment of what could well be her unfolding doom.

Four Dwaer-Stones were flashing brightly as they spun about the Great

Serpent's neck—and it struck, fangs gaping, at the diminished, wounded Dragon in its coils.

"Not worthy, hey?" That thunderous shout burst forth from the rent and bleeding Dragon, even as serpent-fangs bit deep. The Dwaerindim flashed and then dimmed in unison, becoming almost dark, and the snake made a wordless sound of surprise and alarm. The Dragon gasped—and glowed, its ruined body flaring to the same white brilliance that the four Stones had shared in their ring.

Ezendor Blackgult wrestled fiercely for control of the Dwaer, heedless of the pain. He was beating Ambelter, he was winning . . .

Calmly he drew in more mighty magic than he'd ever felt before, searing himself inside as he used not a scrap of Dwaer-force to shield himself, but forged it all into a great slaying thrust that raced back up the fangs sunk so cruelly in him, into the Spellmaster.

And the Great Serpent burned, shriveling in a trice to blackened, screaming bones. Ingryl Ambelter and all his dark dreams fell to ash so swiftly that many of the watching folk of Aglirta could scarce believe what had befallen.

Yet one thing was clear enough: The towering bulk of the Serpent was gone from above the blackened, near-skeletal remnant of the Dragon, and four Dwaer-Stones were falling out of the sky.

Embra made a wordless sound of her own and started to run to where the plunges of at least two of them would end among the tumbled Stones—but a dark, shuddering, constantly changing shape was there before her.

The Koglaur! She clambered desperately toward it, knowing in her dazed pain and all this chaos of magic she couldn't yet weave a spell no matter what the need . . . and ahead of her, saw all four Dwaer, glowing faintly again, race down to strike the shapeshifter as if spell-called to it. The Faceless rose up into the shape of Ingryl Ambelter, spell-wove a gate outlined by four whirling Stones—and stepped through it.

In his wake, all four Dwaer sprang apart, fading away in midair as they raced in opposite directions . . . and leaving in their wake a dumbfounded silence to settle over the riven Flowfoam Palace.

"So did the real Spellmaster die," Flaeros Delcamper murmured, looking to the Lady Orele for answers, "or was it a Faceless, all along?"

"And do we have to go hunting *four* Dwaer-Stones now?" Craer groaned, from the shattered floor of the Throne Chamber below.

Spell-radiance flared in a darkened chamber in the tower of the Master of Bats, momentarily outshining the scrying-globes. Three mages whirled around in time to see what fell out of it, into a weak, weeping, smoking sprawl on the stones. Ithim Bowdragon gasped, but Arkle Huldaerus moved as swiftly as a veteran warrior, striding forward to pluck up the young woman by the throat.

"Are you Gadaster Mulkyn?" he demanded, in a voice that shook with all the magic he could muster—as bats poured down from the ceiling to settle all over his visitor in a flapping cloud.

Dark, tearful eyes flashed. "I know you not, sir," a constricted but furious voice snarled, from under Arkle's hands, "but *I* am Maelra Bowdragon—and I've had quite enough of being forced to do things by mages!"

With a sigh of relief the Master of Bats let go of her throat and stepped back. He was jostled and almost sent sprawling by Ithim Bowdragon, plunging forward to embrace the daughter he'd thought lost—but who'd just spellsought him across much of Asmarand. Uncle Dolmur was not far behind.

The Bowdragons collapsed into joyful hugs and tears. Arkle Huldaerus watched their laughter, feeling more lonely than he ever had before, and suddenly tears were welling in his own eyes.

He turned away, wiping at his eyes furiously. It would not do to miss a single glimpse of what was now unfolding in his scrying-globes.

It would not do at all.

Ezendor Blackgult knew he was dying. The pain alone told him that, even without his watery, blood-filled glimpses of his own charred ribs and limbs, returning to him as he slipped helplessly out of dragon-form—and fell just as helplessly across the body of a wounded and dying Lord of the Serpent.

Lying sprawled on his back with the clear morning sky of Aglirta above him, the Golden Griffon mumbled to no one in particular, "I want to hear birds sing again. I don't know why."

As always, Hawkril Anharu reached him first. The great mountain of an armaragor reached down as gently as any wet-nurse, to half-raise his old master, cradling Blackgult in his arms.

The Golden Griffon smiled wearily up at him as darkness came in waves, taking his breath with it. "Good friend," he said swiftly, while he still could, "have my barony. You more than deserve it. I've done much of . . . what I wanted to do . . . chased many dreams, and . . . even caught a few."

Embra Silvertree was crashing toward them across the jagged, tumbled rubble now, heedless of her own safety. *"Father!"* she cried.

Blackgult kept on speaking, because he had to. "I . . . wanted love, friends, wealth, danger . . . and excitement . . . and I haven't been disappointed."

His daughter reached him and fell to her knees, sobbing, "Father!"

"Hah," the Serpent-priest sneered weakly, from where he lay beside her, "did you think it was going to be *easy* to kill a god?"

Embra stared at the dying man with fire rising in her eyes. "I do believe," she said softly and deliberately, "I feel the Blood Plague taking hold of me at last."

She snatched out her dagger and drove it firmly through one of the priest's eyes, not flinching when his gore fountained over her.

Incredibly, the Lord of the Serpent did not die right away. Choking on his own blood, he cried, "Serpent, aid me!"

Nothing happened, and his next cry was fainter. "Serpent?"

Blood bubbled from the lips of the Lord of the Serpent as his remaining eye glared at Blackgult, and then turned to gaze back up at the woman who'd brought him death, and was still bent over him, dripping his blood.

"I expected so much more," the priest whispered reproachfully. "You've all been such a disappointment." And he turned his head toward his own shoulder and looked away from them. One last tear ran from his eye, and he died.

A serpent slithered from the neck of the priest's robe and reared up to strike at Embra with a malevolent hiss—and she grabbed it just below the head, flung it to an exposed patch of marble floor, and stomped on its head with one booted foot, shuddering.

Then she whirled back to her father, and burst into tears.

One charred arm reached up and caught hold of her arm in a last, vise-hard grip. "You're . . . my daughter, all right," Ezendor Blackgult whispered hoarsely, giving her a fierce, pain-wracked smile. "Live . . . well. Go on to glory, with Hawk . . . Save Aglirta!"

She leaned forward to stroke his face, through her tears, but he struggled up and forward, trembling. As the Golden Griffon thrust himself forward, trying to reach her lips and kiss them, the light went out of his dark eyes . . . and that iron strength ebbed, until his fingers fell away from her arm.

27

The Renunciation of the Dragon

Trembling with grief, Embra Silvertree bent forward the few inches of space her father had died trying to cross, and kissed his dead mouth fiercely.

And a gout of shining blue flame rose from within Ezendor Blackgult and hissed out of him, into her.

Swallowing it, Embra gasped—and froze like that, her lips parted and her eyes staring wildly. Flames of that deep and splendid sapphire hue licked up all around her, appearing from the empty air around her body. In their midst, the tall and slender Lady of Jewels was tugged upright, as if plucked by unseen strings, and held there, motionless in the rushing flames. Blue fire roared up all around her, but touched her not.

The Aglirtans now stumbling cautiously through the ruined Throne Chamber, their king among them, stared at her doubtfully. She gave no sign of seeing or hearing anyone.

"He's dead! Blackgult is dead!" a palace guard gasped, staring down at the man fallen on his face at her feet. "The Dragon is dead!"

Armed men burst in through several archways as he spoke, breathless from their race up from the docks.

"The Serpent's dead, too! Aglirta is free at last!" a courtier cried.

"No," a new voice snapped from behind King Raulin Castlecloaks, as a blood-wet sword burst through the royal breastplate from behind. "*Now* Aglirta is free!"

The king reeled, and then toppled forward as the Tersept of Ironstone shook the gurgling, dying Raulin off his blade, snatching the crown from the king's head in the same motion.

"Behold your new King!" he roared, as he crowned himself.

His armaragors standing with him took up the cry: "King Ironstone!"

"It's customary," Craer Delnbone remarked, as he sprang from atop a broken wall to crash down atop Ironstone's shoulders, slitting the man's throat with a dagger and striking the crown from his head to clang and roll on the floor, "to have just *one* king in a realm at a time. Orele?"

The Lady of the Wise was already picking her way forward through the rubble to where Raulin lay, the sorceress she'd just healed at her side. Wordlessly the old woman turned to Tshamarra, and the last Talasorn sorceress fed her what magic she had left, to heal the king.

The moment it was clear the Lady Overduke's magic was bent on healing and not blasting them down, Ironstone's men surged forward with a roar—but were met by royal warriors headed by Hawkril, Hulgor, Flaeros, and Craer, who sprang to meet them, striking savagely with their blades.

In a trice the Throne Chamber was in an uproar of men swording each other, chambermaids screaming from the balconies, tersepts shouting orders, and hurrying folk. Royal guards led by Suldun Greatsarn rushed into the room to form a defensive ring around the stricken king—and some of the courtiers shifted their shapes into warriors wearing Flowfoam armor, plucked up weapons from among the fallen, and joined them.

More arrivals from the docks charged in with swords drawn, novice Serpent-priests with venomed knives slipped in among the royal warriors and started slaying, and the clang of steel became deafening in the shattered Throne Chamber. Men were dying bloodily everywhere. Embra stood like a living torch of blue flame in the center of the tumult, and tersept turned on tersept to settle old scores.

On her knees above a blood-drenched Raulin Castlecloaks, Tshamarra Talasorn went pale as she spent the last of her power. Swaying, she almost fell over on her face—but Lady Orele put a steadying hand around her shoulders, ignoring an armaragor bearing down on them with bloody sword raised.

The man was still two hurrying strides away when Hulgor Delcamper crashed into him from one side and Flaeros Delcamper hit him from another. The young bard smote his foe so hard that his sword broke, its riven ends singing past the Lady Talasorn's nose. Snarling, Flaeros drove the broken stub of the blade into the man's face, and they crashed to the floor together, rolling—the bard trying to deal more harm to his foe, and the warrior lost in pain. Hulgor ended it for him with a sword-thrust, and kicked the body aside to grin encouragingly at Orele.

She shook her head and sighed. "Lads never grow up, do they?"

The Tersept of Thornwood died screaming an instant later, his fingers hacked away by the cortahars of a rival and a spear run through him—and at the same time, not far away, the Tersept of Harbridge took a hurled Serpent-dagger in the face and went down, tripping over the heaped bodies of his fallen armaragors.

The ruined Throne Chamber was strewn with the dead and dying now, and as the Tersept of Mesper roared out a challenge to his rival of Tarnshars and launched into a lumbering run, Embra Silvertree suddenly threw up her hands and bellowed *"Enough!"* in a voice that rocked Flowfoam and echoed back from the banks of the Silverflow and the crumbling battlements of the Silent House.

Scales rippled into being on her cheeks, and then as swiftly faded again. Dragon scales.

"Sithra dourr," she whispered, her voice still thunderous with the awakened power of the Dragon—and all drawn swords, daggers, spears, and like weapons in the room were plucked into the air. Above the roofless part of the Throne Chamber, the sky was full of swords—and where there was still a ceiling, the weapons were driven deep into smoking stone.

Silence fell as dumbfounded men turned to stare at the Lady of Jewels.

Wild-eyed, her breast heaving and her hair standing on end, Embra Silvertree glared back at them.

"There's been more than enough killing in Aglirta today," she said fiercely. "Let it end, *now.*"

A deeper silence fell, wherein men glanced sidelong at each other, and then hurriedly back to the tall, slender woman still sheathed in wisps of bright blue flame, wondering what she'd do next—and what they dared try, in the face of her fury.

"The King lives," Craer Delnbone remarked, into that stillness.

"H-help me up," Raulin said urgently. Hawkril Anharu took one great stride and plucked the King of Aglirta to his feet.

Raulin Castlecloaks's face was bone-white, and he was still drenched in his own blood, his breastplate missing and the rest of his armor much hacked and dented. Yet he looked both calm and older than he'd ever seemed before as he faced the silent crowd and announced, "I'm very weary of Serpent-priests and warring barons and tersepts alike. Henceforth, let it be known that the penalty for worship of the Serpent, anywhere in Aglirta, is death. There will be no more barons, and any tersept who does not declare loyalty to me—and prove it, by service in the army I shall whelm today, to scour the Vale—shall lose his rank and his life. Loyal Aglirtans, to me! No longer shall—"

"No," the Lady Silvertree said firmly, from behind him. "No, Raulin, this is not the way. Loyalty and trust must be earned . . . and not by greater tyranny than that practiced by those you deem traitors."

She bent, and picked up the crown. "I think Aglirta deserves better."

There was a brief murmur from the watching crowd as she lifted the crown, and the sunlight caught it, making it gleam in her hands.

"What do you mean?" Raulin whispered, whirling around. "You know I never wanted the throne . . ."

"Precisely why you've done better than a more ambitious man would have," the Lady of Jewels replied, "yet still there's unrest in the Vale, and swords out, and Serpent-mischief."

She turned slowly to look around at all the faces staring back at her. "I could change all that," she told them quietly. "I am the Dragon. A new Serpent is rising even now, but he'll be but a lone, weak man if none worship him—and for now, I hold sway over Aglirta, to do whatever I desire."

She turned again to regard Raulin, and added gently, "And I desire Raulin Castlecloaks to be free of the throne."

"Aye! Down with the King!" someone shouted, from among the watching warriors.

Embra whirled to face whence that cry had come. "No! Say rather: 'Up with the King!' For years upon years the King slept, and Aglirta was the Kingless Land. The curse of the realm then was ambitious, warring men— each baron ruling as his own king, and desiring the rest of the Vale. 'Tis the curse of the realm *now*. You folk of Aglirta have too many rulers."

She climbed a heap of rubble so that everyone could see her, and turned slowly to look at them all with the crown shining in her hands. "There was a time when I would never have dared challenge what was right and lawful, what nobles and kings said and did. That time is past. Hear then *my* will. I desire Raulin Castlecloaks to rule as Regent of all Aglirta. There will be no King, hereafter, and no barons—only tersepts who garrison and give judgment and watch over folk around them in the name of the regent. All of these titled folk shall rule in the name of the people."

Embra sighed, looked down at the crown, and added, "The regent will travel the realm constantly, at the head of an army that will build and fix and tend crops and settle disputes and improve roads as well as fighting. Flowfoam will become a court and a place of healing where folk are tended by priests of the Three, who shall be permitted no temples elsewhere, but only open-air altars. No one shall worship the Serpent in Aglirta upon pain of exile, and in like manner none shall venerate the Dragon."

There was a stirring of released breath from all around her, as folk lost themselves in relief that there was to be no attempted tyranny of sorcery, and started to consider her words.

"I renounce this ancient war of Serpent and Dragon," Embra added, "and so long as I curb my power, and none worship me or the Scaled One, the new Serpent can never become stronger than I am. The madness and the turning-to-beasts were fell Serpent-magic; they will end when the last Serpent-priests are slain or driven forth from Aglirta. The Dwaer are hidden, sealed where they're scattered to by my power—and I shall know if anyone disturbs them. My companions will renounce something else with me: our title of 'Overduke.' Our task here is done."

She tossed the crown into the air and made a swift and simple gesture—and the royal circlet of Aglirta burst apart into ringing shards that dissolved in flame . . . and faded to empty air ere they hit the ground.

Another shared sigh arose all around her, and Embra stepped down from the height of tumbled stones, saying as she went, "Yet we'll always be guardians of Aglirta. If Aglirta should need us, you'll see us again."

She strode to join the rest of the Four, adding over her shoulder, "*Try* not to let Aglirta have need of us."

There was a moment of shocked silence, and then Flaeros Delcamper cried, "Behold the Guardians of Aglirta!"

"*The Guardians of Aglirta!*" most of the crowd roared back, their cry thunderous, suddenly eager.

"Wait!" a tersept snarled. "Castlecloaks, are you going to stand for this?"

Silence fell again, very suddenly—and into it Raulin said firmly, "I am, and welcome it dearly. I intend to find and meet with every priest of the Three and every tersept and former baron to hear their personal acceptance of Embra's wise way. Those who refuse to accept it will have to leave Aglirta, or face the swords of those who stand with me. I also want to hear from every man and lass of Aglirta the names of any Aglirtans they deem worthy of sitting in court judgment over them—I'll need such people as officers in my regency. Embra's right: We've seen far too much of sword and spell and Serpent in Aglirta, and too little of honest toil and earned coin and good harvests and feasts—and peace to enjoy those feasts in!"

"Well said!" the Lady Orele said crisply, and from among the warriors Lorgauth the Smith agreed loudly.

"For Aglirta!" Flaeros Delcamper cried, in the manner of grand bards Darsar over. "The Guardians have spoken! The regent has spoken! For Aglirta!"

"For Aglirta!" came the thunderous reply, and then everyone began talking at once.

"Well, *that's* settled," Craer commented, cradling an exhausted Tshamarra in his arms as he watched Hawkril embrace a trembling Embra Silvertree. "So how about the first of those feasts, then? I'm starving!"

There was a general roar of approval from the folk standing nearby, and a cry swiftly started of "Feast! Feast!" Throats all over the Throne Chamber echoed those words, and folk stirred into action, rushing once more—hurrying past the sprawled, fly-ridden corpses of Ezendor Blackgult, many Lords and Brothers of the Serpent, and dozens of dead Aglirtans.

With his arms wrapped around his softly weeping lady, Hawkril Anharu gazed down at the man who'd been his master for so many years. The grave would be next to Sarasper's. "Four no longer," he murmured—and then discovered he was crying too.

Epilogue

The taverns and feasthouses of Sirlptar were astir with merchants arguing excitedly about one man's arrival in their streets. Word had raced like a storm breeze through the city: Regent Raulin Castlecloaks of Aglirta had come to Sirlptar.

Prelude to an invasion, some said hotly. Come to beg union, or coins from Sirl city to rebuild the Vale, others claimed. In need of seeing what real wealth could bring but he could only dream of, a few insisted. Here like everyone else, to shop or pay debts—or even to collect them, others reasoned, though what some penniless lad from war-torn Aglirta could have lent anyone in Sirlptar was hard to say.

Wherefore curious crowds of the idle, those too wealthy to work, and those whose profession it was to peer and overhear things followed the lad and his sizable entourage wherever they went—which was, eventually, down to the bustling docks, specifically to a wharf of some age and little importance where a long, slender sea-rel creaked at the pilings.

There the sometime king greeted the master of that vessel—one Telgaert, whose ship was the *Fair Wind*—who seemed to be expecting him. The crowd drew close to hear what might unfold, and saw the regent embrace a handsome young lord of about his own age.

"May you have a fair wind for Ragalar, Flaer," Raulin said huskily, his throat suddenly tight. "You always come when I need you. I'll miss you."

"Not nearly as much as I'll miss you, and all green Aglirta, too," the bard replied. "Send word if ever you need us, or want to see us, or hunger to spend some time smelling the sea in Varandaur."

"Aye," Hulgor Delcamper put in, clapping Raulin on the shoulder, "where Orele can mother you like a warcaptain!" He roared with laughter as the aged Lady of Chambers gave him a glare and a prod with her cane.

"Gentles," Master Telgaert murmured, waving a hand at the waters, "the tide turns already."

"And we're late, as usual," a short, slender man who had the sleek look of a successful procurer said heartily. "But of course. So let's be kissing and cuddling and getting you Delcamper rabble aboard, hey?"

The slender woman beside him winced. "There *are* gentler ways of say-ing that, Craer."

"What, the sly nothings courtiers tongue all the time? Aren't you sick of them by now, Tash?"

"Longfingers," a taller woman said firmly from behind him, "say farewell, get out of the way, and shut your mouth for once—or we'll all soon be able to watch how well overclever scions of House Delnbone swim!" Embra raised the toe of her boot meaningfully.

"Like unto an eel," Craer boasted, bowing with a flourish.

"Well, *that* doesn't surprise me," Tshamarra Talasorn told the sky just above her innocently, "given what I see of my lord in our bedchambers, of nights."

The procurer assumed a scandalized expression, and drew back from his lady to utter a shocked protest—only to have his ear grasped firmly by the Lady Orele, who towed him around to face her, kissed him firmly on the lips, said, "Farewell, lad. Call on us when you grow up," and marched toward the waiting ship.

When she reached its gangplank, calmly ignoring the mirth behind her and the rude gestures Craer was enthusiastically making at her back, she nodded to the slender woman in leathers who waited there—a grave nod of recognition that was returned in kind.

"Orathlee," the woman of the ship identified herself with a warmly wel-coming smile, holding out a hand to help her aged passenger aboard. Two of the Wise would have much to talk about, on the run to Ragalar.

Flaeros Delcamper was blushing like a flame as he followed, and Hulgor Delcamper was grinning in his wake, for Embra Silvertree's kisses had been both long and deep, and those of Tshamarra Talasorn only slightly less so.

Two or three of the Delcamper manservants held out their faces hope-fully as they trooped past to help load baggage, but the two sorceresses merely grinned and waved them away—and at least one of those men took his leave wearing an expression of clear relief. Sorceresses were not to be safely trifled with, and the Dragon of the Arrada even less so.

In a surprisingly short time lines were cast off, farewells were called, and the *Fair Wind* sailed. The sleek ship caught the breeze immediately and scudded swiftly out of sight, and the regal party turned away from the docks.

It took them only about three chattering paces to become aware that amid the hurrying sailors, cellarers, and carters were some individuals who did not move, but stood like statues grimly awaiting the regal party—and that these persons were forming a ring around the Aglirtans.

Hawkril growled deep in his throat and laid a hand on the hilt of his warsword—and the folk of the docks melted away from around him with a deft wariness that bespoke familiarity with many brawls and spilled blood, leaving the regal party facing their foes.

A dozen men. Sirl mages, by their garments, wizards for hire. Behind them stood a row of wealthy merchants from the Isles of Ieirembor, smiling in triumph.

Although she knew very well that the Ieiremborans still sought revenge for Blackgult's failed invasion, and probably saw this as a perfect opportunity to either slaughter the ruler of Aglirta, or win from him concessions or a rich ransom, Tshamarra Talasorn assumed the role of the bewildered outlander, and asked crisply, "Yes, sirs? *What* is the meaning of this?"

The wizards merely smirked. One man of the Isles cleared his throat importantly, stepped forward to speak, and—kept silent as Craer and Hawkril drew their blades with a flourish and stepped forward to defend the regent. Behind them, Raulin swallowed nervously and drew his own sword.

Tshamarra raised her hands with a ready spell crackling warningly around them, and stepped forward. "Desist, wizards," she warned, "or there'll be slaughter this day on the docks of Sirlptar."

The mages sneered at her and shook back their sleeves to lift their own hands. The fires of risen magics crackled around them, too.

"Not so mighty without your Dwaer-Stones, are you?" one of them chuckled.

Embra Silvertree smiled back at him. "Oh, we manage," she replied softly—and soared up into Dragon-form, towering great and terrible amid the chaos of their bursting enchantments and frantic slaying-spells.

Screams broke over the docks of Sirlptar, and folk fled in all directions. Tshamarra smote one mage reeling with a spell, Craer brought down another with a hurled dagger to the throat, and above them the Dragon leaned down and breathed fire.

Her huge gout of rolling flame broke over three of the mages . . . and left nothing of them but dancing cinders. Others abruptly remembered important business elsewhere and vanished—either in a winking of mage-light or in a terrified sprint toward the nearest alley.

In the space of a gasped breath twelve Sirl wizards were gone from the docks, leaving a handful of terrified Ieiremborans frantically beating at their blazing robes and garments. One of them ran along the wharves with a ter-rified wail until he reached a spot where he could leap into the sea and douse the flames.

Embra let him go, but lowered her great head to look straight into the eyes of the remaining merchants, and said, "Come to Aglirta with hostile magic, or the words of the Serpent on your tongue, and you can expect a like reception." She used the power of the Dragon to magnify her voice so that it rolled out across Sirlptar like thunder, carrying to every ear and for some miles beyond. "Those who come in peace, to trade, we welcome—but *never* mistake our welcome for weakness."

Embra's words boomed clearly in the taproom of the Sighing Gargoyle, causing every man there to stiffen and fall silent.

In a table in one corner of the room that Flaeros Delcamper would have recognized, four drinkers smiled a little ruefully at each other across a small forest of empty winebottles. Maelra Bowdragon shuddered, too, but Uncle Dolmur patted her thigh comfortingly under the table, and her father clapped her shoulder reassuringly above it, and she sighed a long sigh and then managed another smile.

"I suppose this means we'll have to invent something to trade in, or keep clear of the Vale henceforth," the Master of Bats observed.

"Oh, I don't know," Craer Delnbone replied, stepping forward out of the brief flash of a teleport-spell with Tshamarra Talasorn at his side. "We're short of bats in Aglirta."

He handed a chittering, wing-flapping bat back to Arkle Huldaerus, and added a trifle archly, "Though we won't be, if you keep sending them to spy on us in such excessively obvious numbers."

The four mages around the table eyed each other in startled silence for a moment—and then, suddenly, everyone started to laugh.

Dramatis Personae

AENTRA, ALAIS: personal chambermaid, dresser, and lover of the Tersept of Stornbridge (*see* Stornbridge, Rarandar). Alais is shorter, darker, and more lush of figure and bold of manner than her fellow chambermaid Jhaundra (*see* Istrim, Jhaundra), and is the favorite of Lord Stornbridge. Most folk of Stornbridge Castle like Alais because she has no shred of arrogance or temper, drifting through life on clouds of merriment—and because she likes to help folk (including men—even relative strangers—desiring warm companionship).

AMBELTER, INGRYL: onetime Spellmaster of Silvertree who desires to be much more, this dangerous man was once the strongest wizard of the Dark Three mages who served Baron Faerod Silvertree. Ambitious, shrewd, and worldly, he's a creative, ruthless, and very powerful spellweaver. Though slain in *The Kingless Land,* Ingryl seems to have found a way to live on, beyond death. His spells have won him control over the Melted (q.v.), the stumbling zombie creations of the dead wizard Corloun.

ANHARU, HAWKRIL: Overduke of Aglirta, known as "the Boar of Blackgult" when he was an armaragor (unranked battle knight) in the service of the Baron Blackgult, whom he was once personal bodyguard to. A man of unusually large build and strength, Hawk is a member of the Band of Four and the longtime friend and sword-companion of Craer Delnbone, who often calls him "Tall Post."

ARANGLAR, BENTHE: known to one and all as "Aranglar the Weaver" for his livelihood, this mild-mannered and locally respected man works out of his house in the upcountry Aglirtan village of Bowshun, and is married to a popular seamstress (*see* Aranglar, Thaelae).

ARANGLAR, THAELAE: a pretty, kindhearted, and skilled seamstress whose specialties are swift mending and elegant adornments (embroidery). She lives in the Aglirtan village of Bowshun, and is married to the local weaver (*see* Aranglar, Benthe).

ARTHROON, BELGUR: an ambitious and powerful priest of the Church of the Serpent, who holds the rank of Scaled Master and is sufficiently senior to be considered a Lord of the Serpent. Arthroon is a cruel, scheming, and energetic man. He bullies priests of lower rank tirelessly and gleefully, in particular Fangbrother Darl Khavan (q.v.), who has become his unofficial servant.

AUMTHUR, DARLAERIUS: an aging sage of Aglirta, retired to safer Sirlptar in his failing years. His writings on many topics, published in chapbook form, are widely read up and down the coast of Asmarand, and considered authoritative, even by many who disagree with some of "old Aumthur's" opinions. He's only the latest—but one of the most eloquent—to advance the theory that magic (particularly when "great constructions" of magic such as the Arrada are involved) creates "offices" or roles that can be filled by successive individuals if an incumbent is slain or fails. For example, Aumthur believes that several different men have in turn "been" the Great Serpent.

Band of Four, the: our heroes, the Overdukes of Aglirta, who began their careers together as an independent band of four adventurers in *The Kingless Land* (see Anharu, Hawkril; Blackgult, Ezendor; Codelmer, Sarasper; Delnbone, Craer; and Silvertree, Embra).

BELKLARRAVUS, GLARSIMBER: Baron of Brightpennant, formerly the Tersept (non-noble ruler) of Sart but made baron by King Kelgrael Snowsar in *The Vacant Throne*. This stout, brawny warrior was infamous from his days as a mercenary warcaptain as "the Smiling Wolf of Sart." He fought alongside the Band of Four, was slain in *A Dragon's Ascension,* and lies buried on Flowfoam Isle.

BLACKGULT, EZENDOR: Regent of Aglirta and Baron (Lord) of Blackgult, known as the Golden Griffon for his heraldic badge. Long-time rival to Faerod Silvertree for rule of Aglirta, Blackgult was the leader of a disastrous attempted conquest of the Isles of Ieirembor just prior to *The Kingless Land,* which resulted in the seizure of his lands by Silvertree and all of his warriors (including Craer and Hawkril of the Four) being declared outlaw. A sophisticated, intelligent warrior and esthete, Blackgult has dabbled in spellcraft and collected many enchanted items, using their powers to wear another human shape: that of the seldom-seen bard Inderos Stormharp, Master Bard of Darsar, famous as the greatest living bard of Asmarand (if not all Darsar). He is the true father of Embra Silvertree.

Bloodblade: *see* Duthjack "Bloodblade", Sendrith

BOAZSHYN, KLARANGAS: a swift-witted, fearless Lord of the Serpent (senior priest of the Church of the Serpent). Bald due to a little-understood disease, he's neither lovely nor slender, and is known to all as "Boazshyn of Ool" for the town in which he dwells. Long successful in business, he enjoys fine wine, young boys, and deft swindles—and is both a user of poisons on others, and himself immune to many, due to frequent and deliberate samplings of such substances.

BOWDRAGON, CATHALEIRA: most powerful of the youngest generation of the sorcerous Bowdragon family, she was apprenticed to the Aglirtan archwizard Tharlorn of the Thunders. When he tired of her charms and ambitions, he slew Cathaleira, using her sentience to animate a monster he dubbed "the mage-slayer." Trapped in that form, she perished (in *The Vacant Throne*) in battle with dozens of frightened Aglirtans in a wayside inn.

BOWDRAGON, DOLMUR: the eldest Bowdragon brother, current patriarch of the family and a mighty archwizard in his own right. A thoughtful, even-tempered, and serious man who considers future implications far more than do most mages of power.

BOWDRAGON, ITHIM: the youngest Bowdragon brother, a weak and sensitive man who fathered Jhavarr and five daughters, the eldest of whom is Maelra.

BOWDRAGON, JHAVARR: an arrogant, rash, and powerful young sorcerer of a family known for its magical might, who sought to avenge the death of his "sister" (actually cousin; the current Bowdragon younglings were raised together, and regard each other as siblings) Cathaleira Bowdragon and is thought to have been slain himself in spell-battle in the skies over Aglirta in *A Dragon's Ascension*.

BOWDRAGON, MAELRA: the raven-haired, beautiful, hot-tempered, and icy-tongued eldest daughter of Ithim Bowdragon. Her restlessness grew throughout *A Dragon's Ascension* to become something far more dangerous to her and to Darsar than mere ambition.

BOWDRAGON, MULTHAS: a hot-tempered Bowdragon brother who earned himself the unlovely nicknames "the Blackheart" and "the Roaring-Bearded Storm" for his hot-tempered, arrogant, blustering behavior. Bearded and darkly handsome, he's the father of no less than seven daughters.

BRAEROS, HAUNTHUR: trusted veteran guard of Flowfoam Palace, loyal to King Raulin Castlecloaks. Once an armaragor in the service of Baron (later Regent) Ezendor Blackgult (q.v.).

BRANJACK, AMMERT: an easygoing, talkative farmer whose holding lies just north of the Aglirtan village of Fallingbridge; friend to Dunhuld Drunter (q.v.) and Buckland Ruld (q.v.).

BRAUMDUR, ILVRETH: a burly, ugly, muscular brute of a hunter (poacher) and retired mercenary warrior who dwells in the woods at the edge of the Aglirtan village of Bowshun. A friend to the hunter Muryk Eregar (q.v.).

Brightpennant: *see* Belklarravus, Glarsimber

CARDASSA, ITHCLAMMERT: Baron of Cardassa, "the Old Crow" or "Crow of Cardassa," famous as a strict, loyal, and fair "upright" baron who was slain for his loyalty to King Kelgrael Snowsar in *The Vacant Throne*.

CARONTHOM: "Fangmaster" and First Voice in the councils of the Church of the Serpent. The most senior surviving Lord of the Serpent, he functions as acting head of the faith of the Serpent, working in concert with

Raunthur (q.v.) the Wise, until the rise of a new Great Serpent. A clever, wily and powerful man, shrewd in judgment of people and tactics, Caronthom is swift and ruthless when he needs to be.

CASTLECLOAKS, RAULIN TILBAR: King of Aglirta and thereby the owner of a dozen more grand and largely meaningless titles, but best known (derisively) as "the Boy King" because of his youth. Son of the respected bard Helgrym Castlecloaks, Raulin was briefly a battle-companion to the Band of Four, who enthroned him in *A Dragon's Ascension.*

Cathaleira: *see* Bowdragon, Cathaleira

CHAEVUR, CHALANCE: guard of Stornbridge Castle and cortahar in the service of the Tersept of Stornbridge, Lord Rarandar Stornbridge (q.v.). A stolid, slow-witted, loyal man known for stubborn patience more than battle-prowess.

CHELDRAEM, VYNTHUR: a glib-tongued, swift-witted Lord of the Serpent, one of the most greedy, worldly, and trade-oriented senior priests of the Church of the Serpent. Dwelling in the Aglirtan town of Ibryn under the scrutiny of another Serpent-Lord, Halhoaze Maskalos (q.v.), Cheldraem is judged both untrustworthy and "un-devout" by many Serpent-priests, and keeps his Church position (and life) only by his financial support of Caronthom (q.v.) and Raunthur (q.v.).

CODELMER, SARASPER: "Longfangs," a healer and onetime courtier who for years hid in the Silent House and other places about Aglirta, often in one of three beast shapes he could adopt: bat, ground snake, or (his most favored) the man-eating "wolf-spider" or longfangs. This old, gruff, and homely man was a member of the Band of Four and friend to Craer Delnbone (q.v.) when the latter first entered the service of the Baron Blackgult. Sarasper became the Dragon of legend and died in battle against the Serpent (in *A Dragon's Ascension*), and is buried on Flowfoam Isle beside Baron Brightpennant. King Castlecloaks dubbed him "Lord Dragon" at his burial.

CORAUMAUNTH, BRAE: the mightiest archwizard of Sirlptar in his day, some four centuries ago, and the author of at least six thick spellbooks. Some sages believe those grimoires survive in such good condition today because Coraumaunth bound his life-essence into them, and "lives on" within the books, observing what happens around them and stealing into the minds of all who handle them.

Corloun: *see entry for* Ambelter, Ingryl

Dark Three, the: a trio of evil, powerful and treacherous wizards who served the Baron Faerod Silvertree. They all perished in *The Kingless Land,* and in descending order of rank, power, and age, were: Spellmaster Ingryl Ambelter; Klamantle Beirldoun; and Markoun Yarynd. Ambelter has proven rather hard to keep in the grave (*see* Ambelter, Ingryl).

DELCAMPER, FLAEROS: young bard of the wealthy Delcamper merchant family of Ragalar, known (sometimes mockingly) as "the Flower of the Delcampers," and a friend to King Raulin Castlecloaks of Aglirta.

DELCAMPER, HULGOR: one of the uncles of Flaeros Delcamper. A big, florid, hunt- and wine-loving man, swift with his sword and swifter with his temper.

DELNBONE, CRAER: Overduke of Aglirta; longtime procurer (scout and thief) in the service of the Baron Blackgult; a small, agile, and irritatingly clever-tongued man. Member of the Band of Four and longtime friend and sword-companion of Hawkril Anharu, who often calls him "Longfingers."

DRUNTER, DUNHULD: short, stout farmer, whose holding lies north of the Aglirtan village of Fallingtree, near that of his friend Ammert Branjack (q.v.). He's a friend of Fallingtree's blacksmith, Buckland Ruld (q.v.).

DUTHJACK "BLOODBLADE", SENDRITH: "the Hope of Aglirta," a capable, charismatic mercenary warrior who once served the Baron Blackgult, and later became the leader of "Bloodblade's Band," an outlaw fighting band he led in a failed attempt to slay the Risen King and put himself on the throne. Bloodblade tried to take the throne again in *A Dragon's Ascension,* and paid for this second failure with his life.

EIREVAUR, INSKUR: Coinmaster of Stornbridge, a clever, dishonest rogue of slender build, dark good looks, and a whimsical sense of humor. Personally loyal to the Tersept of Stornbridge (*see* Stornbridge, Rarandar) but increasingly fearful of the growing power of the Church of the Serpent, whose influence over Lord Stornbridge has always been strong. Eirevaur would be pleased to find an easy way to slip out of Aglirta—but even more pleased to awaken one morning and find the Church of the Serpent suddenly wiped from the face of Darsar. Eirevaur is not a man to be trusted with coins, though he's patient and subtle in his thefts.

EIYRASKUL, THAUNDUR: the Wizard of Storms, a long-ago mage of Arlund who was a rival of the Bowdragon family. Entrapped in spell-battle against them, he was entombed alive deep under Bowdragon House in Arlund, where his life-essence has been slowly drained (like that of almost a dozen other wizards) to power the ongoing enchantments of what's now the home of Dolmur Bowdragon (q.v.).

EREGAR, MURYK: a tall, rangy, battle-scarred former armaragor who makes his living as a hunter in the woods north of the Aglirtan village of Bowshun. Locally respected for providing meat through harsh winters, but a true friend to few (one of whom is the poacher Ilvreth Braumdur, q.v.).

Eroeha: *see* Serpent, the

Faceless, the/Faceless Ones, the: *see* Koglaur

Faerla: *see* Valath, Faerla

GAMARA, FLORIMELE: Lady Factor of Sart, a breathtakingly beautiful but wily, cruel, and dishonest trade agent of the Aglirtan town of Sart, posted by the Tersept of Sart to the court of King Raulin Castlecloaks (q.v.) on Flowfoam. Florimele seduces men as often as she changes gowns, and cares nothing for anyone except—Florimele. She's rumored to have a huge fortune hidden in cellars in Sirlptar and other coastal Asmarandan cities, most of them beneath houses she (secretly) owns.

GARAUNT, TAMRYST: a now-dead wizard of Aglirta who allied himself with the Church of the Serpent, and did spell-battle on their behalf whilst riding the Winged Serpent, a monster augmented by the spells of many Serpent-priests. In one such fray, above the waters of the River Silverflow, Garaunt slew the Dragon of the day, the bard Taleth Tanathavur (q.v.), but in calling on the Arrada to do so, was mind-blasted by the Great Serpent seeking to win free of slumber, and ended his days witless and wandering, abandoned by the Church that no longer found any use for him.

GESTEL, GELGARTH: a bold, restless, slender youth, son of the miller Haumur Gestel of the Aglirtan village of Fallingtree. A dreamer and prankster who knows how to work hard, but spends much time arranging matters so that he doesn't have to.

GHULDART, HORLE: a young, extremely powerful-in-magic Priest of the Serpent, low in rank but high in ambition. For some time he's dreamed of mastering the Arrada and becoming the Great Serpent—if only he can get the chance.

GOLBERT, NAMURTH: a stout, grizzled, successful cloth and wine merchant of Aglirta, whose country house stands southwest of the Aglirtan town of Gilth (he has a grander house in Sirlptar, and larger landholdings elsewhere). Golbert is married and childless, but secretly hopes to sire a child on his wife's young, pretty maidservant, Nathalessra Nathuin (q.v.).

Golden Griffon, the: *see* Blackgult, Ezendor

GOLKUTH, IMRAE: "the Skull That Does Not Sleep," an archmage of Sirlptar, now passed into undeath (by his own magics) in the form of a flying, talking, spellcasting skull. Golkuth features in many whispered late-night Sirl fireside tales, but is rarely seen in Asmarand. His present whereabouts, aims, and doings are unknown.

GREATSARN, SULDUN: trusted bodyguard of King Raulin Castle-cloaks, a grim, attentive (but kindly to Raulin) veteran armaragor, once a swordcaptain of Cardassa. A man of absolute loyalty and attentive professionalism.

HALANTHAN, JALREK: authoritative Aglirtan scribe, author of the oft-consulted record *A Year-Scroll of Aglirta.* Jalrek is fussy, vain, and opinionated, but a shrewd judge of folk and possessed of a dry, wry sense of humor that causes much snorting mirth when his writings are read aloud in Aglirtan taverns.

HANENHATHER, MELVAR: a secretive Lord of the Serpent allied to both Zolaus Yedren (q.v.) and Caronthom (q.v.). Sardonic, superior, and cunning, Hanenhather is a skilled actor who plays the role of a quiet, simpleminded, dreamy priest in Church councils, but acts as a sort of "secret agent" for both Yedren and Caronthom (both of whom know about his services to the other). Hanenhather skillfully balances one against the other, professing his loyalty to them and to the greater Church, and has often submitted to mind-reading spells from both Serpent-lords that have proven to them that he loves power and secrets, but has no personal ambition to become Great Serpent or head of the Church, or to betray either of them—only to weed out the corrupt and the weak among the Serpent-clergy. Both Yedren and Caronthom value him and let him act more or less as he pleases—in between "delicate missions" for them . . . and both are careful to never put him in the position of having to act against one of them at the behest of the other. Hanenhather rarely goes anywhere without his personal servant, Brother of the Serpent Preldyn Landrun (q.v.).

HARSADRIN, CORSIL: a sarcastic, arrogant, and athletic Lord of the Serpent, a restless and young senior-rank priest in the Church of the Serpent. Often a vocal foe of Caronthom (q.v.) and Raunthur (q.v.) in Church councils—but often a foe of just about everyone else, too, saved from swift demise by his private mutual-aid pacts and gifts of spells to many Serpent-priests. As Caronthom has several times been heard to sigh, "Harsadrin's always up to *something.*"

HAUNDRAKH, RAUMSKURR: a great philosopher and pundit of Sirlptar, now fallen into drooling, wrinkled dotage (he's known to be at least six-score summers old!). Though he can no longer walk, see, or speak coherently, and never leaves his palatial Sirl house, his words remain in use, as clever sayings quoted daily by folk of Asmarand.

HLEKTAUR, ORNRO: a cold, cruel, fundamentalist Lord of the Serpent, one of the most repressive and authority-loving senior priests of the Church of the Serpent. A resident of the Aglirtan town of Dranmaer, Hlektaur only reluctantly supports Caronthom (q.v.) and Raunthur (q.v.) in their guidance over the Church, often railing against their "practical, personal chases after greed and expediency, that stray from the Holy Path of the Great Serpent." Just what that Holy Path is, only Hlektaur seems to know, but it appears to involve a lot of torture, slavery of women, spying on others, and random beatings to keep all Aglirtans—and traveling out-landers—within reach in a constant state of cringing.

HULDAERUS, ARKLE: "the Master of Bats," formerly Lord Wizard of Ornentar, an ambitious, cruel, grasping mage known for using bat-related magic, commanding bats, and taking bat-shape. The minstrel Vilcabras once said at a Moot that "Aglirta's worst nightmare would be Huldaerus and Silvertree, working together—a terror for Silverflow Vale one year, and all Darsar the next," and Huldaerus soon killed him for that utterance.

ILGER, MARTOS: Armsmaster of Flowfoam; a longtime, trusted guard of Flowfoam Palace, loyal to King Raulin Castlecloaks. As Armsmaster, Ilger trains "underguards" (novice guards) constantly—and has grown greatly in wealth and status from his days as a cowering cortahar of Sil-vertree.

ILMARK, YRAUN: a skilled stonemason of Sirlptar, miscalled "Elmargh" by Quar Thraunt (q.v.), the Masterpriest of the Serpent who often hires him for tomb-breakings and fortress delves (which are Church of the Serpent activities whenever a member, business associate, or victim of the Serpent-worshippers dies and the Church suspects hidden treasure can be gained). Ilmark is valued for his complete silence about what he's hired for—and the Church makes sure he knows he remains alive because of it. In turn, he often reminds them of the rarity of honest workers in Sirlptar . . . or anywhere else.

IRONSTONE, BLASKAR: a stern, scowling Tersept of Aglirta who looks every inch the grim armaragor he once was. His ambitions have grown since the events of *A Dragon's Ascension*. Born Blaskar Olendryn, he rose to his terseptry (conferred by King Kelgrael Snowsar after his Awaken-ing) through diligent service to the previous Tersept of Ironstone, Hornargh Mrael, who died in the battles recounted in *The Vacant Throne*.

ISTRIM, JHAUNDRA: personal chambermaid, dresser, and lover of the Tersept of Stornbridge (*see* Stornbridge, Rarandar). Jhaundra is taller, fairer, and more demure than her fellow chambermaid Alais Aentra (q.v.), and is a (terrified, reluctant) spy on Lord Stornbridge for the Church of the Serpent.

JOSMER, XORMAR: a soft-spoken, skulking, sly little "weasel of a man" (in the words of Imra Klaedra, q.v.) born in Elmerna and a longtime dweller in Sirlptar. He's a fair vintner specializing in blending and tinting wines, and a master poisoner, and for this latter skill has been hired so often by the Church of the Serpent that Serpent-priests almost consider him a lay member of the Church clergy. At the time of *The Dragon's Doom,* he's been resident in Storn-bridge Castle, ostensibly selling wines locally, for some twoscore days.

Kelgrael: *see* Snowsar, Kelgrael

KELHANDROS, ORBRIM: a Lord of the Serpent, one of the most worldly and battle-wise senior priests of the Church of the Serpent. For-merly an armaragor and then the leader of a mercenary war-band, Kelhan-dros is a tall, cold-eyed, always-alert swordsman turned mage turned Priest of the Serpent. Strong and agile, a good listener and a shrewd judge of unfolding events, hidden aims, and consequences to come, Kelhandros was recruited by Raunthur (q.v.) to the worship of the Serpent, and made Master Cellarer of the Church (head of all procurement and deployment of supplies, from food to tools to horses and their hay). Stationed in a Church-owned fortress in Sart, he's firmly loyal to Caronthom (q.v.) and Raunthur, and sees internal dissent and intrigues as the greatest danger to the Church.

KHAVAN, DARL: a timid, oft-terrified Fangbrother in the Church of the Serpent, increasingly used as a fetch-and-carry servant by Scaled Master Belgur Arthroon (q.v.). Born in Carraglas, he went to Sirlptar in search of riches as a merchant trader—and soon fell into debt to the Church, who recruited him to steal from, swindle, manipulate, and ultimately slay Sirl merchants. When Sirlptar grew too dangerous for him, Khavan pleaded to be made a priest "to do the holy work of the Serpent," and his wish was granted, beginning with years of wandering Aglirta making exacting maps of back lanes, ruins, caves, and the like for the Church.

KLAEDRA, IMRA: Mistress of the Pantry in Stornbridge Castle and a longtime agent of the Church of the Serpent. An accomplished preserver-of-foods, seasoner (spice refiner, gleaner, and storer) and cook, Klaedra is pos-sessed of a lush figure, a love of men, some acting skills—and a complete ruthlessness in her dealings with anyone she doesn't fear (which is everyone not associated with the Church of the Serpent).

Koglaur, the: the "Faceless" or "Faceless Ones," legendary lurking human-like shapeshifting beings who watch over Aglirta and meddle in its affairs for mysterious reasons of their own.

Lady of Jewels, the: *see* Silvertree, Embra

LAERLOR, ORMOND: mage of Aglirta, thought by most sages to be long dead—but by others to have been imprisoned somewhere in the Vale by a rival mage to be life-drained to power lasting enchantments upon a tower or stronghold. Just which rival or tower, no one can agree upon. "Laerlor may yet live!" was briefly a catch-phrase denoting faint hope, but its meaning later soured into "false hope."

Lameira: *see* Nuinar, Lameira

LANDRUN, PRELDYN: a prudent—even fearful—low-ranking Priest of the Serpent who serves as the personal servant of Lord of the Serpent Melvar Hanenhather (q.v.).

LASHANTRA, NAEVRELE: a fun-loving noble lady of Coelortar, cousin to Tshamarra Talasorn (q.v.) and unwed heiress to the large Lashantra family fortune. Always merry and energetic, Naevrele travels Darsar constantly on whims, in search of sensation after adventure. She's as likely to be found dancing for coins on tavern tables as attending feasts and revels of the wealthy, and once, on a dare, stole all the coins wagered during a long day of tavern gaming by warriors of Blackgult on leave in Sirlptar, slipping them into pockets that covered the inside of a cloak. Posing as a tavern dancer and therefore wearing nothing but her own skin, she boldly left the scene of the theft, retrieving the cloak outside (she'd thrust it through a high tavern window onto the sill). She was chased and caught by Craer Delnbone (q.v.), who took his own revenge—and payment—from her.

LAUNSRAR, RYEL: a greedy and luxury-loving Tersept of Launsrar, who allied himself with Baron Faerod Silvertree (q.v.) and ultimately died in the battles recounted in *The Vacant Throne*. One of his pay-coaches (from Silvertree) was stolen from under his nose by the procurer Craer Delnbone (q.v.), who was then in the service of Baron Ezendor Blackgult (q.v.) and assigned to spy on Launsrar's doings.

Lessra: *see* Nathuin, Nathalessra

LETHSAIS, GAUNDEL: a handsome, romance-loving Lord of the Serpent, one of the most luxury-loving and decadent senior priests of the

Church of the Serpent. A permanent resident of the Aglirtan town of Telbonter, Lethsais has devoted himself to seducing every woman—and many men—to come within his reach, and building an ever-growing network of intimates and former intimates who view him as their ally, friend, and fellow conspirator. He holds frequent revels, and intrigues tirelessly to make all decisions for nearby barons and tersepts, manipulating them whenever possible so they believe those decisions are their own. His overly public ways and independent streak don't sit well with Lords of the Serpent Caronthom (q.v.) and Raunthur (q.v.), but he scorns their attempted guidance of the Church as "regressive, doomed to failure, and presumptuous on their part from the outset."

LORGAUTH, SUNDRAR: a well-known and respected blacksmith of Aglirta, who plies his trade up and down the Silverflow on docks and from his own barge. Most of his work is emergency repairs to metal-work on barges, wagons, crates, chests, and draft-beast harnesses. His forge-mark is an arc of three close-spaced stars, the center one above the flanking marks.

Lorivar: *see* Mrantyn, Lorivar

LOTHOAN, FELROR: a young, low-ranking, but ambitious and bold Priest of the Serpent, restless for more personal power—soon.

MASKALOS, HALHOAZE: a suspicious-of-all Lord of the Serpent, one of the most careful and loyal to superiors senior priests of the Church of the Serpent. Stationed by Caronthom (q.v.) and Raunthur (q.v.) in the Aglirtan town of Ibryn to keep watch over his sly fellow Serpent-Lord Vynthur Cheldraem (q.v.), Maskalos is feared among Church clergy for his never-failing memory, attention to detail, and careful, inspired spying. As one forgotten (and now-dead) priest once said of Maskalos, "He looks at you—and he *knows*."

Master of Bats, the: *see* Huldaerus, Arkle

MAUMANTHAR, DELVARKH: sage and archwizard of Houlborn, an astonishingly tall and gaunt man whose magic has kept him alive for centuries. Rarely seen outside his dark and dusty tower these days, he's famous among mages for his spell-won longevity and for the many tomes of magical lore and advice (each containing a handful of spells) he wrote in his first century of life. These include *Circles of Flame, A Wizard's Way to Might, Spells for the Seasons,* and *Doors to the Secrets.* Copies of these works are rarely seen for sale, and change hands for steep sums when they do turn up (often pursued by angry wizards from whom they were stolen).

MAURIVAN, WORVYN: a cold, cruel priest of the Church of the Serpent, who holds the rank of Fangbrother and is assigned to guide (order about and spy on) the Tersept Rarandar Stornbridge (q.v.). Maurivan is arrogant, impatient, and very capable.

MELJRUNE, ILVRYM: widely considered the most powerful archwizard of all Darsar in his day (some three centuries back), "Mad Meljrune" was a handsome, sinister man of Carraglas who always wore crimson robes, a goatee as sharp as a dagger, and long, thin waxed mustaches. Meljrune penned several large and highly-valued spellbooks, to which cling a curious legend: that he lives still, in some silent otherwhere, and returns to do magical harm to anyone who keeps any of his tomes for more than a score of years. Enough mages believe this tale—bolstered by the curious deaths of the wizards Thongolon and Qester Dree—that Meljrune's books change hands fairly often.

Melted, the: men burned beyond death into a zombie-like animated state by a special fire-spell of the mage Corloun; their flesh droops and disfigures and they become conduits of his magic (he can cast spells from afar, through their touch, or cause them to explode in flames). *See* Ambelter, Ingryl.

MIRMORN, MAELREE: Undercook of Stornbridge Castle, and "Ree" to her coworkers, this large, meaty, strong-willed woman is the best cook in Stornbridge (particularly when producing roasts), and is more sharp-witted than most believe her to be. "That sour-faced ox" is how the Tersept's Champion, Onskur Pheldane (q.v.) once unkindly described her. She can be short-tempered and vicious, but is generally kindly—though the feeling of power imparted to her by secretly serving the Serpents fills her with wicked glee.

MORAUNTAUVAR, NAUNTHUR: self-styled "mightiest mage of Sirlptar" at the time of *The Dragon's Doom,* this eccentric, sardonic, and greedy wizard has secretly hired himself out to the Church of the Serpent, to aid them in seizing the throne of Aglirta with his spells.

MRANTYN, LORIVAR: a longtime, trusted guard of Flowfoam Palace, loyal to King Raulin Castlecloaks.

MULKYN, GADASTER: first and most infamous Spellmaster of Silvertree; an aging, ruthless evil archwizard who was tutor to Ingryl Ambelter—and whom Ingryl slew (before the events of *The Kingless Land*) by a succession of life- and magic-stealing spells that forced Gadaster into a strange unlife. The "Old Beast of Silvertree" retains his sentience, but has for decades served as little more than a captive means of healing for Ambelter.

NAEL, NARSO: an aging, plain-spoken former farmer who's risen to become a Lord of the Serpent. One of the most "common" and level-headed senior priests of the Church of the Serpent, Nael dwells in the Aglirtan town of Rithrym. He's universally known as "Old Nael" because his son, also named Narso Nael, is also a priest of the faith (though of much lower rank). Old Nael openly supports Caronthom (q.v.) and Raunthur (q.v.)—not because he loves them, their methods, or their policies, but because he believes them the most prudent of the powerful Serpent-lords, best able to give the Church stability through a minimum of internal strife, which is what Old Nael hates and fears most of all.

NARVUL, FARSTEN: a strong, burly, short-tempered retired armaragor of Silvertree, now a butcher in the Aglirtan village of Bowshun. Friend to the local shopkeeper Ulbert Thunn (q.v.).

NATHUIN, NATHALESSRA: the quiet, long-suffering maidservant of the shrewish wife of Namurth Golbert (q.v.), a rich Aglirtan merchant. Nathalessra dislikes the goodwife, but secretly admires Golbert's successes and worldly wisdom, and does not spurn his thus-far-surreptitious advances.

NAUMUN, TARACE: a sly, always-scheming Lord of the Serpent, a wealthy and worldly senior priest of the Church of the Serpent. A resident of the city of Sirlptar, Naumun is a firm foe of Caronthom (q.v.) and Raunthur (q.v.) in Church councils, and believes their intrigues and fearmongering have kept the faith from being embraced by many folk of Asmarand—whereas if they followed *his* approach, of making the faith a mighty trade organization that rewarded all its members with coin in return for their service (a handful for those at the bottom, and vaults-full for those at the top), the Church of the Serpent would have long since risen to great popularity—and power—in Darsar, winning all the benefits of great influence without the drawbacks of actually ruling anywhere.

NUINAR, LAMEIRA: a sharp-tongued, opinionated Maid of Chambers (servant) in the Delcamper castle of Varandaur, highly valued by Natha Orele (q.v.) for her hard work and attention to detail. Lameira customarily works with her firm friend Faerla Valath (q.v.).

ORATHLEE: a beautiful young woman of the Wise (those folk who can foresee in dreams or by divers means, or have other inner magical gifts they can call on without casting spells, but are outcast by priests of the Three as "spirit-touched") who guides merchants of Sirlptar in their investments—for fees. Orathlee was once a slave in Sarinda, and bears disfiguring brands on both breasts.

ORELE, NATHA: oldest Lady of Chambers in the Delcamper castle of Varandaur; addressed as "Lady" and (as a former consort of several Delcamper uncles) considered almost noble in her own right. Clear-witted and imperious, she walks with the aid of a silver-handled cane. Known as "Old Wrinkles," "Old Boot," and "Sweethips" to Hulgor Delcamper (q.v.), Orele is known to be one of the Wise.

ORMSIVUR, FARANDROS: a tall, handsome, taciturn Lord of the Serpent, one of the most personally wealthy senior priests of the Church of the Serpent. A dweller in Sirlptar, Ormsivur bankrolls many Church activities, and is often (but only in whispers) accused of stinting funds to those faithful and policies he dislikes, but giving extra to those he favors. For his part, Ormsivur admits nothing and says little, but refuses to attend council meetings unless they are held in Sirlptar, or openly support Caronthom (q.v.) and Raunthur (q.v.) in their guidance over the Church.

ORNAUGH, IYSTYM: a novice priest of the Serpent, often dismissed as a fool by priests of higher rank for his worst faults: curiosity coupled with naivete.

OTHGLAEL, ORSOR: a guard of Stornbridge Castle and cortahar in the service of the Tersept of Stornbridge, Lord Rarandar Stornbridge (q.v.). Lazy, laconic, and bored with his duties, but a good bowman and shrewd enough never to put a boot or remark wrong in the presence of Lord Storn-bridge or any Serpent-priest. Increasingly, Orsor suspects every second or third Castle servant of being a Serpent spy, and is attaining that state of wariness that most Aglirtans call "dead cold scared."

PHELDANE, ONSKUR: Champion of Stornbridge, personal body-guard and envoy of its Tersept, Lord Rarandar Stornbridge (q.v.). A burly, blustering giant of a man, given to rages and to forcing himself on any woman he fancies, the Tersept's Champion is hated in Stornbridge almost as much as he's feared, thanks to his casual vandalism, bullying, and treatment of Storn women. He rarely fights fair, and almost never loses a battle.

PHELINNDAR, ORLIN ANDAMUS: Baron of Phelinndar and an urbane, treacherous man who keeps to himself as much as possible, avoid-ing the intrigues and risings-to-arms of most barons of Aglirta. He has good reason to do so: since sometime before King Kelgrael Snowsar named him to his barony, Orlin—then Orlin Breselt, Tersept of Downdaggers—has been the secret owner of a Dwaer-stone.

PHELTARTH, HARRAMUN: a handsome outlander from Felsheiryn who came to the Church of the Serpent because he craved power. Risen to become a Lord of the Serpent through enthusiastic support of Caronthom (q.v.), Pheltarth dwells in Adelnwater, and capably administers several Church-owned businesses (notably barge and caravan-wagon concerns that serve to smuggle Church supplies, contraband, captives, slaves, and other "quiet cargoes").

QUENNSAR, TALBURT: Seneschal of Mrorn Castle in the time when the Barons Blackgult and Silvertree contested for supremacy in Aglirta, "Haughty Talburt" was a man of legendary rudeness, eccentricities, and stilted manners. A widower, he dwelt in Mrorn Castle with a small band of superb cortahars (trained, led, and equipped by his hand) and his beau-tiful daughter, Seldrene, until Craer Delnbone (q.v.), then a procurer in the service of Baron Blackgult, tricked him into fulfilling Seldrene's long-held dream: escaping from Mrorn Castle into adventure with a handsome young man. Craer provided the handsome looks, the adventure, a whirl-wind romance, and deliverance to Sirlptar—and Talburt's furious attempts at pursuit led him to his death at the hands of cortahars of Silvertree.

RATHTAEN, ELDEMAR: a kindly and well-liked Lord of the Serpent, a senior priest of the Church of the Serpent who uses aid and good deeds to knit the faith together rather than fear and cold commands—traits that often bring him into gentle, polite conflict with First Voice Caronthom (q.v.) and Raunthur (q.v.) the Wise of the Church. They and most of his fellow Serpent-priests see him as vital to the morale and continued existence of the Church; in the words of Raunthur, he's "the glue that binds all our fangs together, and keeps them from turning upon each other."

RAULDRON, NAURELD: a handsome, always-alert Lord of the Serpent, an active, scheming senior priest of the Church of the Serpent. In the upland Aglirtan town of Tselgara, Rauldron has quietly founded a flourishing "circle" (company) of woodcarvers. He openly supports Caronthom (q.v.) and Raunthur (q.v.) in their guidance over the Church.

RAUNTHUR, PHELMAER: the Wise, second most senior surviving Lord of the Serpent (after his ally Caronthom q.v.). Raunthur is a prudent, pragmatic, and shrewd man who sees quiet local domination of every barony of Aglirta—and ultimately, every region of Asmarand—as the future of the faith. His nickname was won through exhaustive knowledge of both Church custom and history, and general lore about all things Aglirtan and Sirl. If conspiracies are hatching among merchants, wizards, priests of other faiths, or rulers anywhere up and down the Asmarandan coast, Raunthur knows about them or has anticipated their arising. In most matters of Church intrigue thus far, he's been "one stride ahead" of foes and rivals. Perhaps the most (inwardly, among his fellow priests of the Church) respected Serpent-priest of all.

Risen King, the: *see* Snowsar, Kelgrael

ROLD, DURLSTAN: Master of the *Silver Fin,* a barge that sails the River Silverflow between Sirl harbor to the docks of Tselgara. Rold has been a barge captain for some three decades when the events recounted in *The Dragon's Doom* begin.

RULD, BUCKLAND: locally popular blacksmith of the Aglirtan village of Fallingtree. Good-natured and more swift-witted than many a smith, he's a friend to most folk of Fallingtree and the surrounding lands, including the farmers Ammert Branjack (q.v.) and Dunhuld Drunter (q.v.).

RYETHREL, DEVYN: Lornsar of Stornbridge, the captain of all Storn cortahars, Ryethrel is a sour, short-tempered fighting man personally loyal to the Tersept of Stornbridge, Lord Rarandar Stornbridge (q.v.). Born on the Isles of Ieirembor, Ryethrel became an armaragor who fought against the invasion of Baron Ezendor Blackgult (q.v.)—and burned down Sea Rock Hall on the island of Nantantuth, slaying not only some of Blackgult's warriors, but dozens of Ieiremborans. A bully and a coward, Ryethrel is swifter-witted, faster with a sword, and more wily than his rival Storn lord, Onskur Pheldane (q.v.).

SALAUNTHUS, ILBUR: an old, scarred senior Priest of the Serpent, highly ranked in the Church of the Serpent but not a Lord of the Serpent, Salaunthus is trusted by Caronthom (q.v.) and Raunthur (q.v.) to loyally and secretly conduct the work he's happiest doing: experimenting endlessly with spells, perfecting magical effects "to order."

Sarasper: *see* Codelmer, Sarasper

Scaled Ones, the: *see* Serpents, the

Seneschal of Mrorn Castle, the: *see* Quennsar, Talburt

Serpent, the: "the Serpent in the Shadows," "the Sacred Serpent," "the Great Serpent," "the Fanged One" a great evil being worshipped by the Church of the Serpent. Long ago he was a human wizard (name now forgotten; it's thought he worked to purge records of it) who helped enchant the Dwaerindim, but went mad or was mad, and murdered several rival mages to strengthen the Dwaer enchantment. When confronted by the other mages of the Shaping, he fled into serpent-form to fight his way free of their spells and was imprisoned by them in serpent-shape; now a gigantic serpent bound into slumber by a mighty magic worked by the King of Aglirta (fated to sleep when he does); worshipped by humans who revere him as divine, and to whom he grants spells through a magical network known as the Arrada. Present-day worshippers of him (who are wizards using his secret spell-lore, though they call themselves priests to further the false belief that the Serpent is a god) call him "Eroeha," but this is believed to be a corrupt form of the Serpent's human rank or title, not his name. This ancient entity was slain by the Band of Four in *A Dragon's Ascension,* but his priests redoubled their efforts to conquer Aglirta, believing a new Great Serpent would inevitably arise to master the Arrada and lead them.

Serpents, the: worshippers of the Serpent (humans who often become snake-like); they refer formally to themselves as "the Faithful of the Serpent," but others call them "the Cowled Priests," "the Fanged Faithful," "the Scaly Ones," "the Serpent-spawn," and worse; those with snake-like heads and forked tongues are known (not to their faces) as "Hissing Ones."

SILVERTREE, EMBRA: Overduke of Aglirta and Lady Baron (Baroness) of Silvertree, widely known as the Lady of Jewels (for her opulent, gem-studded gowns); a beautiful sorceress who's grown to become the unofficial leader of the Band of Four. Daughter of the cruel Faerod Silvertree (q.v.), who intended her to become a captive "Living Castle," Embra was in truth fathered by Ezendor Blackgult (q.v.).

SILVERTREE, FAEROD: a cruel and grasping Baron of Silvertree, who came very close to ruling all Aglirta in *The Kingless Land,* and was widely feared because of his wicked deeds and ruthless reach. He made Flowfoam Palace his home, fortifying the isle into Castle Silvertree. Most Aglirtans thought him dead at the end of the events recounted in *The Kingless Land,* but he survived in hiding, as the local Lord (equivalent to mayor) of the upland Aglirtan village of Tarlarnastar, only to perish in *The Vacant Throne.*

SNOWSAR, KELGRAEL: the Risen King, the Lost King, the Sleeping King, the Sleeper of Legend, the Last Snowsar; King of Aglirta, the Lion of Aglirta, the Crown of Aglirta, Lord of all Aglirta, Master of the River and its Vale; rightful crowned ruler of Aglirta. This wise and perceptive warrior and wizard slept for centuries in a spell-hidden "otherwhere" while warring barons tore his realm apart. When he sleeps, the Serpent is bound also into slumber by his spells; when he awakens, so too does the Serpent.

Stormharp, Inderos: *see* Blackgult, Ezendor

STORNBRIDGE, RARANDAR: Tersept of Aglirta, a sly-tongued, craven, and handsome coward of a man. Born Rarandar Thrael, of an educated Sirl family who trained him to be a scribe and coinmaster to nobility, and then grew in wealth enough to fancy themselves noble and give their four sons training in arms and horsemanship, Rarandar offered his services to Faerod Silvertree as a factor (trade agent) and spy, and served with diligence enough to be rewarded with a terseptry in the brief time when Baron Silvertree acted as *de facto* ruler of much of Aglirta. As Tersept of Stornbridge, Rarandar surrounded himself with men of morals as flexible as his own, and soon fell under the sway of Serpent-priests, who kept Lord Storn-bridge far more wealthy, and his subjects far less unruly, than either should have been. At the time of *The Dragon's Doom,* the loyalties of Tersept of Stornbridge are regarded with polite suspicion by King Castlecloaks.

Suldun: *see* Greatsarn, Suldun

TALASORN, TSHAMARRA: the Lady Talasorn, youngest and most kindhearted (though still sharp-tongued) of the four proud, beautiful sorcer-ess daughters of the wizard Reavur Talasorn and his wife Iyrinda. Unlike her sisters Olone, Dacele, and Araithe, Tshamarra survived the events of *A Dragon's Ascension,* to become the battle-companion of the Band of Four. Craer Delnbone (q.v.) of the Four, with whom she's grown close, calls her "Tash."

TANATHAVUR, TALETH: a wandering bard of Aglirta who manifested as the Dragon in his day, and fell in battle against the wizard Tamryst Garaunt (q.v.), champion of the Church of the Serpent. Tanathavur was blasted to smoke and ashes above the River Silverflow; it's said that "True Bards" can still smell the stink of his death, and his last shouted snatches of song, when they pass the place of his passing.

TELGAERT, TASLAR: owner and master of the ship *Fair Wind,* of no particular home port. The *Fair Wind* is a sea-rel: a fast, narrow coastal-running vessel that delivers small cargoes swiftly, up and down the Asmaranta Coast. Telgaert is a kindly, swift-witted, handsome man—and secretly one of the Wise, though largely untrained.

TESMER, CORTH: a longtime, trusted guard of Flowfoam Palace, loyal to King Raulin Castlecloaks, and now deemed capable (thanks to covert tests of his loyalty and his quick wits, nondescript facial features, and stolid endurance) of serving as a spy or "undercloak agent" for the King.

Thaelae: *see* Aranglar, Thaelae

THALAS, PHEREK: a steward (servant) of Stornbridge Castle of grasp-ing ways and sly schemes.

THANNASO, HORM: Master Jailer of the Royal Dungeons (the cells beneath Flowfoam Palace), known to one and all as "Old Thannaso." A blind and limping retired warrior, Thannaso is gruff, kindly, and alert, seeming to always "smell" trouble. Wise to the ways of prisoners, he possesses keen hearing.

THELVAUN, JORTH: a scarred, bitter, ruthless Lord of the Serpent, one of the most elderly senior priests of the Church of the Serpent. He believes he should be leading the faith rather than Caronthom (q.v.) and Raunthur (q.v.), and sometimes says so, but is secretly glad to stand in the background and leave the perilous "place by the fire" to others.

THORNTRUMPET: Herald of Aglirta, one of the roving officers of blazonry long ago granted quasi-independence by the Court (there were originally seven such "Flowfoam heralds"—not to be confused with local, baronial heralds—but only four of the offices have survived). The current Thorntrumpet was born Raeld Brandlar in Adelnwater, but took the name of his office after his ailing predecessor (now dead) trained him and "renounced the banner" in his favor. Thorntrumpet is young, energetic, and well regarded.

THRAUNT, QUAR: a Serpent-priest of the rank of Masterpriest, known for his swift temper, arrogance, and bouts of gloating. He's unpopular with superiors, who have increasingly chosen missions of peril for him—which he has shown a frankly surprising tendency of surviving.

THULDRAN, TOROLD: a young Priest of the Serpent, rising in reputation (though not yet in rank) within the Church of the Serpent because of his capable service. Less openly ambitious, bold, and cruel than most Serpent clergy.

THUNN, ULBERT: a stout, sour, and no-nonsense shopkeeper in the Aglirtan village of Bowshun, friend to the local butcher Farsten Narvul (q.v.).

URBRINDUR, MALVUS: Seneschal of Stornbridge Castle and most trusted confidant of the Tersept of Stornbridge (*see* Rarandar Stornbridge). A sharp-tongued, sarcastic, suspicious man, haughty and quick-tempered. Slender, athletic, graying with age, and possessed of a long memory for slights and shortcomings. The most hated man in Stornbridge Castle—no matter who's visiting.

VALATH, FAERLA: a scatterbrained, careless, but enthusiastic and romantic Maid of Chambers (servant) in the Delcamper castle of Varandaur. Youngest and least well behaved of the Maids of Chambers; the despair of Lady Orele. Faerla customarily serves with her good friend Lameira Nuinar (q.v.).

YEDREN, ZOLAUS: a tall, handsome, and charismatic Lord of the Serpent, one of the most active and energetic senior priests of the Church of the Serpent—traits that keep him alive in the face of his defiance of First Voice Caronthom (q.v.) and Raunthur (q.v.) the Wise. Yedren is utterly fearless, always speaks politely, and is very popular among young priests of the Serpent of the lower ranks, who see him as their champion against a cold, cruel hierarchy.